THE EMANCIPATED

George Gissing

Edited and with a new introduction by
PIERRE COUSTILLAS
Director, Centre for Victorian Studies
University of Lille

Rutherford . Madison . Teaneck
Fairleigh Dickinson University Press

First American edition published in 1977 by
Associated University Presses, Inc.,
Cranbury, N.J. 08512

© New editorial material, Pierre Coustillas, 1977

The Emancipated first published in 1890 by
Richard Bentley & Son

Library of Congress Catalog Card Number: 77-80328
ISBN 0-8386-2171-6

Printed in Great Britain

Contents

Bibliographical Note

The Emancipated was first published in three volumes by Richard Bentley & Son in late March 1890, bound in ornamented boards with brown cloth back and ornamented end-papers. 1,000 copies were printed but only 625 were bound, and 492 sold. In 1892 Lawrence & Bullen bought the copyright of the novel and published a six-shilling one-volume edition in maroon cloth in December 1893. George Bell & Sons bought 750 copies in sheets from Lawrence & Bullen in September 1894, and another 500 two months later. These lots constitute the two impressions in Bell's Indian and Colonial Library, dated respectively 1894 and 1895. Lawrence & Bullen reissued the book in 1895 (third edition); so did A. H. Bullen under his own imprint in 1901, and Sidgwick & Jackson in 1911.

In America the novel was not published until October 1895 under the imprint of Way & Williams, a Chicago firm. They reissued the book in 1897, offering it as the 'third edition', but no 'second edition' is on record. The English three-volume edition was reprinted, the three volumes bound in one, by the AMS Press in 1969.

The manuscript is in the Berg Collection of the New York Public Library.

Introduction

It is generally admitted that Gissing took a new departure with *The Emancipated*, probably because, coming after *The Nether World*, his darkest working-class novel, it offers an undeniable contrast which the author himself stressed in his diary and in his correspondence. During his first protracted Continental journey, he felt an altogether new man, an idealist student of art who could afford to forget for a time the world to which he had been confined for over a decade. England suddenly looked foreign to him, and it is to some extent true that he never saw it after 1888 as he had seen it before. His main concern hitherto had been with the lower classes, with squalor and starvation, and the series of proletarian novels had culminated with a book which was at once an arraignment of society and a tribute to his first wife's memory. After *The Nether World*, he never again treated working-class life at any length. 'Lou and Liz', a short story published in 1893, can hardly be reckoned an exception on account of its brevity; furthermore it was written at the request of Clement Shorter, who specifically wanted a story like the bank-holiday scene in *The Nether World*. Years later, when the editor of the *Cornhill Magazine* asked him in February 1900 to contribute an article on the life of the lower classes in London, Gissing felt that he could not possibly undertake such a task; the subject no longer was a living one to him; besides some younger writers had dealt in a very successful manner with the London poor recently and with greater sympathy than he ever had.[1] Clearly, the turning-point in his inspiration was his first visit to Italy from October 1888 to February 1889, but it had been prepared by Nell's death. Just as he was later to relieve his conscience of the

Manchester episode in *Born in Exile*, he bade farewell to the life of the people in *The Nether World*.

Gissing did not embark for Italy with the idea of looking for fresh material. What he undertook was a cultural trip. Still the notion of turning his new experiences to account in his next novel germinated in his mind weeks before he sailed back home. On 21 January, 1889 he wrote in his diary that he had thought of a possible story while taking a walk on the Viale de' Colli in Florence, and a letter of the same day to Katie, his brother's wife, shows that the necessity of having a new book ready by the end of the summer began to worry him. On 9 February he recorded further cogitations as well as some satisfactory names for his characters. The name of Cecily Doran, the emancipated young lady who comes to grief, was probably suggested to him by Raphael's famous picture of St Cecilia which he saw at Bologna at the Academy of Fine Arts on 30 January – 'a divine picture', he wrote to Eduard Bertz – before he gave it a symbolical role in the story.[2] But he did not resume preparatory work until 20 March, 1889, planning to lay the early chapters in England. Scarcely had he set pen to paper when he changed his mind. His diary shows him on 24 March working at the description with which the novel was to begin: 'several hours writing some 20 lines, a terrible business.' This was only the first of many false starts. As usual, he was trying to write before he was quite ready. Besides giving greater mental attention to the details of the narrative he resorted to various expedients in order to gather momentum – among these were De Quincey's essay on style, Aristophanes' *Frogs* and a history of Rome. If his five months' stay abroad had been profitable in many ways, it obviously had also put him out of gear for fiction writing. Composition was a positive torment. Even the Neapolitan background demanded strenuous efforts: one morning at the British Museum provided the information required. By 16 April he was still in ch. IV after a good deal of rewriting which involved 'a considerable alteration in the story', and he collapsed again at the end of the month, remarking on 1 May, when he took a fresh start, that 'this perpetual rewriting seems to be a necessity of my method.' Indeed it was, for not until 3 June, in the quiet of his Wakefield home, did he set to work on what was to be the book as we know it, even though quite a few passages from his old manuscript were put to use. Volume I lay completed on 22 June and Volume

II was launched into forthwith. In view of the fact that he was now writing apace, doing 4 or 5 pages in his small handwriting every day, one is astonished at his suddenly deciding on 2 July that his story would be divided into two parts, with an interval of about three years. After pondering for a few days on the details of his next chapters, he went ahead bravely and finished Volume II on 16 July. Progress with Volume III was a little slower – ch. VIII and IX gave him more trouble than any before – but by 13 August he had written the last lines, which however he thought it necessary to rewrite two days later.

Although by no means an autobiographical novel, *The Emancipated* incorporates numberless elements which were borrowed from Gissing's recent experiences. They were vivid in his brain and lay recorded in his diary and other papers. They mainly concern the setting in a general way, but also particular places like Frau Häberle's boarding-house in Vico Brancaccio in Naples, where he was to stay again on his return from Greece in the autumn of 1889, or the Albergo del Sole at Pompeii. In actual life as in the book we find in the latter inn a party of German travellers in lively conversation with an Englishman struggling to express himself in the Teutonic language. The exclamations of the Germans are identical, and Clifford Marsh takes the part of that curious Yorkshireman, John Shortridge, whose family life is so graphically described in the diary. When Edward Spence wonders at the fantastic noise coming up from Fuorigrotta, he voices Gissing's own surprise when leaning out of his window at nightfall. The tinkling of the bells carried by the goats and cows delighted the novelist as they do his characters; the cabmen amused him and so they do those of his personages who observe Italian manners with intelligent and tolerant eyes. The inscription on the fountain at Sorrento is transcribed from a diary jotting for 23 November, 1888, and the feeling of 'gratitude to our old schoolmasters' uttered by Reuben Elgar was certainly shared by Gissing, whose intellectual enjoyment of Latin and Greek could hardly be surpassed. In the same way we come across an aesthetic judgment on the girls of Venice passed by the author before he put it into Elgar's mouth. In some cases autobiographical inspiration extends beyond the Italian background. Thus Mrs. Lessingham's home at Craven Hill is patterned on that of the Gaussens, who settled there every year for the London season; or again the relations between Mallard and his family in Yorkshire recall Gissing's imperfect intimacy with his own people.

With her provincial sensitiveness Ellen Gissing interpreted *The Emancipated* as an attack upon herself, her opinions and mode of life, and she had a tiff with her brother because she suspected she had served as a model for Miriam Baske. Had she known of it, the provisional title – 'The Puritan' – would have stirred her to greater bitterness. The two or three letters Gissing wrote in defence of his own point of view throw useful light on the book itself as well as on his relations with his sister and on his deeper thoughts on puritanism. Thus on April 3, 1890:

> First of all, it is a delusion to suppose that I identify you with Miriam. Nothing of the kind. You have grown up in a far more liberal atmosphere. Her like I have known, & the type is not uncommon; but you have never been, as far as I know, in that extreme phase. Then again, I by no means attack all people who hold a supernatural faith. The object of my onslaught is *formalism*, – an obstinate belief in things that were disproved by sheer arithmetic long ago, which even such an old-fashioned book as Newman's 'Phases of Faith' (I only wish you could read it) rendered forever untenable. I mean, of course, Sabbatarianism, & everything connected with it, – which, as you are aware, has never existed anywhere but in England, (putting aside the Swiss puritans & the Pharisees). – If you think over the book, you will see that *formalism* alone is spoken of as deadening; mere spiritual belief, never. That is simply not dealt with at all. It did not enter into my purpose. I should simply have been repeating the work of such books as 'Robert Elsmere'.
>
> If you doubt the existence of such people as Miriam, it surprises me. Kingsley knew the type, as you will see in the beginning of 'Alton Locke'. But perhaps you don't & were merely hurt because you misconceived my purpose.
>
> No; minus a little faith in forms, you would be broad-minded. Nay, you *are* broad-minded, in many ways & directions. And of your true enjoyment of art in various shapes I never entertained a moment's doubt. That is all misconception on your part. You have read & studied probably more than most girls of your age. It would be monstrously unjust if I closed my eyes to all this, & you would be right to feel angry with me. Again & again I have told you how I admire your persistency in working under so

many disadvantages. Never should I ridicule *you*, however savagely I strike at the worn-out fetters which here & there hang heavily on you.

You will find it always the same with me. I never attack spiritual faith in itself, – but I shall never cease to use all my power against such illusions as, for instance, that which imagines Sunday to be different from any other day (in plain defiance of the New Testament & ecclesiastical history, as strong Christians have again & again pointed out).

If only you would read 'Phases of Faith', – a most minute history of spiritual slow emancipation, written by Cardinal Newman's brother long years ago. It would enable you to understand the all but frenzy with which I regard forms whose persistence is due to literal & absolute ignorance, & nothing else. Suppose I lived in a country where it was a grave article of faith that all men in New Zealand had but one eye; & then, after a visit to New Zealand, when I came back & declared that such was not the case, I found everybody foaming against me for my heresy? What would be my state of mind? Precisely what it now is, when I encounter belief (*not* in the existence of God, or anything of that kind), but in supposed *facts* which have been plainly demonstrated not to be facts, but mistakes.

I do not even feel strongly impatient with a literal belief in the New Testament. Let me repeat: I quarrel only with people who will believe all the New Testament *except* that part which declares that the burden of the old law was thenceforth done away with.

Newman, a man of vast learning, who devoted many years to the elaborate study of these things (being actually in orders, I think), would put all this far more clearly & authoritatively before you than I can.[3]

The self-confidence reflected in this letter was not only that of the elder brother addressing his younger sister, of the professional writer rebuking the impercipient reader, or of the agnostic pooh-poohing the believer. It was the attitude of the artist trusting in his work. 'The general opinion here', he wrote from London, 'is that the book makes a great advance on my others. I myself think that it is the best yet in style and characterization.'[4] He rejoiced that he had broken new ground while remaining faithful to his former outlook. Indeed, if the Italian background gives *The Emancipated* a colour and a place of its own, the story nevertheless reveals many affinities with his other works, and, among the earlier ones, not only with those in which he ventured into the middle-class world, that is *Isabel Clarendon* and *A Life's Morning*. Here as elsewhere, he was a moralist, a close observer of human motives, an apostle of spiritual freedom, a candid denouncer of humbug. 'Echo and Prelude', the title of chapter XIII of Part I would be an appropriate heading for a study of the points this novel has in common with its predecessors and successors.

A number of true and bogus artists – painters, writers, musicians – people Gissing's fiction from *Workers in the Dawn* (1880) to *Will Warburton* (1905). Clifford Marsh, 'a man excelling in speciousness', is one of those painters – men of scant talent, brazen-faced posers or clever exploiters of public ignorance – who may succeed in making money but are more likely to produce daubs for which no one will ever care. He stands far below Gilbert Gresham and Norbert Franks in the novels just mentioned. He is also one of those charlatans, self-pitying or infirm of purpose, who pollute the fields of literature, politics or religion and as often as not delude one or two women besides themselves. In an oft-quoted letter to Morley Roberts, Gissing said that the most significant of his work was that which dealt with a class of young men distinctive of his time – 'well educated, fairly bred, but without money' –, but he could have extended the category to the young men who cleverly manage to sponge on their relatives (Clifford Marsh and Reuben Elgar are instances in the present novel) or who spend their money on unprofitable schemes, philanthropic or commercial. Mrs. Lessingham calls these people 'the young men of promise', a phrase which Gissing turned over and over in his mind for some twenty years. Was not Dyce Lashmar called 'The Coming Man', 'The Young Man Eloquent', and more obliquely 'The Friend of Woman', before he was more bluntly styled a charlatan? Jasper Milvain was 'A Man of his Day' and James Dalmaine, in *Thyrza*, 'A Man with a Future'. In all cases irony prevails. The younger Whiffle in *Workers*, Bruno Chilvers in *Born in Exile* are similar impostors. The originality of Clifford Marsh consists in his finding salvation in business, while Reuben Elgar goes the way of most scoundrels. His Christian name, which he himself detests, puts him on a level with Milvain and Lashmar. Gissing was here subtler than

Dickens or Trollope; his symbolic use of names places him, more adequately, by the side of Hardy.

It would be wearisome to analyse at length the network of associations between *The Emancipated* and the other Gissing novels, although they would make us feel the very texture of the writer's thoughts. A few instances will enable us to follow some of the channels into which they flowed. The title of the novel itself was anticipated by that of ch. XIII of *Workers in the Dawn*, 'Emancipation', which is concerned with Helen Norman's spiritual evolution through the reading of Strauss's *Life of Jesus*, prior to her discovery of Schopenhauer, who figures unnamed in *The Emancipated*. The central paragraph on p. 174 referring to Mallard, and his remark to Miriam Baske that 'in a world where pain is the most obvious fact, the task of mercy must surely take precedence of most others', bear the stamp of the German philosopher. Waymark in *The Unclassed* had already spoken in this strain, and so would Reardon and Biffen in *New Grub Street*. The burden of life weighs on a number of characters in a tragic or semi-comic manner: Madeline Denyer dies a living death, poor Mr. Musselwhite lives a dying life. On other planes, Spence's detestation of the commercial aspects of existence has been foreshadowed in *Thyrza* and will be prolonged in *The Crown of Life*. Zillah Denyer, as depicted in ch. III, toiling 'day by day at perky little primers and compendia, and only [learning] one chapter that it might be driven out of her head by the next', is a pathetic illustration of the effects of inadequate education upon a fourth-rate brain, an idea taken up at length in *In the Year of Jubilee* with Samuel Barmby and Jessica Morgan. Also, when journalising, Cecily Doran seems to hold the pen once owned by Helen Norman in her Tübingen days, while Mrs. Travis, that much tried wife who functions as a link between Cecily and Madeline, might conveniently pass into *The Odd Women*, so akin to their difficulties are her own conjugal troubles.

Despite all the woes that befall the Emancipated, the story is not as gloomy as most reviewers of the first edition deplored it was. With the exception of Madeline Denyer, whose tragic fate can only be blamed on the malignity of chance, the characters are given their due – indeed some are better rewarded than their intelligence wisdom justifies. Gissing had so far written novels nearly all of which betrayed passionate commitments detrimental to their artistic balance. Here as in *Isabel Clarendon* he adopts a quiet tone which the reader of *Demos* or *The Nether World* finds restful. It is this aspect that C. J. Francis stressed at the beginning of his important article on *The Emancipated*: 'The escape it offers from the claustrophobic mood of the previous novels, – in all its aspects, setting, subject, tone, feeling, – is quite remarkable, like a cool drink or a cleansing shower: it breathes freedom as does no other, and this gives point to its theme and the arguments about free choice and determinism which fill it.'[5] Here we meet no characters like John Pether, Jane Vine or Mad Jack; the sky may well sink a little around us when we visit Bartles and its Dissenters or the Denyer boarding-house in London, but on the whole, because of the foreignness of the setting, there prevails an atmosphere of freedom and spaciousness. All the characters have their limitations but they are far more internal than environmental. The baser worries of life interfere but little with their activities or lack of activity. And Gissing does not identify himself closely with any of his young men. Ross Mallard may appear to be his spokesman off and on, but he has his faults and makes mistakes. He is never an exponent character to the same extent as Osmond Waymark, Bernard Kingcote or Sidney Kirkwood had been. Under Italian skies, Gissing largely forgets his personal involvement with the social problems of his country; he places himself on the spiritual and cultural level of existence. Geographical distance makes him serene and allows his intellectual and artistic enthusiasm to follow a broader course. He has become capable of an objectivity hitherto rather sought after than achieved.

The theme of emancipation is satisfactorily integrated with the scenery, with art (mainly in the form of painting, sculpture and literature) and with Italian life in its daily aspects. Naples and its surroundings in Part I, Rome in Part II are significant factors in the characterization. The *dramatis personae* do not visit the sites of ancient civilization or the Roman museums gratuitously; they are influenced by them and reveal themselves by their behaviour in such places. The setting also has an obvious symbolical dimension: the love scene between Reuben Elgar and Cecily Doran in the dead city of Pompeii somehow contains the seeds of its unhappy outcome. Not only is mutual passion soon to die down, but the fruit of that passion – Cecily's baby – is also fated to pass away. Remoteness from her soul-killing Lancashire environment gradually brings Miriam to see Bartles as a stronghold of hypocrisy and religious mummery. Cecily's romanticism flames up in sight of Vesuvius just as Reuben's temperamental instability develops in southern climes. This aspect of *The Emancipated* has prompted recent commentators to compare the story with *Middlemarch*, a comparison fully justified in itself and supported by a side reference to this novel in a letter from Gissing to Eduard Bertz of 11 September 1889.[6] In *The Appropriate Form*, Barbara Hardy has noted how Miriam 'is prepared for her rescue into love by the sensual challenge of painting', and how, like Dorothea Brooke, 'she changes her view on art', adding that 'after Mallard . . . realizes that she is still alarmed by sculpture, there comes an interestingly explicit dialogue between Mallard and another male character in which this is expressly accounted for by the mention of nudity.'[7] The comparison with E. M. Forster's *Where Angels Fear to Tread* and *A Room with a View* is even more compelling, though, as Shigeru Koike has rightly observed, in these novels the agent of the revelations experienced by Philip Herriton, Caroline Abbott and Lucy Honeychurch is only 'contemporary Italy, the Italians, their real life', while in Gissing's novel the historic and artistic past of the country play a much more significant part.[8] And the fact that this part is not necessarily positive, that indeed it may prove the reverse with easily excitable temperaments, confirms the impression of authorial non-commitment.

There is at the level of themes a similar balance between the unsightly and the beautiful (Bartles and Naples); between freedom and constraint (Reuben and Miriam are examples of each); between truth and falsehood, notably on the human and artistic planes; between passion and reason, especially as far as Cecily is concerned; between the eternal and the ephemeral; between the natural and the artificial. Irony is present from beginning to end. It starts with the title. Few people are spared. There is the easy yet excellent satire of boarding-house life abroad and of the average Englishman or woman abroad; the satire of Italomania and Italophobia, the satire of emancipation and of its opposite, slavery to prejudices as well as to uncontrolled passion. The only people to escape open criticism are Edward and Eleanor Spence; they enjoy happiness because they have rejected romantic and dogmatic attitudes alike. The only dictates they welcome are those of reason, which they are too reasonable to think they can obey in every circumstance. They know each other well, and the gentle shafts they aim at each other prevent their self-satisfaction and basic mutual contentment from degenerating into sentimentalism or foolishness. On her first appearance, Mrs. Lessingham seems to be possessed of the same virtues, but it soon turns out that she is an educator with a system; so Gissing, who had read *The Ordeal of Richard Feverel* with admiration and profit, gives her no chance. Like the girl in her charge, she suffers chastisement. Mrs. Lessingham cultivates self-assurance and to her astonishment reaps the fruits of self-conceit. Gissing disposes of her in a way which appears as gratuitous as Trollope's doing away with Mrs. Proudie, but on second thoughts one is bound to admit that the circumstances of her death harmonize with her mental attitudes. She ultimately pays the penalty of excess.

Although we find Mallard realizing Gissing's persistent dream of raising the women he loved to his own intellectual level, the virtues of education are not exaggerated here as they were in *The Unclassed* or an early short story like 'The Lady of the Dedication'. The training of the mind is one thing, the training of instincts quite another thing. Experience, as is shown by Cecily's trials, is the supreme, perhaps the only teacher. No one, we are given to understand, can claim to be proof against the wildest impulses of his temperament. Only a few lucky individuals can reach moderate happiness – material and domestic, intellectual and spiritual –, so infinite is human capacity for self-delusion, so innumerable the obstacles on the way to full personal development. More explicitly than in his previous novels Gissing depicts men and women in quest of happiness. Through their experiences he aims at defining the conditions and philosophy of contentment for the minority of individuals who do not have to work for a living, a minority which two world wars and greater social justice have condemned to extinction. His answers to the questions raised by the characters' dilemmas is that of an outsider, not that of a man directly involved, hence the sober mood of this novel, if compared with his next two, *New Grub Street* and *Born in Exile*, in which he reviewed with passion and bitterness his own predicament. It was only in the late nineties, with *The Whirlpool*, when disease had made him an invalid, that he felt capable – within the covers of a book – of the wisdom in which Henry Ryecroft glories. In view of the decreasing vitality and defeatism implied by such wisdom, *The Emancipated* is among the corpus of Gissing's more thoughtful works, very nearly an optimistic novel. Mallard is one

of the few congenial heroes whom we leave with moderate
confidence in the future, and there are signs that Cecily might
before long find a more suitable partner in Mr. Seaborne. Piers
Otway, the youthful protagonist of *The Crown of Life*, achieves
greater success than Mallard, but it is to be feared that the brain
which conceived him overlooked the lesson implied by the early
adventures of Cecily Doran. Gissing's last song of love expressed
all too clearly the triumph of hope over experience.

Notes

1 Letter of 25 February 1900 (University of Texas at Austin).
2 Letter of 13 February 1889, *Letters of George Gissing to Eduard Bertz*
   (London, 1961), p. 45.
3 *More Books* (The Bulletin of the Boston Public Library), December
   1947, pp. 376-77.
4 Letter to Ellen of 1 April 1890, *More Books*, November 1947,
   pp. 335-36.
5 C. J. Francis, 'The Emancipated', *Gissing Newsletter*, January 1975,
   p. 2.
6 *Op. cit.*, p. 71.
7 Barbara Hardy, *The Appropriate Form: An Essay on the Novel* (London,
   1964), p. 126.
8 Shigeru Koike, 'The Education of George Gissing', in *English
   Criticism in Japan*, ed. Earl Miner (Tokyo, 1972), p. 249.

The Two Versions of the Novel

Together with *The Unclassed* (1884 and 1895) and *Thyrza* (1887 and 1891), *The Emancipated* is one of the three novels of which two English versions are extant. The French versions of *New Grub Street* and of *The Odd Women* also correspond to revised editions, but the copies of the English edition bearing Gissing's corrections seem to have disappeared, and no authoritative English text matching the revised French version is in either case available.

It was Arthur Henry Bullen, the Elizabethan scholar and publisher, who gave Gissing an opportunity to revise *The Emancipated*. He had published *Denzil Quarrier* in February 1892 and was preparing to bring out *The Odd Women* when he offered to reissue all the novels that were not kept in print by their original publishers, that is all those that were not included in Smith, Elder's half-crown and two-shilling series. Gissing suggested *The Emancipated* rather than *Isabel Clarendon*, *The Unclassed* or *Workers in the Dawn* because it was a comparatively recent book with which he had not yet become deeply dissatisfied. After some difficulties with Bentley who was prepared to sell the copyright of the novel only if he could recoup himself for his losses, an agreement was reached, and Gissing went through a copy of the three-decker on 11 and 12 December, 1892. He did not record any mental torture as he was to do about *The Unclassed* three years later – only his having 'made many corrections'. Indeed as late as 3 July, 1896 we find him referring to *The Emancipated* with some satisfaction in a letter to Clara Collet: 'You know I am always glad when you feel able to praise my writing. There *are* a few good things in 'The Emancipated', especially some fair descriptive passages. As for the women, – well I had a pretty clear notion of Miriam. Cecily seems to me now colourless.'

The revision was much less extensive than that of *The Unclassed* or even that of *Thyrza*, doubtless because he had not yet cast off the yoke of the three-decker technique. About 240 lines in the first edition were cancelled, that is some 10 pages out of 900. The revised version offers many examples of rephrasing affecting a few words; additions are very rare and never exceed a few words either.

Alterations readily fall into several categories:

(i) correction of misprints and orthographic slips: Posilipo/Posilippo (p. 3); any of his painting(s) (69); would have been (an) insult (88); faculty/facility (222); Marian/Miriam (370); please do come/please to come (434). Hyphenation and punctuation were also improved.

(ii) substitution of one word or phrase for another with a view to replacing an unfelicitous, ambiguous, pedantic, or unduly aggressive word: terminated/bounded (12); aggravation/provocation (20); discretion/prudence (37); nastly little primers/perky little primers (39); vile little town/murky little town (75); called to each other in Latin/talked. . . (78); trained palate/learned palate (135); for supremacy with that tribe/with them (325); easiness/ease (344); bourgeois world/humdrum world (446); a brightening in her eyes/in her face (448).

(iii) deletion of unnecessary and/or tautological words: there was *certainly* a strong affection between her and Miriam Elgar (19); but letters *gradually* grew shorter (19); exquisite *girlish* frankness (82); upon his brows, *ambrosial, soul-shadowing* (90); *distinctly* above his own social standing (118).

(iv) rewriting of ponderous sentences: a local importance which she prized so much as to determine on living as hitherto/to which she was not indifferent (19); remained so as to be present when the visitors/remained when the visitors (37); unless one took it for such that her sober garments exhibited a perfect neatness and a complete inoffensiveness/unless it were that her sober garments exhibited perfect neatness and complete inoffensiveness (37); secretly hid it within/secreted it within (153); dead by when/dead when (153): I know of that, of course/I know that, of course (394).

(v) cancellation of superfluous details and short incidental remarks: Greek and Latin were not indeed linguistically known

to her – one must pick one's phrases in speaking of Madeline –
but/Greek and Latin were beyond her scope, but (38); . . . to
meet. *What a road it is!* Unlike the Sorrento side (73); with some
warmth, *though he yet preserved the tone of self-accusation* (181);
. . . impulses – *as we are all apt to do, alike in great and little things –*
she attributed (367).

(vi) changes concerning people and places: Madame Glück
became Mrs. Glück; the Via Roma (42 and 97) was replaced by
the Toledo while two literary allusions to Herrick and to Tennyson
disappeared. On p. 37, line 9, Madeline Denyer was introduced
thus: 'Madeline, a couple of years younger, enjoyed a more healthy
physique and a less common comeliness, but in attire she seemed
to aim at Herrick's "fine distraction" and 'sweet disorder", without
being able to compass the corresponding "wild civility". '. On page
46, line 10, 'but they were unsophisticated' is a correction for
'but then these were children of nature, and would doubtless
have indulged in profane laughter at sight of an early portrait of
Alfred Tennyson.' . . . .

More important with regard to Gissing's changing attitude
to the art of fiction between 1889 and 1892 is the systematic
removal of all traces of authorial intervention in the first person
singular or plural and of addresses to the reader in the second
person singular or plural. One example of each will suffice to
illustrate this point: (i) At the time of which I write/In 1878;
(ii) you may readily attribute to her/might probably be attributed
to her. One exception only has been found, on page 274, line 6:
'With what result you are aware.' In spite of these corrections,
the author's effacement in the revised version is only relative.
Indeed it is in quite a few cases purely superficial, witness this
example on p. 20, line 28: 'She was not, perhaps, singular in her
concernment with such a personal problem.' Gissing was content
to substitute 'perhaps' for 'I believe'.

The most extensive deletions (from 2 to 40 lines) are about
twenty in number. Here are those which have not been recorded
for other reasons above:

(i) narrative and didactic details on the magnificence of the
Neapolitan scenery (12, line 1), on the correspondence between
Miriam and Cecily (19, line 26), on singing (21, line 12), on
Clifford Marsh (118, line 30: 'Frankness as to his circumstances
was inevitable, and we know what had been the result'), on
pictures shown by Mallard to Miriam (321, line 2) and on

Miriam's hairdress (434, line 22).

(ii) lengthy psychological comment and parenthetic authorial remarks on his characters. They concern Mrs. Bradshaw (32, line 30), the Denyers (36, line 30), Reuben Elgar and men of his temperament (115, line 24; 309, line 16), Publius Octavius Rufus (169, line 21), Miriam's feelings (347, line 5, and 348, line 6), Mallard's thoughts of Miriam (353, line 29), on Cecily's character and position (356, line 24 and 357, line 31).

(iii) a characteristic passage eloquent of Gissing's enthusiasm about the Greek temples at Paestum: 'Dear and glorious temples! sanctuaries still for all to whom poetry is religion. These stones, have they not echoed to Hellenic speech? When Latin worship had fled from them, when the Saracen had done his worst, when the Norman pirate had pillaged all he could to adorn his Christian church at Amalfi, – time and solitude became warders of what remained, hallowing the austere beauty of these abandoned fanes to be a monument of the world where gods and men walked together' (308, after 'chinks').

(iv) an address to the average man which is typical of the early novels: 'Oh, good, happy, respectable people! How kindly did Nature deal with you, when she framed you to be placid and useful members of society – to fall becomingly in love at five and twenty, and wait peacefully for marriage in the ninth year after, when your means are adequate; to see children grow up about you as your hairs grizzle, and witness in them the repetition of your own orderly youth! Right is it, right and good, that you should kneel at your bedsides and render thanks for the day of prose that has been granted you. In prose is your blessedness; seek to know nothing else; shun the poet and all his works as you do the devil with whom you are theoretically so familiar. You might have been born with a core of fire in your bosoms, instead of the ingenious organ which pumps the gentle current of life along your unfretted veins. Think of it, and render double thanks. . .' (142, after 'to yell'). Akin to this passage is a short aside to the reader (296, line 11, after 'world') about Elgar's book: 'You conceive readily enough what kind of work he wished to produce; this and that example from existing literature occur to you.'

(v) some long anticipatory comment about Cecily's failure to exercise a moral influence on her husband which occurred between the last two paragraphs on p. 296: 'And there began Cecily's misfortune, for, of course, it is idle to use the word 'fault' in such connection. When by the blessing of her love a strong woman has put joyous activity in the heart of a man whose life has suffered misdirection and vain tumult, there is one supreme gift she must yet bestow if her influence is to remain beneficent: she must teach him self-knowledge and resignation therein. No harder task than this, for love only can perform it, and yet the undertaking is love's greatest peril. Cecily was foredoomed to failure by the fact that she was only now beginning to know herself, and, as a consequence, to perceive how greatly her love had been the outcome of youthful illusion. When each new discovery of Reuben's limitations was a pang and a fear to her, how could she encourage him against his own discouragements? When she herself avoided looking forward, and that in conscious cowardice, how was she to bid him keep a steadfast face?

Pretence in this case is worse than useless, and Cecily was incapable of sustained disguise.'

After perusing such passages, one is inevitably led to think that in 1892 Gissing was prepared to trust his readers' judgment far more than he did in 1889. The most substantial deletions would nowadays be pronounced offensive by those critics who, having suffered mental torture when reading authorial digressions in Trollope and George Eliot, have become unduly sensitive to any overexplicit expression of the writer's stance. Among the many reasons why *The Emancipated* must be allowed a new lease of life, there is one of particular artistic significance: it was between the first and the second version of this novel that Gissing became committed to the new, more impersonal approach to fiction. When Eduard Bertz, after reading *Born in Exile*, expressed fears that the tone of the book might henceforth become that of his friend's work, he wrote placatingly: 'No, I hope to be more and more objective in my work; I hope to, and mean to.' *The Odd Women* shows that he was true to his word, and his revision of *The Emancipated* testifies to the same determination.

THE EMANCIPATED

A NOVEL

BY

GEORGE GISSING

AUTHOR OF "THE ODD WOMEN," "NEW GRUB STREET," ETC.

LONDON

LAWRENCE AND BULLEN

16, HENRIETTA STREET, W.C.

1893

LONDON.
PRINTED BY WOODFALL AND KINDER,
70 TO 76, LONG ACRE, W.C.

CONTENTS.

PART II.

CHAPTER X.

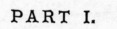

PART I.

THE EMANCIPATED.

CHAPTER I.

By a window looking from Posillipo upon the Bay of Naples sat an English lady, engaged in letter-writing. She was only in her four-and-twentieth year, but her attire of subdued mourning indicated widowhood already at the stage when it is permitted to make quiet suggestion of freedom rather than distressful reference to loss; the dress, however, was severely plain, and its grey coldness, which would well have harmonized with an English sky in this month of November, looked alien in the southern sunlight. There was no mistaking her nationality; the absorption, the troubled earnestness with which she bent over her writing, were peculiar to a cast of features such as can be found only in our familiar island; a physiognomy not quite pure in out-line, vigorous in general effect and in detail delicate; a proud young face, full of character and capacity, beautiful in chaste control. Sorrowful it was not, but its paleness and thinness expressed something more than imperfect health of body; the blue-grey eyes, when they wandered for a moment in an effort of recollection, had a look of weariness, even of ennui; the lips moved as if in nervous impatience until she had found the phrase or the thought for which her pen waited. Save for these intervals, she wrote with quick decision, in a large clear hand, never underlining, but frequently supplying the emphasis of heavy stroke in her penning of a word. At the end of her letters came a signature excellent in individuality: "Miriam Baske."

The furniture of her room was modern, and of the kind demanded by wealthy *forestieri* in the lodgings they condescend to occupy. On the variegated tiles of the floor were strewn rugs and carpets; the drapery was bright, without much reference to taste in the ordering of hues; a handsome stove served at present to support leafy plants, a row of which also stood on the balcony before the window. Round the ceiling ran a painted border of foliage and flowers. The chief ornament of the walls was a large and indifferent copy of Raphael's "St. Cecilia;" there were, too, several *gouache* drawings of local scenery: a fiery night-view of Vesuvius, a panorama of the Bay, and a very blue Blue Grotto. The whole was blithe, sunny, Neapolitan; sufficiently unlike a sitting-room in Redbeck House, Bartles, Lancashire, which Mrs. Baske had in her mind as she wrote.

A few English books lay here and there, volumes of unattractive binding, and presenting titles little suggestive of a holiday in Campania; works which it would be misleading to call theological; the feeblest modern echoes of fierce old Puritans, half shame-faced modifications of logic which, at all events, was wont to conceal no consequence of its savage premises. More noticeable were some architectural plans unrolled upon a settee; the uppermost represented the elevation of a building designed for religious purposes, painfully recognizable by all who know the conventicles of sectarian England. On the blank space beneath the drawing were a few comments, lightly pencilled.

Having finished and addressed some half a dozen brief letters, Mrs. Baske brooded for several minutes before she began to write on the next sheet of paper. It was intended for her sister-in-law, a lady of middle age, who shared in the occupancy of Redbeck House. At length she penned the introductory formula, but again became absent, and sat gazing at the branches of a pine-tree which stood in strong relief against cloudless blue. A sigh, an impatient gesture, and she went on with her task.

"It is very kind of you to be so active in attending to the things which you know I have at heart. You say I shall find everything as I could wish it on my return, but you cannot think what a stranger to Bartles I already feel. It will soon be six months since I lived my real life there; during my illness I might as well have been absent, then came those weeks in the Isle of Wight, and now this exile. I feel it as exile, bitterly. To be sure Naples is beautiful, but it does not interest me. You need not envy me the bright sky, for it gives me no pleasure. There is so much to pain and sadden; so much that makes me angry. On Sunday I was miserable. The Spences are as kind as any one could be, but——I won't write about it; no doubt you understand me.

"What do you think ought to be done about Mrs. Ackworth and her daughter? It is shameful, after all they have received from me. Will you tell them that I am gravely displeased to hear of their absenting themselves from chapel. I have a very good mind to write to Mr. Higginson and beg him to suspend the girl from his employment until she becomes regular in her attendance at worship. Perhaps that would seem malicious, but she and her mother ought to be punished in some way. Speak to them very sternly.

"I do not understand how young Brooks has dared to tell you I promised him work in the greenhouse. He is irreclaimable; the worst character that ever came under my notice; he shall not set foot on the premises. If he is in want, he has only himself to blame. I do not like to think of his wife suffering, but it is the attribute of sins such as his that they involve the innocent with the guilty ; and then she has shown herself so wretchedly weak. Try, however, to help her secretly if her distress becomes too acute.

"It was impertinent in Mrs. Walker to make such reference to me in public. This is the result of my absence and helplessness. I shall write to her—two lines."

A flush had risen to her cheek, and in adding the last two words she all but pierced through the thin note-paper. Then her hand trembled so much that she was obliged to pause. At the same] moment there sounded a tap at the door, and, on Mrs. Baske's giving permission, a lady entered. This was Mrs. Spence, a cousin of the young widow; she and her husband had an apartment here in the Villa Sannazaro, and were able to devote certain rooms to the convenience of their relative during her stay at Naples. Her age was about thirty; she had a graceful figure, a manner of much|refinement, and a bright, gentle, intellectual face, which just now bore an announcement of news.

"They have arrived!"

"Already?" replied the other, in a tone of civil interest.

"They decided not to break the journey after Genoa. Cecily and Mrs. Lessingham are too tired to do anything but get settled in their rooms, but Mr. Mallard has come to tell us."

Miriam laid down her pen, and asked in the same voice as before:

"Shall I come?"

"If you are not too busy." And Mrs. Spence added, with a smile, "I should think you must have a certain curiosity to see each other, after so long an acquaintance at second-hand."

"I will come in a moment."

Mrs. Spence left the room. For a minute Miriam sat reflecting, then rose. In moving towards the door she chanced to see her image in a mirror—two of a large size adorned the room—and it checked her step; she regarded herself gravely, and passed a smoothing hand over the dark hair above her temples.

By a corridor she reached her friends' sitting-room, where Mrs. Spence sat in the company of two gentlemen. The elder of these was Edward Spence. His bearded face, studious of cast and small-featured, spoke a placid, self-commanding character; a lingering smile, and the pleasant wrinkles about his brow, told of a mind familiar with many by-ways of fancy and reflection. His companion, a man of five-and-thirty, had a far more striking countenance. His complexion was of the kind which used to be called adust— burnt up with inner fires; his visage was long and some-what harshly designed, very apt, it would seem, to the expression of bitter ironies or stern resentments, but at present bright with friendly pleasure. He had a heavy moustache, but no beard; his hair tumbled in disorder. To matters of costume he evidently gave little thought, for his clothes, though of the kind a gentleman would wear in travelling, had seen their best days, and the waist-coat even lacked one of its buttons; his black necktie was knotted into an indescribable shape, and the ends hung loose.

Him Mrs. Spence at once presented to her cousin as "Mr. Mallard." He bowed ungracefully; then, with a manner naturally frank but constrained by obvious shyness, took the hand Miriam held to him.

"We are scarcely strangers, Mr. Mallard," she said in a self-possessed tone, regarding him with steady eyes.

"Miss Doran has spoken of you frequently on the journey," he replied, knitting his brows into a scowl as he smiled and returned her look. "Your illness made her very anxious. You are much better, I hope?"

"Much, thank you."

Allowance made for the difference of quality in their voices, Mrs. Baske and Mallard resembled each other in speech. They had the same grave note, the same decision.

"They must be very tired after their journey," Miriam added, seating herself.

"Miss Doran seems scarcely so at all; but Mrs. Lessingham is rather over-wearied, I'm afraid."

"Why didn't you break the journey at Florence or Rome?" asked Mrs. Spence.

"I proposed it, but other counsels prevailed. All through Italy Miss Doran was distracted between desire to get to Naples and misery at not being able to see the towns we passed. At last she buried herself in the 'Revue des Deux Mondes,' and refused even to look out of the window."

"I suppose we may go and see her in the morning?" said Miriam.

"My express instructions are," replied Mallard, "that you are on no account to go. They will come here quite early. Miss Doran begged hard to come with me now, but I wouldn't allow it."

"Is it the one instance in which your authority has prevailed?" inquired Spence. "You seem to declare it in a tone of triumph."

"Well," replied the other, with a grim smile, leaning forward in his chair, "I don't undertake to lay down rules for the young lady of eighteen as I could for the child of twelve. But my age and sobriety of character still ensure me respect."

He glanced at Mrs. Baske, and their eyes met. Miriam smiled rather coldly, but continued to observe him after he had looked away again.

"You met them at Genoa?" she asked presently, in her tone of habitual reserve.

"Yes. I came by sea from London, and had a couple of days to wait for their arrival from Paris."

"And I suppose you also are staying at Mrs. Gluck's?"

"Oh no! I have a room at old quarters of mine high up in the town, Vico Brancaccio. I shall only be in Naples a few days."

"How's that?" inquired Spence,

"I'm going to work at Amalfi and Paestum."

"Then, as usual, we shall see nothing of you," said Mrs. Spence. "Pray, do you dine at Mrs. Gluck's this evening?"

"By no means."

"May we, then, have the pleasure of your company? There is no need to go back to Vico Brancaccio. I am sure Mrs. Baske will excuse you the torture of uniform."

With a sort of grumble, the invitation was accepted. A little while after, Spence proposed to his friend a walk before sunset.

"Yes; let us go up the hill," said Mallard, rising abruptly. "I need movement after the railway."

They left the villa, and Mallard grew less restrained in his conversation.

"How does Mrs. Baske answer to your expectations?" Spence asked him.

"I had seen her photograph, you know."

"Where?"

"Her brother showed it me—one taken at the time of her marriage."

"What is Elgar doing at present?"

"It's more than a year since we crossed each other," Mallard replied. "He was then going to the devil as speedily as can in reason be expected of a man. I happened to encounter him one morning at Victoria Station, and he seemed to have just slept off a great deal of heavy drinking. Told me he was going down to Brighton to see about selling a houseful of furniture there—his own property. I didn't inquire how or why he came possessed of it. He is beyond help, I imagine. When he comes to his last penny, he'll probably blow his brains out; just the fellow to do that kind of thing."

"I suppose he hasn't done it already? His sister has heard nothing of him for two years at least, and this account of yours is the latest I have received."

"I should think he still lives. He would be sure to make a *coup de théâtre* of his exit."

"Poor lad!" said the elder man, with feeling. "I liked him."

"Why, so did I; and I wish it had been in my scope to keep him in some kind of order. Yes, I liked him much. And as for brains, why, I have scarcely known a man who so impressed me with a sense of his ability. But you could see that he was doomed from his cradle. Strongly like his sister in face."

"I'm afraid the thought of him troubles her a good deal."

"She looks ill."

"Yes; we are uneasy about her," said Spence. Then, with a burst of impatience: "There's no getting her mind away from that pestilent Bartles. What do you think she is projecting now? It appears that the Dissenters of Bartles are troubled concerning their chapel; it isn't large enough. So Miriam proposes to pull down her own house, and build them a chapel on the site, of course at her own expense. The ground being her freehold, she can unfortunately do what she likes with it; the same with her personal property. The thing has gone so far that a Manchester firm of architects have prepared plans; they are lying about in her room here."

Mallard regarded the speaker with humorous wonder.

"And the fact is," pursued Spence, "that such an undertaking as this will impoverish her. She is not so wealthy as to be able to lay out thousands of pounds and leave her position unaltered."

"I suppose she lives only for her religious convictions?"

"I don't profess to understand her. Her character is not easily sounded. But no doubt she has the puritanical spirit in a rather rare degree. I daily thank the fates that my wife grew up apart from that branch of the family. Of all the accursed—— But this is an old topic; better not to heat one's self uselessly."

"A Puritan at Naples," mused Mallard. "The situation is interesting."

"Very. But then she doesn't really live in Naples. From the first day she has shown herself bent on resisting every influence of the place. She won't admit that the climate benefits her; she won't allow an expression of interest in anything Italian to escape her. I doubt whether we shall ever get her even to Pompeii. One afternoon I persuaded her to walk up here with me, and tried to make her confess that this view was beautiful. She grudged making any such admission. It is her nature to *distrust* the beautiful."

"To be sure. That is the badge of her persuasion."

"Last Sunday we didn't know whether to compassionate her or to be angry with her. The Bradshaws are at Mrs. Gluck's. You know them by name, I think? There again, an interesting study, in a very different way. Twice in the day she shut herself up with them in their rooms, and they held a dissident service. The hours she spent here were passed in the solitude of her own room, lest she should witness our profane enjoyment of the fine weather. Eleanor refrained from touching the piano, and at meals kept the gravest countenance, in mere kindness. I doubt whether that is right. It isn't as though we were dealing with a woman whose mind is hopelessly—immatured; she is only a girl still, and I know she has brains if she could be induced to use them."

"Mrs. Baske has a remarkable face, it seems to me," said Mallard.

"It enrages me to talk of the matter."

They were now on the road which runs along the ridge of Posillipo; at a point where it is parted only by a low wall from the westward declivity, they paused and looked towards the setting sun.

"What a noise from Fuorigrotta!" murmured Spence, when he had leaned for a moment on the wall. "It always amuses me. Only in this part of the world could so small a place make such a clamour."

They were looking away from Naples. At the foot of the
vine-covered hillside lay the noisy village, or suburb, named
from its position at the outer end of the tunnel which the
Romans pierced to make a shorter way between Naples and
Puteoli; thence stretched an extensive plain, set in a deep
amphitheatre of hills, and bounded by the sea. Vineyards
and maizefields, pine-trees and poplars, diversify its surface,
and through the midst of it runs a long, straight road,
dwindling till it reaches the shore at the hamlet of Bagnoli.
Follow the enclosing ridge to the left, to where its slope cuts
athwart plain and sea and sky; there close upon the coast
lies the island rock of Nisida, meeting-place of Cicero and
Brutus after Cæsar's death. Turn to the opposite quarter
of the plain. First rises the cliff of Camaldoli, where from
their oak-shadowed lawn the monks look forth upon as fair
a prospect as is beheld by man. Lower hills succeed, hiding
Pozzuoli and the inner curve of its bay; behind them, too,
is the nook which shelters Lake Avernus; and at a little
distance, by the further shore, are the ruins of Cumæ, first
home of the Greeks upon Italian soil. A long promontory
curves round the gulf; the dark crag at the end of it is Cape
Misenum, and a little on the hither side, obscured in remoteness, lies what once was Baiæ. Beyond the promontory
gleams again a blue line of sea. The low length of Procida
is its limit, and behind that, crowning the view, stands the
mountain-height of Ischia.

Over all, the hues of an autumn evening in Campania.
From behind a bulk of cloud, here and there tossed by high
wind currents into fantastic shapes, sprang rays of fire,
burning to the zenith. Between the sea-beach at Bagnoli
and the summit of Ischia, tract followed upon tract of colour
that each moment underwent a subtle change, darkening
here, there fading into exquisite transparencies of distance,
till by degrees the islands lost projection and became mere
films against the declining day. The plain was ruddy with
dead vine-leaves, and golden with the decaying foliage of

the poplars; Camaldoli and its neighbour heights stood gorgeously enrobed. In itself, a picture so beautiful that the eye wearied with delight; in its memories, a source of solemn joy, inexhaustible for ever.

"I suppose," said Mallard, in the undertone of reflection, "the pagan associations of Naples are a great obstacle to Mrs. Baske's enjoyment of the scenery."

"She admits that."

"By-the-bye, what are likely to be the relations between her and Miss Doran?"

"I have wondered. They seem to keep on terms of easy correspondence. But doesn't Cecily herself throw any light on that point?"

Mallard made a pause before answering.

"You must remember that I know very little of her. I have never spoken more intimately with her than you yourself have. Naturally, since she has ceased to be a child, I have kept my distance. In fact, I shall be heartily glad when the next three years are over, and we can shake hands with a definite good-bye."

"What irritates you?" inquired Spence, with a smile which recognized a phase of his friend's character.

"The fact of my position. A nice thing for a fellow like me to have charge of a fortune! It oppresses me—the sense of responsibility; I want to get the weight off my shoulders. What the deuce did her father mean by burdening me in this way?"

"He foresaw nothing of the kind," said Spence, amused. "Only the unlikely event of Trench's death left you sole trustee. If Doran purposed anything at all—why, who knows what it may have been?"

Mallard refused to meet the other's look; his eyes were fixed on the horizon.

"All the same, the event was possible, and he should have chosen another man of business. It's worse than being rich on my own account. I have dreams of a national repudiation of debt; I imagine dock-companies failing and banks stopping payment. It disturbs my work; I am tired of it. Why can't I transfer the affair to some trustworthy and competent person; yourself, for instance? Why didn't Doran select you, to begin with—the natural man to associate with Trench?"

"Who never opened a book save his ledger; who was the model of a reputable dealer in calicoes; who——"

"I apologize," growled Mallard. "But you know in what sense I spoke."

"Pray, what has Cecily become since I saw her in London?" asked the other, after a pause, during which he smiled his own interpretation of Mallard's humour.

"A very superior young person, I assure you," was the reply, gravely spoken. "Miss Doran is a young woman of her time; she ranks with the emancipated; she is as far above the Girton girl as that interesting creature is above the product of an establishment for young ladies. Miss Doran has no prejudices, and, in the vulgar sense of the word, no principles. She is familiar with the Latin classics and with the Parisian feuilletons; she knows all about the newest religion, and can tell you Sarcey's opinion of the newest play. Miss Doran will discuss with you the merits of Sarah Bernhardt in 'La Dame aux Camélias,' or the literary theories of the brothers Goncourt. I am not sure that she knows much about Shakespeare, but her appreciation of Baudelaire is exquisite. I don't think she is naturally very cruel, but she can plead convincingly the cause of vivisection. Miss Doran——"

Spence interrupted him with a burst of laughter.

"All which, my dear fellow, simply means that you——"

Mallard, in his turn, interrupted gruffly.

"Precisely: that I am the wrong man to hold even the position of steward to one so advanced. What have I to do with heiresses and fashionable ladies? I have my work to get on with, and it shall not suffer from the intrusion of idlers."

"I see you direct your diatribe half against Mrs. Lessingham. How has she annoyed you?"

"Annoyed me? You never were more mistaken. It's with myself that I am annoyed."

"On what account?"

"For being so absurd as to question sometimes whether my responsibility doesn't extend beyond stock and share. I ask myself whether Doran—who so befriended me, and put such trust in me, and paid me so well in advance for the duties I was to undertake—didn't take it for granted that I should exercise some influence in the matter of his daughter's education? Is she growing up what he would have wished her to be? And if——"

"Why, it's no easy thing to say what views he had on this subject. The lax man, we know, is often enough severe with his own womankind. But as you have given me no description of what Cecily really is, I can offer no judgment. Wait till I have seen her. Doubtless she fulfils her promise of being beautiful?"

"Yes; there is no denying her beauty."

"As for her *modernité*, why, Mr. Ross Mallard is a singular person to take exception on that score."

"I don't know about that. When did I say that the modern woman was my ideal?"

"When had you ever a good word for the system which makes of woman a dummy and a kill-joy?"

"That has nothing to do with the question," replied Mallard, preserving a tone of gruff impartiality. "Have I been faithful to my stewardship? When I consented to Cecily's—to Miss Doran's passing from Mrs. Elgar's care to that of Mrs. Lessingham, was I doing right?"

"Mallard, you are a curious instance of the Puritan conscience surviving in a man whose intellect is liberated. The note of your character, including your artistic character, is this conscientiousness. Without it, you would have had worldly success long ago. Without it, you wouldn't talk nonsense of Cecily Doran. Had you rather she were co-operating with Mrs. Baske in a scheme to rebuild all the chapels in Lancashire ? "

" There is a medium."

" Why, yes. A neither this nor that, an insipid refinement, a taste for culture moderated by reverence for Mrs. Grundy."

" Perhaps you are right. It's only occasionally that I am troubled in this way. But I heartily wish the three years remaining were over."

" And the 'definite good-bye' spoken. A good phrase, that of yours. What possessed you to come here just now, if it disturbs you to be kept in mind of these responsibilities ? "

"I should find it hard to tell you. The very sense of responsibility, I suppose. But, as I said, I am not going to stay in Naples."

" You'll come and give us a ' definite good-bye ' before you leave ? "

Mallard said nothing, but turned and began to move on. They passed one of the sentry-boxes which here along the ridge mark the limits of Neapolitan excise ; a boy-soldier, musket in hand, cast curious glances at them. After walking in silence for a few minutes, they began to descend the eastern face of the hill, and before them lay that portion of the great gulf which pictures have made so familiar. The landscape was still visible in all its main details, still softly suffused with warm colours from the west. About the cone of Vesuvius a darkly purple cloud was gathering ; the twin height of Somma stood clear and of a rich brown. Naples, the many-coloured, was seen in profile, climbing from the Castel dell' Ovo, around which the sea slept, to the rock of Sant' Elmo ; along the curve of the Chiaia lights had begun to glimmer. Far withdrawn, the craggy promontory of Sorrento darkened to profoundest blue ; and Capri veiled itself in mist.

CHAPTER II.

CECILY DORAN.

VILLA SANNAZARO had no architectural beauty; it was a building of considerable size, irregular, in need of external repair. Through the middle of it ran a great archway, guarded by copies of the two Molossian hounds which stand before the Hall of Animals in the Vatican; beneath the arch, on the right-hand side, was the main entrance to the house. If you passed straight through, you came out upon a terrace, where grew a magnificent stone-pine and some robust agaves. The view hence was uninterrupted, embracing the line of the bay from Posillipo to Cape Minerva. From the parapet bordering the platform you looked over a descent of twenty feet, into a downward sloping vineyard. Formerly the residence of an old Neapolitan family, the villa had gone the way of many such ancestral abodes, and was now let out among several tenants.

The Spences were established here for the winter. On the occasion of his marriage, three years ago, Edward Spence relinquished his connection with a shipping firm, which he represented in Manchester, and went to live in London; a year and a half later he took his wife to Italy, where they had since remained. He was not wealthy, but had means sufficient to his demands and prospects. Thinking for himself in most matters, he chose to abandon money-making at the juncture when most men deem it incumbent upon them to press their efforts in that direction; business was repugnant to him, and he saw no reason why he should sacrifice his own existence to put a possible family in more than easy circumstances. He had the inclinations of a student, but was untroubled by any desire to distinguish himself, freedom from the demands of the office meant to him the possibility of living where he chose, and devoting to his books the best part of the day instead of its fragmentary leisure. His choice in marriage was most happy. Eleanor Spence had passed her maiden life in Manchester, but with parents of healthy mind and of more literature than generally falls to the lot of a commercial family. Pursuing a natural development, she allied herself with her husband's freedom of intellect, and found her nature's opportunities in the life which was to him most suitable. By a rare chance, she was the broader-minded of the two, the more truly impartial. Her emancipation from dogma had been so gradual, so unconfused by external pressure, that from her present standpoint she could look back with calmness and justice on all the stages she had left behind. With her cousin Miriam she could sympathize in a way impossible to Spence, who, by-the-bye, somewhat misrepresented his wife in the account he gave to Mallard of their Sunday experiences. Puritanism was familiar to her by more than speculation; in the compassion with which she regarded Miriam there was no mixture of contempt, as in her husband's case. On the other hand, she did not pretend to read completely her cousin's heart and mind; she knew that there was no simple key to Miriam's character, and the quiet study of its phases from day to day deeply interested her.

Cecily Doran had been known to Spence from childhood; her father was his intimate friend. But Eleanor had only made the girl's acquaintance in London, just after her marriage, when Cecily was spending a season there with her aunt, Mrs. Lessingham. Mallard's ward was then little more than fifteen; after several years of weak health, she had entered upon a vigorous maidenhood, and gave such promise of free, joyous, aspiring life as could not but strongly affect the sympathies of a woman like Eleanor. Three years prior to that, at the time of her father's death, Cecily

was living with Mrs. Elgar, a widow, and her daughter
Miriam, the latter on the point of marrying (at eighteen)
one Mr. Baske, a pietistic mill-owner, aged fifty. It then
seemed very doubtful whether Cecily would live to mature
years; she had been motherless from infancy, and the
difficulty with those who brought her up was to repress an
activity of mind which seemed to be one cause of her bodily
feebleness. In those days there was a strong affection
between her and Miriam Elgar, and it showed no sign of
diminution in either when, on Mrs. Elgar's death, a year and
a half after Miriam's marriage, Cecily passed into the care of
her father's sister, a lady of moderate fortune, of parts and
attainments, and with a great love of cosmopolitan life. A
few months more and Mrs. Baske was to be a widow, child-
less, left in possession of some eight hundred a year, her
house at Bartles, and a local importance to which she was
not indifferent. With the exception of her brother, away in
London, she had no near kin. It would now have been a
great solace to her if Cecily Doran could have been her companion; but the young girl was in Paris, or Berlin, or St.
Petersburg, and, as Miriam was soon to learn, the material
distance between them meant little in comparison with the
spiritual remoteness which resulted from Cecily's education
under Mrs. Lessingham. They corresponded, however, and
at first frequently; but letters grew shorter on both sides,
and arrived less often. The two were now to meet for the
first time since Cecily was a child of fourteen.

The ladies arrived at the villa about eleven o'clock.
Miriam had shown herself indisposed to speak of them,
both last evening, when Mallard was present, and again
this morning when alone with her relatives; at breakfast
she was even more taciturn than usual, and kept her room
for an hour after the meal. Then, however, she came to
sit with Eleanor, and remained when the visitors were
announced.

Mrs. Lessingham did not answer to the common idea of a

strong-minded woman. At forty-seven she preserved much natural grace of bearing, a good complexion, pleasantly mobile features. Her dress was in excellent taste, tending to elaboration, such as becomes a lady who makes some figure in the world of ease. Little wrinkles at the outer corners of her eyes assisted her look of placid thoughtfulness ; when she spoke, these were wont to disappear, and the expression of her face became an animated intelligence, an eager curiosity, or a vivacious good-humour. Her lips gave a hint of sarcasm, but this was reserved for special occasions ; as a rule her habit of speech was suave, much observant of amenities. One might have imagined that she had enjoyed a calm life, but this was far from being the case. The daughter of a country solicitor, she married early —for love, and the issue was disastrous. Above her right temple, just at the roots of the hair, a scar was discoverable ; it was the memento of an occasion on which her husband aimed a blow at her with a mantelpiece ornament, and came within an ace of murder. Intimates of the household said that the provocation was great—that Mrs. Lessingham's gift of sarcasm had that morning displayed itself much too brilliantly. Still, the missile was an extreme retort, and on the whole it could not be wondered at that husband and wife resolved to live apart in future. Mr. Lessingham was, in fact, an aristocratic boor, and his wife never puzzled so much over any intellectual difficulty as she did over the question how, as a girl, she came to imagine herself enamoured of him. She was not, perhaps, singular in her concernment with such a personal problem.

"It is six years since I was in Italy," she said, when greetings were over, and she had seated herself. "Don't you envy me my companion, Mrs. Spence ? If anything could revive one's first enjoyment, it would be the sight of Cecily's."

Cecily was sitting by Miriam, whose hand she had only just relinquished. Her anxious and affectionate inquiries moved Miriam to a smile which seemed rather of indulgence than warm kindness.

"How little we thought where our next meeting would be!" Cecily was saying, when the eyes of the others turned upon her at her aunt's remark.

Noble beauty can scarcely be dissociated from harmony of utterance ; voice and visage are the correspondent means whereby spirit addresses itself to the ear and eye. One who had heard Cecily Doran speaking where he could not see her, must have turned in that direction, have listened eagerly for the sounds to repeat themselves, and then have moved forward to discover the speaker. The divinest singer may leave one unaffected by the tone of her speech. Cecily could not sing, but her voice declared her of those who think in song, whose minds are modulated to the poetry, not to the prose, of life.

Her enunciation had the peculiar finish which is acquired in intercourse with the best cosmopolitan society, the best in a worthy sense. Four years ago, when she left Lancashire, she had a touch of provincial accent,—Miriam, though she spoke well, was not wholly free from it,—but now it was impossible to discover by listening to her from what part of England she came. Mrs. Lessingham, whose admirable tact and adaptability rendered her unimpeachable in such details, had devoted herself with artistic zeal to her niece's training for the world ; the pupil's natural aptitude ensured perfection in the result. Cecily's manner accorded with her utterance ; it had every charm derivable from youth, yet nothing of immaturity. She was as completely at her ease as Mrs. Lessingham, and as much more graceful in her self-control as the advantages of nature made inevitable.

Miriam looked very cold, very severe, very English, by the side of this brilliant girl. The thinness and pallor of her features became more noticeable; the provincial faults of her dress were painfully obvious. Cecily was not robust, but her form lacked no development appropriate to her years, and its beauty was displayed by Parisian handiwork. In this respect, too, she had changed remarkably since Miriam last saw her, when she was such a frail child. Her hair of dark gold showed itself beneath a hat which Eleanor Spence kept regarding with frank admiration, so novel it was in style, and so perfectly suitable to its wearer. Her gloves, her shoes, were no less perfect; from head to foot nothing was to be found that did not become her, that was not faultless in its kind.

At the same time, nothing that suggested idle expense or vanity. To dwell at all upon the subject would be a disproportion, but for the note of contrast that was struck. In an assembly of well-dressed people, no one would have remarked Cecily's attire, unless to praise its quiet distinction. In the Spences' sitting-room it became another matter; it gave emphasis to differences of character; it distinguished the atmosphere of Cecily's life from that breathed by her old friends.

"We are going to read together Goethe's 'Italienische Reise,'" continued Mrs. Lessingham. "It was of quite infinite value to me when I first was here. In each town I *tuned* my thoughts by it, to use a phrase which sounds like affectation, but has a very real significance."

"It was much the same with me," observed Spence.

"Yes, but you had the inestimable advantage of knowing the classics. And Cecily, I am thankful to say, at least has something of Latin; an ode of Horace, which I look at with fretfulness, yields her its meaning. Last night, when I was tired and willing to be flattered, she tried to make me believe it was not yet too late to learn."

"Surely not," said Eleanor, gracefully.

"But Goethe—you remember he says that the desire to see Italy had become an illness with him. I know so well what that means. Cecily will never know; the happiness has come before longing for it had ceased to be a pleasure."

It was not so much affection as pride that her voice expressed when she referred to her niece ; the same in her look, which was less tender than gratified and admiring. Cecily smiled in return, but was not wholly attentive ; her eyes constantly turned to Miriam, endeavouring, though vainly, to exchange a glance.

Mrs. Lessingham was well aware of the difficulty of addressing to Mrs. Baske any remark on natural topics which could engage her sympathy, yet to ignore her presence was impossible.

"Do you think of seeing Rome and the northern cities when your health is established ? " she inquired, in a voice which skilfully avoided any presumption of the reply. " Or shall you return by sea ? "

" I am not a very good sailor," answered Miriam, with sufficient suavity, " and I shall probably go back by land. But I don't think I shall stop anywhere."

" It will be wiser, no doubt," said Mrs. Lessingham, " to leave the rest of Italy for another visit. To see Naples first, and then go north, is very much like taking dessert before one's substantial dinner. I'm a little sorry that Cecily begins here ; but it was better to come and enjoy Naples with her friends this winter. I hope we shall spend most of our time in Italy for a year or two."

Conversation took its natural course, and presently turned to the subject—inexhaustible at Naples—of the relative advantages of this and that situation for an abode. Mrs. Lessingham, turning to the window, expressed her admiration of the view it afforded.

" I think it is still better ·from Mrs. Baske's sitting-room," said Eleanor, who had been watching Cecily, and thought that she might be glad of an opportunity of private talk with Miriam. And Cecily at once availed herself of the suggestion.

" Would you let me see it, Miriam ? " she asked. " If it is not troublesome——"

Miriam rose, and they went out together. In silence they passed along the corridor, and when they had entered her room Miriam walked at once to the window. Then she half turned, and her eyes fell before Cecily's earnest gaze.

"I did so wish to be with you in your illness!" said the girl, with affectionate warmth. "Indeed, I would have come if I could have been of any use. After all the trouble you used to have with my wretched headaches and ailments——"

"You never have anything of the kind now," said Miriam, with her indulgent smile.

"Never. I am in what Mr. Mallard calls aggressive health. But it shocks me to see how pale you still are, Miriam. I thought the voyage and these ten days at Naples—— And you have such a careworn look. Cannot you throw off your troubles under this sky?"

"You know that the sky matters very little to me, Cecily."

"If I could give you only half my delight! I was awake before dawn this morning, and it was impossible to lie still. I dressed and stood at the open window. I couldn't see the sun itself as it rose, but I watched the first beams strike on Capri and the sea; and I tried to make a drawing of the island as it then looked,—a poor little daub, but it will be precious in bringing back to my mind all I felt when I was busy with it. Such feeling I have never known; as if every nerve in me had received an exquisite new sense. I keep saying to myself, 'Is this really Naples?' Let us go on to the balcony. Oh, you *must* be glad with me!"

Freed from the constraint of formal colloquy, and overcoming the slight embarrassment caused by what she knew of Miriam's thoughts, Cecily revealed her nature as it lay beneath the graces with which education had endowed her. This enthusiasm was no new discovery to Miriam, but in the early days it had attached itself to far other things. Cecily seemed to have forgotten that she was ever in sympathy with the mood which imposed silence on her friend. Her eyes drank light from the landscape; her beauty was transfigured by passionate reception of all the influences this scene could exercise upon heart and mind. She leaned on the railing of the balcony, and gazed until tears of ecstasy made her sight dim.

"Let us see much of each other whilst we are here," she said suddenly, turning to Miriam. "I could never have dreamt of our being together in Italy; it is a happy fate, and gives me all kinds of hope. We will be often alone together in glorious places. We will talk it over; that is better than writing. You shall understand me, Miriam. You shall get as well and strong as I am, and know what I mean when I speak of the joy of living. We shall be sisters again, like we used to be."

Miriam smiled and shook her head.

"Tell me about things at home. Is Miss Baske well?"

"Quite well. I have had two letters from her since I was here. She wished me to give you her love."

"I will write to her. And is old Don still alive?"

"Yes, but very feeble, poor old fellow. He forgets even to be angry with the baker's boy."

Cecily laughed with a moved playfulness.

"He has forgotten me. I don't like to be forgotten by any one who ever cared for me."

There was a pause. They came back into the room, and Cecily, with a look of hesitation, asked quietly,—

"Have you heard of late from Reuben?"

Miriam, with averted eyes, answered simply, "No." Again there was silence, until Cecily, moving about the room, came to the "St. Cecilia."

"So my patron saint is always before you. I am glad of that. Where is the original of this picture, Miriam? I forget."

"I never knew."

"Oh, I wished to speak to you of Mr. Mallard. You met him yesterday. Had you much conversation ? "

" A good deal. He dined with us."

" Did he ? I thought it possible. And do you like him ? "

" I couldn't say until I knew him better."

" It isn't easy to know him, I think," said Cecily, in a reflective and perfectly natural tone, smiling thoughtfully. " But he is a very interesting man, and I wish he would be more friendly with me. I tried hard to win his confidence on the journey from Genoa, but I didn't seem to have much success. I fancy"—she laughed—"that he is still in the habit of regarding me as a little girl, who wouldn't quite understand him if he spoke of serious things. When I wished to talk of his painting, he would only joke. That annoyed me a little, and I tried to let him see that it did, with the result that he refused to speak of anything for a long time."

" What does Mr. Mallard paint ? " Miriam asked, half absently.

" Landscape," was the reply, given with veiled surprise. " Did you never see anything of his ? "

" I remember; the Bradshaws have a picture by him in their dining-room. They showed it me when I was last in Manchester. I'm afraid I looked at it very inattentively, for it has never re-entered my mind from that day to this. But I was ill at the time."

" His pictures are neglected," said Cecily, " but people who understand them say they have great value. If he has anything accepted by the Academy, it is sure to be hung out of sight. I think he is wrong to exhibit there at all. Academies are foolish things, and always give most encouragement to the men who are worth least. When there is talk of such subjects, I never lose an opportunity of mentioning Mr. Mallard's name, and telling all I can about his work. Some day I shall, perhaps, be able to help him. I will insist on every friend of mine who buys pictures at all possessing at least one of Mr. Mallard's; then, perhaps, he will condescend to talk with me of serious things."

She added the last sentence merrily, meeting Miriam's look with the frankest eyes.

"Does Mrs. Lessingham hold the same opinion?" Miriam inquired.

"Oh yes! Aunt, of course, knows far more about art than I do, and she thinks very highly indeed of Mr. Mallard. Not long ago she met M. Lambert at a friend's house in Paris—the French critic who has just been writing about English landscape—and he mentioned Mr. Mallard with great respect. That was splendid, wasn't it?"

She spoke with joyous spiritedness. However modern, Cecily, it was clear, had caught nothing of the disease of pococurantism. Into whatever pleased her or enlisted her sympathies, she threw all the glad energies of her being. The scornful remark on the Royal Academy was, one could see, not so much a mere echo of advanced opinion, as a piece of championship in a friend's cause. The respect with which she mentioned the name of the French critic, her exultation in his dictum, were notes of a youthful idealism which interpreted the world nobly, and took its stand on generous beliefs.

"Mr. Mallard will help you to see Naples, no doubt," said Miriam.

"Indeed, I wish he would. But he distinctly told us that he has no time. He is going to Amalfi in a few days, to work. I begged him at least to go to Pompeii with us, but he frowned—as he so often does—and seemed unwilling to be persuaded; so I said no more. There again, I feel sure he was afraid of being annoyed by trifling talk in such places. But one mustn't judge an artist like other men. To be sure, anything I could say or think would be trivial compared with what is in *his* mind."

"But isn't it rather discourteous?" Miriam observed impartially.

"Oh, I could never think of it in that way! An artist is privileged; he must defend his time and his sensibilities. The common terms of society have no application to him. Don't you feel that, Miriam?"

"I know so little of art and artists. But such a claim seems to me very strange."

Cecily laughed.

"This is one of a thousand things we will talk about. Art is the grandest thing in the world; it means everything that is strong and beautiful—statues, pictures, poetry, music. How could one live without art? The artist is born a prince among men. What has he to do with the rules by which common people must direct their lives? Before long, you will feel this as deeply as I do, Miriam. We are in Italy, Italy!"

"Shall we go back to the others?" Miriam suggested, in a voice which contrasted curiously with that exultant cry.

"Yes; it is time."

Cecily's eyes fell on the plans of the chapel, which were still lying open.

"What is this?" she asked. "Something in Naples? Oh no!"

"It's nothing," said Miriam, carelessly. "Come, Cecily."

The visitors took their leave just as the midday cannon boomed from Sant' Elmo. They had promised to come and dine in a day or two. After their departure, Miriam showed as little disposition to make comments as she had to indulge in expectation before their arrival. Eleanor and her husband put less restraint upon themselves.

"Heavens!" cried Spence, when they were alone; "what astounding capacity of growth was in that child!"

"She is a swift and beautiful creature!" said Eleanor, in a warm undertone characteristic of her when she expressed admiration.

"I wish I could have overheard the interview in Miriam's room."

"I never felt more curiosity about anything. Pity one is

not a psychological artist. I should have stolen to the keyhole and committed eavesdropping with a glow of self-approval."

"I half understand our friend Mallard."

"So do I, Ned."

They looked at each other and smiled significantly.

That evening Spence again had a walk with the artist. He returned to the villa alone, and only just in time to dress for dinner. Guests were expected, Mr. and Mrs. Bradshaw of Manchester, old acquaintances of the Spences and of Miriam. When it had become known that Mrs. Baske, advised to pass the winter in a mild climate, was about to accept an invitation from her cousin and go by sea to Naples, the Bradshaws, to the astonishment of all their friends, offered to accompany her. It was the first time that either of them had left England, and they seemed most unlikely people to be suddenly affected with a zeal for foreign travel. Miriam gladly welcomed their proposal, and it was put into execution.

When Spence entered the room his friends had already arrived. Mr. Bradshaw stood in the attitude familiar to him when on his own hearthrug, his back turned to that part of the wall where in England would have been a fireplace, and one hand thrust into the pocket of his evening coat.

"I tell you what it is, Spence!" he exclaimed, "I'm very much afraid I shall be committing an assault. Certainly I shall if I don't soon learn some good racy Italian. I must make out a little list of sentences, and get you or Mrs. Spence to translate them. Such as 'Do you take me for a fool?' or 'Be off, you scoundrel!' or 'I'll break every bone in your body!' That's the kind of thing practically needed in Naples, I find."

"Been in conflict with coachmen again?" asked Spence, laughing.

"Slightly! Never got into such a helpless rage in my life. Two fellows kept up with me this afternoon for a couple of miles or so. Now, what makes me so mad is the assumption of these blackguards that I don't know my own mind. I go out for a stroll, and the first cabby I pass wants to take me to Pozzuoli or Vesuvius—or Jericho, for aught I know. It's no use showing him that I haven't the slightest intention of going to any such place. What the deuce! does the fellow suppose he can persuade me or badger me into doing what I've no mind to do ? Does he take me for an ass? It's the insult of the thing that riles me! The same if I look in at a shop window; out rushes a gabbling swindler, and wants to drag me in——"

"Only to *take* you in, Mr. Bradshaw," interjected Eleanor.

"Good! To take me in, with a vengeance. Why, if I've a mind to buy, shan't I go in of my own accord ? And isn't it a sure and certain thing that I shall never spend a halfpenny with a scoundrel who attacks me like that ? "

"How can you expect foreigners to reason, Jacob ? " exclaimed Mrs. Bradshaw.

"You should take these things as compliments," remarked Spence. "They see an Englishman coming along, and as a matter of course they consider him a person of wealth and leisure, who will be grateful to any one for suggesting how he can kill time. Having nothing in the world to do but enjoy himself, why shouldn't the English lord drive to Baiæ and back, just to get an appetite ? "

"Lord, eh ? " growled Mr. Bradshaw, rising on his toes, and smiling with a certain satisfaction.

Threescore years all but two sat lightly on Jacob Bush Bradshaw. His cheek was ruddy, his eyes had the lustre of health ; in the wrinkled forehead you saw activity of brain, and on his lips the stubborn independence of a Lancashire employer of labour. Prosperity had set its mark upon him, that peculiarly English prosperity which is so intimately associated with spotless linen, with a good cut of clothes, with scant but valuable jewellery, with the absence of any perfume save that which suggests the morning tub. He was a manufacturer of silk. The provincial accent notwithstanding, his conversation on general subjects soon declared him a man of logical mind and of much homely information. A sufficient self-esteem allied itself with his force of character, but robust amiability prevented this from becoming offensive; he had the sense of humour, and enjoyed a laugh at himself as well as at other people. Though his life had been absorbed in the pursuit of solid gain, he was no scorner of the attainments which lay beyond his own scope, and in these latter years, now that the fierce struggle was decided in his favour, he often gave proof of a liberal curiosity. With regard to art and learning, he had the intelligence to be aware of his own defects; where he did not enjoy, he at least knew that he ought to have done so, and he had a suspicion that herein also progress could be made by stubborn effort, as in the material world. Finding himself abroad, he had set himself to observe and learn, with results now and then not a little amusing. The consciousness of wealth disposed him to intellectual generosity; standing on so firm a pedestal, he did not mind admitting that others might have a wider outlook. Italy was an impecunious country; personally and patriotically he had a pleasure in recognizing the fact, and this made it easier for him to concede the points of superiority which he had heard attributed to her. Jacob was rigidly sincere; he had no touch of the snobbery which shows itself in sham admiration. If he liked a thing he said so, and strongly; if he felt no liking where his guide-book directed him to be enthusiastic, he kept silence and cudgelled his brains.

Equally ingenuous was his wife, but with results that argued a shallower nature. Mrs. Bradshaw had the heartiest and frankest contempt for all things foreign; in Italy she deemed herself among a people so inferior to the English that even to discuss the relative merits of the two nations would have been ludicrous. Life "abroad" she could not

take as a serious thing; it amused or disgusted her, as the
case might be—never occasioned her a grave thought. The
proposal of this excursion, when first made to her, she
received with mockery; when she saw that her husband
meant something more than a joke, she took time to consider, and at length accepted the notion as a freak which
possibly would be entertaining, and might at all events be
indulged after a lifetime of sobriety. Entertainment she
found in abundance. Though natural beauty made little
if any appeal to her, she interested herself greatly in
Vesuvius, regarding it as a serio-comic phenomenon which
could only exist in a country inhabited by childish triflers.
Her memory was storing all manner of Italian absurdities
—everything being an absurdity which differed from English
habit and custom—to furnish her with matter for mirthful
talk when she got safely back to Manchester and civilization. With respect to the things which Jacob was constrain-
ing himself to study—antiquities, sculptures, paintings,
stored in the Naples museum—her attitude was one of
jocose indifference or of half-tolerant contempt. Puritanism
diluted with worldliness and a measure of common sense
directed her views of art in general. Works such as the
Farnese Hercules and the group about the Bull she looked
upon much as she regarded the wall-scribbling of some
dirty-minded urchin; the robust matron is not horrified by
such indecencies, but to be sure will not stand and examine
them. "Oh, come along, Jacob!" she exclaimed to her
husband, when, at their first visit to the Museum, he went
to work at the antiques with his Murray. "I've no patience!
you ought to be ashamed of yourself!"

The Bradshaws were staying at the *pension* selected by
Mrs. Lessingham. Naturally the conversation at dinner
turned much on that lady and her niece. With Cecily's
father Mr. Bradshaw had been well acquainted, but Cecily
herself he had not seen since her childhood, and his
astonishment at meeting her as Miss Doran was great.

" What kind of society do they live among? " he asked of Spence. "Tip-top people, I suppose?"

" Not exactly what we understand by tip-top in England. Mrs. Lessingham's family connections are aristocratic, but she prefers the society of authors, artists—that kind of thing."

" Queer people for a young girl to make friends of, eh?"

" Well, there's Mallard, for instance."

"Ah, Mallard, to be sure."·

Mrs. Bradshaw looked at her hostess and smiled knowingly.

" Miss Doran is rather fond of talking about Mr. Mallard," she remarked. " Did you notice that, Miriam?"

"Yes, I did."

Jacob broke the silence.

" How does he get on with his painting? " he asked—and it sounded very much as though the reference were to a man busy on the front door.

"He's never likely to be very popular," replied Spence, adapting his remarks to the level of his guests' understanding. "There was something of his in this year's Academy, and it sold at a tolerable price."

" That thing of his that I bought, you remember—I find people don't see much in it. They complain that the colour's so dull. But then, as I always say, what else could you expect on a bit of Yorkshire moor in winter? Is he going to paint anything here? Now, if he'd do me a bit of the bay, with Vesuvius smoking."

"That would be something like!" assented Mrs. Bradshaw.

When the ladies had left the dining-room, Mr. Bradshaw, over his cigarette, reverted to the subject of Cecily.

" I suppose the lass has had a first-rate education?"

"Of the very newest fashion for girls. I am told she reads Latin."

"By Jove!" cried the other, with sudden animation.

" That reminds me of something I wanted to talk about. When I was leaving Manchester, I got together a few books, you know, that were likely to be useful over here. My friend Lomax, the bookseller, suggested them. ' Got a classical dictionary ? ' says he. ' Not I ! ' As you know, my schooling never went much beyond the three R's, and hanged if I knew what a classical dictionary was. ' Better take one,' says Lomax. " You'll want to look up your gods and goddesses.' So I took it, and I've been looking into it these last few days."

" Well ? "

Jacob had a comical look of perplexity and indignation. He thumped the table.

" Do you mean to tell me that's the kind of stuff boys are set to learn at school ? "

" A good deal of it comes in."

" Then all I can say is, no wonder the colleges turn out such a lot of young blackguards. Why, man, I could scarcely believe my eyes ! You mean to say that, if I'd had a son, he'd have been brought up on that kind of literature, and without me knowing anything about it ? Why, I've locked the book up; I was ashamed to let it lay on the table."

" It's the old Lemprière, I suppose," said Spence, vastly amused. " The new dictionaries are toned down a good deal ; they weren't so squeamish in the old days."

" But the lads still read the books these things come out of, eh ? "

" Oh yes. It has always been one of the most laughable inconsistencies in English morality. Anything you could find in the dictionary is milk for babes compared with several Greek plays that have to be read for examinations."

" It fair caps me, Spence ! Classical education that is, eh ? That's what parsons are bred on ? And, by the Lord, you say they're beginning it with girls ? "

" Very zealously."

" Nay——! "

Jacob threw up his arms, and abandoned the effort to express himself.

Later, when the guests were gone, Spence remembered this, and, to Eleanor's surprise, he broke into uproarious laughter.

" One of the best jokes I ever heard! A fresh, first-hand judgment on the morality of the Classics by a plain-minded English man of business." He told the story. " And Bradshaw's perfectly right; that's the best of it."

CHAPTER III.

THE BOARDING-HOUSE ON THE MERGELLINA.

THE year was 1878. A tourist searching his Baedeker for a genteel but not oppressively aristocratic *pension* in the open parts of Naples would have found himself directed by an asterisk to the establishment kept by Mrs. Gluck on the Mergellina ;—frequented by English and Germans, and very comfortable. The recommendation was a just one. Mrs. Gluck enjoyed the advantage of having lived as many years in England as she had in Germany ; her predilections leaned, if anything, to the English side, and the arrival of a " nice " English family always put her in excellent spirits. She then exhibited herself as an Anglicized matron, perfectly familiar with all the requirements, great and little, of her guests, and, when minutiæ were once settled, capable of meeting ladies and gentlemen on terms of equality in her drawing-room or at her table, where she always presided. Indeed, there was much true refinement in Mrs. Gluck. You had not been long in her house before she found an opportunity of letting you know that she prided herself on connection with the family of the great musician, and under her roof there was generally some one who played or sang well. It was her desire that all who sat at her dinner-table—the English people, at all events—should be in evening dress. She herself had no little art in adorning herself so as to appear, what she was, a lady, and yet not to conflict with the ladies whose presence honoured her.

In the drawing-room, a few days after the arrival of Mrs. Lessingham and her niece, several members of the household were assembled in readiness for the second dinner-bell. There was Frau Wohlgemuth, a middle-aged lady with severe brows, utilizing spare moments over a German work on Greek sculpture. Certain plates in the book had caught the eye of Mrs. Bradshaw, with the result that she regarded this innocent student as a person of most doubtful character, who, if in ignorance admitted to a respectable boarding-house, should certainly have been got rid of as soon as the nature of her reading had been discovered. Frau Wohlgemuth had once or twice been astonished at the severe look fixed upon her by the buxom English lady, but happily would never receive an explanation of this silent animus. Then there was Fräulein Kriel, who had unwillingly incurred even more of Mrs. Bradshaw's displeasure, in that she, an unmarried person, had actually looked over the volume together with its possessor, not so much as blushing when she found herself observed by strangers. The remaining persons were an English family, a mother and three daughters, their name Denyer.

Mrs. Denyer was florid, vivacious, and of a certain size She had seen much of the world, and prided herself on cosmopolitanism; the one thing with which she could not dispense was intellectual society. This would be her second winter at Naples, but she gave her acquaintances to understand that Italy was by no means the country of her choice;

she preferred the northern latitudes, because there the intellectual atmosphere was more bracing. But for her daughters' sake she abode here: "You know, my girls *adore* Italy."

Of these young ladies, the two elder—Barbara and Madeline were their seductive names—had good looks. Barbara, perhaps twenty-two years old, was rather colourless, somewhat too slim, altogether a trifle limp; but she had a commendable taste in dress. Madeline, a couple of years younger, presented a more healthy physique and a less common comeliness, but in the matter of costume she lacked her sister's discretion. Her colours were ill-matched, her ornaments awkwardly worn; even her hair sought more freedom than was consistent with grace. The youngest girl, Zillah, who was about nineteen, had been less kindly dealt with by nature; like Barbara, she was of very light complexion, and this accentuated her plainness. She aimed at no compensation in attire, unless it were that her sober garments exhibited perfect neatness and complete inoffensiveness. Zillah's was a good face, in spite of its unattractive features; she had a peculiarly earnest look, a reflective manner, and much conscientiousness of speech.

Common to the three was a resolve to be modern, advanced, and emancipated, or perish in the attempt. Every one who spoke with them must understand that they were no everyday young ladies, imbued with notions and prejudices recognized as feminine, frittering away their lives amid the follies of the drawing-room and of the circulating library. Culture was their pursuit, heterodoxy their pride. If indeed it were true, as Mrs. Bradshaw somewhat acrimoniously declared, that they were all desperately bent on capturing husbands, then assuredly the poor girls went about their enterprise with singular lack of prudence.

Each had her *rôle*. Barbara's was to pose as the adorer of Italy, the enthusiastic glorifier of Italian unity. She spoke Italian feebly, but, with English people, never lost an opportunity of babbling its phrases.   Speak to her of Rome, and before long she was sure to murmur rapturously, " Roma capitale d'Italia ! "—the watch-word of antipapal victory. Of English writers she loved, or affected to love, those only who had found inspiration south of the Alps.   The proud mother repeated a story of Barbara's going up to the wall of Casa Guidi and kissing it.   In her view, the modern Italians could do no wrong ; they were divinely regenerate. She praised their architecture.

Madeline—whom her sisters addressed affectionately as " Mad "—professed a wider intellectual scope ; less given to the melting mood than Barbara, less naïve in her enthusiasms, she took for her province æsthetic criticism in its totality, and shone rather in censure than in laudation. French she read passably ; German she had talked so much of studying that it was her belief she had acquired it ; Greek and Latin were beyond her scope, but from modern essayists who wrote in the flamboyant style she had gathered enough knowledge of these literatures to be able to discourse of them with a very fluent inaccuracy.   With all schools of painting she was, of course, quite familiar ; the great masters —vulgarly so known—interested her but moderately, and to praise them was, in her eyes, to incur a suspicion of philistinism.   From her preceptors in this sphere, she had learnt certain names, old and new, which stood for more exquisite virtues, and the frequent mention of them with a happy vagueness made her conversation very impressive to the generality of people.   The same in music.   It goes without saying that Madeline was an indifferentist in politics and on social questions ; at the introduction of such topics, she smiled.

Zillah's position was one of more difficulty.   With nothing of her sisters' superficial cleverness, with a mind that worked slowly, and a memory irretentive, she had a genuine desire to instruct herself, and that in a solid way.   She alone studied with real persistence, and, by the irony of fate, she alone continually exposed her ignorance, committed gross blunders, was guilty of deplorable lapses of memory. Her unhappy lot kept her in a constant state of nervousness and shame. She had no worldly tact, no command of her modest resources, yet her zeal to support the credit of the family was always driving her into hurried speech, sure to end in some disastrous pitfall. Conscious of æsthetic defects, Zillah had chosen for her speciality the study of the history of civilization. But for being a Denyer, she might have been content to say that she studied history, and in that case her life might also have been solaced by the companionship of readable books ; but, as modernism would have it, she could not be content to base her historical inquiries on anything less than strata of geology and biological elements, with the result that she toiled day by day at perky little primers and compendia, and only learnt one chapter that it might be driven out of her head by the next. Equally out of deference to her sisters, she smothered her impulses to conventional piety, and made believe that her spiritual life supported itself on the postulates of science. As a result of all which, the poor girl was not very happy, but in that again did she not give proof of belonging to her time ?

There existed a Mr. Denyer, but this gentleman was very seldom indeed in the bosom of his family. Letters—and remittances — came from him from the most surprising quarters of the globe. His profession was that of speculator at large, and, with small encouragement of any kind, he toiled unceasingly to support his wife and daughters in their elegant leisure. At one time he was eagerly engaged in a project for making starch from potatoes in the south of Ireland. When this failed, he utilized a knowledge of Spanish—casually picked up, like all his acquirements—and was next heard of at Vera Cruz, where he dealt in cochineal, indigo, sarsaparilla, and logwood. Yellow fever interfered with his activity, and after a brief sojourn with his family in the United States, where they had joined him with the idea of making a definite settlement, he heard of something promising in Egypt, and thither repaired. A spare, vivacious, pathetically sanguine man, always speaking of the day when he would " settle down " in enjoyment of a moderate fortune, and most obviously doomed never to settle at all, save in the final home of mortality.

Mrs. Lessingham and her niece entered the room. On Cecily, as usual, all eyes were more or less openly directed. Her evening dress was simple—though with the simplicity not to be commanded by every one who wills—and her demeanour very far from exacting general homage ; but her birthright of distinction could not be laid aside, and the suave Mrs. Gluck was not singular in recognizing that here was such a guest as did not every day grace her *pension.* Barbara and Madeline Denyer never looked at her without secret pangs. In appearance, however, they were very friendly, and Cecily had met their overtures from the first with the simple goodwill natural to her. She went and seated herself by Madeline, who had on her lap a little portfolio.

" These are the drawings of which I spoke," said Madeline, half opening the portfolio.

" Mr. Marsh's ? Oh, I shall be glad to see them ! "

" Of course, we ought to have daylight, but we'll look at them again to-morrow. You can form an idea of their character."

They were small water-colours, the work—as each declared in fantastic signature—of one Clifford Marsh, spoken of by the Denyers, and by Madeline in particular, as a personal friend. He was expected to arrive any day in Naples. The subjects, Cecily had been informed, were natural scenery ; the style, impressionist. Impressionism was no novel term to Cecily, and in Paris she had had her attention intelligently directed to good work in that kind ; she knew, of course, that, like every other style, it must be judged with reference to its success in achieving the end proposed. But

the first glance at the first of Mr. Marsh's productions perplexed her. A study on the Roman Campagna, said Madeline. It might just as well, for all Cecily could determine,
have been a study of cloud-forms, or of a storm at sea, or of
anything, or of nothing; nor did there seem to be any
cogent reason why it should be looked at one way up rather
than the other. Was this genius, or impudence?

"You don't know the Campagna, yet," remarked Madeline, finding that the other kept silence. "Of course, you
can't appreciate the marvellous truthfulness of this impression; but it gives you new emotions, doesn't it?"

Mrs. Lessingham would have permitted herself to reply
with a pointed affirmative. Cecily was too considerate of
others' feelings for that, yet had not the habit of smooth
falsehood.

"I am not very familiar with this kind of work," she
said. "Please let me just look and think, and tell me your
own thoughts about each."

Madeline was not displeased. Already she had discovered
that in most directions Miss Doran altogether exceeded her
own reach, and that it was not safe to talk conscious nonsense to her. The tone of modesty seemed unaffected, and,
as Madeline had reasons for trying to believe in Clifford
Marsh, it gratified her to feel that here at length she might
tread firmly and hold her own. The examination of the
drawings proceeded, with the result that Cecily's original
misgiving was strongly confirmed. What would Ross Mallard say? Mallard's own work was not of the impressionist
school, and he might suffer prejudice to direct him; but she
had a conviction of how his remarks would sound were this
portfolio submitted to him. Genius—scarcely. And if not,
then assuredly the other thing, and that in flagrant degree.

Most happily, the dinner-bell came with its peremptory
interruption.

"I must see them again to-morrow," said Cecily, in her
pleasantest voice.

At table, the ladies were in a majority. Mr. Bradshaw was the only man past middle life. Next in age to him came Mr. Musselwhite, who looked about forty, and whose aquiline nose, high forehead, light bushy whiskers, and air of vacant satisfaction, marked him as the aristocrat of the assembly. This gentleman suffered under a truly aristocratic affliction—the ever-reviving difficulty of passing his day. Mild in demeanour, easy in the discharge of petty social obligations, perfectly inoffensive, he came and went like a vivified statue of gentlemanly *ennui*. Every morning there arrived for him a consignment of English newspapers; these were taken to his bedroom at nine o'clock, together with a cup of chocolate. They presumably occupied him until he appeared in the drawing-room, just before the hour of luncheon, when, in spite of the freshness of his morning attire, he seemed already burdened by the blank of time, always sitting down to the meal with an audible sigh of gratitude. Invariably he addressed to his neighbour a remark on the direction of the smoke from Vesuvius. If the neighbour happened to be uninformed in things Neapolitan, Mr. Musselwhite seized the occasion to explain at length the meteorologic significance of these varying fumes. Luncheon over, he rose like one who is summoned to a painful duty; in fact, the great task of the day was before him —the struggle with time until the hour of dinner. You would meet him sauntering sadly about the gardens of the Villa Nazionale, often looking at his watch, which he always regulated by the cannon of Sant' Elmo: or gazing with lack-lustre eye at a shop-window in the Toledo; or sitting with a little glass of Marsala before him in one of the fashionable *cafés*, sunk in despondency. But when at length he appeared at the dinner-table, once more fresh from his toilet, then did a gleam of animation transform his countenance; for the victory was won; yet again was old time defeated. Then he would discourse his best. Two topics were his: the weather, and "my brother the baronet's place in Lincolnshire." The manner of his monologue on this second and more fruitful subject was really touching. When so fortunate as to have a new listener, he began by telling him or her that he was his father's fourth son, and consequently third brother to Sir Grant Musselwhite—" who goes in so much for model-farming, you know." At the hereditary "place in Lincolnshire" he had spent the bloom of his life, which he now looked back upon with tender regrets. He did not mention the fact that, at the age of five-and-twenty, he had been beguiled from that Arcadia by wily persons who took advantage of his innocent youth, who initiated him into the metropolitan mysteries which sadden the soul and deplete the pocket, who finally abandoned him upon the shoal of a youngest brother's allowance when his father passed away from the place in Lincolnshire, and young Sir Grant, reigning in the old baronet's stead, deemed himself generous in making the family scapegrace any provision at all. Yet such were the outlines of Mr. Musselwhite's history. Had he been the commonplace spendthrift, one knows pretty well on what lines his subsequent life would have run; but poor Mr. Musselwhite was at heart a domestic creature. Exiled from his home, he wandered in melancholy, year after year, round a circle of continental resorts, never seeking relief in dissipation, never discovering a rational pursuit, imagining to himself that he atoned for the disreputable past in keeping far from the track of his distinguished relatives.

Ah, that place in Lincolnshire! To the listener's mind it became one of the most imposing of English ancestral abodes. The house was of indescribable magnitude and splendour. It had a remarkable "turret," whence, across many miles of plain, Lincoln Cathedral could be discovered by the naked eye; it had an interminable drive from the lodge to the stately portico; it had gardens of fabulous fertility; it had stables which would have served a cavalry regiment In what region were the kine of Sir Grant Musselwhite unknown to fame? Who had not heard of his dairy-produce? Three stories was Mr. Musselwhite in the habit of telling, scintillating fragments of his blissful youth; one was of a foxcub and a terrier; another of a heifer that went mad; the third, and the most thrilling, of a dismissed coachman who turned burglar, and in the dead of night fired shots at old Sir Grant and his sons. In relating these anecdotes, his eye grew moist and his throat swelled.

Mr. Musselwhite's place at table was next to Barbara Denyer. So long as Miss Denyer was new, or comparatively new, to her neighbour's reminiscences, all went well between them. Barbara condescended to show interest in the place in Lincolnshire; she put pertinent questions; she smiled or looked appropriately serious in listening to the three stories. But this could not go on indefinitely, and for more than a week now conversation between the two had been a trying matter. For Mr. Musselwhite to sustain a dialogue on such topics as Barbara had made her own was impossible, and he had no faculty even for the commonest kind of impersonal talk. He devoted himself to his dinner in amiable silence, enjoying the consciousness that nearly an hour of occupation was before him, and that bed-time lay at no hopeless distance.

Moreover, there was a boy—yet it is doubtful whether he should be so described; for, though he numbered rather less than sixteen years, experience had already made him *blasé*. He sat beside his mother, a Mrs. Strangwich. For Master Strangwich the ordinary sources of youthful satisfaction did not exist; he talked with the mature on terms of something more than equality, and always gave them the impression that they had still much to learn. This objectionable youth had long since been everywhere and seen everything. The *naïveté* of finding pleasure in novel circumstances moved him to a pitying surprise. Speak of the glories of the Bay of Naples, and he would remark, with hands in pockets and head thrown back, that he thought a good deal more of the Golden Horn. If climate came up for discussion, he gave an impartial vote, based on much personal observation, in favour of Southern California. His parents belonged to the race of modern nomads, those curious beings who are reviving an early stage of civilization as an ingenious expedient for employing money and time which they have not intelligence enough to spend in a settled habitat. It was already noticed in the *pension* that Master Strangwich paid somewhat marked attentions to Madeline Denyer; there was no knowing what might come about if their acquaintance should be prolonged for a few weeks.

But Madeline had at present something else to think about than the condescending favour of Master Strangwich. As the guests entered the dining-room, Mrs. Gluck informed Mrs. Denyer that the English artist who was looked for had just arrived, and would in a few minutes join the company. "Mr. Marsh is here," said Mrs. Denyer aloud to her daughters, in a tone of no particular satisfaction. Madeline glanced at Miss Doran, who, however, did not seem to have heard the remark.

And, whilst the guests were still busy with their soup, Mr. Clifford Marsh presented himself. Within the doorway he stood for a moment surveying the room; with placid eye he selected Mrs. Denyer, and approached her just to shake hands; her three daughters received from him the same attention. Words Mr. Marsh had none, but he smiled as smiles the man conscious of attracting merited observation. Indeed, it was impossible not to regard Mr. Marsh with curiosity. His attire was very conventional in itself, but somehow did not look like the evening uniform of common men : it sat upon him with an artistic freedom, and seemed the garb of a man superior to his surroundings. The artist was slight, pale, rather feminine of feature ; he had delicate hands, which he managed to display to advantage ; his auburn hair was not long behind, as might have been expected, but rolled in a magnificent mass upon his brows.

Many were the affectations whereby his countenance rendered itself unceasingly interesting. At times he wrinkled his forehead down the middle, and then smiled at vacancy—a humorous sadness; or his eyes became very wide as he regarded, yet appeared not to see, some particular person; or his lips drew themselves in, a symbol of meaning reticence. All this, moreover, not in such degrees as to make him patently ridiculous; by no means. Mr. and Mrs. Bradshaw might exchange frequent glances, and have a difficulty in preserving decorum; but they were unsophisticated. Mrs. Lessingham smiled, indeed, when there came a reasonable pretext, but not contemptuously. Mr. Marsh's aspect, if anything, pleased her; she liked these avoidances of the commonplace. Cecily did not fail to inspect the new arrival. She too was well aware that hatred of vulgarity constrains many persons who are anything but fools to emphasize their being in odd ways, and it might still—in spite of the impressionist water-colours—be proved that Mr. Marsh had a right to vary from the kindly race of men. She hoped he was really a person of some account; it delighted her to be with such. And then she suspected that Madeline Denyer had something more than friendship for Mr. Marsh, and her sympathies were moved.

"What sort of weather did you leave in England?" Mrs. Denyer inquired, when the artist was seated next to her.

"I came away from London on the third day of absolute darkness," replied Mr. Marsh, genially.

"Oh dear!" exclaimed Mrs. Gluck; and at once translated this news for the benefit of Frau Wohlgemuth, who murmured, "Ach!" and shook her head.

"The fog is even yet in my throat," proceeded the artist, to whom most of the guests were listening. "I can still see nothing but lurid patches of gaslight on a background of solid mephitic fume. There are fine effects to be caught, there's no denying it; but not every man has the requisite

physique for such studies. As I came along here from the
railway-station, it occurred to me that the Dante story might
have been repeated in my case; the Neapolitans should
have pointed at me and whispered, 'Behold the man who
has been in hell!'"

Cecily was amused; she looked at Madeline and exchanged
a friendly glance with her. At the same time she was
becoming aware that Mr. Marsh, who sat opposite, vouchsafed her the homage of his gaze rather too frequently and
persistently. It was soon manifest to her, moreover, that
Madeline had noted the same thing, and not with entire
equanimity. So Cecily began to converse with Mrs. Lessingham, and no longer gave heed to the artist's utterances.

She was going to spend an hour with Miriam this evening,
without express invitation. Mr. Bradshaw would drive up
the hill with her, and doubtless Mr. Spence would see her
safely home. Thus she saw no more for the present of the
Denyers' friend.

Those ladies had a private sitting-room, and thither, in
the course of the evening, Clifford Marsh repaired. Barbara
and Zillah, with their mother, remained in the drawing-
room. On opening the door to which he had been directed,
Marsh found Madeline bent over a book. She raised her
eyes carelessly, and said:

"Oh, I hoped it was Barbara."

"I will tell her at once that you wish to speak to her."

"Don't trouble."

"No trouble at all."

He turned away, and at once Madeline rose impatiently
from her chair, speaking with peremptory accent.

"Please do as I request you! Come and sit down."

Marsh obeyed, and more than obeyed. He kicked a stool
close to her, dropped upon it with one leg curled underneath
him, and leaned his head against her shoulder. Madeline
remained passive, her features still showing the resentment
his manner had provoked.

"I've come all this way just to see you, Mad, when I've no right to be here at all."

"Why no right?"

"I told you to prepare yourself for bad news."

"That's a very annoying habit of yours. I hate to be kept in suspense in that way. Why can't you always say at once what you mean? Father does the same thing constantly in his letters. I'm sure we've quite enough anxiety from him; I don't see why you should increase it."

Without otherwise moving, he put his arm about her.

"What is it, Clifford? Tell me, and be quick."

"It's soon told, Mad. My step-father informs me that he will continue the usual allowance until my twenty-sixth birthday—eighteenth of February next, you know—and no longer than that. After then, I must look out for myself."

Madeline wrinkled her brows.

"What's the reason?" she asked, after a pause.

"The old trouble. He says I've had quite long enough to make my way as an artist, if I'm going to make it at all. In his opinion, I am simply wasting my time and his money. No cash results; that is to say, no success. Of course, his view."

The girl kept silence. Marsh shifted his position slightly, so as to get a view of her face.

"Somebody else's too, I'm half afraid," he murmured dubiously.

Madeline was thinking of a look she had caught on Miss Doran's face when the portfolio disclosed its contents; of Miss Doran's silence; of certain other persons' looks and silence—or worse than silence. The knitting of her brows became deeper; Marsh felt an uneasy movement in her frame.

"Speak plainly," he said. "It's far better."

"It's very hot, Clifford. Sit on a chair; we can talk better."

"I understand."

He moved a little away from her, and looked round the room with a smile of disillusion.

"You needn't insult me," said Madeline, but not with the former petulance. "Often enough you have done that, and yet I don't think I have given you cause."

Still crouching upon the stool, he clasped his hands over his knee, jerked his head back—a frequent movement, to settle his hair—and smiled with increase of bitterness.

"I meant no insult," he said, "either now or at other times, though you are always ready to interpret me in that way. I merely hint at the truth, which would sound disagreeable in plain terms."

"You mean, of course, that I think of nothing— have never thought of anything—but your material prospects?"

"Why didn't you marry me a year ago, Mad?"

"Because I should have been mad indeed to have done so. You admit it would have caused your step-father at once to stop his allowance. And pray what would have become of us?"

"Exactly. See your faith in me, brought to the touch-stone!"

"I suppose the present day would have seen you as it now does?"

"Yes, if you had embarrassed me with lack of confidence. Decidedly not, if you had been to me the wife an artist needs. My future has lain in your power to make or mar. You have chosen to keep me in perpetual anxiety, and now you take a suitable opportunity to overthrow me altogether; or rather, you try to. We will see how things go when I am free to pursue my course untroubled."

"Do so, by all manner of means!" exclaimed Madeline, her voice trembling. "Perhaps I shall prove to have been your friend in this way, at all events. As your wife in London lodgings on the third floor, I confess it is very unlikely I should have aided you. I haven't the least belief in projects of that kind. At best, you would have been forced into some kind of paltry work just to support me— and where would be the good of our marriage? You know perfectly well that lots of men have been degraded in this way. They take a wife to be their Muse, and she becomes the millstone about their neck; then they hate her—and I don't blame them. What's the good of saying one moment that you know your work can never appeal to the multitude, and the next, affecting to believe that our marriage would make you miraculously successful?"

"Then it would have been better to part before this."

"No doubt—as it turns out."

"Why do you speak bitterly? I am stating an obvious fact."

"If I remember rightly, you had some sort of idea that the fact of our engagement might help you. That didn't seem to me impossible. It is a very different thing from marriage on nothing a year."

"You have no faith in me; you never had. And how *could* you believe in what you don't understand? I see now what I have been forced to suspect—that your character is just as practical as that of other women. Your talk of art is nothing more than talk. You think, in truth, of pounds, shillings and pence."

"I think of them a good deal," said Madeline, "and I should be an idiot if I didn't. What is art if the artist has nothing to live on? Pray, what are *you* going to do henceforth? Shall you scorn the mention of pounds, shillings and pence? Come to see me when you have had no dinner to-day, and are feeling very uncertain about breakfast in the morning, and I will say, 'Pooh! your talk about art was after all nothing but talk; you are a sham!'"

Marsh's leg began to ache. He rose and moved about the room. Madeline at length turned her eyes to him; he was brooding genuinely, and not for effect. Her glance discerned this.

"Well, and what *are* you going to do, in fact ? " she asked.

"I'm hanged if I know, Mad; and there's the truth."

He turned and regarded her with wide eyes, seriously perceptive of a blank horizon.

"I've asked him to let me have half the money, but he refuses even that. His object is, of course, to compel me into the life of a Philistine. I believe the fellow thinks it's kindness; I know my mother does. She, of course, has as little faith in me as you have."

Madeline did not resent this. She regarded the floor for a minute, and, without raising her eyes, said :

"Come here, Clifford."

He approached. Still without raising her eyes, she again spoke.

"Do you believe in yourself ? "

The words were impressive. Marsh gave a start, uttered an impatient sound, and half turned away.

"Do you believe in yourself, Clifford ? "

"Of course I do ! " came from him blusterously.

"Very well. In that case, struggle on. If you care for the kind of help you once said I could give you, I will try to give it still. Paint something that will sell, and go on with the other work at the same time."

"Something that will sell ! " he exclaimed, with disgust. "I can't, so there's an end of it."

"And an end of your artist life, it seems to me. Unless you have any other plan ? "

"I wondered whether you could suggest any."

Madeline shook her head slowly. They both brooded in a cheerless way. When the girl again spoke, it was in an undertone, as if not quite sure that she wished to be heard.

"I had rather you were an artist than anything else, Clifford."

Marsh decided not to hear. He thrust his hands deeper into his pockets, and trod about the floor heavily. Madeline made another remark.

"I suppose the kind of work that is proposed for you would leave you no time for art?"

"Pooh! of course not. Who was ever Philistine and artist at the same time?"

"Well, it's a bad job. I wish I could help you. I wish I had money.

"If you had, *I* shouldn't benefit by it," was the exasperated reply.

"Will you please to do what you were going to do at first, and tell Barbara I wish to speak to her?"

"Yes, I will."

His temper grew worse. In his weakness he really had thought it likely that Madeline would suggest something hopeful. Men of his stamp constantly entertain unreasonable expectations, and are angry when the unreason is forced upon their consciousness.

"One word before you go, please," said Madeline, standing up and speaking with emphasis. "After what you said just now, this is, of course, our last interview of this kind. When we meet again—and I think it would be gentlemanly in you to go and live somewhere else—you are Mr. Marsh, and I, if you please, am Miss Denyer."

"I will bear it in mind."

"Thank you." He still lingered near the door. "Be good enough to leave me."

He made an effort and left the room. When the door had closed, Madeline heaved a deep sigh, and was for some minutes in a brown, if not a black, study. Then she shivered a little, sighed again, and again took up the volume she had been reading. It was Daudet's "Les Femmes d'Artistes."

Not long after, all the Denyers were reunited in their sitting-room. Mrs. Denyer had brought up an open letter.

"From your father again," she said, addressing the girls conjointly. "I am sure he wears me out This is worse than the last. 'The fact of the matter is, I must warn you very seriously that I can't supply you with as much as I have been doing. I repeat that I am serious this time. It's a horrible bore, and a good deal worse than a bore. If I could keep your remittances the same by doing on less myself, I would, but there's no possibility of that. I shall be in Alexandria in ten days, and perhaps Colossi will have some money for me, but I can't count on it. Things have gone deuced badly, and are likely to go even worse, as far as I can see. Do think about getting less expensive quarters. I wish to heaven poor little Mad could get married! Hasn't Marsh any prospects yet?'"

"That's all at an end," remarked Madeline, interrupting. "We've just come to an understanding."

Mrs. Denyer stared.

"You've broken off?"

"Mr. Marsh's allowance is to be stopped. His prospects are worse than ever. What's the good of keeping up our engagement?"

There was a confused colloquy between all four. Barbara shrugged her fair shoulders; Zillah looked very gravely and pitifully at Madeline. Madeline herself seemed the least concerned.

"I won't have this!" cried Mrs. Denyer, finally. "His step-father is willing to give him a position in business, and he must accept it; then the marriage can be soon."

"The marriage will decidedly *not* be soon, mother!" replied Madeline, haughtily. "I shall judge for myself in this, at all events."

"You are a silly, empty-headed girl!" retorted her mother, with swelling bosom and reddening face. "You have quarrelled on some simpleton's question, no doubt. He will accept his step-father's offer; we know that well enough. He ought to have done so a year ago, and our difficulties would have been lightened. Your father means what he says?"

"Wolf!" cried Barbara, petulantly.

"Well, I can see that the wolf has come at last, in good earnest. My girl, you'll have to become more serious. Barbara, *you* at all events, cannot afford to trifle."

"I am no trifler!" cried the enthusiast for Italian unity and regeneracy.

"Let us have proof of that, then." Mrs. Denyer looked at her meaningly.

"Mother," said Zillah, earnestly, "do let me write to Mrs. Stonehouse, and beg her to find me a place as nursery governess. I can manage that, I feel sure."

"I'll think about it, dear. But, Madeline, I insist on your putting an end to this ridiculous state of things. You will *order* him to take the position offered."

"Mother, I can do nothing of the kind. If necessary, I'll go for a governess as well."

Thereupon Zillah wept, protesting that such desecration was impossible. The scene prolonged itself to midnight. On the morrow, with the exception of Mrs. Denyer's resolve to subdue Marsh, all was forgotten, and the Denyer family pursued their old course, putting off decided action until there should come another cry of "Wolf!"

CHAPTER IV.

MIRIAM'S BROTHER.

BUT for the aid of his wife's more sympathetic insight, Edward Spence would have continued to interpret Miriam's cheerless frame of mind as a mere result of impatience at being removed from the familiar scenes of her religious activity, and of disquietude amid uncongenial surroundings. "A Puritan at Naples"—that was the phrase which represented her to his imagination; his liking for the picturesque and suggestive led him to regard her solely in that light. No strain of modern humanitarianism complicated Miriam's character. One had not to take into account a possible melancholy produced by the contrast between her life of ease in the South, and the squalor of laborious multitudes under a sky of mill-smoke and English fog. Of the new philan- thropy she spoke, if at all, with angry scorn, holding it to be based on rationalism, radicalism, positivism, or whatsoever name embodied the conflict between the children of this world and the children of light. Far from Miriam any desire to abolish the misery which was among the divinely- appointed conditions of this preliminary existence. No ; she was uncomfortable, and content that others should be so, for discomfort's sake. It fretted her that the Sunday in Naples could not be as universally dolorous as it was at Bartles. It revolted her to hear happy voices in a country abandoned to heathendom.

" Whenever I see her looking at old Vesuvius," said Spence to Eleanor, his eye twinkling, " I feel sure that she muses on the possibility of another tremendous outbreak. She regards him in a friendly way ; he is the minister of vengeance."

Eleanor's discernment was not long in bringing her to a modification of this estimate.

" I am convinced, Ned, that her thoughts are not so con- stantly at Bartles as we imagine. In any case, I begin to understand what she suffers from most. It is want of occu- pation for her mind. She is crushed with *ennui.*"

" This is irreverence. As well attribute *ennui* to the Prophet Jeremiah meditating woes to come."

" I allow you your joke, but I am right for all that. She has nothing to think about that profoundly interests her ; her books are all but as sapless to her as to you or me. She is sinking into melancholia."

" But, my dear girl, the chapel ! "

"She only pretends to think of it. Miriam is becoming a hypocrite; I have noted several little signs of it since Cecily came. She poses—and in wretchedness. Please to recollect that her age is four-and-twenty."

"I do so frequently, and marvel at human nature."

"I do so, and without marvelling at all, for I see human nature justifying itself. I'll tell you what I am going to do, I shall propose to her to begin and read Dante."

"The 'Inferno.' Why, yes."

"And I shall craftily introduce to her attention one or two wicked and worldly little books, such as, 'The Improvisatore,' and the 'Golden Treasury,' and so on. Any such attempts at first would have been premature; but I think the time has come."

Miriam knew no language but her own, and Eleanor by no means purposed inviting her to a course of grammar and exercise. She herself, with her husband's assistance, had learned to read Italian in the only rational way for mature-minded persons—simply taking the text and a close translation, and glancing from time to time at a skeleton accidence. This, of course, will not do in the case of fools, but Miriam Baske, all appearances notwithstanding, did not belong to that category. On hearing her cousin's proposition, she at first smiled coldly; but she did not reject it, and in a day or two they had made a fair beginning of the 'Inferno.' Such a beginning, indeed, as surprised Eleanor, who was not yet made aware that Miriam worked at the book in private with feverish energy—drank at the fountain like one perishing of thirst. Andersen's exquisite story was not so readily accepted, yet this too before long showed a book-marker. And Miriam's countenance brightened; she could not conceal this effect. Her step was a little lighter, and her speech became more natural.

A relapse was to be expected; it came at the bidding of sirocco. One morning the heavens lowered, grey, rolling; it might have been England. Vesuvius, heavily laden at first with a cloud like that on Olympus when the gods are wrathful, by degrees passed from vision, withdrew its form into recesses of dun mists. The angry blue of Capri faded upon a troubled blending of sea and sky; everywhere the horizon contracted and grew mournful; rain began to fall.

Miriam sank as the heavens darkened. The strength of which she had lately been conscious forsook her; all her body was oppressed with languor, her mind miserably void. No book made appeal to her, and the sight of those which she had brought from home was intolerable. She lay upon a couch, her limbs torpid, burdensome. Eleanor's company was worse than useless.

" Please leave me alone," she said at length. " The sound of your voice irritates me."

An hour went by, and no one disturbed her mood. Her languor was on the confines of sleep, when a knock at the door caused her to stir impatiently and half raise herself. It was her maid who entered, holding a note.

" A gentleman has called, ma'am. He wished me to give you this."

Miriam glanced at the address, and at once stood up, only her pale face witnessing the lack of energy of a moment ago.

" Is he waiting ? "

" Yes, ma'am."

The note was of two or three lines :—" Will you let me see you ? Of course I mean alone. It's a long time since we saw each other.—R. E."

" I will see him in this room."

The footstep of the maid as she came back along the tiled corridor was accompanied by one much heavier. Miriam kept her eyes turned to the door; her look was of pained expectancy and of sternness. She stood close by the window, as if purposely drawing as far away as possible. The visitor was introduced, and the door closed behind him.

He too, stood still, as far from Miriam as might be. His age seemed to be seven- or eight-and-twenty, and the cast of his features so strongly resembled Miriam's that there was no doubt of his being her brother. Yet he had more beauty as a man than she as a woman. Her traits were in him developed so as to lose severity and attain a kind of vigour, which at first sight promised a rich and generous nature ; his excellent forehead and dark imaginative eyes indicated a mind anything but likely to bear the trammels in which Miriam had grown up. In the attitude with which he waited for his sister to speak there was both pride and shame ; his look fell before hers, but the constrained smile on his lips was one of self-esteem at issue with adversity. He wore the dress of a gentleman, but it was disorderly. His light overcoat hung unbuttoned, and in his hand he crushed together a hat of soft felt.

"Why have you come to see me, Reuben?" Miriam asked at length, speaking with difficulty and in an offended tone.

"Why shouldn't I, Miriam?" he returned quietly, stepping nearer to her. "Till a few days ago I knew nothing of the illness you have had, or I should, at all events, have written. When I heard you had come to Naples, I—well, I followed. I might as well be here as anywhere else, and I felt a wish to see you."

"Why should you wish to see me? What does it matter to you whether I am well or ill?"

"Yes, it matters, though of course you find it hard to believe."

"Very, when I remember the words with which you last parted from me. If I was hateful to you then, how am I less so now?"

"A man in anger, and especially one of my nature, often says more than he means. It was never *you* that were hateful to me, though your beliefs and your circumstances might madden me into saying such a thing."

"My beliefs, as I told you then, are a part of myself—*are* myself."

She said it with irritable insistence—an accent which would doubtless have been significant in the ears of Eleanor Spence.

"I don't wish to speak of that. Have you recovered your health, Miriam?"

"I am better."

He came nearer again, throwing his hat aside.

"Will you let me sit down? I've had a long journey in third-class, and I feel tired. Such weather as this doesn't help to make me cheerful. I imagined Naples with a rather different sky."

Miriam motioned towards a chair, and looked drearily from the window at the dreary sea. Neither spoke again for two or three minutes. Reuben Elgar surveyed the room, but inattentively.

"What is it you want of me?" Miriam asked, facing him abruptly.

"Want? You hint that I have come to ask you for money?'

"I shouldn't have thought it impossible. If you were in need—you spoke of a third-class journey—I am, at all events, the natural person for your thoughts to turn to."

Reuben laughed dispiritedly.

"No, no, Miriam; I haven't quite got to that. You are the very last person I should think of in such a case."

"Why?"

"Simply because I am not quite so contemptible as you think me. I don't quarrel with my sister, and come back after some years to make it up just because I want to make a demand on her purse."

"You haven't accustomed me to credit you with high motives, Reuben."

"No. And I have never succeeded in making you understand me. I suppose it's hopeless that you ever will. We are too different. You regard me as a vulgar reprobate, who by some odd freak of nature happens to be akin to you. I can picture so well what your imagination makes of me. All the instances of debauchery and general blackguardism that the commerce of life has forced upon your knowledge go towards completing the ideal. It's a pity. I have always felt that you and I might have been a great deal to each other if you had had a reasonable education. I remember you as a child rebelling against the idiocies of your training, before your brain and soul had utterly yielded; then you were my sister, and even then, if it had been possible, I would have dragged you away and saved you."

"I thank Heaven," said Miriam, "that my childhood was in other hands than yours!"

"Yes; and it is very bitter to me to hear you say so."

Miriam kept silence, but looked at him less disdainfully.

"I suppose," he said, "the people you are staying with have much the same horror of my name as you have."

"You speak as loosely as you think. The Spences can scarcely respect you."

"You purpose remaining with them all the winter?"

"It is quite uncertain. With what intentions have you come here? Do you wish me to speak of you to the Spences or not?"

He still kept looking about the room. Perhaps upon him too the baleful southern wind was exercising its influence, for he sat listlessly when he was not speaking, and had a weary look.

"You may speak of me or not, as you like. I don't see that anything's to be gained by my meeting them; but I'll do just as you please."

"You mean to stay in Naples?"

"A short time. I've never been here before, and, as I said, I may as well be here as anywhere else."

"When did you last see Mr. Mallard?"

"Mallard? Why, what makes you speak of him?"

"You made his acquaintance, I think, not long after you last saw me."

"Ha! I understand. That was why he sought me out. You and your friends sent him to me as a companion likely to 'do me good.'"

"I knew nothing of Mr. Mallard then—nothing personally. But he doesn't seem to be the kind of man whose interest you would resent."

"Then you know him?" Reuben asked, in a tone of some pleasure.

"He is in Naples at present."

"I'm delighted to hear it. Mallard is an excellent fellow, in his own way. Somehow I've lost lost sight of him for a long time. He's painting here, I suppose? Where can I find him?"

"I don't know his address, but I can at once get it for you. You are sure that he will welcome you?"

"Why not? Have you spoken to him about me?"

"No," Miriam replied distantly.

"Why shouldn't he welcome me, then? We were very good friends. Do you attribute to him such judgments as your own?"

His way of speaking was subject to abrupt changes. When, as in this instance, he broke forth impulsively, there was a corresponding gleam in his fine eyes and a nervous tension in all his frame. His voice had an extraordinary power of conveying scornful passion; at such moments he seemed to reveal a profound and strong nature.

"I am very slightly acquainted with Mr. Mallard," Miriam answered, with the cold austerity which was the counterpart in her of Reuben's fiery impulsiveness, "but I understand that he is considered trustworthy and honourable by people of like character."

Elgar rose from his chair, and in doing so all but flung it down.

"Trustworthy and honourable! Why, so is many a greengrocer. How the artist would be flattered to hear this estimate of his personality! The honourable Mallard! I must tell him that."

"You will not dare to repeat words from my lips!" exclaimed Miriam, sternly. "You have sunk lower even than I thought."

"What limit, then, did you put to my debasement? In what direction had I still a scrap of trustworthiness and honour left?"

"Tell me that yourself, instead of talking to no purpose in this frenzied way. Why do you come here, if you only wish to renew our old differences?"

"You were the first to do so."

"Can I pretend to be friendly with you, Reuben? What word of penitence have you spoken? In what have you amended yourself? Is not every other sentence you speak a defence of yourself and scorn upon me?"

"And what right have you to judge me? Of course I defend myself, and as scornfully as you like, when I am despised and condemned by one who knows as little of me as the first stranger I pass on the road. Cannot you come forward with a face like a sister's, and leave my faults for my own conscience? *You* judge me! What do you, with your nun's experiences, your heart chilled, your paltry view of the world through a chapel window, know of a man whose passions boil in him like the fire in yonder mountain? I should subdue my passions. Excellent text for a copy-book in a girls' school! I should be another man than I am; I should remould myself; I should cool my brain with doctrine. With a bullet, if you like; say that, and you will tell the truth. But with the truth you have nothing to do; too long ago you were taught that you must never face that. Do you deal as truthfully with yourself as I with my own heart? I wonder, I wonder."

Miriam's eyes had fallen. She stood quite motionless, with a face of suffering.

"You want me to confess my sins?" Reuben continued, walking about in uncontrollable excitement. "What is your chapel formula? Find one comprehensive enough, and let me repeat it after you; only mind that it includes hypocrisy, for the sake of the confession. I tell you I am conscious of no sins. Of follies, of ignorances, of miseries— as many as you please. And to what account should they all go? Was I so admirably guided in childhood and boy-hood that my subsequent life is not to be explained? It succeeded in your case, my poor sister. Oh, nobly! Don't be afraid that I shall outrage you by saying all I think. But just think of *me* as a result of Jewish education applied to an English lad, and one whose temperament was plain enough to eyes of ordinary penetration. My very name! Your name, too! You it has made a Jew in soul; upon me it weighs like a curse as often as I think of it. It symbolizes all that is making my life a brutal failure—a failure—a failure!"

He threw himself upon the couch and became silent, his strength at an end, even his countenance exhausted of vitality, looking haggard and almost ignoble. Miriam stirred at length, for the first time, and gazed steadily at him.

"Reuben, let us have an end of this," she said, in a voice half choked. "Stay or go as you will; but I shall utter no more reproaches. You must make of your life what you can. As you say, I don't understand you. Perhaps the mere fact of my being a woman is enough to make that impossible. Only don't throw your scorn at me for believing what you can't believe. Talk quietly; avoid those subjects; tell me, if you wish to, what you are doing or think of doing."

"You should have spoken like this earlier, Miriam. It would have spared my memory its most wretched burden."

" How ? "

" You know quite well that I valued your affection, and that it had no little importance in my life. Instead of still having my sister, I had only the memory of her anger and injustice, and of my own cursed temper."

" I had no influence for good."

" Perhaps not in the common sense of the words. I am not going to talk humbug about a woman's power to make a man angelic; that will do for third-rate novels and plays. But I shouldn't have thrown myself away as I have done if you had cared to know what I was doing."

" Did I not care, Reuben ? "

" If so, you thought it was your duty not to show it. You thought harshness was the only proper treatment for a case such as mine. I had had too much of that."

" What did you mean just now by speaking as though you were poor ? "

" I have been poor for a long time—poor compared with what I was. Most of my money has gone—on the fool's way. I haven't come here to lament over it. It's one of my rules never, if I can help it, to think of the past. What has been, has been; and what will be, will be. When I fume and rage like an idiot, that's only the blood in me getting the better of the brain; an example of the fault that always wrecks me. Do you think I cannot see myself? Just now, I couldn't keep back the insensate words—insensate because useless—but I judged myself all the time as distinctly as I do now it's over."

" Your money gone, Reuben? " murmured his sister, in consternation.

" You might have foreseen that. Come and sit down by me, Miriam. I am tired and wretched. Where is the sun ? Surely one may have sunshine at Naples ! "

He was now idly fretful. Miriam seated herself at his side, and he took her hand.

"I thought you might perhaps receive me like this at first. I came only with that hope. I wish you looked better, Miriam. How do you employ yourself here?"

"I am much out of doors. I get stronger."

"You spoke of old Mallard. I'm glad he is here, really glad. You know, Mallard's a fellow of no slight account; I should think you might even like him."

"But yourself, Reuben?"

"No, no; let me rest a little. I'm sick and tired of myself. Let's talk of old Mallard. And what's become of little Cecily Doran?"

"She is here—with her aunt."

"She here too! By Jove! Well, of course, I shall have nothing to do with them. Mallard still acting as her guardian, I suppose. Rather a joke, that. I never could get him to speak on the subject. But I feel glad you know him. He's a solid fellow, tremendously conscientious; just the things you would like in a man, no doubt. Have you seen any of his paintings?"

Miriam shook her head absently, unable to find voice for the topic, which was remote from her thoughts.

"He's done fine things, great things. I shall look him up, and we'll drink a bottle of wine together."

He kept stroking Miriam's hand, a white hand with blue veins—a strong hand, though so delicately fashioned. The touch of the wedding-ring again gave a new direction to his discursive thoughts.

"After this, shall you go back to that horrible hole in Lancashire?"

"I hope to go back home, certainly."

"Home, home!" he muttered, impatiently. "It has made you ill, poor girl. Stay in Italy a long time, now you are once here. For you to be here at all seems a miracle; it gives me hopes."

Miriam did not resent this, in word at all events. She was submitting again to physical oppression; her head drooped, and her abstracted gaze was veiled with despondent lassitude. Reuben talked idly, in loose sentences.

"Do you think of me as old or young, Miriam?" he asked, when both had kept silence for a while.

"I no longer think of you as older than myself."

"That is natural. I imagined that. In one way I am old enough, but in another I am only just beginning my life, and have all my energies fresh. I shall do something yet; can you believe it?"

"Do what?" she asked, wearily.

"Oh, I have plans; all sorts of plans."

He joined his hands together behind his head, and began to stir with a revival of mental energy.

"But plans of what sort?"

"There is only one direction open to me. My law has of course gone to—to limbo; it was always an absurdity. Most of my money has gone the same way, and I'm not sorry for it. If I had never had anything, I should have set desperately to work long ago. Now I am bound to work, and you will see the results. Of course, in our days, there's only one road for a man like me. I shall go in for literature."

Miriam listened, but made no comment.

"My life hitherto has not been wasted," Elgar pursued, leaning forward with a new light on his countenance. "I have been gaining experience. Do you understand? Few men at my age have seen more of life—the kind of life that is useful as literary material. It's only quite of late that I have begun to appreciate this, to see all the possibilities that are in myself. It has taken all this time to outgrow the miserable misdirection of my boyhood, and to become a man of my time. Thank the fates, I no longer live in the Pentateuch, but at the latter end of the nineteenth century. Many a lad has to work this deliverance for himself nowadays. I don't wish to speak unkindly any more, Miriam, but I must tell you plain facts. Some fellows free themselves by dint of hard study. In my case that was made impossible by all sorts of reasons—temperament mainly, as you know. I was always a rebel against my fetters; I had not to learn that liberty was desirable, but how to obtain it, and what use to make of it. All the disorder through which I have gone was a struggle towards self-knowledge and understanding of my time. You and others are wildly in error in calling it dissipation, profligacy, recklessness, and so on. You at least, Miriam, ought to have judged me more truly; you, at all events, should not have classed me with common men."

His eyes were now agleam, and the beauty of his countenance fully manifest. He held his head in a pose of superb confidence. There was too much real force in his features to make this seem a demonstration of idle vanity. Miriam regarded him, and continued to do so.

"To be sure, my powers are in your eyes valueless," he pursued; "or rather, your eyes have never been opened to anything of the kind. The nineteenth century is nothing to you; its special opportunities and demands and characteristics would revolt you if they were made clear to your intelligence. If I tell you I am before everything a man of my time, I suppose this seems only a cynical confession of all the weaknesses and crimes you have already attributed to me? It shall not always be so! Why, what are you, after all, Miriam? Twenty-three, twenty-four—which is it? Why, you are a child still; your time of education is before you. You are a child come to Italy to learn what can be made of life!"

She averted her face, but smiled, and not quite so coldly as of wont. She could not but think of Cecily, whose words a few days ago had been in spirit so like these, so like them in the ring of enthusiasm.

"Some day," Elgar went on, exalting himself more and more, "you shall wonder in looking back on this scene between us—wonder how you could have been so harsh to me. It is impossible that you and I, sole brother and sister, should move on constantly diverging paths. Tell me —you are not really without some kind of faith in my abilities ? "

" You know it has always been my grief that you put them to no use."

" Very well. But it remains for you to learn what my powers really are, and to bring yourself to sympathize with my direction. You are a child—there is my hope. You shall be taught—yes, yes ! Your obstinacy shall be over-come ; you shall be made to see your own good ! "

" And who is to be so kind as to take charge of my educa-tion ? " Miriam asked, without looking at him, in an idly contemptuous tone.

" Why not old Mallard ? " cried Reuben, breaking suddenly into jest. " The tutorship of children is in his line."

Miriam showed herself offended.

" Please don't speak of me. I am willing to hear what you purpose for yourself, but don't mix my name with it."

Elgar resumed the tone of ambition. Whether he had in truth definite literary schemes could not be gathered from the rhetoric on which he was borne. His main conviction seemed to be that he embodied the spirit of his time, and would ere long achieve a work of notable significance, the fruit of all his experiences. Miriam, though with no sign of strong interest, gave him her full attention.

" Do you intend to work here ? " she asked at length.

" I can't say. At present I am anything but well, and I shall get what benefit I can from Naples first of all. I suppose the sun will shine again before long ? This sky is depressing."

He stood up, and went to the windows ; then came back with uncertain step.

" You'll tell the Spences I've been ? "

" I think I had better. They will know, of course, that I have had a visitor."

" Should I see them ? " he asked, with hesitation.

" Just as you please."

" I shall have to, sooner or later. Why not now ? "

Miriam pondered.

" I'll go and see if they are at leisure."

During her absence, Elgar examined the books on the table. He turned over each one with angry mutterings. The chapel plans were no longer lying about ; only yesterday Miriam had rolled them up and put them away— temporarily. Before the " St. Cecilia " he stood in thoughtful observation, and was still there when Miriam returned. She had a look of uneasiness.

" Miss Doran and her aunt are with Mrs. Spence, Reuben."

" Oh, in that case——" he began carelessly, with a wave of the arm.

" But they will be glad to see you."

" Indeed ? I look rather seedy, I'm afraid."

" Take off your overcoat."

" I'm all grimy. I came here straight from the railway."

" Then go into my bedroom and make yourself presentable."

A few moments sufficed for this. As she waited for his return, Miriam stood with knitted brows, her eyes fixed on the floor. Reuben reappeared, and she examined him.

" You're bitterly ashamed of me, Miriam."

She made no reply, and at once led the way along the corridor.

Mrs. Spence had met Reuben in London, since her marriage ; by invitation he came to her house, but neglected to repeat the visit. To Mrs. Lessingham he was personally a stranger. But neither of these ladies received the honour of much attention from him for the first few moments after he had entered the room ; his eyes and thoughts were occupied with the wholly unexpected figure of Cecily Doran. In his recollection, she was a slight, pale, shy little girl, fond of keeping in corners with a book, and seemingly marked out for a life of dissenting piety and provincial surroundings. She had interested him little in those days, and seldom did anything to bring herself under his notice. He last saw her when she was about twelve. Now he found himself in the presence of a beautiful woman, every line of whose countenance told of instruction, thought, spirit; whose bearing was refined beyond anything he had yet understood by that word; whose modest revival of old acquaintance made his hand thrill at her touch, and his heart beat confusedly as he looked into her eyes. With difficulty he constrained himself to common social necessities, and made show of conversing with the elder ladies. He wished to gaze steadily at the girl's face, and connect past with present; to revive his memory of six years ago, and convince himself that such development was possible. At the same time he became aware of a reciprocal curiosity in Cecily. When he turned towards her she met his glance, and when he spoke she gave him a smile of pleased attentiveness. The consequence was that he soon began to speak freely, to pick his words, to balance his sentences and shun the commonplace.

"I saw Florence and Rome in '76," he replied to a question from Mrs. Lessingham. "In Rome my travelling companion fell ill, and we returned without coming further south. It is wrong, however, to say that I *saw* anything; my mind was in far too crude a state to direct my eyes to any purpose. I stared about me a good deal, and got some notions of topography, and there the matter ended for the time."

"The benefit came with subsequent reflection, no doubt," said Mrs. Lessingham, who found one of her greatest pleasures in listening to the talk of young men with brains. Whenever it was possible, she gathered such individuals about her and encouraged them to discourse of themselves, generally quite as much to their satisfaction as to her own.

Already she had invited with some success the confidence of Mr. Clifford Marsh, who proved interesting, but not unfathomable; he belonged to a class with which she was tolerably familiar. Reuben Elgar, she perceived at once, was not without characteristics linking him to that same group of the new generation, but it seemed probable that its confines were too narrow for him. There was comparatively little affectation in his manner, and none in his aspect; his voice rang with a sincerity which claimed serious audience, and his eyes had something more than surface gleamings. Possibly he belonged to the unclassed and the unclassable, in which case the interest attaching to him was of the highest kind.

"Subsequent reflection," returned Elgar, "has, at all events, enabled me to see myself as I then was; and I suppose self-knowledge is the best result of travel."

"If one agrees that self-knowledge is ever a good at all," said the speculative lady, with her impartial smile.

"To be sure." Elgar looked keenly at her, probing the significance of the remark. "The happy human being will make each stage of his journey a phase of more or less sensual enjoyment, delightful at the time and valuable in memory. The excursion will be his life in little. I envy him, but I can't imitate him."

"Why envy him?" asked Eleanor.

"Because he is happy; surely a sufficient ground."

"Yet you give the preference to self-knowledge."

"Yes, I do. Because in that direction my own nature tends to develop itself. But I envy every lower thing in creation. I won't pretend to say how it is with other people who are forced along an upward path; in my own case every step is made with a groan, and why shouldn't I confess it?"

"To do so enhances the merit of progress," observed Mrs. Lessingham, mischievously.

"Merit? I know nothing of merit. I spoke of myself

being *forced* upwards. If ever I feel that I am slipping back, I shall state it with just as little admission of shame."

Miriam heard this modern dialogue with grave features. At Bartles, such talk would have qualified the talker for social excommunication, and every other pain and penalty Bartles had in its power to inflict. She observed that Cecily's interest increased. The girl listened frankly; no sense of anything improper appeared in her visage. Nay, she was about to interpose a remark.

" Isn't there a hope, Mr. Elgar, that this envy of which you speak will be one of the things that the upward path leaves behind ? "

" I should like to believe it, Miss Doran," he answered, his eyes kindling at hers. " It's true that I haven't yet gone very far."

" I like so much to believe it that I *do* believe it," the girl continued impulsively.

" Your progress in that direction exceeds mine."

" Don't be troubled by the compliment," interjected Eleanor, before Cecily could speak. " There is no question of merit."

Mrs. Lessingham laughed.

The rain still fell, and the grey heavens showed no breaking. Shortly after this, Elgar would have risen to take his leave, but Mrs. Spence begged him to remain and lunch with them. The visitors from the Mergellina declined a similar invitation.

Edward Spence was passing his morning at the Museum. On his return at luncheon-time, Eleanor met him with the intelligence that Reuben Elgar had presented himself, and was now in his sister's room.

" *In formâ pauperis*, presumably," said Spence, raising his eyebrows.

" I can't say, but I fear it isn't impossible. Cecily and her aunt happened to call this morning, and he had some talk with them."

"Is he very much of a blackguard?" inquired her husband, disinterestedly.

"Indeed, no. That is to say, externally and in his conversation. It's a decided improvement on our old impressions of him."

"I'm glad to hear it," was the dry response.

"He has formed himself in some degree. Hints that he is going to produce literature."

"Of course." Spence laughed merrily. "The last refuge of a scoundrel."

"I don't like to judge him so harshly, Ned. He has a fine face."

"And is Miriam killing the fatted calf?"

"His arrival seems to embarrass rather than delight her."

"Depend upon it, the fellow has come to propose a convenient division of her personal property."

When he again appeared, Elgar was in excellent spirits. He met Spence with irresistible frankness and courtesy; his talk made the luncheon cheery, and dismissed thought of sirocco. It appeared that he had as yet no abode; his luggage was at the station. A suggestion that he should seek quarters under the same roof with Mallard recommended itself to him.

"I feel like a giant refreshed," he declared, in privately taking leave of Miriam. "Coming to Naples was an inspiration."

She raised her lips to his for the first time, but said nothing.

———————

CHAPTER V.

THE ARTIST ASTRAY.

FROM the Strada di Chiaia, the narrow street winding between immense houses, all day long congested with the merry tumult of Neapolitan traffic, where herds of goats and milch cows placidly make their way among vehicles of every possible and impossible description; where *cocchieri* crack their whips and belabour their hapless cattle, and yell their "Ah—h—h! Ah—h—h!"—where teams of horse, ox, and ass, the three abreast, drag piles of country produce, jingling their fantastic harness, and primitive carts laden with red-soaked wine-casks rattle recklessly along; where bare-footed, girdled, and tonsured monks plod on their no-business, and every third man one passes is a rotund ecclesiastic, who never in his life walked at more than a mile an hour; where, at evening, carriages returning from the Villa Nazionale cram the thoroughfare from side to side, and make one aware, if one did not previously know it, that parts of the street have no pedestrians' pavement;—from the Strada di Chiaia (now doomed, alas! by the exigencies of *lo sventramento* and *il risanamento*) turn into the public staircase and climb through the dusk, with all possible attention to where you set your foot, past the unmelodious beggars, to the Ponte di Chiaia, bridge which spans the roadway and looks down upon its crowd and clamour as into a profound valley; thence proceed uphill on the lava paving, between fruit-shops and sausage-shops and wine-shops, always in an atmosphere of fried oil and roasted chestnuts and baked pine-cones; and presently turn left into a still narrower street, with tailors and boot-makers and smiths all at work

in the open air ; and pass through the Piazzetta Mondragone, and turn again to the left, but this time downhill;
then lose yourself amid filthy little alleys, where the scent
of oil and chestnuts and pine-cones is stronger than ever;
then emerge on a little terrace where there is a noble view
of the bay and of Capri; then turn abruptly between walls
overhung with fig-trees and orange-trees and lemon-trees,—
and you will reach Casa Rolandi.

It is an enormous house, with a great arched entrance
admitting to the inner court, where on the wall is a
Madonna's shrine, lamp-illumined of evenings. A great
staircase leads up from floor to floor. On each story are
two tenements, the doors facing each other. In 1878, one
of the apartments at the very top—an ascent equal to that
of a moderate mountain—was in the possession of a certain
Signora Bassano, whose name might be read on a brass
plate. This lady had furnished rooms to let, and here it
was that Ross Mallard established himself for the few days
that he proposed to spend at Naples.

Already he had lingered till the few days were become
more than a fortnight, and still the day of his departure was
undetermined. This was most unwonted waste of time, not
easily accounted for by Mallard himself. A morning of
sunny splendour, coming after much cloudiness and a good
deal of rain, plucked him early out of bed, strong in the
resolve that to-morrow should see him on the road to Amalfi.
He had slept well—an exception in the past week—and his
mind was open to the influences of sunlight and reason.
Before going forth for breakfast he had a letter to write, a
brief account of himself addressed to the murky little town
of Sowerby Bridge, in Yorkshire. This finished, he threw
open the big windows, stepped out on to the balcony, and
drank deep draughts of air from the sea. In the street
below was passing a flock of she-goats, all ready to be
milked, each with a bell tinkling about her neck. The goat-
herd kept summoning his customers with a long musical

whistle. Mallard leaned over and watched the clean-fleeced, slender, graceful animals with a smile of pleasure. Then he amused himself with something that was going on in the house opposite. A woman came out on to a balcony high up, bent over it, and called, "Annina! Annina!" until the call brought another woman on to the balcony immediately below; whereupon the former let down a cord, and her friend, catching the end of it, made it fast to a basket which contained food covered with a cloth. The basket was drawn up, the women gossiped and laughed for a while in pleasant voices, then they disappeared. All around, the familiar Neapolitan clamour was beginning. Church bells were ringing as they ring at Naples—a great crash, followed by a rapid succession of quivering little shakes, then the crash again. Hawkers were crying fruit and vegetables and fish in rhythmic cadence; a donkey was braying obstreperously.

Mallard had just taken a light overcoat on his arm, and was ready to set out, when some one knocked. He turned the key in the door, and admitted Reuben Elgar.

"I'm off to Pompeii," said Elgar, vivaciously.

"All right. You'll go to the 'Sole'? I shall be there myself to-morrow evening."

"I'm likely to stay several days, so we shall have more talk."

They left the house together, and presently parted with renewed assurance of meeting again on the morrow.

Mallard went his way thoughtfully, the smile quickly passing from his face. At a little *caffè*, known to him of old, he made a simple breakfast, glancing the while over a morning newspaper, and watching the children who came to fetch their *due soldi* of coffee in tiny tins. Then he strolled away and supplemented his meal with a fine bunch of grapes, bought for a penny at a stall that glowed and was fragrant with piles of fruit. Heedless of the carriage-drivers who shouted at him and even dogged him along street after street, he sauntered in the broad sunshine, plucking his grapes and relishing them. Coming out by the sea-shore, he stood for a while to watch the fishermen dragging in their nets—picturesque fellows with swarthy faces and sun-tanned legs of admirable outline, hauling slowly in files at interminable rope, which boys coiled lazily as it came in; or the oyster-dredgers, poised on the side of their boats over the blue water. At the foot of the sea-wall tumbled the tideless breakers; their drowsy music counselled enjoyment of the hour and carelessness of what might come hereafter.

With no definite purpose, he walked on and on, for the most part absorbed in thought. He passed through the long *grotta* of Posillipo, gloomy, chilly, and dank; then out again into the sunshine, and along the road to Bagnoli. On walls and stone-heaps the little lizards darted about, innumerable; in vineyards men were at work dismantling the vine-props, often singing at their task. From Bagnoli, still walking merely that a movement of his limbs might accompany his busy thoughts, he went along by the sea-shore, and so at length, still long before midday, had come to Pozzuoli. A sharp conflict with the swarm of guides who beset the entrance to the town, and again he escaped into quietness, wandered among narrow streets, between blue, red, and yellow houses, stopping at times to look at some sunny upper window hung about with clusters of *sorbe* and *pomidori*. By this time he had won appetite for a more substantial meal. In the kind of eating-house that suited his mood, an obscure *bettola* probably never yet patronized by Englishman, he sat down to a dish of maccheroni and a bottle of red wine. At another table were some boatmen, who, after greeting him, went on with their lively talk in a dialect of which he could understand but few words.

Having eaten well and drunk still better, he lit a cigar and sauntered forth to find a place for dreaming. Chance led him to the patch of public garden, with its shrubs and young palm-trees, which looks over the little port. Here, when once he had made it clear to a succession of rhetorical boatmen that he was not to be tempted on to the sea, he could sit as idly and as long as he liked, looking across the sapphire bay and watching the bright sails glide hither and thither. With the help of sunlight and red wine, he could imagine that time had gone back twenty centuries—that this was not Pozzuoli, but Puteoli; that over yonder was not Baia, but Baiæ; that the men among the shipping talked to each other in Latin, and perchance of the perishing Republic.

But Mallard's fancy would not dwell long in remote ages. As he watched the smoke curling up from his cigar, he slipped back into the world of his active being, and made no effort to obscure the faces that looked upon him. They were those of his mother and sisters, thought of whom carried him to the northern island, now grim, cold, and sunless beneath its lowering sky. These relatives still lived where his boyhood had been passed, a life strangely unlike his own, and even alien to his sympathies, but their house was still all that he could call home. Was it to be always the same?

Fifteen years now, since, at the age of twenty, he painted his first considerable landscape, a tract of moorland on the borders of Lancashire and Yorkshire. This was his native ground. At Sowerby Bridge, a manufacturing town, which, like many others in the same part of England, makes a blot of ugliness on country in itself sternly beautiful, his father had settled as the manager of certain rope-works. Mr. Mallard's state was not unprosperous, for he had invented a process put in use by his employers, and derived benefit from it. He was a man of habitual gravity, occasionally severe in the rule of his household, very seldom unbending to mirth. Though not particularly robust, he employed his leisure in long walks about the moors, walks sometimes prolonged till after midnight, sometimes begun long before dawn. His acquaintances called him unsociable, and doubt-less he was so in the sense that he could not find at Sowerby Bridge any one for whose society he greatly cared. It was even a rare thing for him to sit down with his wife and children for more than a few minutes; if he remained in the house, he kept apart in a room of his own, musing over, rather than reading, a little collection of books—one of his favourites being Defoe's "History of the Devil." He often made ironical remarks, and seemed to have a grim satisfaction when his hearers missed the point. Then he would chuckle, and shake his head, and go away muttering.

Young Ross, who made no brilliant figure at school, and showed a turn for drawing, was sent at seventeen to the factory of Messrs. Gilstead, Miles and Doran, to become a designer of patterns. The result was something more than his father had expected, for Mr. Doran, who had his abode at Sowerby Bridge, quickly discovered that the lad was meant for far other things, and, by dint of personal intervention, caused Mr. Mallard to give his son a chance of becoming an artist.

A remarkable man, this Mr. Doran. By nature a Bohemian, somehow made into a Yorkshire mill-owner; a strong, active, nobly featured man, who dressed as no one in the factory regions ever did before or probably ever will again— his usual appearance suggesting the common notion of a bushranger; an artist to the core; a purchaser of pictures by unknown men who had a future—at the sale of his collection three Robert Cheeles got into the hands of dealers, all of them now the boasted possessions of great galleries; a passionate lover of music—he had been known to make the journey to Paris merely to hear Diodati sing; finally, in common rumour a profligate whom no prudent householder would admit to the society of his wife and daughters. However, at the time of young Mallard's coming under his notice he had been married about a year. Mrs. Doran came from Manchester; she was very beautiful, but had slight education, and before long Sowerby Bridge remarked that the husband was too often away from home.

Doran and the elder Mallard, having once met, were disposed to see more of each other; in spite of the difference

of social standing, they became intimates, and Mr. Mallard
had at length some one with whom he found pleasure in conversing. He did not long enjoy the new experience. In the
winter that followed, he died of a cold contracted on one of
his walks when the hills were deep in snow.

Doran remained the firm friend of the family. Local talk
had inspired Mrs. Mallard with a prejudice against him, but
substantial services mitigated this, and the widow was in
course of time less uneasy at her son's being practically
under the guardianship of this singular man of business.
Mallard, after preliminary training, was sent to the studio
of a young artist whom Doran greatly admired, Cullen
Banks, then struggling for the recognition he was never to
enjoy, death being beforehand with him. Mrs. Mallard was
given to understand that no expenses were involved save those
of the lad's support in Manchester, where Banks lived, and
Mallard himself did not till long after know that his friend
had paid the artist a fee out of his own pocket. Two things
did Mallard learn from Doran himself which were to have a
marked influence on his life—a belief that only in landscape
can a painter of our time hope to do really great work, and
a limitless contempt of the Royal Academy. In Manchester
he made the acquaintance of several people with whom Doran
was familiar, among them Edward Spence, then in the ship-
ping-office, and Jacob Bush Bradshaw, well on his way to
making a fortune out of silk. On Banks's death, Mallard,
now nearly twenty-one, went to London for a time. His
patrimony was modest, but happily, if the capital remained
intact, sufficient to save him from the cares that degrade and
waste a life. His mother and sisters had also an income
adequate to their simple habits.

In the meantime, Mrs. Doran was dead. After giving
birth to a daughter, she fell into miserable health; her
husband took her abroad, and she died in Germany. Thereafter Sowerby Bridge saw no more of its bugbear; Doran
abandoned commerce and became a Bohemian in earnest—

save that his dinner was always assured. He wandered over Europe ; he lived with Bohemian society in every capital ; he kept adding to his collection of pictures (stored in a house at Woolwich, which he freely lent as an abode to a succession of ill-to-do artists) ; and finally he was struck with paralysis whilst conducting to their home the widow and child of a young painter who had suddenly died in the Ardennes. The poor woman under his protection had to become his guardian. He was brought to the house at Woolwich, and there for several months lay between life and death. A partial recovery followed, and he was taken to the Isle of Wight, where, in a short time, a second attack killed him.

His child, Cecily, was twelve years old. For the last five years she had been living in the care of Mrs. Elgar at Manchester. This lady was an intimate friend of Mrs. Doran's family, and in entrusting his child to her, Doran had given a strong illustration of one of the singularities of his character. Though by no means the debauchee that Sowerby Bridge declared him, he was not a man of conventional morality ; yet, in the case of people who were in any way entrusted to his care, he showed a curious severity of practice. Ross Mallard, for instance ; no provincial Puritan could have instructed the lad more strenuously in the accepted moral code than did Mr. Doran on taking him from home to live in Manchester. In choosing a wife, he went to a family of conventional Dissenters ; and he desired his daughter to pass the years of her childhood with people who he knew would guide her in the very straitest way of Puritan doctrine. What his theory was in this matter (if he had one) he told nobody. Dying, he left it to the discretion of the two trustees to appoint a residence for Cecily, if for any reason she could not remain with Mrs. Elgar. This occasion soon presented itself, and Cecily passed into the care of Doran's sister, Mrs. Lessingham, who was just entered upon a happy widowhood. Mallard, most unexpectedly left sole trustee, had no choice but to assent to this arrangement ; the only other home possible for the girl was with Miriam at Redbeck House, but Mr. Baske did not look with favour on that proposal. Hitherto, Mr. Trench, the elder trustee, who lived in Manchester, had alone been in personal relations with Mrs. Elgar and little Cecily; even now Mallard did not make the personal acquaintance of Mrs. Elgar (otherwise he would doubtless have met Miriam), but saw Mrs. Lessingham in London, and for the first time met Cecily when she came to the south in her aunt's care. He knew what an extreme change would be made in the manner of the girl's education, and it caused him some mental trouble; but it was clear that Cecily might benefit greatly in health by travel, and, as for the moral question, Mrs. Lessingham strongly stirred his sympathies by the dolorous account she gave of the child's surroundings in the north. Cecily was being intellectually starved; that seemed clear to Mallard himself after a little conversation with her. It was wonderful how much she had already learnt, impelled by sheer inner necessity, of things which in general she was discouraged from studying. So Cecily left England, to return only for short intervals, spent in London. Between that departure and this present meeting, Mallard saw her only twice; but the girl wrote to him with some regularity. These letters grew more and more delightful. Cecily addressed herself with exquisite frankness as to an old friend, old in both senses of the word; collected, they made a history of her rapidly growing mind such as the shy artist might have glorified in possessing. In reality, he did nothing of the kind; he wished the letters would not come and disturb him in his work. He sent gruff little answers, over which Cecily laughed, as so characteristic.

Yes, there was a distinct connection between those homely memories and picturings which took him in thought to Sowerby Bridge, and the image of Cecily Doran which had caused him to waste all this time in Naples. They represented two worlds, in both of which he had some part; but it was only too certain with which of them he was

the more closely linked. What but mere accident put
him in contact with the world which was Cecily's ? Through
her aunt she had aristocratic relatives ; her wealth made her
a natural member of what is called society; her beauty and
her brilliancy marked her to be one of society's ornaments.
What could she possibly be to him, Ross Mallard, landscape-
painter of small if any note, as unaristocratic in mind and
person as any one that breathed ? To put the point with
uncompromising plainness, and therefore in all its absurdity,
how could he possibly imagine Cecily Doran called Mrs.
Mallard ?

The thing was flagrantly, grossly, palpably absurd. He
tingled in the ears in trying to represent to himself how
Cecily would think of it, if by any misfortune it were ever
suggested to her.

Then why not, in the name of common sense, cease to
ponder such follies, and get on with the work which waited
for him ? Why this fluttering about a flame which scorched
him more and more dangerously ? It was not the first time
that he had experienced temptations of this kind; a story of
five years ago, its scene in London, should have reminded
him that he could stand a desperate wrench when convinced
that his life's purpose depended upon it. Here were three
years of trusteeship before him—he could not, or would not,
count on her marrying before she came of age. Her letters
would still come ; from time to time doubtless he must meet
her. It had all resulted from this confounded journey taken
together ! Why, knowing himself sufficiently, did he consent to meet the people at Genoa, loitering there for a
couple of days in expectancy ? Why had he come to Italy
at all just now ?

The answers to all such angry queries were plain enough,
however he had hitherto tried to avoid them. He was a
lonely man like his father, but not content with loneliness ;
friendship was always strong to tempt him, and when the
thought of something more than friendship had been

suffered to take hold upon his imagination, it held with terrible grip, burning, torturing. He had come simply to meet Cecily; there was the long and short of it. It was a weakness, such as any man may be guilty of, particularly any artist who groans in lifelong solitude. Let it be recognized; let it be flung savagely into the past, like so many others encountered and overcome on his course.

The other day, when it was rainy and sunless, he had seemed all at once to find his freedom. In a moment of mental languor, he was able to view his position clearly, as though some other man were concerned, and to cry out that he had triumphed; but within the same hour an event befell which revived all the old trouble and added new. Reuben Elgar entered his room, coming directly from Villa Sannazaro, in a state of excitement, talking at once of Cecily Doran as though his acquaintance with her had been unbroken from the time when she was in his mother's care to now. Irritation immediately scattered the thoughts Mallard had been ranging; he could barely make a show of amicable behaviour; a cold fear began to creep about his heart. The next morning he woke to a new phase of his conflict, the end further off than ever. Unable to command thought and feeling, he preserved at least the control of his action, and could persevere in the resolve not to see Cecily; to avoid casual meetings he kept away even from the Spences. He shunned all places likely to be visited by Cecily, and either sat at home in dull idleness or strayed about the swarming quarters of the town, trying to entertain himself with the spectacle of Neapolitan life. To-day the delicious weather had drawn him forth in a heedless mood. And, indeed, it did not much matter now whether he met his friends or not; he had spoken the word—to-morrow he would go his way.

At the very moment of thinking this thought, when his cigar was nearly finished and he had begun to stretch his limbs, wearied by remaining in one position, shadows and footsteps approached him. He looked up, and——

"Mr. Mallard! So we have caught you at last! It only needed this to complete our enjoyment. Now you will go across to Baiæ with us."

Cecily, with Mrs. Baske and Spence. She had run eagerly forward, and her companions were advancing at a more sober pace. Mallard rose with his grim smile, and of course forgot that it is customary to doff one's beaver when ladies approach; he took the offered hand, said "How do you do?" and turned to the others.

"A fair capture!" exclaimed Spence. "Just now, at lunch, we were speculating on such a chance. The cigar argues a broken fast, I take it."

"Yes, I have had my maccheroni."

"We are going to take a boat over to Baiæ. Suppose you come with us."

"Of course Mr. Mallard will come," said Cecily, her face radiant. "He can make no pretence of work interrupted."

Already the group was surrounded by boatmen offering their services. Spence led the way down to the quay, and after much tumult a boat was selected and a bargain struck, the original demand made by the artless sailors being of course five times as much as was ever paid for the transit. They rowed out through the cluster of little craft, then hoisted a sail, and glided smoothly over the blue water.

"Where is Mrs. Lessingham?" Mallard inquired of Cecily.

"At the Hôtel Bristol, with some very disagreeable people who have just landed on their way from India—a military gentleman, and a more military lady, and a most military son, relatives of ours. We spent last evening with them, and I implored to be let off to-day."

Mallard propped himself idly, and from under the shadow of his hat often looked at her. He had begun to wonder at the unreservéd joy with which she greeted his joining the party. Of course she could have no slightest suspicion of what was in his mind; one moment's thought of him in such a light must have altered her behaviour immediately. Altered in what way? That he in vain tried to imagine; his knowledge of her did not go far enough. But he could not be wrong in attributing unconsciousness to her. Moreover, with the inconsistency of a man in his plight, he resented it. To sit thus, almost touching him, gazing freely into his face, and yet to be in complete ignorance of suffering which racked him, seemed incompatible with fine qualities either of heart or mind. What rubbish was talked about woman's insight, about her delicate sympathies!

"Mrs. Spence is very sorry not to see you occasionally, Mr. Mallard."

It was Miriam who spoke. Mallard was watching Cecily, and now, on turning his head, he felt sure that Mrs. Baske had been observant of his countenance. Her eyes fell whilst he was seeking words for a reply.

"I shall call to see her to-morrow morning," he said, "just to say good-bye for a time."

"You really go to-morrow?" asked Cecily, with interest, but nothing more.

"Yes. I hope to see Mrs. Lessingham for a moment also. Can you tell me when she is likely to be at home?"

"Certainly between two and three, if you could come then."

He waited a little, then looked unexpectedly at Miriam. Again her eyes were fixed on him, and again they fell with something of consciousness. Did *she*, perchance, understand him?

His speculations concerning Cecily became comparative. In point of age, the distance between Cecily and Miriam was of some importance; the fact that the elder had been a married woman was of still more account. On the first day of his meeting with Mrs. Baske, he had thought a good deal about her; since then she had slipped from his mind, but now he felt his interest reviving. Surely she was as remote from him as a woman well could be, yet his attitude towards her had no character of intolerance; he half wished that he could form a closer acquaintance with her. At present, the thought of calm conversation with such a woman made a soothing contrast to the riot excited in him by Cecily. Did she read his mind? For one thing, it was not impossible that the Spences had spoken freely in her presence of himself and his odd relations to the girl; there was no doubting how *they* regarded him. Possibly he was a frequent subject of discussion between Eleanor and her cousin. Mature women could talk with each other freely of these things.

On the other hand, whatever Mrs. Lessingham might have in her mind, she certainly would not expose it in dialogue with her niece. Cecily was in an unusual position for a girl of her age; she had, he believed, no intimate friend; at all events, she had none who also knew him. Girls, to be sure, had their own way of talking over delicate points, just as married women had theirs, and with intimates of the ordinary kind Cecily must have come by now to consider her guardian as a male creature of flesh and blood. What did it mean, that she did not?

A question difficult of debate, involving much that the mind is wont to slur over in natural scruple. Mallard was no slave to the imbecile convention which supposes a young girl sexless in her understanding; he could not, in conformity with the school of hypocritic idealism, regard Cecily as a child of woman's growth. No. She had the fruits of a modern education; she had a lucid brain; of late she had mingled and conversed with a variety of men and women, most of them anything but crassly conventional. It was this very aspect of her training that had caused him so much doubt. And he knew by this time what his doubt principally meant; in a measure, it came of native conscientiousness, of prejudice which testified to his origin; but, more than that, it signified simple jealousy. Secretly, he did not like her outlook upon the world to be so unrestrained; he would have preferred her to view life as a simpler matter. Partly for this reason did her letters so disturb him. No; it would have been an insult to imagine her with the moral sensibilities of a child of twelve.

Was she intellectual at the expense of her emotional being? Was she guarded by nature against these disturbances? Somewhat ridiculous to ask that, and then look up at her face effulgent with the joy of life. She who could not speak without the note of emotion, who so often gave way to lyrical outbursts of delight, who was so warm-hearted in her friendship, whose every movement was in glad harmony with the loveliness of her form,—must surely have the corresponding capabilities of passion.

After all—and it was fetching a great compass to reach a point so near at hand—might she not take him at his own profession? Might she not view him as a man indeed, and one not yet past his youth, but still as a man who suffered no trivialities to interfere with the grave objects of his genius? She had so long had him represented to her in that way—from the very first of their meetings, indeed. Grant her mature sense and a reflective mind, was that any reason why she should probe subtly the natural appearance of her friend, and attribute to him that which he gave no sign of harbouring? Why must she be mysteriously conscious of his inner being, rather than take him ingenuously for what he seemed? She had instruction and wit, but she was only a girl; her experience was as good as *nil*. Mallard repeated that to himself as he looked at Mrs. Baske. To a great extent Cecily did, in fact, inhabit an ideal world. She was ready to accept the noble as the natural. Untroubled herself, she could contemplate without scepticism the image of an artist finding his bliss in solitary toil. This was the ground of the respect she had for him; disturb this idea, and he became to her quite another man—one less interesting, and, it might be, less lovable in either sense of the word.

Spence maintained a conversation with Miriam, chiefly referring to the characteristics of the scene about them; he ignored her peculiarities, and talked as though everything must necessarily give her pleasure. Her face proved that at all events the physical influences of this day in the open air were beneficial. The soft breeze had brought a touch of health to her cheek, and languid inattention no longer marked her gaze at sea and shore; she was often absent, but never listless. When she spoke, her voice was subdued and grave; it always caused Mallard to glance in her direction.

At Baiæ they dismissed the boat, purposing to drive back to Naples. In their ramble among the ruins, Mallard did his best to be at ease and seem to share Cecily's happiness; in any case, it was better to talk of the Romans than of personal concerns. When in after-time he recalled this day, it seemed to him that he had himself been well contented; it dwelt in his memory with a sunny glow. He saw Cecily's unsurpassable grace as she walked beside him, and her look of winning candour turned to him so often, and he fancied that it had given him pleasure to be with her. And pleasure there was, no doubt, but inextricably blended with complex miseries. To Cecily his mood appeared more gracious than she had ever known it; he did not disdain to converse on topics which presupposed some knowledge on her part, and there was something of unusual gentleness in his tone which she liked.

"Some day," she said, "we shall talk of Baiæ in London, in a November fog."

"I hope not."

"But such contrasts help one to get the most out of life," she rejoined, laughing. "At all events, when some one happens to speak to me of Mr. Mallard's pictures, I shall win credit by casually mentioning that I was at Baiæ in his company in such-and-such a year."

"You mean, when I have painted my last?"

"No, no! It would be no pleasure to me to anticipate that time."

"But natural, in talking with a veteran."

It was against his better purpose that he let fall these words; they contained almost a hint of his hidden self, and he had not yet allowed anything of the kind to escape him. But the moment proved too strong.

"A veteran who fortunately gives no sign of turning grey," replied Cecily, glancing at his hair.

An interruption from Spence put an end to this dangerous dialogue. Mallard, inwardly growling at himself, resisted the temptation to further *tête-à-tête*, and in a short time the party went in search of a conveyance for their return. None offered that would hold four persons; the ordinary public carriages have convenient room for two only, and a separation was necessary. Mallard succeeded in catching Spence's eye, and made him understand with a savage look that he was to take Cecily with him. This arrangement was effected, and the first carriage drove off with those two, Cecily exchanging merry words with an old Italian who had rendered no kind of service, but came to beg his *mancia* on the strength of being able to utter a few sentences in English.

For the first time, Mallard was alone with Mrs. Baske. Miriam had not concealed surprise at the new adjustment of companionship; she looked curiously both at Cecily and at Mallard whilst it was going on. The first remark which the artist addressed to her, when they had been driving for a few minutes, was perhaps, she thought, an explanation of the proceeding.

"I shall meet your brother again at Pompeii to-morrow, Mrs. Baske."

"Have you seen much of him since he came?" Miriam asked constrainedly. She had not met Mallard since Reuben's arrival.

"Oh yes. We have dined together each evening."

Between two such unloquacious persons, dialogue was naturally slow at first, but they had a long drive before them. Miriam presently trusted herself to ask,—

" Has he spoken to you at all of his plans—of what he is going to do when he returns to England ? "

" In general terms only. He has literary projects."

" Do you put any faith in them, Mr. Mallard ? "

This was a sudden step towards intimacy. As she spoke, Miriam looked at him in a way that he felt to be appealing. He answered the look frankly.

"I think he has the power to do something worth doing. Whether his perseverance will carry him through it, is another question."

" He speaks to me of you in a way that—— He seems, I mean, to put a value on your friendship, and I think you may still influence him. I am very glad he has met you here."

" I have very little faith in the influence of one person on another, Mrs. Baske. For ill—yes, that is often seen ; but influence of the kind you suggest is the rarest of things."

" I'm afraid you are right."

She retreated into herself, and, when he looked at her, he saw cold reserve once more on her countenance. Doubtless she did not choose to let him know how deeply this question of his power concerned her. Mallard felt something like compassion ; yet not ordinary compassion either, for at the same time he had a desire to break down this reserve, and see still more of what she felt. Curious ; that evening when he dined at the villa, he had already become aware of this sort of attraction in her, an appeal to his sympathies together with the excitement of his combative spirit—if that expressed it.

" No man," he remarked, " ever did solid work except in his own strength. One can be encouraged in effort, but the effort must originate in one's self."

Miriam kept silence. He put a direct question.

" Have you yourself encouraged him to pursue this idea ? "

" I have not *dis*couraged him."

" In your brother's case, discouragement would probably be the result if direct encouragement were withheld."

Again she said nothing, and again Mallard felt a desire to subdue the pride, or whatever it might be, that had checked the growth of friendliness between them in its very beginning. He remained mute for a long time, until they were nearing Pozzuoli, but Miriam showed no disposition to be the first to speak. At length he said abruptly :

" Shall you go to the San Carlo during the winter ? "

" The San Carlo ? " she asked inquiringly.

" The opera."

Mallard was in a strange mood. Whenever he looked ahead at Cecily, he had a miserable longing which crushed his heart down, down ; in struggling against this, he felt that Mrs. Baske's proximity was an aid, but that it would be still more so if he could move her to any unusual self-revelation. He had impulses to offend her, to irritate her prejudices—anything, so she should but be moved. This question that fell from him was mild in comparison with some of the subjects that pressed on his harassed brain.

" I don't go to theatres," Miriam replied distantly.

" That is losing much pleasure."

" The word has very different meanings.'

She was roused. Mallard observed with a perverse satisfaction the scorn implied in this rejoinder. He noted that her features had more decided beauty than when placid.

" I imagine," he resumed, smiling at her, " that the life of an artist must seem to you frivolous, if not something worse. I mean an artist in the sense of a painter.

" I cannot think it the highest kind of life," Miriam replied, also smiling, but ominously.

" As Miss Doran does," added Mallard, his eyes happening
to cath Cecily's face as it looked backwards, and his tongue
speaking recklessly.

"There are very few subjects on which Miss Doran and I
think alike."

He durst not pursue this; in his state of mind, the
danger of committing some flagrant absurdity was too
great. The subject attracted him like an evil temptation,
for he desired to have Miriam speak of Cecily. But he
mastered himself.

" The artist's life may be the highest of which a particular man is capable. For instance, I think it is so in my
own case."

Miriam seemed about to keep silence again, but ultimately she spoke. The voice suggested that upon her too
there was a constraint of some kind.

" On what grounds do you believe that ? "

His eyes sought her face rapidly. Was she ironical at
his expense? That would be new light upon her mind, for
hitherto she had seemed to him painfully literal. Irony
meant intellect; mere scorn or pride might signify anything
but that. And he was hoping to find reserves of power in
her, such as would rescue her from the imputation of com-
monplaceness in her beliefs. Testing her with his eye, he
answered meaningly :

" Not, I admit, on the ground of recognized success."

Miriam made a nervous movement, and her brows
contracted. Without looking at him, she said, in a voice
which seemed rather to resent his interpretation than to be
earnest in deprecating it :

" You know, Mr. Mallard, that I meant nothing of the
kind."

" Yet I could have understood you, if you had. Naturally
you must wonder a little at a man's passing his life as I do.
You interpret life absolutely; it is your belief that it can
have only one meaning, the same for all, involving certain

duties of which there can be no question, and admitting certain relaxations which have endured the moral test. A man may not fritter away the years that are granted him ; and that is what I seem to you to be doing, at best."

" Why should you suppose that I take upon myself to judge you ? "

" Forgive me ; I think it is one result of your mental habits that you judge all who differ from you."

This time she clearly was resolved to make no reply. They were passing through Pozzuoli, and she appeared to forget the discussion in looking about her. Mallard watched her, but she showed no consciousness of his gaze.

" Even if the world recognized me as an artist of distinction," he resumed, " you would still regard me as doubtfully employed. Art does not seem to you an end of sufficient gravity. Probably you had rather there were no such thing, if it were practicable."

" There is surely a great responsibility on any one who makes it the *end* of life."

This was milder again, and just when he had anticipated the opposite.

" A responsibility to himself, yes. Well, when I say that I believe this course is the highest I can follow, I mean that I believe it employs all my best natural powers as no other would. As for highest in the absolute sense, that is a different matter. Possibly the life of a hospital nurse, of a sister of mercy—something of that kind—comes nearest to the ideal."

She glanced at him, evidently in the same kind of doubt about his meaning as he had recently felt about hers.

" Why should you speak contemptuously of such people ? "

" Contemptuously ? I speak sincerely. In a world where pain is the most obvious fact, the task of mercy must surely take precedence of most others."

" I am surprised to hear you say this."

It was spoken in the tone most characteristic of her, that of a proud condescension.

"Why, Mrs. Baske?"

She hesitated a little, but made answer:

"I don't mean that I think you unfeeling, but your interests seem to be so far from such simple things."

"True."

Again a long silence. The carriage was descending the road from Pozzuoli; it approached the sea-shore, where the gentle breakers were beginning to be tinged with evening light. Cecily looked back and waved her hand.

"When you say that art is an end in itself," Miriam resumed abruptly, "you claim, I suppose, that it is a way of serving mankind?"

Mallard was learning the significance of her tones. In this instance, he knew that the words "serving mankind" were a contemptuous use of a phrase she had heard, a phrase which represented the philosophy alien to her own.

"Indeed, I claim nothing of the kind," he replied, laughing. "Art may, or may not, serve such a purpose; but be assured that the artist never thinks of his work in that way."

"You make no claim, then, even of usefulness?"

"Most decidedly, none. You little imagine how distasteful the word is to me in such connection."

"Then how can you say you are employing your best natural powers?"

She had fallen to ingenuous surprise, and Mallard again laughed, partly at the simplicity of the question, partly because it pleased him to have brought her to such directness.

"Because," he answered, "this work gives me keener and more lasting pleasure than any other would. And I am not a man easily pleased with my own endeavours, Mrs. Baske. I work with little or no hope of ever satisfying myself—that is another thing. I have heard men speak of my kind of art as 'the noble pursuit of Truth,' and so on. I don't care for such phrases; they may mean something, but as a rule come of the very spirit so opposed to my own—that which feels it necessary to justify art by bombast. The one object I have in life is to paint a bit of the world just as I see it. I exhaust myself in vain toil; I shall never succeed; but I am right to persevere, I am right to go on pleasing myself."

Miriam listened in astonishment.

"With such views, Mr. Mallard, it is fortunate that you happen to find pleasure in painting pictures."

"Which, at all events, do people no harm."

She turned upon him suddenly.

"Do you encourage my brother in believing that his duty in life is to please himself?"

"It has been my effort," he replied gravely.

"I don't understand you," Miriam said, in indignation.

"No, you do not. I mean to say that I believe your brother is not really pleased with the kind of life he has too long been leading; that to please himself he must begin serious work of some kind."

"That is playing with words, and on a subject ill-chosen for it."

"Mrs. Baske, do you seriously believe that Reuben Elgar can be made a man of steady purpose by considerations that have primary reference to any one or anything but himself?"

She made no answer.

"I am not depreciating him. The same will apply (if you are content to face the truth) to many a man whom you would esteem. I am sorry that I have lost your confidence, but that is better than to keep it by repeating idle formulas that the world's experience has outgrown."

Miriam pondered, then said quietly:

"We have different thoughts, Mr. Mallard, and speak different languages."

"But we know a little more of each other than we did. For my part, I feel it a gain."

During the rest of the drive they scarcely spoke at all; the few sentences exchanged were mere remarks upon the scenery. Both carriages drew up at the gate of the villa, where Miriam and Mallard alighted. Spence, rising, called to the latter.

"Will you accompany Miss Doran the rest of the way?"

"Certainly."

Mallard took his seat in the other carriage; and, as it drove off, he looked back. Miriam was gazing after them.

Cecily was a little tired, and not much disposed to converse. Her companion being still less so, they reached the Mergellina without having broached any subject.

"It has been an unforgettable day," Cecily said, as they parted.

CHAPTER VI.

CAPTIVE TRAVELLERS.

HE had taken leave of the Spences and Mrs. Baske, yet was not sure that he should go. He had said good-bye to Mrs. Lessingham and to Cecily herself, yet made no haste to depart. It drew on to evening, and he sat idly in his room in Casa Rolandi, looking at his traps half packed. Then of a sudden up he started. "Imbecile! Insensate! I give you fifteen minutes to be on your way to the station. Miss the next train—and sink to the level of common men!" Shirts, socks—straps, locks; adieux, tips—horses, whips! Clatter through the Piazzetta Mondragone; down at breakneck speed to the Toledo; across the Piazza del Municipio; a good-bye to the public scriveners sitting at their little tables by the San Carlo; sharp round the corner, and along by the Porto Grande with its throng of vessels. All the time he sings a tune to himself, caught up in the streets of the tuneful city; an air lilting to the refrain—

> "Io ti voglio bene assaje
> E tu non pienz' a me!"

Just after nightfall he alighted from the train at Pompeii. Having stowed away certain impedimenta at the station, he took his travelling-bag in his hand, broke with small ceremony through porters and hotel-touts, came forth upon the high-road, and stepped forward like one to whom the locality is familiar. In a minute or two he was overtaken by a little lad, who looked up at him and said in an insinuating voice, "Albergo del Sole, signore?"

"Prendi, bambino," was Mallard's reply, as he handed the bag to him. "Avanti!"

A divine evening, softly warm, dim-glimmering. The dusty road ran on between white trunks of plane-trees; when the station and the houses near it were left behind, no other building came in view. To the left of the road, hidden behind its long earth-rampart, lay the dead city; far beyond rose the dark shape of Vesuvius, crested with beacon-glow, a small red fire, now angry, now murky, now for a time extinguished. The long rumble of the train died away, and there followed silence absolute, scarcely broken for a few minutes by a peasant singing in the distance, the wailing song so often heard in the south of Italy. Silence that was something more than the wonted soundlessness of night; the haunting oblivion of a time long past, a melancholy brooding voiceless upon the desolate home of forgotten generations.

A walk of ten minutes, and there shone light from windows. The lad ran forward and turned in at the gate of a garden; Mallard followed, and approached some persons who were standing at an open door. He speedily made arrangements for his night's lodging, saw his room, and went to the quarter of the inn where dinner was already in progress. This was a building to itself, at one side of the garden. Through the doorway he stepped immediately into a low-roofed hall, where a number of persons sat at table. Pillars supported the ceiling in the middle, and the walls were in several places painted with heads or landscapes, the work of artists who had made their abode here; one or two cases with glass doors showed relics of Pompeii.

Elgar was one of the company. When he became aware of Mallard's arrival, he stood up with a cry of "All hail!" and pointed to a seat near him.

"I began to be afraid you wouldn't come this evening. Try the risotto; it's excellent. Ye gods! what an appetite I had when I sat down! To-day have I ascended Vesuvius. How many bottles of wine I drank between starting and returning I cannot compute; I never knew before what it was to be athirst. Why, their vino di Vesuvio is for all the world like cider; I thought at first I was being swindled— not an impossible thing in these regions. I must tell you a story about a party of Americans I encountered at Bosco Reale."

The guests numbered seven or eight; with one exception besides Elgar, they were Germans, all artists of one kind or another, fellows of genial appearance, loud in vivacious talk. The exception was a young Englishman, somewhat oddly dressed, and with a great quantity of auburn hair that rolled forward upon his distinguished brow. At a certain *pension* on the Mergellina he was well known. He sat opposite Elgar, and had been in conversation with him.

Mallard cared little what he ate, and ate little of anything. Neither was he in the mood for talk; but Elgar, who had finished his solid meal, and now amused himself with grapes (in two forms), spared him the necessity of anything but an occasional monosyllable. The young man was elated, and grew more so as he proceeded with his dessert; his cheeks were deeply flushed; his eyes gleamed magnificently.

In the meantime Clifford Marsh had joined in conversation with the Germans; his use of their tongue was far from idiomatic, but by sheer determination to force a way through linguistic obstacles, he talked with a haphazard fluency which was amusing enough. No false modesty imposed a check upon his eloquence. It was to the general table that he addressed himself on the topic that had arisen; in an English dress his speech ran somewhat as follows :—

"Gentlemen, allow me to say that I have absolutely no faith in the future of which you speak! It is my opinion that democracy is the fatal enemy of art. How can you speak of ancient and mediæval states? Neither in Greece nor in Italy was there ever what we understand by a democracy."

"Factisch! Der Herr hat Recht!" cried some one, and several other voices strove to make themselves heard; but the orator raised his note and overbore interruption.

"You must excuse me, gentlemen, if I say that—however it may be from other points of view—from the standpoint of art, democracy is simply the triumph of ignorance and brutality." ("Gewisz!" — "Nimmermehr!" — "Vortrefflich!") "I don't care to draw distinctions between forms of the thing. Socialism, communism, collectivism, parliamentarism,—all these have one and the same end: to put men on an equality; and in proportion as that end is approached, so will art in every shape languish. Art, gentlemen, is nourished upon inequalities and injustices!" ("Ach!"—"Wie kann man so etwas sagen!"—"Hoch! verissime!") "I am not representing this as either good or bad. It may be well that justice should be established, even though art perish. I simply state a fact!" ("Doch!"— "Erlauben Sie!") "Supremacy of the vulgar interest means supremacy of ignoble judgment in all matters of mind. See what plutocracy already makes of art!"

Here one of the Germans insisted on a hearing; a fine fellow, with Samsonic locks and a ringing voice.

"Sir! sir! who talks of a genuine democracy with mankind in its present state? Before it comes about, the multitude will be instructed, exalted, emancipated, humanized!"

"Sir!" shouted Marsh, "who talks of the Millennium? I speak of things possible within a few hundred years. The multitude will *never* be humanized. Civilization is attainable only by the few; nature so ordains it."

"Pardon me for saying that is a lie! I use the word controversially."

"It is a manifest truth!" cried the other. "Who ever doubted it but a *Dummkopf?* I use the word with reference to this argnment only."

So it went on for a long time. Mallard and Elgar knew no German, so could derive neither pleasure nor profit from the high debate.

"Are you as glum here as in London?" Reuben asked of his companion, in a bantering voice. "I should have pictured you grandly jovial, wreathed perhaps with ruddy vine-leaves, the light of inspiration in your eye, and in your hand a mantling goblet! Drink, man, drink! you need a stimulant, an exhilarant, an anti-phlegmatic, a counter-irritant against English spleen. You are still on the other side of the Alps, of the Channel; the fogs yet cling about you. Clear your brow, O painter of Ossianic wildernesses! Taste the foam of life! We are in the land of Horace, and *nunc est bibendum!*—Seriously, do you *never* relax?"

"Oh yes. You should see me over the fifth tumbler of whiskey at Stornoway."

"Bah! you might as well say the fifth draught of fish-oil at the North Cape. How innocent this wine is! A gallon of it would give one no more than a pleasant glow, the faculty of genial speech. Take a glass with me to the health of your enchanting ward."

"Please to command your tongue," growled Mallard, with a look that was not to be mistaken.

"I beg your pardon. It shall be to the health of that superb girl we saw in the Mercato. But, as far as I can judge yet, the Neapolitan type doesn't appeal to me very strongly. It is finely animal, and of course that has its value; but I prefer the suggestion of a soul, don't you? I remember a model old Langton had in Rome, a girl fresh from the mountains; by Juno! a glorious creature! I dare say you have seen her portrait in his studio; he likes to show it. But it does her nothing like justice; she might have sat for the genius of the Republic. Utterly untaught, and intensely stupid; but there were marvellous things to be read in her face. Ah, but give me the girls of Venice! You know them, how they walk about the piazza; their tall, lithe forms, the counterpart of the gondolier; their splendid black hair, elaborately braided and pierced with large ornaments; their noble, aristocratic, grave features; their long shawls! What natural dignity! What eloquent eyes! I like to imagine them profoundly intellectual, which they are unhappily not."

Marsh had withdrawn from colloquy with the Germans, and kept glancing across the table at his compatriots, obviously wishing that he might join them. Mallard, upon whom Elgar's excited talk jarred more and more, noticed the stranger's looks, and at length leaned forward to speak to him.

"As usual, we are in a minority among the sun-worshippers."

"Sun-worshippers! Good!" laughed the other. "Yes, I have never met more than one or two chance Englishmen at the 'Sole.'"

"But you are at your ease with our friends there.—I think you know as little German as I do, Elgar?"

"Devilish bad at languages! To tell you the truth, I can't endure the sense of inferiority one has in beginning to smatter with foreigners. I read four or five, but avoid speaking as much as possible."

Marsh took an early opportunity of alluding to the argument in which he had recently taken part. The subject was resumed. At Elgar's bidding the waiter had brought cigars, and things looked comfortable; the Germans talked with more animation than ever.

"One of the worst evils of democracy in England," said Reuben, forcibly, "is its alliance with Puritan morality."

"Oh, that is being quickly outgrown," cried Marsh. "Look at the spread of rationalism."

"You take it for granted that Puritanism doesn't survive religious dogma? Believe me, you are greatly mistaken. I am sorry to say I have a large experience in this question. The mass of the English people have no genuine religious belief, but none the less they are Puritans in morality. The same applies to the vastly greater part of those who even repudiate Christianity."

"One must take account of the national hypocrisy," remarked the younger man, with an air of superiority, shaking his head as his habit was.

"It's a complicated matter. The representative English bourgeois is a hypocrite in essence, but is perfectly serious in his judgment of the man next door; and the latter characteristic has more weight than the former in determining his life. Puritanism has aided the material progress of England; but its effect on art! But for it, we should have a school of painters corresponding in greatness to the Elizabethan dramatists. Depend upon it, the democracy will continue to be Puritan. Every picture, every book, will be tried by the same imbecile test. Enforcement of Puritan morality will be one of the ways in which the mob, come to power, will revenge itself on those who still remain its superiors."

Marsh was not altogether pleased at finding his facile eloquence outdone. In comparing himself with Elgar, he was conscious of but weakly representing the tendencies which were a passionate force in this man with the singularly fine head, with such a glow of wild life about him. He abandoned the abstract argument, and struck a personal note.

"However it may be in the future, I grant you the artist has at present no scope save in one direction. For my own part, I have fallen back on landscape. Let those who will, paint Miss Wilhelmina in the nursery, with an interesting doll of her own size; or a member of Parliament rising to deliver a great speech on the liquor traffic; or Mrs. What-do-you-call-her, lecturing on woman's rights. These are the subjects our time affords."

Mallard eyed with fresh curiosity the gentleman who had "fallen back on landscape."

"What did you formerly aim at?" he inquired, with a sort of suave gruffness.

"Things which were hopelessly out of the question. I worked for a long time at a 'Death of Messalina.' That was in Rome. I had a splendid inspiration for Messalina's face. But my hand was paralyzed when I thought of the idiotic comments such a picture would occasion in England. One fellow would say I had searched through history in a prurient spirit for something sensational; another, that I read a moral lesson of terrible significance; and so on."

"A grand subject, decidedly!" exclaimed Elgar, with genuine enthusiasm, which restored Marsh to his own good opinion. "Go on with it! Bid the fools be hanged! Have you your studies here?"

"Unfortunately not. They are in Rome."

Mallard delivered himself of a blunt opinion.

"That is no subject for a picture. Use it for literature, if you like."

The inevitable discussion began, the discussion so familiar nowadays, and which would have sounded so odd to the English painters who were wont to call themselves "historical." Where is the line between subjects for the easel and subjects for the desk? What distinguishes the art of the illustrator from the art of the artist?

That was a great evening round the table at the Albergo del Sole. How gloriously the air thickened with tobacco-smoke! What removal of empty bottles and replacing them with full! The Germans were making it a set *Kneipe;* the Englishmen, unable to drink quite so heroically, were scarce behind in vehemence of debate. Mallard, grimly accepting the help of wine against his inner foes, at length earned Elgar's approval; he had relaxed indeed, and was no longer under the oppression of English fog. But with him such moods were of brief duration; he suddenly quitted the table, and went out into the night air.

The late moon was rising, amber-coloured on a sky of dusky azure. He walked from the garden, across the road, and towards the ruins of the Amphitheatre, which lie some distance apart from the Pompeian streets that have been unearthed; he passed beneath an arch, and stood looking down into the dark hollow so often thronged with citizens of Latin speech. Small wonder that Benvenuto's necromancer could evoke his myriads of flitting ghosts in the midnight Colosseum; here too it needed but to stand for a few minutes in the dead stillness, and the air grew alive with mysterious presences, murmurous with awful whisperings. Mallard enjoyed it for awhile, but at length turned away abruptly, feeling as if a cold hand had touched him.

As he re-entered the inn-precincts, he heard voices still uproarious in the dining-room; but he had no intention of going among them again. His bedroom was one of a row which opened immediately upon the garden. He locked himself in, went to bed, but did not sleep for a long time. A wind was rising, and a branch of a tree constantly tapped against the pane. It might have been some centuries-dead inhabitant of Pompeii trying to deliver a message from the silent world.

The breakfast-party next morning lacked vivacity. Clifford

Marsh was mute and dolorous of aspect; no doubt his personal embarrassments were occupying him. Yesterday's wine had become his foe, instead of an ally urging him to dare all in the cause of "art." He consumed his coffee and roll in the manner of ordinary mortals, not once flourishing his dainty hand or shaking his ambrosial hair. Elgar was very stiff from his ascent of Vesuvius, and he too found that "the foam of life" had an unpleasant after-taste, suggestive of wrecked fortunes and a dubious future. Mallard was only a little gruffer than his wonted self.

"I am going on at once to Sorrento," he said, meeting Elgar afterwards in the garden. "To-morrow I shall cross over the hills to Positano and Amalfi. Suppose you come with me?"

The other hesitated.

"You mean you are going to walk?"

"No. I have traps to carry on from the station. We should have a carriage to Sorrento, and to-morrow a donkey for the baggage."

They paced about, hands in pockets. It was a keen morning; the tramontana blew blusterously, causing the smoke of Vesuvius to lie all down its long slope, a dense white cloud, or a vast turbid torrent, breaking at the foot into foam and spray. The clearness of the air was marvellous. Distance seemed to have no power to dim the details of the landscape. The Apennines glistened with new-fallen snow.

"I hadn't thought of going any further just now," said Elgar, who seemed to have a difficulty in simply declining the invitation, as he wished to do.

"What should you do, then?"

"Spend another day here, I think,—I've only had a few hours among the ruins, you know,—and then go back to Naples."

"What to do there?" asked Mallard, bluntly.

"Give a little more time to the museum, and see more of the surroundings."

"Better come on with me. I shall be glad of your company."

It was said with decision, but scarcely with heartiness. Elgar looked about him vaguely.

"To tell you the truth," he said at last, "I don't care to incur much expense."

"The expenses of what I propose are trivial."

"My traps are at Naples, and I have kept the room there. No, I don't see my way to it, Mallard."

"All right."

The artist turned away. He walked about the road for ten minutes.—Very well; then he too would return to Naples. Why? What was altered? Even if Elgar accompanied him to Amalfi, it would only be for a few days; there was no preventing the fellow's eventual return—his visits to the villa, perhaps to Mrs. Gluck's. Again imbecile and insensate! What did it all matter?

He stopped short. He would sit down and write a letter to Mrs. Baske.—A pretty complication, that! What grounds for such a letter as he meditated?

The devil! Had he not a stronger will than Reuben Elgar? If he wished to carry a point with such a weakling, was he going to let himself be thwarted? Grant it was help only for a few days, no matter; Elgar should go with him.

He walked back to the garden. Good; there the fellow loitered, obviously irresolute.

"Elgar, you'd better come, after all," he said, with a grim smile. "I want to have some talk with you. Let us pay our shot, and walk on to the station."

"What kind of talk, Mallard?"

"Various. Get whatever you have to carry; I'll see to the bill."

"But how can I go on without a shirt?"

"I have shirts in abundance. A truce to your obstacles. March!"

And before very long they were side by side in the vehicle,

speeding along the level road towards Castellammare and the mountains. This exertion of native energy had been beneficial to Mallard's temper; he talked almost genially. Elgar, too, had subdued his restiveness, and began to look forward with pleasure to the expedition.

"I only wish this wind would fall!" he exclaimed. "It's cold, and I hate a wind of any kind."

"Hate a wind? You're effeminate; you're a boulevardier. It would do you good to be pitched in a gale about the coast of Skye. A fellow of your temperament has no business in these relaxing latitudes. You want tonics."

"Too true, old man. I know myself at least as well as you know me."

"Then what a contemptible creature you must be! If a man knows his weakness, he is inexcusable for not overcoming it."

"A preposterous contradiction, allow me to say. A man is what he is, and will be ever the same. Have you no tincture of philosophy? You talk as though one could govern fate."

"And you, very much like the braying jackass in the field there."

Mallard had a savage satisfaction in breaking all bounds of civility. He overwhelmed his companion with abuse, revelled in insulting comparisons. Elgar laughed, and stretched himself on the cushions so as to avoid the wind as much as possible.

They clattered through the streets of Castellammare, pursued by urchins, crying, "Un sordo, signori!" Thence on by the seaside road to Vico Equense, Elgar every now and then shouting his ecstasy at the view. The hills on this side of the promontory climb, for the most part, softly and slowly upwards, everywhere thickly clad with olives and orange-trees, fig-trees and aloes. Beyond Vico comes a jutting headland; the road curves round it, clinging close on the hillside, turns inland, and all at once looks down upon the Piano di Sorrento. Instinctively, the companions rose to their feet, as though any other attitude on the first revelation of such a prospect were irreverent. It is not really a plain, but a gently rising wide and deep lap, surrounded by lofty mountains and ending at a line of sheer cliffs along the sea-front. A vast garden planted for Nature's joy; a pleasance of the gods; a haunt of the spirit of beauty set between sun-smitten crags and the enchanted shore.

"Heaven be praised that you forced me to come!" muttered Elgar, in his choking throat.

Mallard could say nothing. He had looked upon this scene before, but it affected him none the less.

They drove into the town of Tasso, and to an inn which stood upon the edge of a profound gorge, cloven towards the sea-cliffs. Sauntering in the yard whilst dinner was made ready, they read an inscription on a homely fountain:

> " Sordibus abstersis, instructo marmore, priscus
> Fons nitet, et manat gratior unda tibi."

"Eternal gratitude to our old schoolmasters," cried Elgar, "who thrashed us through the Eton Latin grammar! What is Italy to the man who cannot share our feelings as we murmur that distich? I marvel that I was allowed to learn this heathen tongue. Had my parents known what it would mean to me, I should never have chanted my *hic, hæc, hoc.*"

He was at his best this afternoon; Mallard could scarcely identify him with the reckless, and sometimes vulgar, spendthrift who had been rushing his way to ruin in London. His talk abounded in quotation, in literary allusion, in high-spirited jest, in poetical feeling. When had he read so much? What a memory he had! In a world that consisted of but one sex, what a fine fellow he would have been!

"What do you think of my sister?" he asked, *à propos* of nothing, as they idled about the Capo di Sorrento and on the road to Massa,

"An absurd question."

"You mean that I cannot suppose you would tell me the truth."

"And just as little the untruth. I do not know your sister."

"We had a horrible scene that day I turned up. I behaved brutally to her, poor girl."

"I'm afraid you have often done so."

"Often. I rave at her superstition; how can she help it? But she's a good girl, and has wit enough if she might use it. Oh, if some generous, large-brained man would drag her out of that slough of despond!—What a marriage that was! Powers of darkness, what a marriage!"

Mallard was led to no question.

"I shall never understand it, never," went on Elgar, in excitement. "If you had seen that oily beast! I don't know what criterion girls have. Several of my acquaintance have made marriages that set my hair on end. Lives thrown away in accursed ignorance—that's my belief."

Mallard waited for the next words, expecting that they would torture him. There was a long pause, however, and what he awaited did not come.

"Do you hate the name Miriam, as I do?"

"Hate it, no."

"I wonder they didn't call her Keziah, and me Mephibosheth. It isn't a nice thing to detest the memory of one's parents, Mallard. It doesn't help to make one a well-balanced man. How on earth did I get my individuality? And you mustn't think that Miriam is just what she seems —I mean, there *are* possibilities in her; I am convinced of it."

"Did it ever occur to you that your own proceedings may have acted as a check upon those possibilities?"

"I don't know that I ever thought of it," said Elgar, ingenuously.

"You never reflected that her notion of the liberated man is yourself?"

"You are right, Mallard. I see it. What other example had she ? "

They walked as far as Massa Lubrense, a little town on the steep shore ; over against it the giant cliffs of Capri, every cleft and scar and jutting rock discernible through the pellucid air, every minutest ruggedness casting its clear-cut shadow. But the surpassing glory was the prospect at the Cape of Sorrento when they reached it on their walk back. Before them the entire sweep of the gulf, from Ischia to Capri ; Naples in its utmost extent, an unbroken line of delicate pink, from Posillipo to Torre Annunziata. Far below their feet the little *marina* of Sorrento, with its row of boats drawn up on the strand ; behind them noble limestone heights. The sea was foaming under the tramontana, and its foam took colour from the declining sun.

Next morning they set forth again as Mallard had proposed, their baggage packed on a donkey, a guide with them to lead the way over the mountains to the other shore. A long climb, and at the culminating point of the ridge they rested to look the last on Naples ; thenceforward their faces were set to the far blue hills of Calabria.

"Yonder lies Pæstum," said Mallard, pointing to the dim plain beyond the Gulf of Salerno ; and his companion's eyes were agleam.

Early in the afternoon they reached the coast at Positano, and thence took boat for Amalfi. Elgar was like one possessed at his first sight of the wonderful old town, nested in its mountain gorge, overlooked by wild crags ; this relic saved from the waste of mediæval glory. When they had put up at an inn less frequented and much cheaper than the " Cappuccini," he would not rest until he had used the last hour of sunlight in clambering about the little maze of streets, or rather of mountain paths and burrows beneath houses piled one upon another indistinguishably. Forced back by hunger, he still lingered upon the window-balcony, looking up at the hoary riven tower set high above the town on what seems an inaccessible peak, or at the cathedral and its many-coloured campanile.

How could Mallard help comparing these manifestations of ardent temper with what he had witnessed in Cecily? The resemblance was at moments more than he could endure; once or twice he astonished Elgar with a reply of unprovoked savageness. The emotions of the day, even more than its bodily exercise, had so wearied him that he went early to bed. They had a double-bedded room, and Elgar continued talking for hours. Even without this, Mallard felt that he would have been unable to sleep. To add to his torments, the clock of the cathedral, which was just on the opposite side of the street, had the terrible southern habit of striking the whole hour after the chime at each quarter; by midnight the clangour was all but incessant. Elgar sank at length into oblivion, but to his companion sleep came not. Very early in the morning there sounded the loud blast of a horn, all through the town and away into remoteness. Signify what it might, the practical result seemed to be a rousing of the population to their daily life; lively voices, the tramp of feet, the clatter of vehicles began at once, and waxed with the spread of daylight.

The sun rose, but only to gleam for an hour on clouds and vapours which it had not power to disperse. The mountain summits were hidden, and down their sides crept ominously the ragged edges of mist; a thin rain began to fall, and grew heavier as the sky dulled. Having breakfasted, the two friends spent an hour in the cathedral, which was dark and chill and gloomy. Two or three old people knelt in prayer, their heads bowed against column or wall; remarking the strangers, they came up to them and begged.

"My spirits are disagreeably on the ebb," said Elgar. "If it's to be a Scotch day, let us do some mountaineering."

They struck up the gorge, intending to pursue the little river, but were soon lost among ascents and descents, narrow stairs, precipitous gardens, and noisy paper-mills. Probably no unassisted stranger ever made his way out of Amalfi on to the mountain slopes. They had scorned to take a guide, but did so at length in self-defence, so pestered were they by all but every person they passed; man, woman, and child beset them for soldi, either frankly begging or offering a direction and then extending their hands. The paper-mills were not romantic; the old women who came along bending under huge bales of rags were anything but picturesque. And it rained, it rained.

Wet and weary, they had no choice but to return to the inn. Elgar's animation had given place to fretfulness; Mallard, after his miserable night, cared little to converse, and would gladly have been alone. A midday meal, with liberal supply of wine, helped them somewhat, and they sat down to smoke in their bedroom. It rained harder than ever; from the window they could see the old tower on the crag smitten with white scud.

"Come now," said Mallard, forcing himself to take a livelier tone, "tell me about those projects of yours. Are you serious in your idea of writing?"

"Perfectly serious."

"And what are you going to write?"

"That I haven't quite determined. I am revolving things. I have ideas without number."

"Too many for use, then. You need to live in some such place as this for a few weeks, and clear your thoughts. 'Company, villanous company,' is the first thing to be avoided."

"No doubt you are right."

But it was half-heartedly said, and with a restless glance towards the window. Mallard, in whose heart a sick weariness conflicted with his will and his desire, went on in a dogged way.

"I want to work here for a time." Work! The syllable was like lead upon his tongue, and the thought a desolation in his mind. "Write to your sister; get her to send your belongings from Casa Rolandi, together with a ream of scribbling-paper. I shall be out of doors most of the day, and no one will disturb you here. Use the opportunity like a man. Fall to. I have a strong suspicion that it is now or never with you."

"I doubt whether I could do anything here."

"Perhaps not on a day like this; but it is happily exceptional. Remember yesterday. Were I a penman, the view from this window in sunlight would make the ink flow nobly."

Elgar was mute for a few minutes.

"I believe I need a big town. Scenes like this dispose me to idle enjoyment. I have thought of settling in Paris for the next six months."

Mallard made a movement of irritation.

"Then why did you come here at all? You say you have no money to waste."

"Oh, it isn't quite so bad with me as all that," replied Elgar, as if he slightly resented this interference with his private affairs.

Yet he had yesterday, in the flow of his good-humour, all but confessed that it was high time he looked out for an income. Mallard examined him askance. The other, aware of this scrutiny, put on a smile, and said with an air of self-conquest:

"But you are right; I have every reason to trust your advice. I'll tell you what, Mallard. To-morrow I'll drive to Salerno, take the train to Naples, pack my traps, and relieve Miriam's mind by an assurance that I'm going to work in your company; then at once come back here."

" I don't see the need of going to Naples. Write a letter. Here's paper; here's pen and ink."

Elgar was again mute. His companion, in an access of intolerable suffering, cried out vehemently:

"Can't you see into yourself far enough to know that you are paltering with necessity? Are you such a feeble creature that you must be at the mercy of every childish whim, and ruin yourself for lack of courage to do what you know you ought to do? If instability of nature had made such work of me as it has of you, I'd cut my throat just to prove that I could at least once make my hand obey my will!"

"It would be but the final proof of weakness," replied Elgar, laughing. "Or, to be more serious, what would it prove either one way or the other? If you cut your throat, it was your destiny to do so; just as it was to commit the follies that led you there. What is all this nonsense about weak men and strong men? I act as I am bound to act; I refrain as I am bound to refrain. You know it well enough."

This repeated expression of fatalism was genuine enough. It manifested a habit of his thought. One of the characteristics of our time is that it produces men who are determinists by instinct; who, anything but profound students or subtle reasoners, catch at the floating phrases of philosophy and recognize them as the index of their being, adopt them thenceforth as clarifiers of their vague self-consciousness. In certain moods Elgar could not change from one seat to another without its being brought to his mind that he had moved by necessity.

"What if that be true?" said Mallard, with unexpected coldness. "In practice we live as though our will were free. Otherwise, why discuss anything?"

"True. This very discussion is a part of the scheme of things, the necessary antecedent of something or other in your life and mine. I shall go to Naples to-morrow; I shall spend one day there; on the day after I shall be with you again. My hand upon it, Mallard. I promise!"

He did so with energy. And for the moment Mallard was the truer fatalist.

Again they left the inn, this time going seaward. Still in rain, they walked towards Minori, along the road which is cut in the mountain-side, high above the beach. They talked about the massive strongholds which stand as monuments of the time when the coast-towns were in fear of pirates. Melancholy brooded upon land and sea; the hills of Calabria, yesterday so blue and clear, had vanished like a sunny hope.

The morrow revealed them again. But again for Mallard there had passed a night of much misery. On rising, he durst not speak, so bitter was he made by Elgar's singing and whistling. Yet he would not have cared to prevent the journey to Naples, had it been in his power. He was sick of Elgar's company; he wished for solitude. When his eyes fell on the materials of his art, he turned away in disgust.

"You'll get to work as soon as I'm gone," cried Reuben, cheerfully.

"Yes."

He said it to avoid conversation.

"Cheer up, old man! I shall not disappoint you this time. You have my promise."

"Yes."

A two-horse carriage was at the door. Mallard looked at it from the balcony, and was direly tempted. No fear of his yielding, however, It was not *his* fate to scamper whither desire pointed him.

"I have already begun to work out an idea," said Elgar, as he breakfasted merrily. "I woke in the night, and it came to me as I heard the bell striking. My mind is always active when I am travelling ; ten to one I shall come back ready to begin to write. I fear there's no decent ink purchasable in Amalfi; I mustn't forget that. By-the-bye, is there anything I can bring you ? "

"Nothing, thanks."

They went down together, shook hands, and away drove the carriage. At the public fountain in the little piazza, where stands the image of Sant' Andrea, a group of women were busy or idling, washing clothes and vegetables and fish, drawing water in vessels of beautiful shape, chattering incessantly—such a group as may have gathered there any morning for hundreds of years. Children darted after the vehicle with their perpetual cry of "Un sord', signor!" and Elgar royally threw to them a handful of coppers, looking back to laugh as they scrambled.

A morning of mornings, deliciously fresh after the rain, the air exquisitely fragrant. On the mountain-tops ever so slight a mist still clinging, moment by moment fading against the blue.

"Yes, I shall be able to work here," said Elgar within himself. "December, January, February; I can be ready with something for the spring."

CHAPTER VII.

THE MARTYR.

CLIFFORD MARSH left Pompeii on the same day as his two chance acquaintances; he returned to his quarters on the Mergellina, much perturbed in mind, beset with many doubts, with divers temptations. "Shall I the spigot wield?" Must the ambitions of his glowing youth come to naught, and he descend to rank among the Philistines? For, to give him credit for a certain amount of good sense, he never gravely contemplated facing the world in the sole strength of his genius. He knew one or two who had done so; before his mind's eye was a certain little garret in Chelsea, where an acquaintance of his, a man of real and various powers, was year after year taxing his brain and heart in a bitter struggle with penury; and these glimpses of Bohemia were far from inspiring Clifford with zeal for naturalization. Elated with wine and companionship, he liked to pose as one who was sacrificing "prospects" to artistic conscientiousness; but, even though he had "fallen back" on landscape, he was very widely awake to the fact that his impressionist studies would not supply him with bread, to say nothing of butter—and Clifford must needs have both.

That step-father of his was a well-to-do manufacturer of shoddy in Leeds, one Hibbert, a good-natured man on the whole, but of limited horizon. He had married a widow above his own social standing, and for a long time was content to supply her idolized son with the means of pursuing artistic studies in London and abroad. But Mr. Hibbert had a strong opinion that this money should by now have begun to make some show of productiveness. Domestic grounds of dissatisfaction ripened his resolve to be firm with young Mr. Marsh. Mrs. Hibbert was extravagant; doubtless her son was playing the fool in the same direction. After all, one could pay too much for the privilege of being snubbed by one's superior wife and step-son. If Clifford were willing to "buckle to " at sober business (it was now too late for him to learn a profession), well and good; he should have an opening at which many a young fellow would jump. Otherwise, let the fastidious gentleman pay his own tailor's bills.

Clifford's difficulties were complicated by his relations with Madeline Denyer. It was a year since he had met Madeline at Naples, had promptly fallen in love with her face and her advanced opinions, and had won her affection in return. Clifford was then firm in the belief that, if he actually married, Mr. Hibbert would not have the heart to stop his allowance; Mrs. Denyer had reasons for thinking otherwise, and her daughter saw the case in the same light. It must be added that he presumed the Denyers to be better off than they really were; in fact, he was to a great extent misled. His dignity, if the worst came about, would not have shrunk from moderate assistance at the hands of his parents-in-law. Madeline knew well enough that nothing of this kind was possible, and in the end made her lover's mind clear on the point. Since then the course of these young people's affections had been anything but smooth. However, the fact remained that there *was* mutual affection—which, to be sure, made the matter worse.

Distinctly so since the estrangement which had followed Marsh's arrival at the boarding-house. He did not take Madeline's advice to seek another abode, and for two or three days Madeline knew not whether to be glad or offended at his remaining. For two or three days only; then she began to have a pronounced opinion on the subject. It was monstrous that he should stay under this roof and sit at this table, after what had happened. He had no delicacy; he was behaving as no gentleman could. It was high time that her mother spoke to him.

Mrs. Denyer solemnly invited the young man to a private interview.

"Mr. Marsh," she began, with pained dignity, whilst Clifford stood before her twiddling his watch-chain, "I really think the time has come for me to ask an explanation of what is going on. My daughter distresses me by saying that all is at an end between you. If that is really the case, why do you continue to live here, when you must know how disagreeable it is to Madeline?"

"Mrs. Denyer," replied Clifford, in a friendly tone. "there has been a misunderstanding between us, but I am very far from reconciling myself to the thought that everything is at an end. My remaining surely proves that."

"I should have thought so. But in that case I am obliged to ask you another question. What can you mean by paying undisguised attentions to another young lady who is living here?"

"You astonish me. What foundation is there for such a charge?"

"At least you won't affect ignorance as to the person of whom I speak. I assure you that I am not the only one who has noticed this."

"You misinterpret my behaviour altogether. Of course, you are speaking of Miss Doran. If your observation had been accurate, you would have noticed that Miss Doran gives me no opportunity of paying her attentions, if I wished. Certainly I have had conversations with Mrs. Lessingham, but I see no reason why I should deny myself that pleasure."

"This is sophistry. You walked about the museum with *both* these ladies for a long time yesterday."

Clifford was startled, and could not conceal it.

"Of course," he exclaimed, "if my movements are watched, with a view to my accusation—— !"

And he broke off significantly.

"Your movements are not watched. But if I happen to hear of such things, I must draw my own conclusions."

"I give you my assurance that the meeting was purely by chance, and that our conversation was solely of indifferent matters—of art, of Pompeii, and so on."

"Perhaps you are not aware," resumed Mrs. Denyer, with a smile that made caustic comment on this apology, "that, when we sit at table, your eyes are directed to Miss Doran with a frequency that no one can help observing."

Marsh hesitated; then, throwing his head back, remarked in an unapproachable manner:

"Mrs. Denyer, you will not forget that I am an artist."

"I don't forget that you profess to be one, Mr. Marsh."

This was retort with a vengeance. Clifford reddened slightly, and looked angry. Mrs. Denyer had reached the point to which her remarks were from the first directed, and it was not her intention to spare the young man's suscepti- bilities. She had long ago gauged him, and not inaccurately on the whole; it seemed to her that he was of the men who can be " managed."

"I fail to understand you," said Marsh, with dignity.

"My dear Clifford, let me speak to you as one who has your well-being much at heart. I have no wish to hurt your feelings, but I have been upset by this silly affair, and it makes me speak a little sharply. Now, I see well enough what you have been about; it is an old device of young gentlemen who wish to revenge themselves just a little for what they think a slight. Of course you have never given a thought to Miss Doran, who, as you say, would never dream of carrying on a flirtation, for she knows how things are between you and Madeline, and she is a young lady of very proper behaviour. In no case, as you of course understand, could she be so indelicate as anything of this kind would imply. No; but you are vexed with Madeline about some silly little difference, and you play with her feelings. There has been enough of it; I must interfere. And now let us talk a little about your position. Madeline has, of course, told me everything. Listen to me, my dear Clifford; you must at once accept Mr. Hibbert's kindly meant proposal—you must indeed."

Marsh had reflected anxiously during this speech. He let a moment of silence pass; then said gravely:

"I cannot consent to do anything of the kind, Mrs. Denyer."

"Oh yes, you can and will, Clifford. Silly boy, don't you see that in this way you secure yourself the future just suited to your talents? As an artist you will never make your way; that is certain. As a man with a substantial business at your back, you can indulge your artistic tastes quite sufficiently, and will make yourself the centre of an admiring circle. We cannot all be stars of the first magnitude. Be content to shine in a provincial sphere, at all events for a time. Madeline as your wife will help you substantially. You will have good society, and better the richer you become. You are made to be a rich man and to enjoy life. Now let us settle this affair with your step-father."

Still Clifford reflected, and again with the result that he appeared to have no thought of being persuaded to such concessions. The debate went on for a long time, ultimately with no little vigour on both sides. Its only immediate result was that Marsh left the house for a few days, retiring to meditate at Pompeii.

In the mean time there was no apparent diminution in Madeline's friendliness towards Cecily Doran. It was not to be supposed that Madeline thought tenderly of the other's beauty, or with warm admiration of her endowments; but she would not let Clifford Marsh imagine that it mattered to her in the least if he at once transferred his devotion to Miss Doran. Her tone in conversing with Cecily became a little more patronizing,—though she spoke no more of impressionism,—in proportion as she discovered the younger girl's openness of mind and her lack of self-assertiveness.

"You play the piano, I think?" she said one day.

"For my own amusement only."

"And you draw?"

"With the same reserve."

"Ah," said Madeline, "I have long since given up these things. Don't you think it is a pity to make a pastime of an art? I soon saw that I was never likely really to *do* any-thing in music or drawing, and out of respect for them I ceased to—to potter. Please don't think I apply that word to you."

"Oh, but it is very applicable," replied Cecily, with a laugh. "I think you are quite right; I often enough have the same feeling. But I am full of inconsistencies—as you are finding out, I know."

Mrs. Lessingham displayed good nature in her intercourse with the Denyers. She smiled in private, and of course breathed to Cecily a word of warning; but the family entertained her, and Madeline she came really to like. With Mrs. Denyer she compared notes on the Italy of other days.

"A sad, sad change !" Mrs. Denyer was wont to sigh. "All the poetry gone ! Think of Rome before 1870, and what it is now becoming. One never looked for intellect in Italy—living intellect, of course, I mean—but natural poetry one did expect and find. It is heart-breaking, this progress ! If it were not for my dear girls, I shouldn't be here ; they adore Italy—of course, never having known it as it was. And I am sure you must feel, as I do, Mrs. Lessingham, the miserable results of cheapened travel. Oh, the people one sees at railway-stations, even meets in hotels, I am sorry to say, sometimes ! In a few years, I do believe, Genoa and Venice will strongly remind one of Margate."

No echo of the cry of "Wolf !" ever sounded in Mrs. Denyer's conversation when she spoke of her husband. That Odysseus of commerce was always referred to as being concerned in enterprises of mysterious importance and magnitude ; she would hint that he had political missions, naturally not to be spoken of in plain terms. Mrs. Lessingham often wondered with a smile what the truth really was ; she saw no reason for making conjectures of a disagreeable kind, but it was pretty clear to her that selfishness, idleness, and vanity were at the root of Mrs. Denyer's character, and in a measure explained the position of the family.

During the last few days, Barbara had exhibited a revival of interest in the " place in Lincolnshire." Her experiments proved that it needed but a moderate ingenuity to make Mr. Musselwhite's favourite topic practically inexhaustible. The "place" itself having been sufficiently described, it was natural to inquire what other " places " were its neighbours, what were the characteristics of the nearest town, how long it took to drive from the " place " to the town, from the " place " to such another "place," and so on. Mr. Musselwhite was undisguisedly grateful for every remark or question that kept him talking at his ease. It was always his dread lest a subject should be broached on which he could say nothing whatever—there were so many such! —and as often as Barbara broke a silence without realizing his fear, he glanced at her with the gentlest and most amiable smile. Never more than glanced; yet this did not seem to be the result of shyness; rather it indicated a lack of mental activity, of speculation, of interest in her as a human being.

One morning he lingered at the luncheon-table when nearly all the others had withdrawn, playing with crumbs, and doubtless shrinking from the *ennui* that lay before him until dinner-time. Near him, Mrs. Denyer, Barbara, and Zillah were standing in conversation about some photographs that had this morning come by post.

" This one isn't at all like you, my dear," said Mrs. Denyer, with emphasis, to her eldest girl. " The other is passable, but I wouldn't have any of these."

" Well, of course I am no judge," replied Barbara, " but I can't agree with you. I much prefer this one."

Mr. Musselwhite was slowly rising.

" Let us take some one else's opinion," said the mother. " I wonder what Mr. Musselwhite would say ? "

The mention of his name caused him to turn his head, half absently, with an inquiring smile. Barbara withdrew a step, but Mrs. Denyer, in the most natural way possible, requested Mr. Musselwhite's judgment on the portraits under discussion.

He took the two in his hands, and, after inspecting them, looked round to make comparison with the original. Barbara met his gaze placidly, with gracefully poised head, her hands joined behind her. It was such a long time before the arbiter found anything to remark, that the situation became a little embarrassing; Zillah laughed girlishly, and her sister's eyes fell.

" Really, it's very hard to decide," said Mr. Musselwhite

at length, with grave conscientiousness. "I think they're both remarkably good. I really think I should have some of both."

"Barbara thinks that this makes her look too childish," said Mrs. Denyer, using her daughter's name with a pleasant familiarity.

Again Mr. Musselwhite made close comparison. It was, in fact, the first time that he had seen the girl's features; hitherto they had been, like everything else not embalmed in his memory, a mere vague perception, a detail of the phantasmic world through which he struggled against his *ennui*.

"Childish? Oh dear, no!" he remarked, almost vivaciously. "It is charming; they are both charming. Really, I'd have some of both, Miss Denyer."

"Then we certainly will," was Mrs. Denyer's conclusion; and with a gracious inclination of the head, she left the room, followed by her daughters. Mr. Musselwhite looked round for another glance at Barbara, but of course he was just too late.

Poor Madeline, in the meantime, was being sorely tried. Whilst Clifford Marsh was away at Pompeii, daily "scenes" took place between her and her mother. Mrs. Denyer would have had her make conciliatory movements, whereas Madeline, who had not exchanged a word with Clifford since the parting in wrath, was determined not to be the first to show signs of yielding. And she held her ground, tearless, resentful, strong in a sense of her own importance.

When he again took his place at Mrs. Gluck's table, Clifford had the air of a man who has resigned himself to the lack of sympathy and appreciation—nay, who defies everything external, and in the strength of his genius goes serenely onwards. Never had he displayed such self-consciousness; not for an instant did he forget to regulate the play of his features. Mrs. Denyer he had greeted distantly; her daughters, more distantly still. He did not look more than once or twice in Miss Doran's direction, for Mrs. Denyer's reproof had made him conscious of an excess in artistic homage. His neighbour being Mr. Bradshaw, he conversed with him agreeably, smiling seldom. He seemed neither depressed nor uneasy; his countenance wore a grave and noble melancholy, now and then illumined with an indescribable ardour.

The Bradshaws had begun to talk of leaving Naples, but this seemed to be the apology for enjoying themselves which is so characteristic of English people. Even Mrs. Bradshaw found her life from day to day very pleasant, and in consequence never saw her friends at the villa without expressing much uneasiness about affairs at home, and blaming her husband for making so long a stay. Both of them were now honoured with the special attention of Mr. Marsh. Clifford was never so much in his element as when conversing of art and kindred matters with persons who avowed their deficiencies in that sphere of knowledge, yet were willing to learn; relieved from the fear of criticism, he expanded, he glowed, he dogmatized. With Mrs. Lessingham he could not be entirely at his ease; her eye was occasionally disturbing to a pretender who did not lack discernment. But in walking about the museum with Mr. Bradshaw, he was the most brilliant of ciceroni. Jacob was not wholly credulous, for he had spoken of the young man with Mrs. Lessingham, but he found such companionship entertaining enough from time to time, and Clifford's knowledge of Italian was occasionally a help to him.

A day or two of moderate intimacy with any person whatsoever always led Clifford to a revelation of his private circumstances; it was not long before Mr. Bradshaw was informed not only of Mr. Hibbert's harshness, but of the painful treatment to which Clifford was being subjected at the hands of Mrs. Denyer and Madeline. The latter point was handled with a good deal of tact, for Clifford had it in view that through Mr. Bradshaw his words would one way or other reach Mrs. Lessingham, and so perchance come to Miss Doran's ears. He made no unworthy charges; he spoke not in anger, but in sorrow; he was misunderstood, he was depreciated, by those who should have devoted themselves to supporting his courage under adversity. And as he talked, he became the embodiment of calm magnanimity; the rhetoric which was meant to impress his listener had an exalting effect upon himself—as usual.

"You mean to hold out, then?" asked the bluff Jacob, with a smile which all but became a chuckle.

"I am an artist," was the noble reply. "I cannot abandon my life's work."

"But how about bread and cheese? They are necessary to an artist, as much as to other men, I'm afraid."

Clifford smiled calmly.

"I shall not be the first who has starved in such a cause."

Jacob roared as he related this conversation to his wife.

"I must keep an eye on the lad," he said. "When I hear he's given in, I'll write him a letter of congratulation."

CHAPTER VIII.

PROOF AGAINST ILLUSION.

AN interesting conversation took place one morning between Mrs. Spence and Mrs. Lessingham with regard to Cecily. They were alone together at the villa; Cecily and Miriam had gone for a drive with the Bradshaws. After speaking of Reuben Elgar, Mrs. Lessingham passed rather abruptly to what seemed a disconnected subject.

"I don't think it's time yet for Cecily to give up her set studies. I should like to find some one to read with her regularly again before long—say Latin and history; there would be no harm in a little mathematics. But there's a difficulty in finding the suitable person." She smiled. "I'm afraid only a lady will answer the purpose."

"Better, no doubt," assented Eleanor, also with a smile.

"And ladies who would be any good to Cecily are not at one's disposition every day. What an admirable mind she has! I never knew any one acquire with so little effort. Of course, she has long ago left me behind in everything. The only use I can be to her is to help her in gaining knowledge of the world—not to be learnt entirely out of books, we know."

"What is your system with her?"

"You see that I have one," said Mrs. Lessingham, gratified, and rustling her plumage a little as a lady does when she is about to speak in confidence of something that pleases her. "Of course, I very soon understood that the ordinary *surveillance* and restrictions and moral theories were of little use in her case. (I may speak with you quite freely, I am sure.) I'm afraid the results would have been very sad if Cecily had grown up in Lancashire."

"I doubt whether she would have grown up at all."

"Indeed, it seemed doubtful. If her strength had not utterly failed, she must have suffered dreadfully in mind. I studied her carefully during the first two years; then I was able to pursue my method with a good deal of confidence. It has been my aim to give free play to all her faculties; to direct her intelligence, but never to check its growth—as is commonly done. We know what is meant by a girl's education, as a rule; it is not so much the imparting of knowledge as the careful fostering of special ignorances. I think I put it rightly?"

"I think so."

"It is usual to say that a girl must know nothing of this and that and the other thing—these things being, in fact, the most important for her to understand. I won't say that every girl can safely be left so free as I have left Cecily; but when one has to deal with exceptional intelligence, why not yield it the exceptional advantages? Then again, I had to bear in mind that Cecily has strong emotions. This seemed to me only another reason for releasing her mind from the misconceptions it is usual to encourage. I have done my best to help her to see things as they *are*, not as moral teachers would like them to be, and as parents make-believe to their girls that they are indeed."

Mrs. Lessingham ended on a suave note of triumph, and smiled very graciously as Eleanor looked approval.

"The average parent says," she pursued, "that his or her daughter must be kept pure-minded, and therefore must grow up in a fool's paradise. I have no less liking for purity, but I understand it in rather a different sense; certain examples of the common purity that I have met with didn't entirely recommend themselves to me. Then again, the average parent says that the daughter's lot in life is marriage, and that after marriage is time enough for her to throw away the patent rose-coloured spectacles. I, on the other hand, should be very sorry indeed to think that Cecily has no lot in life besides marriage; to me she seemed a human being to be instructed and developed, not a pretty girl to be made ready for the market. The rose coloured spectacles had no part whatever in my system. I have known some who threw them aside at marriage, in the ordinary way, with the result that they thenceforth looked on everything very obliquely indeed. I'm sorry to say that it was my own fate to wear those spectacles, and I know only too well how hard a struggle it cost me to recover healthy eyesight."

"Mine fell off and got broken long before I was married," said Eleanor, "and my parents didn't think it worth while to buy new ones."

"Wise parents! No, I have steadily resisted the theory

that a girl must know nothing, think nothing, but what is likely to meet the approval of the average husband—that is to say, the foolish, and worse than foolish, husband. I see no such difference between girl and boy as demands a difference in moral training; we know what comes of the prevalent contrary views. And in Cecily's case, I believe I have vindicated my theory. She respects herself; she knows all that lack of self-respect involves. She has been fed on wholesome victuals, not on adulterated milk. She is not haunted with that vulgar shame which passes for maiden modesty. Do you find fault with her, as a girl?"

"I should have to ponder long for an objection."

"And what is the practical result? In whatever society she is, I am quite easy in mind about her. Cecily will never do anything foolish. It's only the rose-coloured spectacles that cause stumbling. And I mean by 'stumbling' all the silliness to which girls are subject. Ah! if I could live *my* girlhood over again, and with some sensible woman to guide me! If I could have been put on my guard against idiotic illusions, as Cecily is!"

"We mustn't expect too much of education," Eleanor ventured to remark. "There is no way of putting experience into a young girl's head. It would say little for her qualities if a girl could not make a generous mistake."

"Such mistakes are not worthy of being called generous, as a rule. They are too imbecile. That state of illusion is too contemptible. There is very little danger of Cecily's seeing any one in a grossly false light."

Eleanor did not at once assent.

"You seem to doubt that?" added the other, with a searching look.

"I think she is as well guarded as a girl can be; but, as I said before, education is no substitute for experience. Don't think me captious, however. I sympathize entirely with the course you have taken. If I had a daughter, I should like her to be brought up on the same principles."

"Cecily is very mature for her age," continued Mrs. Lessingham, with evident pleasure in stating and restating her grounds of confidence. "She feels strongly, but never apart from judgment. Now and then she astonishes me with her discernment of character; clearness of thought seems almost to anticipate in her the experience on which you lay such stress. Have you noticed her with Mr. Mallard? How differently many girls would behave! But Cecily understands him so well; she knows he thinks of her as a child, and nothing could be more simply natural than her friendship for him. I suppose Mr. Mallard is one of the artists who never marry?"

"I don't know him well enough to decide that," answered Eleanor, with a curious smile.

It was in the evening of this day, when the Spences and Miriam were sitting together after dinner, that a servant announced a visit of Reuben Elgar, adding that he was in his sister's room. Miriam went to join him.

"You can spare me a minute or two?" he asked cheerily, as she entered.

"Certainly. You are just back from Pompeii?"

"From Castellamare—from Sorrento the indescribable —from Amalfi the unimaginable—from Salerno! Leave Naples without seeing those places, and hold yourself for ever the most wretched of mortals! Old Mallard forced me to go with him, and I am in his debt to eternity!"

This exalted manner of speech was little to Miriam's taste, especially from her brother. Sobriety was what she desired in him. It seemed a small advantage that his extravagance should exhibit itself in this way rather than in worse; the danger was still there.

"Sit down, and talk more quietly. You say Mr. Mallard *forced* you to go?"

"I was coming back to Naples from Pompeii. By-the-bye, I went up Vesuvius, and descended shoeless. The guides ought to have metal boots on hire. I was coming

back, but Mallard clutched me by the coat-collar. Even
now I've come sorely against his will. I left him at Amalfi.
I'm going to settle my affairs here to-morrow, and join him
again. He's persuaded me to try and work at Amalfi."

"How long do you think of staying there?"

"It all depends. Perhaps I shan't be able to do anything,
after all."

"But surely that depends on yourself."

"Not a bit! If I were a carpenter or bricklayer, one
might say so—in a sense. But such work as I am going to
do is a question of mood, influences, caprices——"

Miriam reflected.

"Mr. Mallard was unwilling to let you return here?"

"Naturally. He knows my uncertainty. But I have promised him; I shall keep my word."

"He is working himself?"

"Will be by now; we had a horrible day of rain at Amalfi.
He seems rather glummer than usual, but that won't hinder
his work. I wish I had the old fellow's energy. After all,
though, one can force one's self to use pencils and brushes;
it's a different thing when all has to come from the brain.
If you haven't a quiet mind——"

"What disturbs you?" Miriam asked, watching him.

"Oh, there's always something. I wish you could give
me a share of your equanimity. Never mind, I shall try.
By-the-bye, I ought to have a word with Mrs. Lessingham
and Cecily before I go. Are they likely to be here to-
morrow?"

"I can't say."

"Then I shall call at their place. When will they be at
home?"

"Do you think you ought to do that?" Miriam asked,
without looking at him.

"Why on earth not?"

His brow darkened, and he seemed about to utter something not unlike his vehemencies on the day of arrival.

"You must judge for yourself, of course," said Miriam. "We won't talk about it."

Reuben nodded agreement carelessly. Then he began to talk of his proposed work, and presently they went to join the Spences. For an hour or more, Reuben held forth rapturously on what he had seen these last few days. He could not rest seated, but paced up and down the room, gesticulating, fervidly eloquent.

"Do play me something, will you, Mrs. Spence?" he asked at length. (His cousinship with Eleanor had never been affirmed by intimate association, and he had not the habit of addressing her by the personal name.) "Just for ten minutes; then I'll be off and trouble you no more. Something to invigorate! A rugged piece!"

Eleanor made a choice from Beethoven, and, whilst she played, Elgar leant forward on the back of a chair. Then he bade them good-bye, his pulse at fever-time.

Half-past ten next morning found him walking hither and thither on the Mergellina, frequently consulting his watch. He decided at length to approach the house in which his acquaintances dwelt. Passing through the *portone*, whom should he encounter but Clifford Marsh, known to him only from the casual meeting at Pompeii, not by name. They stopped to speak. Elgar inquired if the other lived at Mrs. Gluck's.

"For the present."

"I have friends here," Reuben added. "You know Mrs. Lessingham?"

"Oh yes," replied Clifford, eyeing his collocutor. "If you are calling to see those ladies," he continued, "they went out half an hour ago. I saw them drive away."

Elgar muttered his annoyance. Though he disliked doing so, he asked Marsh whether he knew when the ladies were likely to return. Clifford declared his ignorance. The two looked at each other, smiled, said good morning, and turned different ways.

Reuben walked about the sea-front for a couple of hours. "Who is that confounded fellow?" he kept asking in his mind, adding the highly ludicrous question, "What business has he to know them?" His impatience waxed; now and then he strode at such a pace that perspiration covered him. The most trivial discomposure had often much the same effect on him; if he happened to have a difficulty in finding his way, for instance, he would fume himself into exasperated heat.

"What business have they to live in a vulgar boarding-house? It's abominable bad taste and indiscretion in that woman. In fact, I don't like Mrs. Lessingham.—And what the devil has it to do with me?"

He strode up to the villa. Possibly they were there; yet he didn't like to call—for various reasons. He fretted about the roads, this way and that, till hunger oppressed him. Having eaten at the first restaurant he came to, he directed his steps towards the Mergellina again. At two o'clock he reached the house and made inquiry. The ladies had not yet returned.

He struck off towards the Chiaia, again paced backwards and forwards, cursed at carriage-drivers who plagued him, tried to amuse himself on the Santa Lucia. And pray what was all this fuss about? When he rose this morning, he had half a mind to start at once for Amalfi, and not see Mrs. Lessingham and her niece at all; he "didn't know that he cared much." He had met Cecily Doran twice. The second time was on the Strada Nuova di Posillipo, where he encountered a carriage in which Cecily and her aunt were taking the air; he talked with them for three minutes. It was the undeniable fact that he had broken away from "old Mallard" merely to see Cecily again. He had never tried to blind himself to it; that kind of thing was not in his way. None the less was it a truth that he thought himself capable of saying good-bye to the wonderful girl, and posting off to his literary work. Why expose himself to temptation?

Because he chose to; because it was pleasant; surely an excellent reason.

If only he hadn't come up against that confounded artist-fellow! That had upset him, most absurdly. A half good-looking sort of fellow: a fellow who could prate with a certain *brio;* not unlikely to make something of a figure in the eyes of a girl like Cecily. And what then?

Before now, Elgar had confessed to a friend that he couldn't read the marriage-column in a newspaper without feeling a distinct jealousy of all the male creatures there mentioned.

He sought out a *caffè*, and sat there for an hour, drinking a liquor that called itself lacryma-Christi, but would at once have been detected for a pretender by a learned palate. He drank it for the first time, and tried to enjoy it, but his mind kept straying to alien things. When it was nearly four o'clock, he again went forth, took a carriage, and bade the man drive quickly.

This time he was successful. A servant conducted him by many stairs and passages to Mrs. Lessingham's sitting-room. He entered, and found himself alone with Cecily.

"Mrs. Lessingham will certainly be back very soon," she said, in shaking hands with him. "They told me you had called before, and I thought you would like better to wait a few minutes than to be disappointed again."

"I think of going to Amalfi to-morrow morning, perhaps for a long time," remarked the visitor. "I wished to say good-bye."

The accumulated impatience and nervousness of the whole morning disturbed his pulses and put a weight upon his tongue; he spoke with awkward indecision, held himself awkwardly. His own voice sounded boorish to him after Cecily's accents.

Cecily began to speak of how she had spent the day. Her aunt was making purchases—was later in returning than had been expected. Then she asked for an account of Elgar's doings since they last met. The conversation grew easier; Reuben began to recover his natural voice, and to lose disagreeable self-consciousness in the delight of hearing Cecily and meeting her look. Had he known her better, he would have observed that she spoke with unusual diffidence, that she was not quite so self-possessed as of wont, and that her manner was deficient in the frank gaiety which as a rule made its great charm. Her tone softened itself in questioning; she listened so attentively that, when he had ceased speaking, her eyes always rose to his, as if she had expected something further.

"Who is the young artist that lives here?" Elgar inquired. "I met him at Pompeii, and to-day came upon him here in the courtyard. A slight, rather boyish fellow."

"I think you mean Mr. Marsh," replied Cecily, smiling. "He has recently been at Pompeii, I know."

"You are on friendly terms with him?"

"Not on *un*friendly," she answered, with amusement.

Elgar averted his face. Instantly the flow of his blood was again turbid; he felt an inclination to fling out some ill-mannered remark.

"You must come in contact with all kinds of odd people in a place like this."

"One or two are certainly odd," was the reply, in a gentle tone; "but most of them are very pleasant to be with occasionally. Naturally we see more of the Bradshaws than of any one else. There's a family named Denyer—a lady with three daughters; I don't think you would dislike them. Mr. Marsh is their intimate friend."

It was all but as though she pleaded against a mistaken judgment which troubled her. To Mallard she had spoken of her fellow-boarders in quite a different way, with merry though kindly criticism, or in the strain of generous idealization which so often marked her language.

"Do you know anything of his work?" Elgar pursued.

"I have seen a few of his water-colour drawings."

" He showed you them ? "

"No; one of the Miss Denyers did. He had given them
to her "

"Oh!" He at once brightened. "And how did they
strike you ? "

" I'm sorry to say they didn't interest me much. But I
have no right to sit in judgment."

Elgar had the good taste to say nothing more on the
subject. He let his eyes rest on her down-turned face for a
moment.

"You see a good deal of Miriam, I'm glad to hear."

"I am sometimes afraid I trouble her by going too
often."

"Have no such fear. I wish you were living under the
same roof with her. No one's society could do her so much
good as yours. The poor girl has too long been in need of
such an aid to rational cheerfulness."

They were interrupted by the entrance of an English maid-
servant, who asked whether Miss Doran would have tea
brought at once, or wait till Mrs. Lessingham's return.

" You see how English we are," said Cecily to her visitor.
" I think we'll have it now; Mrs. Lessingham may be here
any moment."

It was growing dusk. Whilst the conversation was
diverted by trifles, two lighted lamps were brought into the
room. Elgar had risen and gone to the window.

" We won't shut out the evening sky," said Cecily, standing not far from him.

The door closed upon the servant who had carried in the
tea-tray. Elgar turned to his companion, and said in a
musing tone, with a smile :

" How long is it since we saw each other every day in
Manchester ? "

" Seven years since that short time you spent with us."

" Seven ; yes. You were not twelve then ; I was not quite
twenty-one. As regards change, a lifetime might have passed

since, with both of us. Yet I don't feel very old, not oppressively ancient."

"And I'm sure I don't."

They laughed together.

"You are younger than you were then," he continued, in
his most characteristic voice, the voice which was musical
and alluring, and suggestive of his nature's passionate
depths and heights. "You have grown into health of body
and soul, and out of all the evil things that would have
robbed you of natural happiness. Nothing ever made me
more glad than first seeing you at the villa. I didn't know
what you had become, and in looking at you I rejoiced on
your account. You would gladden even miserable old age,
like sunlight on a morning of spring."

Cecily moved towards the tea-table in silence. She began
to fill one of the cups, but put the teapot down again and
waited for a moment. Having resumed her purpose, she
looked round and saw Elgar seated sideways on a chair by
the window. With the cup of tea in her hand, she approached him and offered it without speaking. He rose
quickly to take it, and went to another part of the
room.

"I hope Miriam will stay here the whole winter," Cecily
said, as she seated herself by the table.

"I hope so," he assented absently, putting his tea aside.
"How long are you and Mrs. Lessingham likely to stay ?"

"At least till February, I think."

"Shall you get as far as Amalfi some day ?"

"Oh yes ! And Miriam will come with us, I hope. And
to Capri too."

"I must see Capri. I shouldn't wonder if I go there
soon ; probably it would suit my purpose better than Amalfi.
Yet I must be alone, if I am to work. I haven't Mallard's
detachment. That seems to you a paltry confession of
weakness."

"No, indeed. I am told that Mr. Mallard is quite

exceptional in his power of disregarding everything but his work."

"Exceptional in many things, no doubt. I must seem very insignificant in comparison."

"Why should you? Mr. Mallard is so much older; he has long been fixed in his course."

"Older, yes," assented Elgar, with satisfaction. "Perhaps at his age I too may have done something worth doing."

"Who could doubt it?"

"It does me good to hear you say that!"

He moved from his distant place, and threw himself in one of his usual careless attitudes on a nearer chair. "But Miriam has no faith in me, not a jot! Does she speak harshly of me to you?"

"No."

Cecily shook her head, and seemed unable to speak more than the monosyllable.

"But she has nothing encouraging to say? She shows that she looks upon me as one of whom no good can come? That is the impression you have received from her?"

Cecily looked at him gravely.

"She has scarcely spoken of you at all—scarcely more than the few words that were inevitable."

"In itself a condemnation."

Cecily was mute. Before Elgar could say anything more, the door opened. With a sudden radiance on her features, the girl looked up to greet Mrs. Lessingham's entrance.

"How long you have been, aunt!"

"Yes; I am sorry. How do you do, Mr. Elgar? Tea, Cecily, lest I perish!"

From the doorway her quick glance had scrutinized both the young people. Of course she betrayed no surprise; neither did she make exhibition of pleasure. Her greeting of the visitor was gracefully casual, given in passing. She sank upon a low chair as if overcome with weariness. Mrs.

Lessingham had nothing to learn in the arts wherewith social intercourse is kept smooth in spite of nature's improprieties. When she chose, she could be the awe-inspiring chaperon, no less completely than she was at other times the contemner of the commonplace.

"So you leave us to-morrow, Mr. Elgar? I have just met Mr. Spence, and heard the news from him. I am glad you could find a moment to call. You are going to be very busy, I hear, for the rest of the winter."

"I hope so," Elgar replied, walking across the room to fetch his half-emptied teacup.

"We shall look eagerly for the results of your work."

For ten minutes the conversation kept a rather flat course. Cecily only spoke when addressed by her aunt; then quite in her usual way. Elgar took the first opportunity to signal departure. When Cecily gave him her hand, it was with a moment's unfaltering look—a look very different from that which charmed everyday acquaintances at their coming and going, unlike anything man or woman had yet seen on her countenance. The faintest smile hovered about her lips as she said, "Good-bye;" her steadfast eyes added the hope which there was no need to speak.

When he was gone, Mrs. Lessingham sipped her tea in silence. Cecily moved about and presently brought a book to her chair by the tea-table.

"No doubt you had the advantage of hearing Mr. Elgar's projects detailed," said her aunt, with irony which presumed a complete understanding between them.

"No." Cecily shook her head and smiled.

"Curious how closely he and Mr. Marsh resemble each other at times."

"Do you think so?"

"Haven't you noticed it? There are differences, of course. Mr. Elgar is originally much better endowed; though at present I should think he is even less to be depended upon, either intellectually or morally. But they belong to the same species. What numbers of such young men I have met!"

"What are the characteristics of the species, aunt?" Cecily inquired, with a pleasant laugh.

"I dare say you know them almost as well as I do. You might write an essay on 'The Young Man of Promise' of our day. I should be rather too severe; you would treat them with a lighter hand, and therefore more effectually."

In speaking, she kept her eyes on the girl, who appeared to muse the subject with sportful malice.

"I am not sure," said Cecily, "that Mr. Elgar would come into the essay."

"You mean that his promise is too obviously delusive?"

"Not exactly that. I rather think he should have an essay to himself."

"Of what tendency?" asked Mrs. Lessingham, still closely observant.

"Oh, it would need much meditation; but I think I could make it interesting."

With another laugh, she dismissed the subject; nor did her aunt endeavour to revive it.

The morrow was Sunday. Elgar knew at what time his train left for Salerno; the time-table was the same as for other days. Yet he lay in bed till nearly noon, till the train had long since started. No, he should not go to-day.

It irked him to rise at all. He had not slept; his head was hot, and his hands shook nervously. Dressed, he sat down for a minute, and remained seated half an hour, gazing at the wall. When at length he left the house, he walked without seeing anything, stumbling against things and people.

Of course, he knew last night that there was no journey for him to-day. Promise? A promise is void when its fulfilment has become impossible. Very likely Mallard had a conviction that he would not come back at the appointed

time. To-morrow, perhaps ; and perhaps not even to-morrow.
It had got beyond his control.

He ate, and returned to his room. Just now his need was
physical repose, undisturbed indulgence of reverie. And
the reverie of a man in his condition is a singular process.
It consists of a small number of memories, forecasts,
imaginings, repeated over and over again, till one would
think the brain must weary itself beyond endurance. It
can go on for many hours consecutively, and not only remain
a sufficient and pleasurable employment, but render every
other business repulsive, all but impossible.

At evening there came a change. He was now unable to
keep still; he went into the town, and exhausted himself
with walking up and down the hilly streets. Society would
have helped him, but he could find none. He would not
go to the villa; still less could he visit the boarding-house.

What a night! At times he moved about his room like
one in frantic pain, finally flinging himself upon the bed and
lying there till the impulse of his fevered mind broke the
beginnings of sleep. Or he walked the length of the floor,
with measured step, fifty times, counting each time he turned
—a sort of conscious insanity. Or he took his pocket-knife,
and drove the point into the flesh of his arm, satisfied when
the pang became intolerable. Then again a loss of all control in mere frenzy, the desire to shout, to yell. . . .

Elgar was out of the house at sunrise. He went down to
the Chiaia, loitered this way and that, always in the end
facing towards Posillipo. He drank his coffee, but ate
nothing; then again walked along the sea-front. Between
nine and ten he turned into the upward road, and went with
purpose towards Villa Sannazaro.

CHAPTER IX.

IN THE DEAD CITY.

THOUGH it was Sunday, Cecily resolved to go and spend the afternoon with Miriam. She was restless, and could not take pleasure in Mrs. Lessingham's conversation. Possibly her arrival at the villa would be anything but welcome; but she must see Miriam.

She drove up by herself, and first of all saw the Spences. From them she learnt that Miriam, as usual on Sunday, was keeping her own room.

" Do you think I may venture, Mrs. Spence ? "

" Go and announce yourself, my dear. If you are bidden avaunt, come back and cheer us old people with your brightness."

So Cecily went with light step along the corridor, and with light fingers tapped at Miriam's room. The familiar voice bade her enter. Miriam was sitting near the window, on her lap a closed book.

" May I—— ? "

" Of course you may," was the quiet answer.

Cecily closed the door, came forward, and bent to kiss her friend. Then she glanced at the ".St. Cecilia;" then examined herself for a moment in one of the mirrors; then took off her hat, mantle, and gloves.

" I want to stay as long as your patience will suffer me."

" Do so."

" You avoid saying how long that is likely to be."

" How can I tell ? "

" Oh, you have experience of me. You know how trying you find me in certain moods. To-day I am in a very strange mood indeed; very malicious, very wicked. And it is Sunday."

Miriam did not seem to resent this. She looked away at the window, but smiled. Could Cecily have been aware how her face had changed when the door opened, she would not have doubted whether she was truly welcome.

"What book is that, Miriam?"

Cecily had been half afraid to ask; to her surprise it proved to be Dante.

"Do you read this on Sunday?"

Miriam deigned no reply. The other, sitting just in front of her, took up the volume and rustled its leaves.

"How far have you got? This pencil mark? 'Amor ch'a null' amato amar perdona.'"

She read the line in an undertone, slowly towards the close. Miriam's face showed a sudden and curious emotion. Glancing at the book, she said abruptly:

"No; that's an old mark—a difficulty I had. I'm long past that."

"So am I. 'Amor ch'a null'——'"

Miriam stretched out her hand and took the volume with impatience.

"I'm at the end of this canto," she said, pointing. "Never mind it now. I should have thought you would have gone somewhere such a fine afternoon."

"That sounds remarkably like a hint that patience is near its end."

"I didn't mean it for that."

"Then let us get a carriage and drive somewhere together, we two alone."

Miriam shook her head.

"Because it is Sunday?" asked Cecily, with a mischievous smile, leaning her head aside.

"There is an understanding between us, Cecily. Don't break it."

"But I told you my mood was wicked. I feel disposed to break any and every undertaking. I should like to fret and torment and offend you. I should like to ask you why *I* am allowed to enjoy the sunshine, and you not? *Oggi è festa!* What a dreadful sound that must have in your ears Miriam!"

"But they don't apply it to Sunday," returned the other, who seemed to resign herself to this teasing.

"Indeed they do!" With a sudden change of subject, Cecily added, "Your brother came to see us yesterday, to say good-bye."

"Did he?"

"It doesn't interest you. You care nothing where he goes, or what he does—nothing whatever, Miriam. He told me so; but I knew it already."

"He told you so?" Miriam asked, with cold surprise.

"Yes. You are unkind; you are unnatural."

"And you, Cecily, are childish. I never knew you so childish as to-day."

"I warned you. He and I had a long talk before aunt came home."

"I'm sorry he should have thought it necessary to talk about himself."

"What more natural, when he is beginning a new portion of life? Never mind; we won't speak of it. May I play you a new piece I have learnt?"

"Do you mean, of sacred music?"

"Sacred? Why, all music is sacred. There are tunes and jinglings that I shouldn't call so; but neither do I call them music, just as I distinguish between bad or foolish verse, and poetry. Everything worthy of being called art is sacred. I shall keep telling you that till in self-defence you are forced to think about it. And now I shall play the piece whether you like it or not."

She opened the piano. What she had in mind was one of the "Moments Musicaux" of Schubert—a strain of exquisite melody, which ceased too soon. Cecily sat for a few moments at the key-board after she had finished, her head bent; then she came and stood before Miriam.

"Do you like it?"

There was no answer. She looked steadily at the troubled ₋ace, and, as it still kept averted from her, she laid her arms softly, half playfully, about Miriam's neck.

"Why must there always be such a distance between us, Miriam dear? Even when I seem so near to you as this, what a deep black gulf really separates us!"

"You were once on my side of it," said Miriam, her voice softened. "How did you pass to the other?"

"How could I tell you? No one read me lectures, or taught me hard arguments. The change came insensibly, like passing out of a dream into the light of morning. I followed where my nature led, and my thoughts about everything altered. I don't know how it might have been if I had lived on with you. But my happiness was not there."

"Happiness!" murmured the other, scornfully.

"A word you don't, won't understand. Yet to me it means much. Who knows? Perhaps there may come a day when I shall look back upon it, and see it as empty of satisfaction as it now seems to you. But more likely that I shall live to look back in sorrow for its loss."

The dialogue became such as they had held more than once of late, fruitless it seemed, only saddening to both. And Cecily was to-day saddened by it beyond her wont; her excessive gaiety yielded to a dejection which passed indeed, but for a while made her very unlike herself, silent, with troubled eyes.

"I had one valid excuse for coming to see you to-day," she said, when gaiety and dejection had both gone by. "Mr. and Mrs. Bradshaw seriously think of going to Rome at the end of next week, and they wish to have another day at Pompeii. They would like it so much if you would go with them. If you do, I also will; we shall make four for a carriage, and drive there, and come back by train."

"What day?"

"To-morrow, if it be fine. Let me take them your assent."

Miriam agreed.

On Monday morning, as arranged, she was driving down to the Mergellina, when, with astonishment, she saw her brother standing by the roadside, beckoning to her. The carriage stopped, and he came up to speak.

"Where are you off to?" he asked.

"You are still here?"

"I haven't been well. Didn't feel able to go yesterday. I was just coming to see you."

"Not well, Reuben? Why didn't you come before?"

"I couldn't. I want to speak to you. Where are you going?"

She told him the plan for the day. Elgar turned aside, and meditated.

"I'll see you there—at Pompeii somewhere. It'll be on my way."

"I had rather not go at all. I'll ask them to excuse me; Mrs. Lessingham will perhaps take my place, and——"

"No! I'll see you at Pompeii. I shall have no difficulty in finding you."

Miriam looked at him anxiously.

"I don't wish you to meet us there, Reuben."

"And I *do* wish! Let me have my way, Miriam. Say nothing about me, and let the meeting seem by chance."

"I can't do that. You make yourself ridiculous, after——"

"Let me judge for myself. Go on, or you'll be late."

She half rose, as if about to descend from the carriage. Elgar laid his hand on her arm, and clutched it so strongly that she sank back and regarded him with a look of anger.

"Miriam! Do as I wish, dear. Be kind to me for this once. If you refuse, it will make no difference. Have some feeling for me. This one day, Miriam."

Again she looked at him, and reflected. On account of the driver, though of course he could not understand them, they had subdued their voices, and Reuben's sudden action had not been noticeable.

"This one piece of sisterly kindness," he pleaded.

"It shall be as you wish," Miriam replied, her face cast down.

"Thank you, a thousand times. Avanti, cocchiere!"

Scrutiny less keen than Miriam's could perceive that Cecily had not her usual pleasure in to-day's expedition. Even Mrs. Bradshaw, sitting over against her in the carriage, noticed that the girl's countenance lacked its natural animation, wore now and then a tired look; the lids hung a little heavily over the beautiful eyes, and the cheeks were a thought pale. When she forgot herself in conversation, Cecily was the same as ever; mirthful, brightly laughing, fervent in expressing delight; but her thoughts too often made her silent, and then one saw that she was not heart and soul in the present. It was another Cecily than on that day at Baiæ. "She has been over-exciting herself since she came here," was Mrs. Bradshaw's mental remark. Miriam, anxiously observant, made a different interpretation, and was harassed with a painful conflict of thoughts.

Jacob Bush Bradshaw had no eyes for these trivialities. He sat in the squared posture of a hearty Englishman, amusing himself with everything they passed on the road, self-congratulant on the knowledge and experience he had been storing, joking as often as he spoke.

"The lad Marsh would have uncommonly liked an invitation to come with us to-day," he said, about midway in the drive. "What precious mischief we could have made by asking him, Hannah!"

"There's no room for him, fortunately."

"Oh yes; up on the box."

His eye twinkled as he looked at Cecily. She questioned him.

"Where would be the mischief, Mr. Bradshaw?"

"He talks nonsense, my dear," interposed Mrs. Bradshaw. "Pay no attention to him."

Miriam had heard now and then of Clifford Marsh. She met Jacob's smile, and involuntarily checked it by her gravity.

"We might have asked the Denyers as well," said Cecily, "and have had another carriage, or gone by train."

Mr. Bradshaw chuckled for some minutes at this proposal, but his wife would not allow him to pursue the jest.

They lunched at the Hôtel Diomède before entering the precincts of the ruins. Mr. Bradshaw had invariably a splendid appetite, and was by this time skilled in ordering the meals that suited him. The few phrases of Italian which he had appropriated were given forth *ore rotundo*, with Anglo-saxon emphasis on the *o*'s, and accompanied with large gestures. His mere appearance always sufficed to put landlords and waiters into their most urbane mood; they never failed to take him for one of the English nobility—a belief confirmed by the handsomeness of his gratuities. Mrs. Bradshaw was not, perhaps, the ideal lady of rank, but the fine self-satisfaction on her matronly visage, the good-natured disdain with which she allowed herself to be waited upon by foolish foreigners, her solid disregard of everything beyond the circle of her own party, were impressive enough, and exacted no little subservience.

Strong in the experience of two former visits, Mr. Bradshaw would have no guide to-day. Murray in hand, he knew just what he wished to see again, and where to find it. As Miriam was at Pompeii for the first time, he took her especially under his direction, and showed her the city much as he might have led her over his silk-mill in Manchester. Unimbued with history and literature, he knew nothing of the scholar's or the poet's enthusiasm; his gratification lay in exercising his solid intelligence on a lot of strange and often grotesque facts. Here men had lived two thousand years ago. There was no mistake about it; you saw the deep ruts of their wheels along the rugged street; nay, you saw the wearing of their very feet on the comically narrow pavements. And their life had been as different as possible from that of men in Manchester. Everything excited him to merriment.

"Now, this is the house of old Pansa—no doubt an ancestor of friend Sancho"— with a twinkle in his eye. "We'll go over this carefully, Mrs. Baske; it's one of the largest and completest in Pompeii. Here we are in what they called the atrium."

Cecily spoke seldom. Of course, she would have preferred to be alone here with Miriam; best of all—or nearly so—if they could have made the same party as at Baiæ. At times she lingered a little behind the others, and seemed deep in contemplation of some object; or she stood to watch the lizards darting about the sunny old walls. When all were enjoying the view from the top of Jupiter's Temple, she gazed long towards the Sorrento promontory, the height of St. Angelo.

"Amalfi is over on the far side," she said to Miriam. "They are both working there now."

Miriam replied nothing.

When they were in the Street of Tombs, Cecily again paused, by the sepulchre of the Priestess Mamia, whence there is a clear prospect across the bay towards the mountains. Turning back again, she heard a voice that made her tremble with delighted surprise. A wall concealed the speaker from her; she took a few quick steps, and saw Reuben Elgar shaking hands with the Bradshaws. He looked at her, and came forward. She could not say anything, and was painfully conscious of the blood that rushed to her face; never yet had she known this stress of heart-

beats that made suffering of joy, and the misery of being
unable to command herself under observant eyes.

It was years since Elgar and the Bradshaws had met. As
a boy he had often visited their house, but from the time of
his leaving home at sixteen to go to a boarding-school, his
acquaintance with them, as with all his other Manchester
friends, practically ceased. They had often heard of him—
too often, in their opinion. Aware of his arrival at Naples,
they had expressed no wish to see him. Still, now that he
met them in this unexpected way, they could not but assume
friendliness. Jacob, not on the whole intolerant, was willing
enough to take "the lad" on his present merits; Reuben
had the guise and manners of a gentleman, and perhaps
was grown out of his reprobate habits. Mr. Bradshaw and
his wife could not but notice Cecily's agitation at the
meeting; they exchanged wondering glances, and presently
found an opportunity for a few words apart. What was
going on? How had these two young folks become so
intimate? Well, it was no business of theirs. Lucky that
Mrs. Baske was one of the company.

And why should Cecily disguise that now only was her
enjoyment of the day begun—that only now had the sunshine its familiar brightness, the ancient walls and ways
their true enchantment? She did not at once become
more talkative, but the shadow had passed utterly from
her face, and there was no more listlessness in her movements.

"I have stopped here on my way to join Mallard," was
all Reuben said, in explanation of his presence.

All kept together. Mr. Bradshaw resumed his interest
in antiquities, but did not speak so freely about them as
before.

"Your brother knows a good deal more about these things
than I do, Mrs. Baske," he remarked. "He shall give us
the benefit of his Latin."

Miriam resolutely kept her eyes alike from Reuben and

from Cecily. Hitherto her attention to the ruins had been intermittent, but occasionally she had forgotten herself so far as to look and ponder; now she saw nothing. Her mind was gravely troubled; she wished only that the day were over.

As for Elgar, he seemed to the Bradshaws singularly quiet, modest, inoffensive. If he ventured a suggestion or a remark, it was in a subdued voice and with the most pleasant manner possible. He walked for a time with Mrs. Bradshaw, and accommodated himself with much tact to her way of regarding foreign things, whether ancient or modern. In a short time all went smoothly again.

Not since they shook hands had Elgar and Cecily encountered each other's glance. They looked at each other often, very often, but only when the look could not be returned; they exchanged not a syllable. Yet both knew that at some approaching moment, for them the supreme moment of this day, their eyes must meet. Not yet; not casually, and whilst others regarded them. The old ruins would be kind.

It was in the house of Meleager. They had walked among the coloured columns, and had visited the inner chamber, where upon the wall is painted the Judgment of Paris. Mr. Bradshaw passed out through the narrow doorway, and his voice was dulled; Miriam passed with him, and, close after her, Mrs. Bradshaw. Reuben seemed to draw aside for Cecily, but she saw his hand extended towards her—it held a spray of maidenhair that he had just gathered. She took it, or would have taken it, but her hand was closed in his.

"I have stayed only to see you again," came panting from his lips. "I could not go till I had seen you again!"

And before the winged syllables had ceased, their eyes met; nor their eyes alone, for upon both was the constraint of passion that leaps like flame to its desire—mouth to mouth and heart to heart for one instant that concentrated all the joy of being,

What hand, centuries ago crumbled into indistinguishable dust, painted that parable of the youth making his award to Love? What eyes gazed upon it, when this was a home of man and woman warm with life, listening all day long to the music of uttered thoughts? Dark-buried whilst so many ages of history went by, thrown open for the sunshine to rest upon its pallid antiquity, again had this chamber won a place in human hearts, witnessed the birth of joy and hope, blended itself with the destiny of mortals. He who pictured Paris dreamt not of these passionate lips and their unborn language, knew not that he wrought for a world hidden so far in time. Though his white-limbed goddess fade ghostlike, the symbol is as valid as ever. Did not her wan beauty smile youthful again in the eyes of these her latest worshippers?

And they went forth among the painted pillars, once more shunning each other's look. It was some minutes before Cecily knew that her fingers still crushed the spray of maidenhair; then she touched it gently, and secreted it within her glove. It must be dead when she reached home, but that mattered nothing; would it not remain the sign of something deathless?

She believed so. In her vision the dead city had a new and wonderful life; it lay glorious in the light of heaven, its strait ways fit for the treading of divinities, its barren temples reconsecrate with song and sacrifice. She believed there was that within her soul which should survive all change and hazard—survive, it might be, even this warm flesh that it was hard not to think immortal.

She sought Miriam's side, took her hand, held it playfully as they walked on together.

"Why do you look at me so sadly, Miriam?"

"I did not mean to."

"Yet you do. Let me see you smile once to-day."

But Miriam's smile was sadder than her grave look.

CHAPTER X.

THE DECLARATION.

IT was true enough that Clifford Marsh would have relished an invitation to accompany that party of four to Pompeii. For one thing, he was beginning to have a difficulty in passing his days; if the present state of things prolonged itself, his position might soon resemble that of Mr. Musselwhite. But chiefly would he have welcomed the prospect of spending some hours in the society of Miss Doran, and under circumstances which would enable him to shine. Clifford had begun to nurse a daring ambition. Allowing his vanity to caress him into the half-belief that he was really making a noble stand against the harshness of fate, he naturally spent much time in imagining how other people regarded him—above all, what figure he made in the eyes of Miss Doran. There could be no doubt that she knew, at all events, the main items of his story; was it not certain that they must make some appeal to her sympathies? His air of graceful sadness could not but lead her to muse as often as she observed it; he had contemplated himself in the mirror, and each time with reassurance on this point. Why should the attractions which had been potent with Madeline fail to engage the interest of this younger and more emotional girl? Miss Doran was far beyond Madeline in beauty, and, there was every reason to believe, had the substantial gifts of fortune which Madeline altogether lacked. It was a bold thing to turn his eye to her with such a thought, circumstances considered; but the boldness was characteristic of Marsh, with whom at all times self-esteem had the force of an irresistible argument.

He was incapable of passion. Just as he had made a
pretence of pursuing art, because of a superficial cleverness
and a liking for ease and the various satisfactions of his
vanity in such a career, so did he now permit his mind to
be occupied with Cecily Doran, not because her qualities
blinded him to all other considerations, but in pleasant
yielding to a temptation of his fancy, which made a lively
picture of many desirable things, and flattered him into
thinking that they were not beyond his reach. For the
present he could do nothing but wait, supporting his pose of
placid martyrdom. Wait, and watch every opportunity;
there would arrive a moment when seeming recklessness
might advance him far on the way to triumph.

And yet he never for a moment regarded himself as a
schemer endeavouring to compass vulgar ends by machina-
tion. He had the remarkable faculty of viewing himself in
an ideal light, even whilst conscious that so many of his
claims were mere pretence. Men such as Clifford Marsh do
not say to themselves, "What a humbug I am!" When
driven to face their conscience, it speaks to them rather in
this way : "You are a fellow of fine qualities, altogether out
of the common way of men. A pity that conditions do not
allow you to be perfectly honest ; but people in general are
so foolish that you would get no credit for your superiority
if you did not wear a little tinsel, practise a few harmless
affectations. Some day your difficulties will be at an end,
and then you can afford to show yourself in a simpler guise."
When he looked in the glass, Clifford admired himself without reserve; when he talked freely, he applauded his own
cleverness, and thought it the most natural thing that other
people should do so. When he meditated abandoning
Madeline, his sincere view of the matter was that she had
proved herself unworthy : however sensible her attitude, a
girl had no right to put such questions to her lover as she
had done, to injure his self-love. When he plotted with
himself to engage Cecily's interest, he said that it was the

course any lover would have pursued. And in the end he really persuaded himself that he was in love with her.

Yet none the less he thought of Madeline with affection. He was piqued that she made no effort to bring him back to her feet. To be sure, her mother's behaviour probably implied Madeline's desire of reconciliation, but he wished her to make personal overtures; he would have liked to see her approach him with humble eyes, not troubling himself to debate how he should act in that event. With Mrs. Denyer he was once more on terms of apparent friendliness, though he held no private dialogue with her; he was willing that she should suppose him gradually coming over to her views. Barbara and Zillah showed constraint when he spoke with them, but this he affected not to perceive. Only with Madeline he did not converse. Her air of unconcernedness at length proved too much for his patience, and so it came about that Madeline received by post a letter addressed in Clifford's hand. She took it to her bedroom, and broke the envelope with agitation.

"Your behaviour is heartless. Just when I am in deep distress, and need all possible encouragement in the grave struggle upon which I have entered—for I need not tell you that I am resolved to remain an artist—you desert me, and do your best to show that you are glad at being relieved of all concern on my account. It is well for me that I see the result of this test, but, I venture to think, not every woman would have chosen your course. I shall very shortly leave Naples. It will no doubt complete your satisfaction to think of me toiling friendless in London. Remember this as my farewell.—C. M."

The next morning Clifford received what he expected, a reply, also sent by post. It was written in the clearest and steadiest hand, on superfine paper.

"I am sorry you should have repeated your insult in a written form; I venture to think that not every man would have followed this course. For myself, it is well indeed that

I see the result of the test to which you have been exposed. But I shall say and think no more of it. As you leave soon, I would suggest that we should be on the terms of ordinary acquaintances for the remaining time; the present state of things is both disagreeable and foolish. It will always seem to me a very singular thing that you should have continued to live in this house; but that, of course, was in your own discretion.—M. D."

This was on the morning when Cecily and her companions went to Pompeii. Towards luncheon-time, Clifford entered the drawing-room, and there found Mrs. Lessingham in conversation with Madeline. The former looked towards him in a way which seemed to invite his approach.

"Another idle morning, Mr. Marsh?" was her greeting.

"I had a letter at breakfast that disturbed me," he replied, seating himself away from Madeline.

"I'm sorry to hear that."

"Mr. Marsh is very easily disturbed," said Madeline, in a light tone of many possible meanings.

"Yes," admitted Clifford, leaning back and letting his head droop a little; "I can seldom do anything when I am not quite at ease in mind. Rather a misfortune, but not an uncommon one with artists."

The conversation turned on this subject for a few minutes, Madeline taking part in it in a way that showed her resolve to act as she had recommended in her note. Then Mrs. Lessingham rose and left the two together. Madeline seemed also about to move; she followed the departing lady with her eyes, and at length, as though adding a final remark, said to Clifford:

"There are several things you have been so kind as to lend me that I must return before you go, Mr. Marsh. I will make a parcel of them, and a servant shall take them to your room."

"Thank you."

Since the quarrel, Madeline had not worn her ring of

betrothal, but this was the first time she had spoken of returning presents.

"I am sorry you have had news that disturbed you," she continued, as if in calm friendliness. "But I dare say it is something you will soon forget. In future you probably won't think so much of little annoyances."

"Probably not."

She smiled, and walked away, stopping to glance at a picture before she left the room. Clifford was left with knitted brows and uneasy mind ; he had not believed her capable of this sedateness. For some reason, Madeline had been dressing herself with unusual care of late (the result, in fact, of frequent observation of Cecily), and just now, as he entered, it had struck him that she was after all very pretty, that no one could impugn his taste in having formerly chosen her. His reference to her letter was a concession, made on the moment's impulse. Her rejecting it so unmistakably looked serious. Had she even ceased to be jealous ?

In the course of the afternoon, one of Mrs. Gluck's servants deposited a parcel in his chamber. When he found it, he bit his lips. Indeed, things looked serious at last. He passed the hours till dinner in rather comfortless solitude.

But at dinner he was opposite Cecily, and he thought he had never seen her so brilliant. Perhaps the day in the open air—there was a fresh breeze—had warmed the exquisite colour of her cheeks and given her eyes an even purer radiance than of wont. The dress she wore was not new to him, but its perfection made stronger appeal to his senses than previously. How divine were the wreaths and shadowings of her hair ! With what gracile loveliness did her neck bend as she spoke to Mrs. Lessingham ! What hand ever shone with more delicate beauty than hers in the offices of the meal ? It pained him to look at Madeline and make comparison.

Moreover, Cecily met his glance, and smiled—smiled with adorable frankness. From that moment he rejoiced at what had taken place to-day. It had left him his complete freedom. Good; he had given Madeline a final chance, and she had neglected it. In every sense he was at liberty to turn his thoughts elsewhither, and now he felt that he had even received encouragement.

"We had an unexpected meeting with Mr. Elgar," were Cecily's words, when she spoke to her aunt of the day's excursion.

Mrs. Lessingham showed surprise, and noticed that Cecily kept glancing over the columns of a newspaper she had carelessly taken up.

"At Pompeii?"

"Yes; in the Street of Tombs. For some reason, he had delayed on his journey."

"I'm not surprised."

"Why?"

"Delay is one of his characteristics, isn't it?" returned the elder lady, with unaccustomed tartness. "A minor branch of the root of inefficiency."

"I am afraid so."

Cecily laughed, and began to read aloud an amusing passage from the paper. Her aunt put no further question; but after dinner sought Mrs. Bradshaw, and had a little talk on the subject. Mrs. Bradshaw allowed herself no conjectures; in her plain way she merely confirmed what Cecily had said, adding that Elgar had taken leave of them at the railway-station.

"Possibly Mrs. Baske knew that her brother would be there?" surmised Mrs. Lessingham, as though the point were of no moment.

"Oh no! not a bit. She was astonished."

"Or seemed so," was Mrs. Lessingham's inward comment, as she smiled acquiescence. "He has impressed me agreeably," she continued, "but there's a danger that he will never do justice to himself."

"I don't put much faith in him myself," said Mrs. Brad-shaw, meaning nothing more by the phrase than that she considered Reuben a ne'er-do-well. The same words would have expressed her lack of confidence in a servant subjected to some suspicion.

Mrs. Lessingham was closely observant of her niece this evening, and grew confirmed in distrust, in solicitude. Cecily was more than ever unlike herself—whimsical, abstracted, nervous; she flushed at an unexpected sound, could not keep the same place for more than a few minutes. Much before the accustomed hour, she announced her retirement for the night.

"Let me feel your pulse," said Mrs. Lessingham, as if in jest, when the girl approached her.

Cecily permitted it, half averting her face.

"My child, you are feverish."

"A little, I believe, aunt. It will pass by the morning"

"Let us hope so. But I don't like that kind of thing at Naples. I trust you haven't had a chill?"

"Oh dear, no! I never was better in my life!"

"Yet with fever? Go to bed. Very likely I shall look into your room in the night.—Cecily!"

It stopped her at her door. She turned, and took a step back. Mrs. Lessingham moved towards her.

"You haven't forgotten anything that you wished to say to me?"

"Forgotten? No, dear aunt."

"It just come back to my mind that you were on the the point of saying something a little while ago, and I interrupted you."

"No. Good night."

Mrs. Lessingham did enter the girl's room something after midnight, carrying a dim taper. Cecily was asleep, but lay as though fatigue had overcome her after much restless moving upon the pillow. Her face was flushed; one of her hands, that on the coverlet, kept closing itself with a slight spasm. The visitor drew apart and looked about the chamber. Her eyes rested on a little writing-desk, where lay a directed envelope. She looked at it, and found it was addressed to a French servant of theirs in Paris, an excellent woman who loved Cecily, and to whom the girl had promised to write from Italy. The envelope was closed; but it could contain nothing of importance—was merely an indication of Cecily's abiding kindness. By this lay a small book, from the pages of which protruded a piece of white paper. Mrs. Lessingham took up the volume—it was Shelley—and found that the paper within it was folded about a spray of maiden-hair, and bore the inscription "House of Meleager, Pompeii. Monday, December 8, 1878." Over this the inquisitive lady mused, until a motion of Cecily caused her to restore things rapidly to their former condition.

A movement, and a deep sigh; but Cecily did not awake. Mrs. Lessingham again drew softly near to her, and, without letting the light fall directly upon her face, looked at her for a long time. She whispered feelingly, "Poor girl! poor child!" then, with a sigh almost as deep as that of the slumberer, withdrew.

In the morning, Cecily was already dressed when a servant brought letters to the sitting-room. There were three, and one of them, addressed to herself, had only the Naples postmark. She went back to her bedroom with it.

After breakfast Mrs. Lessingham spoke for a while of news contained in her correspondence; then of a sudden asked:

"You hadn't any letters?"

"Yes, aunt; one."

"My child, you are far from well this morning. The fever hasn't gone. Your face burns."

"Yes."

"May I ask from whom the letter was?"

"I have it here—to show you." A choking of her voice broke the sentence. She held out the letter. Mrs. Lessingham found the following lines:—

"DEAR CECILY,

     "I have, of course, returned to Naples, and I earnestly hope I may see you between ten and eleven to-morrow morning. I must see you alone. You cannot reply; I will come and send my name in the ordinary way.

                    "Yours ever,

                        "R. ELGAR."

Mrs. Lessingham looked up. Cecily, who was standing before her, now met her gaze steadily.

"The meaning of this is plain enough," said her aunt, with careful repression of feeling. "But I am at a loss to understand how it has come about."

"I cannot tell you, aunt. I cannot tell myself."

Cecily's true accents once more. It was as though she had recovered all her natural self-command now that the revelation was made. The flush still possessed her cheeks, but she had no look of embarrassment; she spoke in a soft murmur, but distinctly, firmly.

"I am afraid that is only too likely, dear. Come and sit down, little girl, and tell me, at all events, something about it."

"Little girl?" repeated Cecily, with a sweet, affectionate smile. "No; that has gone by, aunt."

"I thought so myself the other day; but—— I suppose you have met Mr. Elgar several times at his sister's, and have said nothing to me about it?"

"That would not have been my usual behaviour, I hope. When did I deceive you, aunt?"

"Never, that I know. Where have you met then?"

"Only at the times and places of which you know."

"Where did you give Mr. Elgar the right to address you in this manner?"

"Only yesterday. I think you mustn't ask me more than that, aunt."

"I'm afraid your companions were rather lacking in discretion," said the other, in a tone of annoyance.

"No; not in the sense you attach to the words. But, aunt, you are speaking as if I *were* a little girl, to be carefully watched at every step."

Mrs. Lessingham mused, looking absently at the letter. She paid no heed to her niece's last words, but at length said with decision:

"Cecily, this meeting cannot take place."

The girl replied with a look of uttermost astonishment.

"It is impossible, dear. Mr. Elgar should not have written to you like this. He should have addressed himself to other people."

"Other people? But you don't understand, aunt. I cannot explain to you. I expected this letter; and we must see each other."

Her voice trembled, failed.

"Shall you not treat my wish with respect, Cecily?"

"Will you explain to me all that you do wish, aunt?"

"Certainly. It is true that you are not a French girl, and I have no desire to regard you as though we were a French aunt and niece talking of this subject in the conventional way. But you are very young, dear, and most decidedly it behoved Mr. Elgar to bear in mind both his and your position. You have no parents, unhappily, but you know that Mr. Mallard is legally appointed the guardian of your interests, and I trust you know also that I am deeply concerned in all that affects you. Let us say nothing, one way or another, of what has happened. Since it *has* happened, it was Mr. Elgar's duty to address himself to me, or to Mr. Mallard, before making private appointments with you."

"Aunt, you can see that this letter is written so as to allow of my showing it to you."

"I have noticed that, of course. It makes Mr. Elgar's way of proceeding seem still more strange to me. He is good enough to ask you to relieve him of what he thinks——"

"You misunderstand him, aunt, entirely. I cannot explain it to you. Only trust me, I beg, to do what I know to be right. It is necessary that I should speak with Mr. Elgar; do not pain me by compelling me to say more. Afterwards, he will wish to see you, I know."

"Please to remember, dear—it astonishes me that you forget it—that I have a responsibility to Mr. Mallard. I have no legal charge of you. With every reason, Mr. Mallard may reproach me if I countenance what it is impossible for him to approve."

Cecily searched the speaker's face.

"Do you mean," she asked gravely, "that Mr. Mallard will disapprove—what I have done?"

"I can say nothing on that point. But I am very sure that he would not approve of this meeting, if he could know what was happening. I must communicate with him at once. Until he comes, or writes, it is your duty, my dear, to decline this interview. Believe me, it is your duty."

Mrs. Lessingham spoke more earnestly than she ever had done to her niece. Indeed, earnest speech was not frequent upon her lips when she talked with Cecily. In spite of the girl's nature, there had never existed between them warmer relations than those of fondness and interest on one side, and gentleness with respect on the other. Cecily was well aware of this something lacking in their common life; she had wished, not seldom these last two years, to supply the want, but found herself unable, and grew conscious that her aunt gave all it was in her power to bestow. For this very reason, she found it impossible to utter herself in the present juncture as she could have done to a mother—as she could have done to Miriam; impossible, likewise, to insist on her heart's urgent desire, though she knew not how she should forbear it. To refuse compliance would have been something more than failure in dutifulness; she would have felt it as harshness, and perhaps injustice, to one with whom she involuntarily stood on terms of ceremony.

"May I write a reply to this letter?" she asked, after a silence.

"I had rather you allowed me to speak for you to Mr. Elgar. To write and to see him are the same thing. Surely you can forget yourself for a moment, and regard this from my point of view."

"I don't know how far you may be led by your sense of responsibility. Remember that you have insisted to me on your prejudice against Mr. Elgar."

"Vainly enough," returned the other, with a smile. "If you prefer it, I will myself write a line to be given to Mr. Elgar when he calls. Of course, you shall see what I write."

Cecily turned away, and stood in struggle with herself. She had not foreseen a conflict of this kind. Surprise, and probably vexation, she was prepared for; irony, argument, she was quite ready to face; but it had not entered her mind that Mrs. Lessingham would invoke authority to oppose her. Such a step was alien to all the habits of their intercourse, to the spirit of her education. She had deemed herself a woman, and free; what else could result from Mrs. Lessingham's method of training and developing her? This disillusion gave a shock to her self-respect; she suffered from a sense of shame; with difficulty she subdued resentment and impulses yet more rebellious. It was ignoble to debate in this way concerning that of which she could not yet speak formally with her own mind; to contend like an insubordinate school-girl, when the point at issue was the dearest interest of her womanhood.

"I think, aunt," she said, in a changed voice, speaking as though her opinion had been consulted in the ordinary way,

" it will be better for you to see Mr. Elgar—if you are willing to do so."

" Quite."

" But I must ask you to let him know exactly why I have not granted his request. You will tell him, if you please, just what has passed between us. If that does not seem consistent with your duty, or dignity, then I had rather you wrote."

"Neither my duty nor my dignity is likely to suffer, Cecily," replied her aunt, with an ironical smile. "Mr. Elgar shall know the simple state of the case. And I will forthwith write to Mr. Mallard."

" Thank you."

There was no further talk between them. Mrs. Lessingham sat down to write. With the note-paper before her, and the pen in hand, she was a long time before she began ; she propped her forehead, and seemed lost in reflection. Cecily, who stood by the window, glanced towards her several times, and in the end went to her own room.

Mrs. Lessingham's letter was not yet finished when a servant announced Elgar's arrival. He was at once admitted. On seeing who was to receive him, he made an instant's pause before coming forward ; there was merely a bow on both sides.

Elgar knew well enough in what mood this lady was about to converse with him. He did not like her, and partly, no doubt, because he had discerned her estimate of his character, his faculties. That she alone was in the room gave him no surprise, though it irritated him and inflamed his impatience. He would have had her speak immediately and to the point, that he might understand his position. Mrs. Lessingham, quite aware of his perfervid state of mind, had pleasure in delaying. Her real feeling towards him was anything but unfriendly ; had it been possible, she would have liked to see much of him, to enjoy his talk. Young men of this stamp amused her, and made strong appeal to certain of her sympathies. But those very sympathies enabled her to judge him with singular accuracy, aided as she was by an outline knowledge of his past. Her genuine affection for Cecily made her, now that the peril had declared itself, his strenuous adversary. For Cecily to marry Reuben Elgar would be a catastrophe, nothing less. She was profoundly convinced of this, and the best elements of her nature came out in the resistance she was determined to make.

A less worthy ground of vexation against Elgar might probably be attributed to her. Skilful in judging men, she had not the same insight where her own sex was concerned, and in the case of Cecily she was misled, or rather misled herself, with curious persistence. Possibly some slight, vague fear had already touched her when she favoured Mrs. Spence with the description of her "system;" not impossibly she felt the need of reassuring herself by making clear her attitude to one likely to appreciate it. But at that time she had not dreamt of such a sudden downfall of her theoretic edifice; she believed in its strength, and did not doubt of her supreme influence with Cecily. It was not to be wondered at that she felt annoyed with the man who, at a touch, made the elaborate structure collapse like a bubble. She imagined Mrs. Spence's remarks when she came to hear of what had happened, her fine smile to her husband. The occurrence was mortifying.

"Miss Doran has put into my hands a letter she received from you this morning, Mr. Elgar."

Reuben waited. Mrs. Lessingham had not invited him to sit down; she also stood.

"You probably wished me to learn its contents?"

"Yes; I am glad you have read it."

"It didn't occur to you that Miss Doran might find the task you imposed upon her somewhat trying?"

Elgar was startled. Just as little as Cecily had he pondered the details of the situation; mere frenzy possessed

him, and he acted as desire bade. Had Cecily been em.
barrassed ? Was she annoyed at his not proceeding with
formality ? He had never thought of her in the light of
conventional obligations, and even now could not bring himself to do so.

"Did Miss Doran wish me to be told that?" he asked,
bluntly, in unconsidered phrase.

"Miss Doran's wish is, that no further step shall be taken
by either of you until her guardian, Mr. Mallard, has been
communicated with."

"She will not see me ? "

"She thinks it better neither to see you nor to write. I
am bound to tell you that this is the result of my advice.
Her own intention was to do as you request in this letter."

"What harm would there have been in that, Mrs. Lessingham? Why mayn't I see her?"

"I really think Miss Doran must be allowed to act as
seems best to her. It is quite enough that I tell you what
she has decided."

"But that is not her decision," broke out Elgar, moving
impetuously. "That is simply the result of your persuasion,
of your authority. Why may I not see her ? "

"For reasons which would be plain enough to any but a
very thoughtless young gentleman. I can say no more."

Her caustic tone was not agreeable. Elgar winced under
it, and had much ado to restrain himself from useless
vehemence.

"Do you intend to write to Mr. Mallard to-day?" he
asked.

"I will write to-day."

Expostulation and entreaty seemed of no avail; Elgar recognized the situation, and with a grinding of his teeth kept
down the horrible pain he suffered. His only comfort was
that Mallard would assuredly come post-haste; he would
arrive by to-morrow evening. But two days of this misery!
Mrs. Lessingham was gratified with his look as he departed;

she had supplied him with abundant matter for speculation, yet had fulfilled her promise to Cecily.

She finished her letter, then went to Cecily's room. The girl sat unoccupied, and listened without replying. That day she took her meals in private, scarcely pretending to eat. Her face kept its flush, and her hands remained feverishly hot. Till late at night she sat in the same chair, now and then opening a book, but unable to read; she spoke only a word or two, when it was necessary.

The same on the day that followed. Seldom moving, seldomer speaking; she suffered and waited.

CHAPTER XI.

THE APPEAL TO AUTHORITY.

"HIC intus homo verus certus optumus recumbo, Publius Octavius Rufus, decurio."

Mallard stood reading this inscription, graven on an ancient sarcophagus preserved in the cathedral of Amalfi. A fool, probably, that excellent Rufus—he said to himself,— but what a happy fool! Unborn as yet, or to him unknown, the faith that would have bidden him write himself a miserable sinner; what he deemed himself in life, what perchance his friends and neighbours deemed him, why not declare it upon the marble when he rested from all his virtues?

"Here lie I, Ross Mallard; who can say no good of myself, yet have as little right to say ill; who had no faith whereby to direct my steps, yet often felt that some such was needful; who spent all my strength on a task which I knew to be vain; who suffered much and joyed rarely; whose happiest day was his last."

Somehow like that would it run, if he were to write his own epitaph at present.

The quiet of the dim sanctuary was helpful to such self-communing. He relished being alone again, and after an hour's brooding had recovered at all events a decent balance of thought, a respite from madness in melancholy.

But he could not employ himself, could not even seek the relief of bodily exertion; his mind grew sluggish, and threw a lassitude upon his limbs. The greater part of the day he spent in his room at the hotel, merely idle. This time he had no energy to attack himself with adjurations and sarcasms; body and soul were oppressed with uttermost fatigue, and for a time must lie torpid. Fortunately he was sure of sleep to-night; the bell of the cathedral might clang its worst, and still not rob him of the just oblivion.

The next day he strayed into the hills, and there in solitude faced the enemy in his heart, bidding misery do its worst. In imagination he followed Reuben Elgar to Naples, saw him speed to Villa Sannazaro, where as likely as not he would meet Cecily. Mallard had no tangible evidence of its being Reuben's desire to see Cecily, but he was none the less convinced that for no other reason had his companion set forth. And jealousy tormented him sorely. It was his first experience of this cruellest passion : what hitherto had been only a name to him, and of ignoble sound, became a disease clutching at his vitals. It taught him fierceness, injustice, base suspicion, brutal conjecture ; it taught him that of which all these are constituents—hatred.

But it did not constrain him to any unworthy action. The temptation that passed through his mind when he looked from the balcony on the carriage that was to convey Elgar, did not return—or only as a bitter desire, impossible of realization. Distant from Naples he must remain, awaiting whatsoever might happen.

Ah, bright, gentle, sweet-faced Cecily ! Inconceivable to her this suffering that lay upon her friend. How it would pain her if she knew of it! With what sad, wondering tenderness her eyes would regard him! How kindly would she lay her soft hand in his, and entreat him to be comforted!

If he asked her, would she not give him that hand, to be his always? Perhaps, perhaps; in her gentleness she would submit to this change, and do her best to love him. And in return he would give her gruff affection, removal from the life to which she was accustomed, loneliness, his uncertain humours, his dubious reputation. How often must he picture these results, and convince himself of the impossibility of anything of the kind?

He knew her better than did Mrs. Lessingham; oh, far better! He had detected in her deep eyes the sleeping passion, some day to awake with suddenness and make the whole world new to her. He knew how far from impossible it was that Reuben Elgar should be the prince to break her charmed slumber. There was the likeness and the unlikeness; common to both that temperament of enthusiasm. On the one hand, Cecily with her unsullied maidenhood; and on the other, Elgar with his reckless experiences—contrasts which so commonly have a mutual attraction. There was the singularity of their meeting after years, and seeing each other in such a new light; the interest, the curiosity inevitably resulting. What likelihood that any distrust would mingle with Cecily's warmth of feeling, were that feeling once excited? He knew her too well.

How Mrs. Lessingham regarded Elgar he did not know. He had no confidence in that lady's discretion; he thought it not improbable that she would speak of Reuben to Cecily in the very way she should not, making him an impressive figure. Then again, what part was Mrs. Baske likely to have in such a situation? Could she be relied upon to represent her brother unfavourably, with the right colour of unfavourableness? Or was it not rather to be feared that the thought of Cecily's influence might tempt her to encourage what otherwise she must have condemned ? He retraced in memory that curious dialogue he had held with Miriam on the drive back from Baiæ; could he gather from it any hints of her probable behaviour ? . . . .

By a sudden revulsion of mind, Mallard became aware that in the long fit of brooding just gone by he had not been occupied with Cecily at all. Busying his thoughts with Mrs. Baske, he had slipped into a train of meditation already begun on the evening in question, after the drive with her. What was Mrs. Baske's true history ? How had she come to marry the man of whom Elgar's phrases had produced such a hateful image ? What was the state, in very deed, of her mind at present ? What awaited her in the future ?

It was curious that Mrs. Baske's face was much more recoverable by his mind's eye than Cecily's. In fact, to see Miriam cost him no effort at all; equally at will, he heard the sound of her voice. There were times when Cecily, her look and utterance, visited him very clearly ; but this was when he did not wish to be reminded of her. If he endeavoured to make her present, as a rule the picturing faculty was irresponsive.

Welcome reverie ! If only he could continue to busy himself with idle speculation concerning the strange young Puritan, and so find relief from the anguish that beset him. Suppose now, he set himself to imagine Miriam in unlikely situations. What if she somehow fell into poverty, was made absolutely dependent on her own efforts ? Suppose she suffered cruelly what so many women have to suffer— toil, oppression, solitude ; what would she become ? Not, he suspected, a meek martyr ; anything but that, Miriam Baske. And how magnificent to see her flash out into revolt against circumstances ! Then indeed she would be interesting.

Nay, suppose she fell in love—desperately, with grim fate against her ? For somehow this came more easily to the fancy than the thought of her loving without obstacle. Presumably she had never loved ; her husband was out of the question. Would she pass her life without that experience? One thing could be affirmed with certainty; if she lost her heart to a man, it would not be to a Puritan. He could conceive her being attracted by a strong and somewhat rude fellow, a despiser of conventionalities, without religion, a man of brains and blood; one whose look could overwhelm her with tumultuous scorn, and whose hand, if need be, could crush her life out at a blow. Why not, however, a highly polished gentleman, critical, keen of speech, deeply read, brilliant in conversation, at once man of the world and scholar? Might not that type have power over her? In a degree, but not so decidedly as the intellectual brute.

Pshaw! what brain-sickness was this! What was he fallen to! Yet it did what nothing else would, amused him for a few minutes in his pain. He recurred to it several times, and always successfully.

Sunday came. This evening would see Elgar back again. No doubt of his return had yet entered his mind. Whether Reuben would in reality settle to some kind of work was a different question; but of course he would come back, if it were only to say that he had kept his promise, but found he must set off again to some place or other. Mallard dreaded his coming. News of some kind he would bring, and Mallard's need was of silence. If he indeed remained here, the old irritation would revive and go on from day to day. Impossible that they should live together long.

It was pretty certain by what train he would journey from Naples to Salerno; easy, therefore, to calculate the probable hour of his arrival at Amalfi. When that hour drew near, Mallard set out to walk a short distance along the road, to meet him. Unlike the Sorrento side of the promontory, the mountains here rise suddenly and boldly out of the sea, towering to craggy eminences, moulded and cleft into infinite variety of slope and precipice, bastion and gorge. Cut upon the declivity, often at vast sheer height above the beach, the

road follows the curving of the hills. Now and then it
makes a deep loop inland, on the sides of an impassable
chasm; and set in each of these recesses is a little town,
white-gleaming amid its orchard verdure, with quaint and
many-coloured campanile, with the semblance of a remote
time. Far up on the heights are other gleaming specks,
villages which seem utterly beyond the traffic of man, solitary for ever in sun or mountain mist.

Mallard paid little heed to the things about him; he
walked on and on, watching for a vehicle, listening for the
tread of horses. Sometimes he could see the white road-
track miles away, and he strained his eyes in observing it.
Twice or thrice he was deceived; a carriage came towards
him, and with agitation he waited to see its occupants, only
to be disappointed by strange faces.

There are few things more pathetic than persistency in
hope due to ignorance of something that has befallen beyond
our ken. It is one of those instances of the irony inherent
in human fate which move at once to tears and bitter
laughter; the waste of emotion, the involuntary folly, the
cruel deception caused by limit of faculties—how they con-
centrate into an hour or a day the essence of life itself!

He walked on and on; as well do this as go back and
loiter fretfully at the hotel. He got as far as the Capo
d' Orso, the headland half-way between Amalfi and Salerno,
and there sat down by the wayside to rest. From this point
Salerno was first visible, in the far distance, between the
sea and the purple Apennines.

Either Elgar was not coming, or he had lingered long
between the two portions of his journey.

Mallard turned back; if the carriage came, it would over-
take him. He plodded slowly, the evening falling around
him in still loveliness, fragrance from the groves of orange
and lemon spread on every motion of the air.

And if he did not come? That must have some strange
meaning. In any case, he must surely write. And ten to

one his letter would be a lie. What was to be expected of him but a lie?

Monday, Tuesday, and now Wednesday morning. Hither-to not even a letter.

When it was clear that Elgar had disregarded his promise, and, for whatever reason, did not even seek to justify or excuse himself, there came upon Mallard a strong mood of scorn, which for some hours enabled him to act as though all his anxiety were at an end. He set himself a piece of work; a flash of the familiar energy traversed his mind. He believed that at length his degradation was over, and that, come what might, he could now face it sturdily. Mere self-deception, of course. The sun veiled itself, and hope was as far as ever.

Never before had he utterly lost the power of working. In every struggle he had speedily overcome, and found in work the one unfailing resource. If he were robbed of this, what stay had life for him henceforth? He could not try to persuade himself that his suffering would pass, sooner or later, and time grant him convalescence; the blackness ahead was too profound. He fell again into torpor, and let the days go as they would; he cared not.

But this morning brought him a letter. At the first glance he was surprised by a handwriting which was not Elgar's; recollecting himself, he knew it for that of Mrs. Lessingham.

"Dear Mr. Mallard,—

"It grieves me to be obliged to send you disquieting news so soon after your departure from Naples, but I think you will agree with me that I have no choice but to write of something that has this morning come to my knowledge. You have no taste for roundabout phrases, so I will say at once in plain words that Cecily and Mr. Elgar have some-how contrived to fall in love with each other—or to imagine that they have done so, which, as regards results, unfortunately amounts to the same thing. I cannot learn by what process it came about, but I am assured by Cecily, in words of becoming vagueness, that they plighted troth, or something of the kind, yesterday at Pompeii. There was a party of four: Mr. and Mrs. Bradshaw, Cecily, and Mrs. Baske. At Pompeii they were unexpectedly (so I am told) joined by Mr. Elgar—notwithstanding that he had taken leave of us on Saturday, with the information that he was about to return to you at Amalfi, and there devote himself to literary work of some indefinite kind. Perhaps you have in the meantime heard from him. This morning Cecily received a letter, in which he made peremptory request for an interview; she showed this to me. My duty was plain. I declared the interview impossible, and Cecily gave way on condition that I saw Mr. Elgar, told him why she herself did not appear, and forthwith wrote to you. Our young gentleman was disconcerted when he found that his visit was to be wasted on my uninteresting self. I sent him about his business—only that, unhappily, he has none—bidding him wait till we had heard from you.

"I fancy this will be as disagreeable to you as it is to me. The poor child is in a sad state, much disposed, I fear, to regard me as her ruthless enemy, and like to fall ill if she be kept long in idle suspense. Do you think it worth while to come to Naples? It is very annoying that your time should be wasted by foolish children. I had given Cecily credit for more sense. For my own part, I cannot think with patience of her marrying Mr. Elgar; or rather, I cannot think of it without dread. We must save her from becoming wise through bitter sorrow, if it can in any way be managed. I hope and trust that nothing may happen to prevent your receiving this letter to-morrow, for I am very uneasy, and not likely to become less so as time goes on.

"Believe me, dear Mr. Mallard,

"Sincerely yours,

"EDITH LESSINGHAM."

At seven o'clock in the evening, Mallard was in Naples. He did not go to Casa Rolandi, but took a room in one of the musty hotels which overlook the port. When he felt sure that Mrs. Gluck's guests must have dined, he presented himself at the house and sent his name to Mrs. Lessingham.

She took his hand with warm welcome.

" Thank you for coming so promptly. I have been getting into such a state of nervousness. Cecily keeps her room, and looks ill; I have several times been on the point of sending for the doctor, though it seemed absurd."

Mallard seated himself without invitation; indeed, he had a difficulty in standing.

" Hasn't she been out to-day ? " he asked, in a voice which might have signified selfish indifference.

" Nor yesterday. Mrs. Spence was here this morning, but Cecily would not see her. I made excuses, and of course said nothing of what was going on. I asked the child if she would like to see Mrs. Baske, but she refused."

Mallard sat as if he had nothing to say, looking vaguely about the room.

" Have you heard from Mr. Elgar ? " Mrs. Lessingham inquired.

" No. I know nothing about him. I haven't been to Casa Rolandi, lest I should meet him. It was better to see you first."

" You were not prepared for this news ? "

" His failure to return made me speculate, of course. I suppose they have met several times at Mrs. Baske's ? "

" That at once occurred to me, but Cecily assures me that is not so. There is a mystery. I have no idea how they saw each other privately at Pompeii on Monday. But, between ourselves, Mr. Mallard, I can't help suspecting that he had learnt from his sister the particulars of the excursion."

" You think it not impossible that Mrs. Baske connived at their meeting in that way ? "

" One doesn't like to use words of that kind, but——"

" I suppose one must use the word that expresses one's meaning," said Mallard, bluntly. "But I didn't think Mrs. Baske was likely to aid her brother for such a purpose. Have you any reason to think the contrary ? "

" None that would carry any weight."

Mallard paused; then, with a restless movement on his chair exclaimed :

" But what has this to do with the matter? What has happened has happened, and there's an end of it. The question is, what ought to be done now ? I don't see that we can treat Miss Doran like a child."

Mrs. Lessingham looked at him. She was resting one arm on a table by which she sat, and supporting her forehead with her hand.

" You propose that things should take their natural course ? "

" They will, whether I propose it or not."

"And if our next information is that they desire to be married as soon as conveniently may be ? "

"That is another matter. They will have no consent of mine to anything of the kind."

" You relieve me."

Mallard looked at her frowningly.

" Miss Doran," he continued, "will not marry Elgar with my consent until she be one-and-twenty. Then, of course, she may do as she likes."

" You will see Mr. Elgar, and make this clear to him ? "

" Very clear indeed," was the grim reply. "As for anything else, why, what can we do ? If they insist upon it, I suppose they must see each other—of course, under reasonable restrictions. You cannot make yourself a duenna of melodrama, Mrs. Lessingham."

" Scarcely. But I think our stay at Naples may reasonably be shortened—unless, of course, Mr. Elgar leaves."

"You take it for granted, I see, that Miss Doran will be guided by our judgment," said Mallard, after musing on the last remark.

"I have no fear of that," replied Mrs. Lessingham with confidence, "if it is made to appear only a question of post-ponement. This will be a trifle compared with my task of yesterday morning. You can scarcely imagine how astonished she was at the first hint of opposition."

"I can imagine it very well," said the other, in his throat. "What else could be expected after——" He checked himself on the point of saying something that would have revealed his opinion of Mrs. Lessingham's "system"—his opinion accentuated by unreasoning bitterness. "From all we know of her," were the words he substituted.

"She is more like her father than I had supposed," said Mrs. Lessingham, meditatively.

Mallard stood up.

"You will let her know that I have been here?"

"Certainly."

"She has expressed no wish to see me?"

"None. I had better report to her simply that you have no objection to Mr. Elgar's visits."

"That is all I would say at present. I shall see Elgar to-night. He is still at Casa Rolandi, I take it?"

"That was the address on his letter."

"Then, good-night. By-the-bye, I had better give you my address." He wrote it on a leaf in his pocket-book. "I will see you again in a day or two, when things have begun to clear up."

"It's too bad that you should have this trouble, Mr Mallard."

"I don't pretend to like it, but there's no help."

And he left Mrs. Lessingham to make her comment on his candour.

Yes, Signor Elgar was in his chamber; he had entered

but a quarter of an hour since. The signor seemed not quite well, unhappily—said Olimpia, the domestic, in her chopped Neapolitan. Mallard vouchsafed no reply. He knocked sharply at the big solid door. There was a cry of " Avanti ! " and he entered.

Elgar advanced a few steps. He did not affect to smile, but looked directly at his visitor, who—as if all the pain of the interview were on him rather than the other—cast down his eyes.

"I was expecting you," said Reuben, without offering his hand.

" So was I you—three days ago."

" Sit down, and let us talk. I'm ashamed of myself, Mallard. I ought at all events to have written."

" One would have thought so."

" Have you seen Mrs. Lessingham ? "

" Yes."

"Then you understand everything. I repeat that I am ashamed of my behaviour to you. For days—since last Saturday—I have been little better than a madman. On Saturday I went to say good-bye to Mrs. Lessingham and her niece; it was *bonâ fide*, Mallard."

"In your sense of the phrase. Go on."

" I tell you, I then meant to leave Naples," pursued Elgar, who had repeated this so often to himself, by way of pallia-tion, that he had come to think it true. " It was not my fault that I couldn't when that visit was over. It happened that I saw Miss Doran alone—sat talking with her till her aunt returned."

Mrs. Lessingham had made no mention of this little matter. Hearing of it, Mallard ejaculated mentally, " Idiot ! "

" It was all over with me. I broke faith with you—as I should have done with any man ; as I should have done if the lives of a hundred people had depended on my coming. I didn't write, because I preferred not to write lies, and if I had told the truth, I knew you would come at once. To be sure, silence might have had the same result, but I had to risk something, and I risked that."

"I marvel at your disinclination to lie."

"What do you mean by saying that?" broke out Elgar, with natural warmth.

"I mean simply what I say. Go on."

"After all, Mallard, I don't quite know why you should take this tone with me. If a man falls in love, he thinks of nothing but how to gain his end; I should think even you can take that for granted. My broken promise is a trifle in view of what caused it."

"Again, in *your* view. In mine it is by no means a trifle. It distinguishes you from honourable men, that's all; a point of some moment, I should think, when your character is expressly under discussion."

"You mean, of course, that I am not worthy of Cecily. I can't grant any such conclusion."

"Let us leave that aside for the present," said Mallard. "Will you tell me how it came to pass that you met Miss Doran and her companions at Pompeii?"

Elgar hesitated; whereupon the other added quickly:

"If it was with Miss Doran's anticipation, I want no details."

"No, it wasn't."

Their looks met.

"By chance, then, of course?" said Mallard, sourly.

Elgar spoke on an impulse, leaning forward.

"Look, I won't lie to you. Miriam told me they were going. I met her that morning, when I was slinking about, and I compelled her to give me her help—sorely against her will. Don't think ill of her for it, Mallard. I frightened her by my violent manner. I haven't seen her since; she can't know what the result has been. None of them at Pompeii suspected—only a moment of privacy; there's no need to say any more about it."

Mallard mused over this revelation. He felt inclined to scorn Elgar for making it. It affected him curiously, and at once took a place among his imaginings of Miriam.

"You shall promise me that you won't betray your knowledge of this," added Reuben. "At all events, not now. Promise me that. Your word is to be trusted, I know."

"It's very unlikely that I should think of touching on the matter to your sister. I shall make no promise."

"Have you seen Cecily herself?" Elgar asked, leaving the point aside in his eagerness to come to what concerned him more deeply.

"No."

"I have waited for your permission to visit her. Do you mean to refuse it?"

"No. If you call to-morrow morning, you will be admitted. Mrs. Lessingham is willing that you should see her niece in private."

"Hearty thanks for that, Mallard! We haven't shaken hands yet, you remember. Forgive me for treating you so ill."

He held out his hand cordially, and Mallard could not refuse it, though he would rather have thrust his fingers among red coals than feel that hot pressure.

"I believe I can be grateful,".pursued Elgar, in a voice that quivered with transport. "I will do my best to prove it."

"Let us speak of things more to the point. What result do you foresee of this meeting to-morrow?"

The other hesitated.

"I shall ask Cecily when she will marry me."

"You may do so, of course, but the answer cannot depend upon herself alone."

"What delay do you think necessary?"

"Until she is of age, and her own mistress," replied Mallard, with quiet decision.

"Impossible! What need is there to wait all that time?"

"Why, there is this need, Elgar," returned the other, more vigorously than he had yet spoken. "There is need that you should prove to those who desire Miss Doran's welfare that you are something more than a young fellow fresh from a life of waste and idleness and everything that demonstrates or tends to untrustworthiness. It seems to me that a couple of years or so is not an over-long time for this, all things considered."

Elgar kept silent.

"You would have seen nothing objectionable in immediate marriage?" said Mallard.

"It is useless to pretend that I should."

"Not even from the point of view of Mrs. Lessingham and myself?"

"You yourself have never spoken plainly about such things in my hearing; but I find you in most things a man of your time. And it doesn't seem to me that Mrs. Lessingham is exactly conventional in her views."

"You imagine yourself worthy of such a wife at present?"

"Plainly, I do. It would be the merest hypocrisy if I said anything else. If Cecily loves me, my love for her is at least as strong. If we are equal in that, what else matters? I am not going to cry *Peccavi* about the past. I have lived, and you know what that means in my language. In what am I inferior as a man to Cecily as a woman? Would you have me snivel, and talk about my impurity and her angelic qualities? You know that you would despise me if I did— or any other man who used the same empty old phrases."

"I grant you that," replied Mallard, deliberately. "I believe I am no more superstitious with regard to these questions than you are, and I want to hear no cant. Let us take it on more open ground. Were Cecily Doran my daughter, I would resist her marrying you to the utmost of my power—not simply because you have lived laxly, but

because of my conviction that the part of your life is to be
a pattern of the whole. I have no faith in you—no faith in
your sense of honour, in your stability, not even in your
mercy. Your wife will be, sooner or later, one of the
unhappiest of women. Thinking of you in this way, and
being in the place of a parent to Cecily, am I doing my duty
or not in insisting that she shall not marry you hastily, that
even in her own despite she shall have time to study you and
herself, that she shall only take the irrevocable step when
she clearly knows that it is done on her own responsibility?
You may urge what you like; I am not so foolish as to
suppose you capable of consideration for others in your
present state of mind. I, however, shall defend myself
from the girl's reproaches in after-years. There will be no
marriage until she is twenty-one."

A silence of some duration followed. Elgar sat with bent
head, twisting his moustaches. At length:

"I believe you are right, Mallard. Not in your judgment
of me, but in your practical resolve."

Mallard examined him from under his eyebrows.

"You are prepared to wait?" he asked, in an uncertain
voice.

"Prepared, no. But I grant the force of your arguments.
I will try to bring myself to patience."

Mallard sat unmoving. His legs were crossed, and he
held his soft felt hat crushed together in both his hands.
Elgar glanced at him once or twice, expecting him to speak,
but the other was mute.

"Your judgment of me," Elgar resumed, "is harsh and
unfounded. I don't know how you have formed it. You
know nothing of what it means to me to love such a girl as
Cecily. Here I have found my rest. It supplies me with
no new qualities, but it strengthens those I have. You
picture me being unfaithful to Cecily—deserting her,
becoming brutal to her? There must be a strange prejudice
in your mind to excite such images." He examined

Mallard's face. "Some day I will remind you of your prophecies."

Mallard regarded him, and spoke at length, in a strangely jarring, discordant voice.

"I said that hastily. I make no prophecies. I wished to say that those seemed to me the probabilities."

"Thank you for the small mercy, at all events," said Elgar, with a laugh.

"What do you intend to do?" Mallard proceeded to ask, changing his position.

"I can make no plans yet. I have pretended to only too often. You have no objection to my remaining here?"

"You must take your own course—with the understanding to which we have come."

"I wish I could make you look more cheerful, Mallard. I owe it to you, for you have given me more gladness than I can utter."

"You can do it."

"How?"

"See her to-morrow morning, and then go back to England, and make yourself some kind of reputable existence."

"Not yet. That is asking too much. Not so soon."

"As you please. We understand each other on the main point."

"Yes. Are you going back to Amalfi?"

"I don't know."

They talked for a few minutes more, in short sentences of this kind, but did not advance beyond the stage of mutual forbearance. Mallard lingered, as though not sure that he had fulfilled his mission. In the end he went away abruptly.

CHAPTER XII.

ON THE HEIGHTS.

In vain, at each meal, did Clifford Marsh await Cecily's appearance. A trifling indisposition kept her to her room, was Mrs. Lessingham's reply to sympathetic inquiries. Mr. and Mrs. Bradshaw, who were seriously making their preparations for journeying northward, held private talk concerning the young lady, and felt they would like to stay a week longer, just to see if their suspicions would be confirmed. Mrs. Denyer found it difficult to assume the becoming air when she put civil questions to Mrs. Lessingham, for she was now assured that to Miss Doran was attributable the alarming state of things between Clifford and Madeline; Marsh would never have been so intractable but for this new element in the situation. Madeline herself on the other hand, was a model of magnanimity; in Clifford's very hearing, she spoke of Cecily with tender concern, and then walked past her recreant admirer with her fair head in a pose of conscious grace.

Even Mr. Musselwhite, at the close of the second day, grew aware that the table lacked one of its ornaments. It was his habit now—a new habit came as a blessing of Providence to Mr. Musselwhite—on passing into the drawing-room after dinner, to glance towards a certain corner, and, after slow, undecided "tackings," to settle in that direction. There sat Barbara Denyer. Her study at present was one of the less-known works of Silvio Pellico, and as Mr. Musselwhite approached, she looked up with an air of absorption. He was wont to begin conversation with the remark, flatteringly toned, " Reading Italian as usual,

Miss Denyer?" but this evening a new subject had been suggested to him.

"I hope Miss Doran is not seriously unwell, Miss Denyer?"

"Oh, I think not."

Mr. Musselwhite reflected, stroking his whiskers in a gentlemanly way.

"One misses her," was his next remark.

"Yes, so much. She is so charming—don't you think, Mr. Musselwhite?"

"Very." He now plucked at the whiskers uneasily. "Oh yes, very."

Barbara smiled and turned her attention to the book, as though she could spare no more time. Mr. Musselwhite, dimly feeling that this topic demanded no further treatment, racked his brains for something else to say. He was far towards Lincolnshire when a rustle of the pages under Barbara's finger gave him a happy inspiration.

"I don't know whether you would care to see English papers now and then, Miss Denyer? I always have quite a number. The *Field*, for instance, and——"

"You are very kind, I don't read much English, but I shall be glad to see anything you like to bring me."

Mrs. Denyer was not wholly without consolation in her troubles about Clifford Marsh.

On the following morning, as she and her daughters were going out, they came face to face with a gentleman who was announcing to the servant his wish to see Miss Doran. Naturally they all glanced at him. Would he be admitted? With much presence of mind, Madeline exclaimed,—

"Oh dear, mamma! I have forgotten that letter. Please wait for me; I won't be a minute."

And she disappeared, the others moving out on to the staircase. When Madeline rejoined them, it was with the intelligence that the visitor *had* been admitted.

"Who can he be?"

"Rather a strange-looking person."

"Miss Doran cannot be ill. She has no brother. What an odd thing!"

They walked on, close serried, murmuring to each other discreetly. . . .

For several minutes there had been perfect stillness in the room, a hush after the music of low, impassioned voices. It was broken, yet scarcely broken, by the sound of lips touching lips—touching to part sweetly, touching again to part more slowly, more sweetly still.

"They will not influence you against me?"

"Never! never!"

"They will try, Cecily. You will hear endless things to my disadvantage—things that I cannot contradict if you ask me."

"I care for nothing, Reuben. I am yours for ever and ever, hear what I may, happen what may!"

"Don't call me by my hateful name, dearest. We will find some other, if I must have a name for you."

"Why, that is like Romeo!"

"So it is; I wish I had no worse than Romeo's reason. I had rather have had the vulgarest Anglo-Saxon name than this Jewish one. Happily, I need have no fear in telling you that; *you* are no Puritan."

"As little as a girl could be." She laughed in her happiness. "Have you the same dislike for your sister's name?"

"Just the same. I believe it partly explains her life."

"She will not be against us, though?"

"Neither for nor against, I am afraid. Yet I have to thank her for the meeting with you at Pompeii. Why haven't you asked me how I came there?"

"I never thought to ask. It seemed so natural. I longed for you, and you stood before me. I could almost believe that my longing had power to bring you, so strong it was. But tell me."

He did so, and again they lost themselves in rapturous dreamland.

"Do you think Mr. Mallard will wish to see me?" she asked timidly.

"I can't be sure. I half think not."

"Yet I half wish he would. I should find it strange and a little difficult, but he couldn't be harsh with me. I think it might do good if he came to see me—in a day or two."

"On what terms have you always been with him? How does he behave to you?"

"Oh, you know him. He still looks upon me rather too much as a child, and he seems to have a pleasure in saying odd, half-rude things; but we are excellent friends—or have been. Such a delightful day as we had at Baiæ! I have always liked him."

"At Baiæ? You didn't go alone with him?"

"No; Miriam was there and Mr. Spence. We found him dreaming at Pozzuoli, and carried him off in the boat with us."

"He never thought much of me, and now he hates me."

"No; that is impossible."

"If you had heard him speaking to me last night, you would think differently. He makes it a crime that I should love you."

"I don't understand it."

"What's more, he has feared this ever since I came; I feel sure of it. When I was coming back from Pompeii, he took me with him to Amalfi all but by force. He dreaded my returning and seeing you."

"But why should he think of such a thing?'

"Why?"

Elgar led her a few paces, until they stood before a mirror.

"Don't look at me. The other face, which is a little paler than it should be."

She hid it against him.

"But you don't love me for my face only? You will see others who have more beauty."

"Perhaps so. Mallard hopes so, in the long time we shall have to wait."

She fixed startled eyes on him.

"He cannot wish me so ill—he cannot! That would be unlike him."

"He wishes *you* no ill, be sure of it."

"Oh, you haven't spoken to him as you should! You haven't made him understand you. Let me speak to him for you."

"Cecily."

"Dearest?"

"Suppose he doesn't wish to understand me. Have you never thought, when he has pretended to treat you as a child, that there might be some reason for it? Did it never occur to you that, if he spoke too roughly, it might be because he was afraid of being too gentle?"

"Never! That thought has never approached my mind. You don't speak in earnest?"

Why could he not command his tongue? Why have suggested this to her imagination? He did not wholly mean to say it, even to the last moment; but unwisdom, as so often, overcame him. It was a way of defending himself; he wished to imply that Mallard had a powerful reason for assailing his character. He had been convinced since last night that Mallard was embittered by jealousy, and he half credited the fear lest jealousy might urge to the use of any weapons against him; he was tempted by the satisfaction of putting Cecily on her guard against interested motives. But he should not have troubled her soul with such suspicions. He read on her face how she was pained, and her next words proved his folly.

" If you are right, I can never speak to him as I might have done. It alters everything; it makes everything harder. You are mistaken."

" I may be. Let us hope I am."

" How I wish I had never seen that possibility! I cannot believe it; yet it will prevent me from looking honestly in his face, as I always have done."

" Forget it. Let us speak only of ourselves."

But she was troubled, and Elgar, angry with himself, spoke impatiently.

" In pity for him, you would love me less. I see that."

" You are not yet satisfied? You find new ways of forcing me to say that I love you. Seem to distrust me, that I may say it over and over; make me believe you really doubt if I can be constant, just that I may hear what my heart says in its distress, and repeat it all to you. Be a little unkind to me, that I may show how your unkindness would wound me, and may entreat you back into your own true self. You can do nothing, say nothing, but I will make it afford new proofs of how I love you."

" I had rather you made yourself less dear to me. The time will be so long. How can I live through it?"

" Will it not help you a little to help me? To know that you are unhappy would make it so much longer to me, my love."

" It will be hell to live away from you! I cannot make myself another man. If you knew what I have suffered only in these two days!"

" There was uncertainty."

" Uncertainty? Then what certainty could I ever have? Every hour spent at a distance from you will be full of hideous misgivings. Remember that every one will be doing the utmost to part us."

" Let them do the utmost twice over! You must have faith in me. Look into my eyes. Is there no assurance, no strength for you? Do they look too happy? That is

because you are still here; time enough for sadness when
you are gone. Oh, you think too humbly of yourself!
Having loved you, and known your love, what else can the
world offer me to live for?"

"Wherever you are, I must come often."

"Indeed you must, or for me too the burden will be
heavier than I can bear."

As the Denyers were coming home, it surprised them to
pass, at a little distance from the house, Clifford Marsh in
conversation with the gentleman who had called upon Miss
Doran. Madeline, exercising her new privilege of perfect
sang-froid, took an opportunity not long after to speak to
Clifford in the drawing-room.

"Who was the gentleman we saw you with?"

"I met him at Pompeii, but didn't know his name till to-
day. He's asked me to dine with him."

"He is a friend of Miss Doran's, I believe?"

"I believe so."

"You accepted his invitation?"

"Yes; I am always willing to make a new acquaintance."

"A liberal frame of mind. Did he give you news of Miss
Doran's health?"

"No."

He smiled mysteriously, only to appear at his ease; and
Madeline, smiling also, turned away.

Cecily reappeared this evening at the dinner-table. She
was changed; Mrs. Gluck and her guests were not again to
behold the vision to which their eyes had become accustomed; that supremacy of simple charm which some of
them had recognized as English girlhood at its best, had
given place to something less intelligible, less instant in its
attractiveness. Perhaps the climate of Naples was proving
not well suited to her.

After dinner, she and Mrs. Lessingham at once went to

their private room. Cecily sat down to write a letter. When she moved, as if the letter were finished, her aunt looked up from a newspaper.

"I've been thinking, Cecily. Suppose we go over to Capri for a change?"

"I am quite willing, aunt."

"I think Mr. Elgar has not been there yet. He might accompany us."

Unprepared for this, Cecily murmured an assent.

"Do you know how much longer he thinks of staying in Italy?"

"We haven't spoken of it."

"Has he given up his literary projects?"

"I'm afraid we didn't speak of that either."

"Shall you be satisfied if he continues to live quite without occupation?"

"I don't for a moment think he purposes that."

"And yet it will certainly be the case as long as he remains here—or wherever else we happen to be living."

Mrs. Lessingham allowed her to ponder this for a few minutes. Then she resumed the train of thought.

"Have you had leisure yet to ask yourself, my dear, what use you will make of the great influence you have acquired over Mr. Elgar's mind?"

"That is not quite the form my thoughts would naturally take, aunt," Cecily replied, with gentleness.

"Yet may it not be the form they should? You are accustomed to think for yourself to a greater extent than girls whose education has been more ordinary; you cannot take it ill if I remind you now of certain remarks I have made on Mr. Elgar lately, and remind you also that I am not alone in my view of him. Don't fear that I shall say anything unkind; but if you feel equal to a woman's responsibilities, you must surely exercise a woman's good sense. Let us say nothing more than that Mr. Elgar has fallen into habits of excessive indolence;

doesn't it seem to you that you might help him out of hem?"

"I think he may not need help as you understand it, now."

"My dear, he needs it perhaps five hundred times more than he did before. If you decline to believe me, I shall be only too much justified by your experience hereafter."

"What would you have me do?"

"What must very soon occur to your own excellent wits, Cecily—for I won't give up all my pride in you. Mr. Elgar should, of course, go back to England, and do something that becomes him; he must decide what. Let him have a few days with us in Capri; then go, and so far recommend himself in our eyes. No one can make him see that this is what his dignity—if nothing else—demands, except yourself. Think of it, dear."

Cecily did think of it, long and anxiously. Thanks to Elgar, her meditations had a dark background such as her own fancy would never have supplied. . . .

He knew not how sadly the image of him had been blurred in Cecily's mind, the man who lay that night in his room overlooking the port. Whether such ignorance were for his aid or his disadvantage, who shall venture to say?

To a certain point, we may follow with philosophic curiosity, step by step, the progress of mental anguish, but when that point is passed, analysis loses its interest; the vocabulary of pain has exhausted itself, the phenomena already noted do but repeat themselves with more rapidity, with more intensity—detail is lost in the mere sense of throes. Perchance the mind is capable of suffering worse than the fiercest pangs of hopeless love combined with jealousy; one would not pretend to put a limit to the possibilities of human woe; but for Mallard, at all events this night did the black flood of misery reach high-water mark.

What joy in the world that does not represent a counter-balance of sorrow? What blessedness poured upon one head but some other must therefore lie down under male-diction? We know that with the uttermost of happiness there is wont to come a sudden blending of troublous humour. May it not be that the soul has conceived a subtle sympathy with that hapless one but for whose sacrifice its own elation were impossible?

CHAPTER XIII.

ECHO AND PRELUDE.

AT Villa Sannazaro, the posture of affairs was already understood. When Eleanor Spence, casually calling at the *pension*, found that Cecily was unable to receive visitors, she at the same time learnt from Mrs. Lessingham to what this seclusion was due. The ladies had a singular little conversation, for Eleanor was inwardly so amused at this speedy practical comment on Mrs. Lessingham's utterances of the other day, that with difficulty she kept her countenance; while Mrs. Lessingham herself, impelled to make the admission without delay, that she might exhibit a philosophic acceptance of fact, had much ado to hide her chagrin beneath the show of half-cynical frankness that became a woman of the world. Eleanor—passably roguish within the limits of becoming mirth—acted the scene to her husband, who laughed shamelessly. Then came explanations between Eleanor and Miriam.

The following day passed without news, but on the morning after, Miriam had a letter from Cecily; not a long letter, nor very effusive, but telling all that was to be told. And it ended with a promise that Cecily would come to the villa that afternoon. This was communicated to Eleanor.

"Where's Mallard, I wonder?" said Spence, when his wife came to talk to him. "Not, I suspect, at the old quarters. It would be like him to go off somewhere without a word. Confound that fellow Elgar!"

"I'm half disposed to think that it serves Mr. Mallard right," was Eleanor's remark.

"Well, for heartlessness commend me to a comfortable woman."

"And for folly commend me to a strong-minded man."

"Pooh! He'll growl and mutter a little, and then get on with his painting."

"If I thought so, my liking for him would diminish. I hope he is tearing his hair."

"I shall go seek him."

"Do; and give my best love to him, poor fellow."

Cecily came alone. She was closeted with Miriam for a long time, then saw Eleanor. Spence purposely kept away from home.

Dante lay unread, as well as the other books which Eleanor placed insidiously in her cousin's room. Letters lay unanswered—among them several relating to the proposed new chapel at Bartles. How did Miriam employ herself during the hours that she spent alone?

Not seldom, in looking back upon her childhood and maidenhood.

Imagine a very ugly cubical brick house of two stories, in a suburb of Manchester. It stands a few yards back from the road. On one side, it is parted by a row of poplars from several mean cottages; on the other, by a narrow field from a house somewhat larger and possibly a little uglier than itself. Its outlook, over the highway, is on to a tract of country just being broken up by builders, beyond which a conglomerate of factories, with chimneys ever belching heavy fumes, closes the view; its rear windows regard a scrubby meadow, grazed generally by broken-down horses, with again a limitary prospect of vast mills.

Imagine a Sunday in this house. Half an hour later than on profane days, Mrs. Elgar descends the stairs. She is a lady of middle age, slight, not ungraceful, handsome; the look of pain about her forehead is partly habitual, but the consciousness of Sunday intensifies it. She moves without a sound. Entering the breakfast-room, she finds there two children, a girl and a boy, both attired in new-seeming garments which are obviously stiff and uncomfortable. The little girl sits on an uneasy chair, her white-stockinged legs dangling, on her lap a large copy of "Pilgrim's Progress;" the boy is half reclined on a shiny sofa, his hands in his pockets, on his face an expression of discontent. The table is very white, very cold, very uninviting.

Ten minutes later appears the master of the house, shaven, also in garments that appear new and uncomfortable, glancing hither and thither with preoccupied eyes. There is some talk in a low voice between the little girl and her mother; then the family seat themselves at table silently. Mr. Elgar turns a displeased look on the boy, and says something in a harsh voice which causes the youngster to straighten himself, curl his lip precociously, and thereafter preserve a countenance of rebellion subdued by fear. His father eats very little, speaks scarcely at all, but thinks, thinks—and most assuredly not of sacred subjects.

Breakfast over, there follows an hour of indescribable dreariness, until the neighbourhood begins to sound with the clanging of religious bells. Mr. Elgar has withdrawn to a little room of his own, where perhaps, he gives himself up to meditation on the duties of a Christian parent, though his incredulous son has ere now had a glimpse at the door, and observed him in the attitude of letter-writing. Mrs. Elgar moves about silently, the pain on her brow deepening as chapel-time approaches. At length the boy and girl go upstairs to be "got ready," which means that they indue

other garments yet more uncomfortable than those they
already wear. This process over, they descend again to the
breakfast-room, and again sit there, waiting for the dread
moment of departure. The boy is more rebellious than
usual; he presently drums with his feet, and even begins to
whistle, very low, a popular air. His sister looks at him,
first with astonished reproach, then in dread.

Satis superque. Again and again Miriam revived these
images of the past. And the more she thought of herself
as a child, the less was she pleased with what her memory
presented. How many instances came back to her of
hypocrisy before her father or mother, hypocrisy which,
strangely enough, she at the time believed a merit, though
perfectly aware of her own insincerity! How many a time
had she suffered from the restraints imposed upon her, and
then secretly allowed herself indulgences, and then again
persuaded herself that by severe attention to formalities she
blotted out her sin!

But the worst was when Cecily Doran came to live in the
house. Cecily was careless in religion, had been subjected
to no proper severity, had not been taught to probe her conscience. At once Miriam assumed an attitude of spiritual
pride—the beginning of an evil which was to strengthen its
hold upon her through years. She would be an example to
the poor little heathen; she talked with her unctuously; she
excited herself, began to find a pleasure in asceticism, and
drew the susceptible girl into the same way. They would
privately appoint periods of fasting, and at several succes-
sive meals irritate their hunger by taking only one or two
morsels; when faintness came upon them, they gloried in
the misery.

And from that stage of youth survived memories far more
painful than those of childhood. Miriam shut her mind
against them.

Her marriage came about in the simplest way; nothing
easier to understand, granted these circumstances. The

friends of the family were few, and all people of the same religious sect, of the same commercial sphere. Miriam had never spoken with a young man whom she did not in her heart despise; the one or two who might possibly have been tempted to think of her as a desirable wife were repelled by her austerity. She had now a character to support; she had made herself known for severe devotion to the things of the spirit. In her poor little world she could not submit to be less than pre-eminent, and only by the way of religion was pre-eminence to be assured. When the wealthy and pious manufacturer sought her hand, she doubted for a while, but was in the end induced to consent by the reflection that not only would she be freer, but at the same time enjoy a greatly extended credit and influence. Her pride silenced every other voice.

Religious hypocrisy is in our day a very rare thing; so little is to be gained by it. To be sure, the vast majority of English people are constantly guilty of hypocritical practices, but that, as a rule, is mere testimony to the rootedness of their orthodox faith. Mr. Elgar, shutting himself up between breakfast and chapel to write business letters— which he pre- or post-dated—was ignoble enough, but not therefore a hypocrite. Had a fatal accident happened to one of his family whilst he was thus employed, he would not have succeeded in persuading his conscience that the sin and the calamity were unconnected. His wife had never admitted a doubt of its being required by the immutable law of God that she should be sad and severe on Sunday, that Reuben should be sternly punished for whistling on that day, that little Miriam should be rewarded when she went through the long services with unnatural stillness and demureness. Nor was Miriam herself a hypocrite when, mistress of Redbeck House, she began to establish her reputation and authority throughout dissenting Bartles.

Her instruction had been rigidly sectarian. Whatever she studied was represented to her from the point of view of its relation to Christianity as her teachers understood it. The Christian faith was alone of absolute significance; all else that the mind of man could contain was of more or less importance as more or less connected with that single interest. To the time of her marriage, her outlook upon the world was incredibly restricted. She had never read a book that would not pass her mother's censorship; she had never seen a work of art; she had never heard any but " sacred " music; she had never perused a journal; she had never been to an entertainment—unless the name could be given to a magic-lantern exhibition of views in Palestine, or the like. Those with whom she associated had gone through a similar training, and knew as little of life.

She had heard of " infidelity ; " yes. Live as long as she might, she would never forget one dreadful day when, in a quarrel with his mother, Reuben uttered words which signified hatred and rejection of all he had been taught to hold divine ; Mrs. Elgar's pallid, speechless horror ; the severe chastisement inflicted on the lad by his father ;—she could never look back on it all without sickness of heart. Thenceforth, her brother and his wild ways embodied for her that awful thing, infidelity. At the age which Cecily Doran had now attained, Miriam believed that there were only a few men living so unspeakably wicked as to repudiate Christianity ; one or two of these, she had learnt from the pulpit, were " men of science," a term which to this day fell on her ears with sinister sound.

Thus prepared for the duties of wife, mother, and leader in society, she shone forth upon Bartles. Her husband, essentially a coarse man, did his utmost, though unconsciously, to stimulate her pride and supply her with incentives to unworthy ambition. He was rich, and boasted of it vulgarly ; he was ignorant, and vaunted the fact, thanking Heaven that for him the purity of religious conviction had never been endangered by the learning that leads astray ; he was proud of possessing a young and handsome wife, and for the first time evoked in her a personal vanity. Day by day was it—most needlessly—impressed upon Miriam that she must regard herself as the chief lady in Bartles, and omit no duty appertaining to such a position. She had an example to set; she was chosen as a support of religion.

Most happily, the man died. Had he remained her consort for ten years, the story of Miriam's life would have been one of those that will scarcely bear dwelling upon, too repulsive, too heart-breaking; a few words of bitterness, of ruth, and there were an end of it. His death was like the removal of a foul burden that polluted her and gradually dragged her down. Nor was it long before she herself understood it in this way, though dimly and uncertainly. She found herself looking on things with eyes which somehow had a changed power of vision. With remarkable abruptness, certain of her habits fell from her, and she remembered them only with distaste, even with disgust. And one day she said to herself passionately that never would she wed again—never, never! She was experiencing for the first time in her life a form of liberty.

Not that her faith had received any shock. To her undeveloped mind every tenet in which she had been instructed was still valid. This is the point to note. Her creed was a habit of the intellect; she held it as she did the knowledge of the motions of the earth. She had never reflected upon it, for in everything she heard or read this intellectual basis was presupposed. With doctrinal differences her reasoning faculty was familiar, and with her to think of religion was to think of the points at issue between one church and another—always, moreover, with pre-judgment in favour of her own.

But the external results of her liberty began to be of importance. She came into frequent connection with her cousin Eleanor; she saw more than hitherto of the Bradshaws' family life; she had business transactions; she read newspapers; she progressed slowly towards some practical acquaintance with the world.

Miriam knew the very moment when the thought of making great sacrifices to build a new chapel for Bartles had first entered her mind. One of her girl friends had just married, and was come to live in the neighbourhood. The husband, Welland by name, was wealthier and of more social importance than Mr. Baske had been; it soon became evident that Mrs. Welland, who also aspired to prominence in religious life, would be a formidable rival to the lady of Redbeck House. On the occasion of some local meeting, Miriam felt this danger keenly; she went home in dark mood, and the outcome of her brooding was the resolve in question.

She had not inherited all her husband's possessions; indeed, there fell to her something less than half his personal estate. For a time, this had not concerned her; now she was beginning to think of it occasionally with discontent, followed by reproach of conscience. Like reproach did she suffer for the jealousy and envy excited in her by Mrs. Welland's arrival. A general uneasiness of mind was gradually induced, and the chapel-building project, with singular confusion of motives, represented to her at once a worldly ambition and a discipline for the soul. It was a long time before she spoke of it, and in the interval she suffered more and more from a vague mental unrest.

Letters were coming to her from Cecily. Less by what they contained than by what they omitted, she knew that Cecily was undergoing a great change. Miriam put at length certain definite questions, and the answers she received were unsatisfactory, alarming. The correspondence became a distinct source of trouble. Not merely on Cecily's account; she was led by it to think of the world beyond her horizon, and to conceive dissatisfactions such as had never taken form to her.

Her physical health began to fall off; she had seasons of

depression, during which there settled upon her superstitious fears. Ascetic impulses returned, and by yielding to them she established a new cause of bodily weakness. And the more she suffered, the more intolerable to her grew the thought of resigning her local importance. Her pride, whenever irritated, showed itself in ways which exposed her to the ridicule of envious acquaintances. At length Bartles was surprised with an announcement of what had so long been in her mind; a newspaper paragraph made known, as if with authority, the great and noble work Mrs. Baske was about to undertake. For a day or two Miriam enjoyed the excitement this produced—the inquiries, the felicitations, the reports of gossip. She held her head more firmly than ever; she seemed of a sudden to be quite re-established in health.

Another day or two, and she was lying seriously ill—so ill that her doctor summoned aid from Manchester.

What a distance between those memories, even the latest of them, and this room in Villa Sannazaro! Its foreign aspect, its brightness, its comfort, the view from the windows, had from the first worked upon her with subtle influences of which she was unconscious. By reason of her inexperience of life, it was impossible for Miriam to analyze her own being, and note intelligently the modifications it underwent. Introspection meant to her nothing but debates held with conscience—a technical conscience, made of religious precepts. Original reflection, independent of these precepts, was to her very simply a form of sin, a species of temptation for which she had been taught to prepare herself. With anxiety, she found herself slipping away from that firm ground whence she was won't to judge all within and about her; more and more difficult was it to keep in view that sole criterion in estimating the novel impressions she received. To review the criterion itself was still beyond her power. She suffered from the conviction that trials foreseen were proving too strong for her. Whenever her youth yielded to the allurement of natural joys, there followed misery of penitence. Not that Miriam did in truth deem it a sin to enjoy the sunshine and the breath of the sea and the beauty of mountains (though such delights might become excessive, like any other, and so veil temptation), but she felt that for one in her position of peril there could not be too strict a watch kept upon the pleasures that were admitted. Hence she could never forget herself in pleasure; her attitude must always be that of one on guard.

The name of Italy signified perilous enticement, and she was beginning to feel it. The people amid whom she lived were all but avowed scorners of her belief, and yet she was beginning to like their society. Every letter she wrote to Bartles seemed to her despatched on a longer journey than the one before; her paramount interests were fading, fading; she could not exert herself to think of a thousand matters which used to have the power to keep her active all day long. The chapel-plans were hidden away; she durst not go to the place where they would have met her eye.

She suffered in her pride. On landing at Naples, she had imagined that her position among the Spences and their friends would not be greatly different from that she had held at Bartles. They were not " religious " people ; all the more must they respect her, feeling rebuked in her presence. The chapel project would enhance her importance. How far otherwise had it proved! They pitied her, compassionated her lack of knowledge, of opportunities. With the perception of this, there came upon her another disillusion In classing the Spences with people who were not " religious," she had understood them as lax in the observance of duties which at all events they recognized as such. By degrees she learnt that they were very far from holding the same views as herself concerning religious obligation ; they were anything but conscience-smitten in the face of her example. Was it, then, possible that persons who lived in a seemly manner could be sceptics, perhaps "infidels"? What of Cecily Doran? She had not dared to ask Cecily face to face how far her disbelief went; the girl seemed to have no creed but that of worldly delight. How had she killed her conscience in so short a time? Obviously, her views were those of Mrs. Lessingham; probably those of Mr. Mallard. Were these people strange and dreadful exceptions, or did they represent a whole world of which she had not suspected the existence?

Yes, she was beginning to feel the allurement of Italy. Instead of sitting turned away from her windows when musing, she often passed an hour with her eyes on the picture they framed, content to be idle, satisfied with form and colour, not thinking at all. Habits of personal idleness crept upon her; she seldom cared to walk, but found pleasure in the motion of a carriage, and lay back on the cushions, instead of sitting quite upright as at first. She began to wish for music; the sound of Eleanor's piano would tempt her to make an excuse for going into the room, and then she would remain, listening. The abundant fruits of the season became a temptation to her palate; she liked to see shops and stalls overflowing with the vineyard's delicious growth.

She knew for the first time the seduction of books. From what unutterable weariness had she been saved when she assented to Eleanor's proposal and began to learn Italian! First there was the fear lest she should prove slow at acquiring, suffer yet another fall from her dignity; but this apprehension was soon removed. She had a brain, and could use it; Eleanor's praise fell upon her ears delightfully. Then there was that little volume of English verse which Eleanor left on the table; its name, "The Golden Treasury," made her imagine it of a religious tone; she was undeceived in glancing through it. Poetry had hitherto made no appeal to her; she did not care much for the little book. But one day Cecily caught it up in delight, and read to her for half an hour; she affected indifference, but had in reality learnt something, and thereafter read for herself.

The two large mirrors in her room had, oddly enough, no unimportant part among the agencies working for her development. It was almost inevitable that, in moving about, she should frequently regard her own figure. From being something of an annoyance, this necessity at length won attractiveness, till she gazed at herself far oftener than she need have done. As for her face she believed it passable, perhaps rather more than that; but the attire that had possessed distinction at Bartles looked very plain, to say the least, in the light of her new experience. One day she saw herself standing side by side with Cecily, and her eyes quickly turned away.

To what was she sinking!

But Dante lay unopened, together with the English books. Miriam had spent a day or two of alternate languor and irritableness, unable to attend to anything serious. Just now she had in her hand Cecily's letter, the letter which told of what had happened. There was no reason for referring to it again; this afternoon Cecily herself had been here. But Miriam read over the pages, and dwelt upon them.

At dinner, no remark was made on the subject that occupied the minds of all three. Afterwards they sat together, as usual, and Eleanor played. In one of the silences, Miriam turned to Spence and asked him if he had seen Mr. Mallard.

"Yes; I found him after a good deal of going about," replied the other, glad to have done with artificial disregard of the subject.

"Does he know that they are going to Capri?"

"He evidently hadn't heard of it. I suppose he'll have a note from Mrs. Lessingham this evening or to-morrow."

Miriam waited a little, then asked:

"What is his own wish? What does he think ought to be arranged?"

"Just what Cecily told you," interposed Eleanor, before her husband could reply.

"I thought he might have spoken more freely to Edward."

"Well," answered Spence, "he is strongly of opinion that Reuben ought to go to England very soon. But I suppose Cecily told you that as well?"

"She seemed to be willing. But why doesn't Mr. Mallard speak to her himself?"

"Mallard isn't exactly the man for this delicate business," said Spence, smiling.

Miriam glanced from him to Eleanor. She would have said no more, had it been in her power to keep silence; but an involuntary persistence, the same in kind as that often manifested by questioning children—an impulsive feeling that the next query must elicit something which would satisfy a vague desire, obliged her to speak again.

"Is it his intention not to see Cecily at all?"

"I think very likely it is, Miriam," answered Eleanor, when her husband showed that he left her to do so.

"I understand."

To which remark Eleanor, when Miriam was gone, attached the interrogative, "I wonder whether she does?" The Spences did not feel it incumbent upon them to direct her in the matter; it were just as well if she followed a mistaken clue.

Two days later, Mrs. Lessingham and her niece, accompanied by Reuben Elgar, departed for Capri. The day after that, Mr. and Mrs. Bradshaw in very deed said good-bye to Naples and travelled northwards. They purposed spending Christmas in Rome, and thence by quicker stages they would return to the land of civilization. Spence went to the station to see them off, and at lunch, after speaking of this and other things, he said to Miriam:

"Mallard wishes to see you. I told him I thought five o'clock this afternoon would be a convenient time."

Miriam assented, but not without betraying surprise and

uneasiness. Subsequently she just mentioned to Eleanor that she would receive the visitor in her own sitting-room. There, as five o'clock drew near, she waited in painful agitation. What it was Mallard's purpose to say to her she could not with any degree of certainty conjecture. Had Reuben told him of the part she had played in connection with that eventful day at Pompeii? What would be his tone? Did he come to ask for particulars concerning her brother? Intend what he might, she dreaded the interview. And yet—fact of which she made no secret to herself—she had rather he came than not. When it was a few minutes past five, and no foot had yet sounded in the corridor, all other feeling was lost in the misgiving that he might have changed his mind. Perhaps he had decided to write instead, and her heart sank at the thought. She felt an overpowering curiosity as to the way in which this event had affected the strange man. Reports were no satisfaction to her; she desired to see him and hear him speak.

The footsteps at last! She trembled, went hot and cold, had a parched throat. Mallard entered, and she did not offer him her hand; perhaps he might reject it. In consequence there was an absurdly formal bow on both sides.

"Please sit down, Mr. Mallard."

She saw that he was looking at the "St. Cecilia," but with what countenance her eyes could not determine. To her astonishment, he spoke of the picture, and in an unembarrassed tone.

"An odd thing that this should be in your room."

"Yes. We spoke of it the first time Cecily came."

Her accents were not firm. At once he fixed his gaze on her, and did not remove it until her temples throbbed and she cast down her eyes in helpless abashment.

"I have had a long letter from your brother, Mrs. Baske. It seems he posted it just before they left for Capri. I can only reply to it in one way, and it gives me so much pain to do so that I am driven to ask your help. He writes begging

me to take another view of this matter, and permit them to
be married before very long. The letter is powerfully
written; few men could plead their cause with such eloquence and force. But it cannot alter my determination.
I must reply briefly and brutally. What I wish to ask you
is, whether with sincerity you can urge my arguments upon
your brother, and give me this assistance in the most obvious
duty?"

"I have no influence with him, Mr. Mallard."

Again he looked at her persistently, and said with deliberation:

"I think you must have some. And this is one of the
cases in which a number of voices may possibly prevail,
though one or two are ineffectual. But—if you will forgive
me my direct words—your voice is, of course, useless if you
cannot speak in earnest."

She was able now to return his look, for her pride was
being aroused. The face she examined bore such plain
marks of suffering that with difficulty she removed her eyes
from it. Nor could she make reply to him, so intensely
were her thoughts occupied with what she saw.

"Perhaps," he said, "you had rather not undertake anything at once." Then, his voice changing slightly, "I have
no wish to seem a suppliant, Mrs. Baske. My reasons for
saying that this marriage shall not, if I can prevent it, take
place till Miss Doran is of age, are surely simple and con-
vincing enough; I can't suppose that it is necessary to insist
upon them to you. But I feel I had no right to leave any
means unused. By speaking to you, I might cause you to
act more earnestly than you otherwise would. That was
all."

"I am very willing to help you," she replied, with carefully courteous voice.

"After all, I had rather we didn't put it in that way,"
Mallard resumed, with a curious doggedness, as if her tone
were distasteful to him. "My own part in the business is

accidental. Please tell me : is it, or not, your own belief that a delay is desirable ? ''

The reply was forced from her.

" I certainly think it is."

" May I ask you if you have reasoned with your brother about it ? "

" I haven't had any communication with him since—since we knew of this." She paused ; but, before Mallard had shown an intention to speak, added abruptly, " I should have thought that Miss Doran might have been trusted to understand and respect your wishes."

" Miss Doran knows my wishes," he answered drily, " but I haven't insisted upon them to her, and am not disposed to do so."

" Would it not be very simple and natural if you did ? "

The look he gave her was stern all but to anger.

" It wouldn't be a very pleasant task to me, Mrs. Baske, to lay before her my strongest arguments against her marrying Mr. Elgar. And if I don't do that, it seems to me that it is better to let her know my wishes through Mrs. Lessingham. As you say, it is to be hoped she will understand and respect them."

He rose from his chair. For some reason, Miriam could not utter the words that one part of her prompted. She wished to assure him that she would do her best with Reuben, but at the same time she resented his mode of addressing her, and the conflict made her tongue-tied.

" I won't occupy more of your time, Mrs. Baske."

She would have begged him to resume his seat. The conversation had been so short ; she wanted to hear him speak more freely. But her request, she knew, would be disregarded. With an effort, she succeeded in holding out her hand ; Mallard held it lightly for an instant.

" I will write to him," fell from her lips, when already he had turned to the door. " If necessary, I will go and see him."

" Thank you," he replied with civility, and left her.

CHAPTER XIV.

ON THE WINGS OF THE MORNING.

" I CANNOT answer your long letter; to such correspondence there is no end. Come and spend a day here with us;
I promise to listen patiently, and you shall hear how things
are beginning to shape themselves in my mind, now I have
had leisure to reflect. Cecily sends a line. Do come. Take
the early boat on Monday; Spence will give you all particulars, and see you off at Santa Lucia. We really have
some very sober plans, not unapproved by Mrs. Lessingham.
Will meet you at the Marina."

Miriam received this on Sunday morning, and went to her
own room to read it. The few lines of Cecily's writing which
were enclosed, she glanced over with careless eye; yet not
with mere carelessness either, but as if something of
aversion disinclined her to peruse them attentively. That
sheet she at once laid aside; Reuben's note she still held in
her hand, and kept re-reading it.

She went to the window and looked over towards Capri.
A slight mist softened its outlines this morning; it seemed
very far away, on the dim borders of sea and sky. For a
long time she had felt the luring charm of that island,
always before her eyes, yet never more than a blue
mountainous shape. Lately she had been reading of it, and
her fancy, new to such picturings, was possessed by the mysterious dread of its history in old time, the grandeur of its
cliffs, the loveliness of its green hollows, and the wonder of
its sea-caves. Her childhood had known nothing of fairy-
land, and now, in this tardy awakening of the imaginative
part of her nature, she thought sometimes of Capri much as

a child is wont to think of the enchanted countries, nameless, regionless, in books of fable.

What thoughts for Sunday! But Miriam was far on the way of those who recognize themselves as overmastered by temptation, and grow almost reckless in the sins they cannot resist. So long it was since she had been able to attend the accustomed public worship, and now its substitute in the privacy of her room had become irksome. She blushed to be practising hypocrisy; the Spences were careful to refrain from interfering with her to-day, and here, withdrawn from their sight, she passed the hours in wearisome idleness—in worse than that.

She could not look again at Cecily's letter. More; she could not let her eyes turn to Raphael's picture. But before the mirrors she paused often and long, losing herself in self-regard.

Early on the morrow, she drove down with Spence to Santa Lucia, and went on board the Capri boat. There were few passengers, a handful of Germans and an English family—father, mother, two daughters, and two sons. Sitting apart, Miriam cast many glances at her country-people, and not without envy. They were comely folk, in the best English health, refined in bearing, full of enjoyment. Now and then a few words of their talk fell upon her ears, and it was merry, kindly, intimate talk, the fruit of a lifetime of domestic happiness. It made her think again of what her own home-life had been. Such companionship of parents and children was inconceivable in her experience. The girls observed her, and, she believed, spoke of her. Must she not look strange in their eyes? Probably they felt sorry for her, as an invalid whose countenance was darkened by recent pain.

The boat made first of all for Sorrento, where a few more persons came on board. Miriam was by this time enjoying the view of the coast. From this point she kept her gaze fixed on Capri. One more delay on the voyage; the steamer stopped near the Blue Grotto, that such of the passengers as wished might visit it before landing. Miriam kept her place, and for the present was content to watch the little boats, as they rocked for a few moments at the foot of the huge cliff and then suddenly disappeared through the entrance to the cavern. When the English family returned, she listened to their eager, wondering conversation. A few minutes more, and she was landing at the Marina, where Reuben awaited her.

He had a carriage ready for the drive up the serpent road to the hotel where Mrs. Lessingham and her niece were staying. His own quarters were elsewhere—at the Pagano, dear to artists.

"Well, have you enjoyed the voyage? What did you think of Sorrento? We watched the steamer across from there; we were up on the road to Anacapri, yonder. You don't look so well as when I saw you last—nothing like."

He waited for no reply to his questions, and talked with nervous brokenness. Seated in the carriage, he could not keep still from one moment to the next. His eyes had the unquiet of long-continued agitation, the look that results from intense excitement when it has become the habit of day after day.

"Mallard has been talking to you," he said suddenly.

"Why do you say that?"

"I know he has, from your letter.—Look at the views!"

"What plans did you speak of?"

"Oh, we'll talk about it afterwards. But Mallard *has* been talking you over?"

Miriam had no resolve by which to guide herself. She knew not distinctly why she had come to Capri. Her familiar self-reliance and cold disregard of anything but a few plain rules in regulating her conduct, were things of the past. She felt herself idly swayed by conflicting influences, unable even to debate what course she should take; the one emotion of which she was clearly conscious was of so strange and disturbing a kind that, so far from impelling her to act, it seemed merely to destroy all her customary motives and leave her subject to the will of others. It was the return of weakness such as had possessed her mind when she lay ill, when she was ceaselessly troubled with a desire for she knew not what, and, unable to utter it, had no choice but to admit the suggestions and biddings of those who cared for her. She could not even resent this language of Reuben's, to which formerly she would have opposed her unyielding pride; his proximity infected her with nervousness, but at the same time made her flaccid before his energy.

"He came and spoke to me about you," she admitted. "But he left me to do as I saw fit."

"After putting the case against me as strongly as it could be put. I know; you needn't tell me anything about the conversation. Let us leave it till afterwards.—You see how this road winds, so that the incline may be gentle enough for carriages. There are stony little paths, just like the beds of mountain streams, going straight down to the Marina. I lost myself again and again yesterday among the gardens and vineyards. Look back over the bay to Naples!"

But in a minute or two the other subject was resumed, again with a suddenness that told of inability to keep from speaking his thoughts.

"You understand, I dare say, why Mallard is making such a fuss?"

"How could I help understanding?"

"But *do* you understand?"

"What do you mean?" she asked irritably.

"Does he speak like a man who is disinterested?"

"It is not my business to discuss Mr. Mallard's motives."

"It certainly is mine—and yours too, if you care anything for me."

They reached the hotel without further debate of this subject. It was not much after one o'clock; all lunched together in private, talking only of Capri. Later they walked to the villa of Tiberius. Elgar kept up an appearance of light-hearted enjoyment; Cecily was less able to disguise her preoccupation. Mrs. Lessingham seemed to have accepted the inevitable. Her first annoyance having passed, she was submitting to that personal charm in Elgar which all women sooner or later confessed; her behaviour to him was indulgent, and marked only with a very gentle reserve when he talked too much paradox.

Elgar went to his hotel for dinner, and left the others to themselves through the evening. The next day was given to wandering about the island. On the return at sunset, Miriam and Reuben had a long talk together, in which it was made manifest that the "plans" were just as vague as ever. Reuben had revived the mention of literary work, that was all, and proposed to make his head-quarters in Paris, in order that he might not be too far from Cecily, who would, it was presumed, remain on the Continent. This evening he dined with the ladies. Afterwards Cecily played. When Miriam and Mrs. Lessingham chanced to be conversing together, Elgar stepped up to the piano, and murmured:

"Will you come out into the garden for a few minutes? There's a full moon; it's magnificent."

Cecily let her fingers idle upon the keys, then rose and went to where her aunt was sitting. There was an exchange of words in a low tone, and she left the room. Elgar at once approached Mrs. Lessingham to take leave of her.

"The Grotta Azzurra to-morrow," he said gaily. "Perhaps you won't care to go again? My grave sister will make a very proper chaperon."

"Let us discuss that when to-morrow comes. Please to limit your moon-gazing to five minutes."

"At the utmost."

From the hotel garden opened a clear prospect towards Naples, which lay as a long track of lights beyond the expanse of deep blue. The coast was distinctly outlined; against the far sky glowed intermittently the fire of Vesuvius. Above the trees of the garden shone white crags, unsubstantial, unearthly in the divine moonlight. There was no sound, yet to intense listening the air became full of sea-music. It was the night of Homer, the island-charm of the Odyssey.

"Answer me quickly, Cecily; we have only a few minutes, and I want to say a great deal. You have talked with Miriam?"

"Yes."

"You know that she repeats what Mallard has instructed her to say? Their one object now is to get me at a distance from you. You see how your aunt has changed—in appearance; her policy is to make me think that she will be my friend when I am away. I can speak with certainty after observing her for so long; in reality she is as firm against me as ever. Don't you notice, too, something strange in Miriam's behaviour?"

"She is not like herself."

"As unlike as could be. Mallard has influenced her strongly. Who knows what he told her?"

"Of you?"

"Perhaps of himself."

"Dear, he could not speak to her in that way!"

"A man in love—and in love with Cecily Doran—can do anything. The Spences are his close friends; they too have been working on Miriam."

"But why, why do you return to this? We have spoken of the worst they can do. To fear anything from their persuasions is to distrust me."

"Cecily, I don't distrust you, but I can't live away from you. I might have gone straight from Naples, but I can't go now; every hour with you has helped to make it impossible. In talking to your aunt and to Miriam, I have been consciously false. Come further this way, into the shadow. Who is over there?"

"Some one we don't know."

Her voice had sunk to a whisper. Elgar led her by the hand into a further recess of the garden; the hand was almost crushed between his own as he continued:

"You must come with me, Cecily. We will go away together, and be married at once."

She panted rather than breathed.

"You must! I can't leave you! I had rather throw myself from these Capri rocks than go away with more than two years of solitude before me."

Cecily made no answer.

"If you think, you will see this is best in every way. It will be kindest to poor Mallard, putting an end at once to any hopes he may have."

"We can't be married without his consent," Cecily whispered.

"Oh yes; I can manage that. I have already thought of everything. Be up early to-morrow morning, and leave the hotel at half-past seven, as if you were going for a walk. Neither your aunt nor Miriam will be stirring by then. Go down the road as far as beyond the next turning, and I will be there with a carriage. At the Marina I will have a boat ready to take us over to Sorrento; we will drive to Castellamare, and there take train direct for Caserta and onwards, so missing Naples altogether. You shall travel as my sister. We will go to London, and be married there. Of course you can't bring luggage, but what does that matter? We can stop anywhere and buy what things you need. I have quite enough money for the present."

"But think of the shock to them all!" she pleaded, trembling through her frame. "How ill I should seem to repay their long kindness! I can't do this, my dearest; oh, I can't do this! I will see Mr. Mallard, as I wished——"

"You shall not see him!" he interrupted violently. "I couldn't bear it. How do I know——"

"How cruel to speak like that to me!"

"Of your own cruelty you never think. You have made me mad with love of you, and have no right to refuse to marry me when I show you the way. If I didn't love you so much, I could bear well enough to let you speak with any one. Your love is very different from mine, or you couldn't hesitate a moment."

"Let me think! I can't answer you to-night."

"To-night, or never!—Oh yes, I understand well enough all your reasons for hesitating. It would mean relinquishing the wedding-dress and the carriages and all the rest of the show that delights women. You are afraid of Mrs. Grundy crying shame when it is known that you have travelled across Europe with me. You feel it will be difficult to resume your friendships afterwards. I grant all these things, but I didn't think they would have meant so much to Cecily."

"You know well that none of these reasons have any weight with me. It is only in joking that you can speak of them. But the unkindness to them all, dear! Think of it!"

"Why say 'to them all'? Wouldn't it be simpler to say 'the unkindness to Mallard'?"

She looked up into his face.

"Why does love make a man speak so bitterly and untruthfully? Nothing could make me do *you* such a wrong."

"Because you are so pure of heart and mind that nothing but truth can be upon your lips. If I were not very near madness, I could never speak so to you. My own dear love, think only of what I suffer day after day! And what folly is it that would keep us apart! Suppose they had none but conscientious motives; in that case, these people take upon themselves to say what is good for us, what we may be allowed and what not; they treat us as children. Of course, it is all for *your* protection. I am not fit to be your husband, my beautiful girl! Tell me—who knows me better, Mallard or yourself?"

"No one knows you as I do, dearest, nor ever will."

"And do you think me too vile a creature to call you my wife?"

"I need not answer that. You are as much nobler than I am as your strength is greater than mine."

"But they would remind you that you are an heiress. I have not made so good a use of my own money as I might have done, and the likelihood is that I shall squander yours, bring you to beggary. Do you believe that?"

"I know it is not true."

"Then what else can they oppose to our wish? Here are all the objections, and all seem to be worthless. Yet there might be one more. You are very young—how I rejoice in knowing it, sweet flower!—perhaps your love of me is a mere illusion. It ought to be tested by time; very likely it may die away, and give place to something truer."

"If so let me die myself sooner than survive such happiness!"

"Why, then what have they to say for themselves? Their opposition is mistake, stubborn error. And are we to sacrifice two whole years, the best time of our lives, to such obstinacy? Either of us may die, Cecily. Suppose it to be my lot, what would be your thoughts then?"

His head bent to hers, and their faces touched.

"Dare you risk that, my love?"

"I dare not."

Her answer trembled upon his hearing as though it came upon the night air from the sea.

"You will come with me to-morrow?"

"I will."

He sought her offered lips, and for a few instants their

whispering in the shadow ceased. Then he repeated rapidly the directions he had already given her.

"Put on your warmest cloak; it will be cold on the water. Now I can say good-night. Kiss me once more, and once more promise."

She pressed her arms about him.

"I am giving you my life. If I had more, I would give it. Be faithful to me!"

"Then, you do doubt me?"

"Never! But say it to-night, to give me strength."

"I will be faithful to you whilst I have life."

She issued from shadows into broad moonlight, looked once round, once at the gleaming crags, and passed again into gloom.

"I think it very unlikely," Mrs. Lessingham was saying to Miriam, in her pleasantest voice of confidence, "that Mr. Mallard will insist on the whole term."

"No doubt that will much depend on the next year," Miriam replied, trying to seem impartial.

"No doubt whatever. I am glad we came here. They are both much quieter and more sensible. In a few days I think your brother will have made up his mind."

"I hope so."

"Cecily lost her head a little at first, but I see that her influence is now in the sober direction, as one would have anticipated. When Mr. Elgar has left us, no doubt Mr. Mallard will come over, and we shall have quiet talk, What an odd man he is! How distinctly I could have foreseen his action in these circumstances! And I know just how it will be, as soon as things have got into a regular course again. Mr. Mallard hates disturbance and agitation. Of course he has avoided seeing Cecily as yet; imagine his exasperated face if he became involved in a 'scene'!"

And Mrs. Lessingham laughed urbanely.

A short and troubled sleep at night's heaviest; then long waiting for the first glimmer of dawn. How unreal the world seemed to her! She tried to link this present morning with the former days, but her life had lost its continuity; the past was past in a sense she had never known; and as for the future, it was like gazing into darkness that throbbed and flashed. It meant nothing to her to say that this was Capri—that the blue waves and the wind of morning would presently bear her to Sorrento; the familiar had no longer a significance; her consciousness was but a point in space and eternity. She had no regret of her undertaking, no fear of what lay before her, but a profound sadness, as though the burden of all mortal sorrows were laid upon her soul.

At seven o'clock she was ready. A very few things that could be easily carried she would take with her; her cloak would hide them. Now she must wait for the appointed moment. It seemed to be very cold; she shivered.

A minute or two before the half-hour, she left her room silently. On the stairs a servant passed her, and looked surprised in giving the " Buon giorno." She walked quickly through the garden, and was on the firm road. At the place indicated stood Elgar beside the carriage, and without exchanging a word they took their seats.

At the Marina, they had but to step from the carriage to the boat. Elgar's luggage was thrown on board, and the men pushed off from the quay.

Bitterly cold, but what a glorious sunrise! Against the flushed sky, those limestone heights of Capri caught the golden radiance and shone wondrously. The green water, gently swelling but unbroken, was like some rarer element, too limpid for this world's shores. With laughter and merry talk between themselves, the boatmen hoisted their sail.

And the gods sent a fair breeze from the west, and it smote upon the sail, and the prow cleft its track of foam, and on they sped over the back of the barren sea.

CHAPTER XV.

" WOLF ! "

IT was a case of between two stools, and Clifford Marsh did not like the bump. From that dinner with Elgar he came home hilariously dismayed; when his hilarity had evaporated with the wine that was its cause, dismay possessed him wholly. Miss Doran was not for him, and in the meantime he had offended Madeline beyond forgiveness. With what countenance could he now turn to her again? Her mother would welcome his surrender—and it was drawing on towards the day when submission even to his stepfather could no longer be postponed—but he suspected that Madeline's resolve to have done with him was strengthened by resentment of her mother's importunities. To be sure, it was some sort of consolation to know that, if indeed he went his way for good, bitterness and regrets would be the result to the Denyer family, who had no great facility in making alliances of this kind; in a few years' time, Madeline would be wishing that she had not let her pride interfere with a chance of marriage. But, on the other hand, there was the awkward certainty that he too would lament making a fool of himself. He by no means liked the thought of relinquishing Madeline; he had not done so, even when heating his brain with contemplation of Cecily Doran. In what manner could he bring about between her and himself a drama which might result in tears and mutual pardon?

But whilst he pondered this, fate was at work on his behalf. On the day which saw the departure of the Bradshaws, there landed at Naples, from Alexandria, a certain

lean, wiry man, with shoulders that stooped slightly, with
grizzled head and parchment visage; a man who glanced
about him in a keen, anxious way, and had other nervous
habits. Having passed the custom-house, he hired a porter
to take his luggage—two leather bags and a heavy chest, all
much the worse for wear— to that same hotel at which
Mallard was just now staying. There he refreshed himself,
and, it being early in the afternoon, went forth again, as if
on business; for decidedly he was no tourist. When he had
occasion to speak, his Italian was fluent and to the point;
he conducted himself as one to whom travel and intercourse
with every variety of men were life-long habits.

His business conducted him to the Mergellina, to the
house of Mrs. Gluck, where he inquired for Mrs. Denyer.
He was led upstairs, and into the room where sat Mrs.
Denyer and her daughters. The sight of him caused com-
motion. Barbara, Madeline, and Zillah pressed around him,
with cries of "Papa!" Their mother rose and looked at
him with concern.

When the greetings were over, Mr. Denyer seated himself
and wiped his forehead with a silk handkerchief. He was
ominously grave. His eyes avoided the faces before him, as
if in shame. He looked at his boots, which had just been
blacked, but were shabby, and then glanced at the elegant
skirts of his wife and daughters; he looked at his shirt-
cuffs, which were clean but frayed, and then gathered
courage to lift his eyes as far as the dainty hands folded
upon laps in show of patience.

"Madeline," he began, in a voice which was naturally
harsh, but could express much tenderness, as now, "what
news of Clifford?"

"He's still here, papa," was the answer, in a very low
voice.

"I am glad of that. Girls, I've got something to tell you.
I wish it was something pleasant."

His parchment cheek showed a distinct flush. The

attempt to keep his eyes on the girls was a failure; he seemed to be about to confess a crime.

"I've brought you bad news, the worst I ever brought you yet. My dears, I can hold out no longer; I'm at the end of my means. If I could have kept this from you, Heaven knows I would have done, but it is better to tell you all plainly."

Mrs. Denyer's brows were knitted; her lips were compressed in angry obstinacy; she would not look up from the floor. The girls glanced at her, then at one another. Barbara tried to put on a sceptical expression, but failed; Madeline was sunk in trouble; Zillah showed signs of tearfulness.

"I can only hope," Mr. Denyer continued, "that you don't owe very much here. I thought, after my last letter"—he seemed more abashed than ever—"you might have looked round for something a little——" He glanced at the ornaments of the room, but at the same time chanced to catch his wife's eye, and did not finish the sentence. "But never mind that; time enough now that the necessity has come. You know me well enough, Barbara, and you Maddy, and you, Zillah, my child, to be sure that I wouldn't deny you anything it was in my power to give. But fortune's gone against me this long time. I shall have to make a new start, new efforts. I'm going out to Vera Cruz again."

He once more wiped his forehead, and took the opportunity to look askance at Mrs. Denyer, dubiously, half reproachfully.

"And what are we to do?" asked his wife, with resentful helplessness.

"I am afraid you must go to England," Mr. Denyer replied apologetically, turning his look to the girls again. "After settling here, and paying the expenses of the journey, I shall have a little left, very little indeed. But I'm going to Vera Cruz on a distinct engagement, and I shall soon be able to send you something. I'm afraid you had better go to Aunt Dora's again; I've heard from her lately, and she has the usual spare rooms."

The girls exchanged looks of dismay. The terrible silence was broken by Zillah, who spoke in quavering accents.

" Papa dear, I have made up my mind to get a place as a nursery governess. I shall very soon be able to do so."

"And I shall do the same, papa—or something of the kind," came abruptly from Madeline.

" You, Maddy ? " exclaimed her father, who had received the youngest girl's announcement with a look of sorrowful resignation, but was shocked at the other's words.

"I am no longer engaged to Mr. Marsh," Madeline proceeded, casting down her eyes. " Please don't say anything, mamma. I have made up my mind. I shall look for employment."

Her father shook his head in distress. He had never enjoyed the control or direction of his daughters, and his long absences during late years had put him almost on terms of ceremony with them. In time gone by, their mother had been to him an object of veneration; it was his privilege to toil that she might live in luxury; but his illusions regarding her had received painful shocks, and it was to the girls that he now sacrificed himself. Their intellect, their attainments, at once filled him with pride and made him humble in their presence. But for his reluctance to impose restraints upon their mode of life, he might have avoided this present catastrophe; he had cried " Wolf ! " indeed, in his mild way, but took no energetic measures when he found his cry disregarded—all the worse for him now that he could postpone the evil day no longer.

" You are the best judge of your own affairs, Madeline," he replied despondently. " I'm very sorry, my girl."

" All I can say is," exclaimed Mrs. Denyer, as if with dignified reticence, " that I think we should have had longer warning of this ! "

"My dear, I have warned you repeatedly for nearly a year."

"I mean *serious* warning. Who was to imagine that things would come to such a pass as this?"

"You never told us there was danger of absolute beggary, papa," remarked Barbara, in a tone not unlike her mother's.

"I ought to have spoken more plainly," was her father's meek answer. "You are quite right, Barbara. I feel that I am to blame."

"I don't think you are at all," said Madeline, with decision. "Your letters were plain enough, if we had chosen to pay any attention to them."

Her father looked up apprehensively, deprecating defence of himself at the cost of family discord. But he was powerless to prevent the gathering storm. Mrs. Denyer gazed sternly at her recalcitrant daughter, and at length discharged upon the girl's head all the wrath with which this situation inspired her. Barbara took her mother's side. Zillah wept and sobbed words of reconciliation. The unhappy cause of the tumult took refuge at the window, sunk in gloom.

However, there was no doubt about it this time; trunks must be packed, bills must be paid, indignities must be swallowed. The Aunt Dora of whom Mr. Denyer had spoken was his own sister, the wife of a hotel-keeper at Southampton. Some seven years ago, in a crisis of the Denyers' fate, she had hospitably housed them for several months, and was now willing to do as much again, notwithstanding the arrogance with which Mrs. Denyer had repaid her. To the girls it had formerly mattered little where they lived; at their present age, it was far otherwise. The hotel was of a very modest description; society would become out of the question in such a retreat. Madeline and Zillah might choose, as the less of two evils, the lot for which they declared themselves ready; but Barbara had no notion of turning governess. She shortly went to her bedroom, and spent a very black hour indeed.

They were to start to-morrow morning. With rage Barbara saw the interdiction of hopes which were just becoming serious. Another month of those after-dinner colloquies in the drawing-room, and who could say what point of intimacy Mr. Musselwhite might have reached. He was growing noticeably more articulate ; he was less absent-minded. Oh, for a month more !

This evening she took her usual place, and at length had the tormenting gratification of seeing Mr. Musselwhite approach in the usual way. Though sitting next to him at dinner, she had said nothing of what would happen on the morrow ; the present was a better opportunity.

"You have no book this evening, Miss Denyer ? "

"No."

"No headache, I hope ? "

"Yes, I have a little headache."

He looked at her with gentlemanly sympathy.

"I have had to see to a lot of things in a hurry. Unexpect-edly, we have to leave Naples to-morrow ; we are going to England."

"Indeed ? You don't say so ! Really, I'm very sorry to hear that, Miss Denyer."

"I am sorry too—to have to leave Italy for such a climate at this time of the year." She shuddered. "But my father has just arrived from Alexandria, and—for family reasons—wishes us to travel on with him."

Mr. Musselwhite seemed to reflect anxiously. He curled his moustaches, he plucked his whiskers, he looked about the room with wide eyes.

"How lonely it will be at the dinner-table ! " he said at length. "So many have gone of late. But I hoped there was no danger of your going, Miss Denyer."

"We had no idea of it ourselves till to-day."

A long silence, during which Mr. Musselwhite's reflections grew intense.

"You are going to London ? " he asked mechanically.

"Not at first. I hardly know. I think we shall be for some time with friends at Southampton."

"Indeed? How odd! I also have friends at Southampton. A son of Sir Edward Mull; he married a niece of mine."

Barbara could have cried with mortification. She muttered she knew not what. Then again came a blank in the dialogue.

"I trust we may meet again," was Mr. Musselwhite's next sentence. It cost him an effort; he reddened a little, and moved his feet about.

"There is no foreseeing. I—we—I am sorry to say my father has brought us rather unpleasant news."

She knew not whether it was a stroke of policy, or grossly imprudent, to make this confession. But it came to her lips, and she uttered it half in recklessness. It affected Mr. Musselwhite strangely. His countenance fell, and a twinge seemed to catch one of his legs; at the same time it made him fluent.

"I grieve to hear that, Miss Denyer; I grieve indeed. Your departure would have been bad enough, but I really grieve to think you should have cause of distress."

"Thank you for your sympathy, Mr. Musselwhite."

"But perhaps we may meet again in England, for all that? Will you permit me to give you my London address —a—a little club that I belong to, and where my friends often send letters? I mean that I should be so very glad if it were ever possible for me to serve you in any trifle. As you know, I don't keep any—any establishment in England at present; but possibly—as you say, there is no anticipating the future. I should be very happy indeed if we chanced to meet, there or abroad."

"You are very kind, Mr. Musselwhite."

"If I might ask you for your own probable address?"

"It is so uncertain. But I am sure mamma would have pleasure in sending it, when we are settled."

"Thank you so very much." He looked up after long

meditation. "I really do *not* know what I shall do when you are gone, Miss Denyer."

And then, without warning, he said good-night and walked away. Barbara, who had thought that the conversation was just about to become interesting, felt her heart sink into unfathomable depths. She went back to her bedroom and cried wretchedly for a long time.

In consequence of private talk with his wife, when the family conclave had broken up, Mr. Denyer went in search of Clifford Marsh. They had met only once hitherto, six months ago, when Mr. Denyer paid a flying visit to London, and had just time to make the acquaintance of his prospective son-in-law. This afternoon they walked together for an hour about the Chiaia, with the result that an understanding of some kind seemed to be arrived at between them.

Mr. Denyer returned to the *pension*, and, when dinner-time approached, surprised Madeline with the proposal that she should come out and dine with him at a restaurant.

"The fact is," he whispered to her, with a laugh, "my appearance is not quite up to the standard of your dinner-table. I'm rather too careless about these things; it's doubtful whether I possess a decent suit. Let us go and find a quiet corner somewhere—if a fashionable young lady will do me so much honour."

Through Madeline's mind there passed a suspicion, but a restaurant-dinner hit her taste, and she accepted the invitation readily. Before long, they drove into the town. Perhaps in recognition of her having taken his part against idle reproaches, her father began, as soon as they were alone, to talk in a grave, earnest way about his affairs; and Madeline, who liked above all things to be respectfully treated, entered into the subject with dutiful consideration. He showed her exactly how his misfortunes had accumulated, how this and that project had been a failure, what unadvised steps he had taken in fear of impending calamity. Snugly seated at the little marble table, they grew very confidential indeed. Mr. Denyer avowed his hope—the hope ever-retreating, though sometimes it had seemed within reach—of being able some day to find rest for the sole of his foot, to settle down with his family and enjoy a quiet close of life. Possibly this undertaking at Vera Cruz would be his last exile; he explained it in detail, and dwelt on its promising aspects. Madeline felt compassionate and remorseful.

Of her own intimate concerns no word was said, but it happened strangely enough, just as they had finished dinner, that Clifford Marsh came strolling into the restaurant. He saw them, and with expressions of surprise explained that he had just turned in for a cup of coffee. Mr. Denyer invited him to sit down with them, and they had coffee together. Clifford kept up a flow of characteristic talk, never directly addressing Madeline, nor encountering her look. He referred casually to his meeting with Mr. Denyer that afternoon.

"I shall be going back myself very shortly. It is probable that there will be something of a change in my circumstances; I may decide to give up a few hours each day to commercial pursuits. It all depends on—on uncertain things."

"You won't come out with me to Vera Cruz?" said Mr. Denyer, jocosely.

"No; I am a man of the old world. I must live in the atmosphere of art, or I don't care to live at all."

Madeline's slight suspicion was confirmed. When they were about to leave the restaurant, Mr. Denyer said that he must go to the railway-station, to make a few inquiries. There was no use in Madeline's going such a distance; would Clifford be so good as to see her safely home? Madeline made a few objections—she would really prefer to accompany her father; she would not trouble Mr. Marsh—but in the end she found herself seated by Clifford in a carriage, passing rapidly through the streets.

Now was Clifford's opportunity; he had prepared for it.

"Madeline—you must let me call you by that name again, even if it is for the last time—I have heard what has happened."

"Happily it does not affect you, Mr. Marsh."

"Indeed it does. It affects me so far, that it alters the whole course of my life. In spite of everything that has seemed to come between us, I have never allowed myself to think of our engagement as at an end. The parcel you sent me the other day is unopened; if you do not open it yourself, no one ever shall. Whatever *you* may do, I cannot break faith. You ought to know me better than to misinterpret a few foolish and hasty words, and appearances that had a meaning you should have understood. The time has come now for putting an end to those misconceptions."

"They no longer concern me. Please to speak of something else."

"You must, at all events, understand my position before we part. This morning I was as firmly resolved as ever to risk everything, to renounce the aid of my relatives if it must be, and face poverty for the sake of art. Now all is changed. I shall accept my step-father's offer, and all its results; becoming, if it can't be helped, a mere man of business. I do this because of my sacred duties to *you*. As an artist, there's no telling how long it might be before I could ask you again to be my wife; as a man of business, I may soon be in a position to do so. Don't interrupt me, I entreat! It is no matter to me if you repulse me now, in your anger. I consider the engagement as still existing between us, and, such being the case, it is plainly my duty to take such steps as will enable me to offer you a home. By remaining an artist, I should satisfy one part of my conscience, but at the expense of all my better feelings; it might even be supposed —though, I trust, not by you—that I made my helplessness an excuse for forgetting you when most you needed kindness. I shall go back to England, and devote myself with energy to the new task, however repulsive it may prove. Whether you think of me or not, I do it for your sake; you cannot rob me of that satisfaction. Some day I shall again stand before you, and ask you for what you once promised. If then you refuse—well, I must bear the loss of all my hopes."

"You may direct your life as you choose," Madeline replied scornfully, "but you will please to understand that I give you no encouragement to hope anything from me. I almost believe you capable of saying, some day, that you took this step because I urged you to it. I have no interest whatever in your future; our paths are separate. Let this be the end of it."

But it was very far from the end of it. When the carriage stopped at Mrs. Gluck's, mutual reproaches were at their height.

"You shall not leave me yet, Madeline," said Clifford, as he alighted. "Come to the other side of the road, and let us walk along for a few minutes. You shall not go in, if I have to hold you by force."

Madeline yielded, and in the light of the moon they walked side by side, continuing their dialogue.

"You are heartless! You have played with me from the first."

"If so, I only treated you as you thought to treat me."

"That you can attribute such baseness to me proves how incapable you are of distinguishing between truth and falsehood. How wretchedly I have been deceived in you!"

From upbraiding, he fell to lamentation. His life was wrecked; he had lost his ideals; and all through her unworthiness. Then, as Madeline was still unrelenting, he began to humble himself. He confessed his levity; he had not considered the risk he ran of losing her respect; all he had done was in pique at her treatment of him. And in the end he implored her forgiveness, besought her to restore him to life by accepting his unqualified submission. To part from her on such terms as these meant despair; the consequences would be tragic. And when he could go no further in amorous supplication, when she felt that her injured pride had exacted the uttermost from his penitence, Madeline at length relented.

"Still," she said, after his outburst of gratitude, "don't think that I ask you to become a man of business. You shall never charge me with that. It is your nature to reproach other people when anything goes wrong with you; I know you only too well. You must decide for yourself; I will take no responsibility."

Yes, he accepted that; it was purely his own choice. Rather than lose her, he would toil at any most ignoble pursuit, amply repaid by the hope she granted him.

They had walked some distance, and were out of sight of the Mergellina, on the ascending road of Posillipo, all the moonlit glory of the bay before them.

"It will be long before we see it again," said Madeline, sadly.

"We will spend our honeymoon here," was Clifford's hopeful reply.

CHAPTER XVI.

LETTERS.

On the thirteenth day after the flight from Capri, Edward Spence, leaving the villa for his afternoon walk, encountered the postman and received from him three letters. One was addressed to Ross Mallard, Esq., care of Edward Spence, Esq.; another, to Mrs. Spence; the third, to Mrs. Baske. As he reascended the stairs, somewhat more quickly than his wont, Spence gave narrow attention to the handwriting on the envelopes. He found Eleanor where he had left her a few minutes before, at the piano, busy with a difficult passage of Brahms. She looked round in surprise, and on seeing the letters started up eagerly.

"Do you know Elgar's hand?" Spence asked. "These two from London are his, I should imagine. This for you is from Mrs. Lessingham, isn't it?"

"Yes; I think this is the news, at last," said Eleanor, inspecting Mrs. Baske's letter, not without feminine emotion. "I'll take it to her. Shall you go over with the other?"

"He'll be here after dinner; the likelihood is that I shouldn't find him."

"Occasionally—very occasionally—you lack tact, my husband. He would hardly care to open this and read it in our presence."

"More than occasionally, my dear girl, you remind me of the woman whose price is above rubies. I'll go over and leave it for him at once. Just to show the male superiority, however, I shall be careful to make my walk a few minutes longer than usual—a thing of which you would be quite incapable whilst the contents of Miriam's letter were unknown to you."

Alone again, Eleanor sent the letter to Miriam's room by a servant, and with uncertain fingers broke the envelope of that addressed to herself. Already she had heard once from Mrs. Lessingham, who ten days ago left Naples to join certain friends in Rome; the first hurried glance over the present missive showed that it contained no intelligence. She had scarcely begun to read it attentively, when the door opened and Miriam came in.

Her face was pale with agitation, and her eyes had the strangest light in them; to one who knew nothing of the circumstances, she would have appeared exultant. Eleanor could not but gaze at her intently.

"From Reuben?"

"Yes." Miriam suppressed her voice, and held out the sheet of note-paper, which fluttered. "Read it."

The body of the letter was as follows :—

"I hope we have caused you no anxiety ; from the first moment when our departure was known, you must have understood that we had resolved to put an end to useless delay. We travelled to London as brother and sister, and to-day have become man and wife. The above will be our address for a short time ; we have not yet decided where we shall ultimately live.

"By this same post I write to Mallard, addressed to him at the villa. I hope he has had the good sense to wait quietly for news.

"Cecily sends her love to you—though she half fears that you will reject it. I cannot see why you should. We have done the only sensible thing, and of course in a month or two it will be just the same, to everybody concerned, as if we had been married in the most foolish way that respectability can contrive. Let us hear from you very soon, dear sister. We talk much of you, and hope to have many a bright day with you yet—more genuinely happy than that we spent in tracking out old Tiberius."

Eleanor looked up, and again was struck with the singular light in her cousin's eyes.

"Well, it only tells us what we anticipated. Of course he made false declarations. If Mr. Mallard were really as grim as he sometimes looks, the result to both of them might be unpleasant."

"But the marriage could not be undone ? " Miriam asked quickly.

"Oh no. Scarcely desirable that it should be."

Miriam took the letter, and in a few minutes went back again to her room.

At nine o'clock in the evening, the Spences, who sat alone, received the foreseen visit from Mallard. They welcomed

him silently. As he sat down, he had a smile on his face;
he drew a letter deliberately from his pocket, and, without preface, began to read it aloud, still in a deliberate
manner.

"Let me first of all make a formal announcement. We
have this morning been married by registrar's licence.
We intend to live for a few weeks at this present address,
where we have taken some furnished rooms until better
arrangements can be made. I lose no time in writing to
you, for of course there is business between us that you will
desire to transact as soon as may be.

"In obtaining the licence, I naturally gave false information regarding Cecily's age; this was an inevitable consequence of the step we had taken. You know my opinions
on laws and customs : for the multitude they are necessary,
and an infraction of them by the average man is, logically
enough, called a sin against society; for Cecily and myself,
in relation to such a matter as our becoming man and wife,
the law is idle form. Personally, I could have wished to
dispense with the absurdity altogether, but, as things are,
this involves an injustice to a woman. I told my falsehoods
placidly, for they were meaningless in my eyes. I have the
satisfaction of knowing that you cannot, without inconsistency, find fault with me.

"And now I speak as one who would gladly be on terms
of kindness with you. You know me, Mallard; you must
be aware how impossible it was for me to wait two years.
As for Cecily, her one word, again and again repeated on
the journey, was, 'How unkind I shall seem to them!' and
I know that it was the seeming disrespect to you which most
of all distressed her. For her sake, I make it my petition
that you will let the past be past. She cannot yet write to
you, but is sad in the thought of having incurred your
displeasure. Whatever you say to me, let it be said
privately; do not hurt Cecily. I mentioned 'business;'
the word and the thing are equally hateful to me. I most

sincerely wish Cecily had nothing, that the vile question of money might never arise. Herein, at all events, you will do me justice; I am no fortune-hunter.

"If you come to London, send a line and appoint a place of meeting. But could not everything be done through lawyers? You must judge; but, again I ask it, do not give Cecily more pain."

The listeners were smiling gravely. After a silence, the letter was discussed, especially its second paragraph. Mallard was informed of the note which Miriam had received.

"I shall go to-morrow," he said, "and 'transact my business.' On the whole, it might as well be done through lawyers, but I had better be in London."

"And then?" asked Eleanor.

"I shall perhaps go and spend a week with the people at Sowerby Bridge. But you shall hear from me."

"Will you speak to Mrs. Baske?"

"I don't think it is necessary. She has expressed no wish that I should?"

"No; but she might like to be assured that her brother won't be prosecuted for perjury."

"Oh, set her mind at ease!"

"Show Mallard the. letter from Mrs. Lessingham," said Spence, with a twinkle of the eyes.

"I will read it to him."

She did so. And the letter ran thus:

"Still no news? I am uneasy, though there can be no rational doubt as to what form the news will take when it comes. The material interests in question are enough to relieve us from anxiety. But I wish they would be quick and communicate with us.

"One reconciles one's self to the inevitable, and, for my own part, the result of my own reflections is that I am something more than acquiescent. After all, granted that these two must make choice of each other, was it not in the fitness of things that they should act as they have done? For us comfortable folk, life is too humdrum; ought we not to be grateful to those who supply us with a strong emotion, and who remind us that there is yet poetry in the world? I should apologize for addressing such thoughts to *you*, dear Eleanor, for you have still the blessing of a young heart, and certainly do not lack poetry. I speak for myself, and after all I am much disposed to praise these young people for their unconventional behaviour.

"What if our darkest anticipations were fulfilled? Beyond all doubt they are now sincerely devoted to each other, and will remain so for at least twelve months. Those twelve months will be worth a life-time of level satisfaction. We shall be poor creatures in comparison when we utter our ' Didn't I tell you so ? '

"Whilst in a confessing mood, I will admit that I had formed rather a different idea of Cecily; I was disposed to think of her as the modern woman who has put unreasoning passion under her feet, and therefore this revelation was at first a little annoying to me. But I see now that my view of her failed by incompleteness. The modern woman need by no means be a mere embodied intellect; she will choose to enjoy as well as to understand, and to enjoy greatly she will sacrifice all sorts of things that women have regarded as supremely important. Indeed, I cannot say that I am disappointed in Cecily; rightly seen, she has justified the system on which I educated her. My object was to teach her to think for herself, to be self-reliant. The *jeune fille,* according to society's pattern, is my abhorrence: an ignorant, deceitful, vain, immoral creature. Cecily is as unlike that as possible; she has behaved independently and with sincerity. I really admire her very much, and hope that her life may not fall below its beginning.

"Let me hear as soon as a word reaches you. I am with charming people, and yet I think longingly of the delightful evenings at Villa Sannazaro, your music and your talk. You and your husband have a great place in my heart; you are of the salt of the earth. Spare me a little affection, for I am again a lonely woman."

This letter also was discussed, and its philosophy appreciated. Mallard spoke little; he had clasped his hands behind his head, and listened musingly.

There was no effusion in the leave-taking, though it might be for a long time. Warm clasping of hands, but little said.

"A good-bye for me to Mrs. Baske," was Mallard's last word.

And his haggard but composed face turned from Villa Sannazaro.

PART II.

CHAPTER I.

A CORNER OF SOCIETY.

IN a London drawing-room, where the murmur of urbane colloquy rose and fell, broken occasionally by the voice of the nomenclator announcing new arrivals, two ladies, seated in a recess, were exchanging confidences. One was a novelist of more ability than repute; the other was a weekly authority on musical performances.

"Her head is getting turned, poor girl. I feel sorry for her."

"Such ridiculous flattery! And really it is difficult to understand. She is pretty, and speaks French; neither the one thing nor the other is uncommon, I believe. Do you see anything remarkable in her?"

"Well, she is rather more than pretty; and there's a certain cleverness in her talk. But at her age this kind of thing is ruinous. I blame Mrs. Lessingham. She should bid her stay at home and mind her baby."

"By-the-bye, what truth is there in that story? The Naples affair, you know?"

"*N'en sais rien.* But I hear odd things about her husband. Mr. Bickerdike knew him a few years ago. He ran through a fortune, and fell into most disreputable ways of life. Somebody was saying that he got his living as 'bus-conductor, or something of the kind."

"I could imagine that, from the look of him."

It was Mrs. Lessingham's Wednesday evening. The house

at Craven Hill opened its doors at ten o'clock, and until midnight there was no lack of company. Singular people, more or less ; distinguished from society proper by the fact that all had a modicum of brains. Some came from luxurious homes, some from garrets. Visitors from Paris were frequent; their presence made a characteristic of the salon. This evening, for instance, honour was paid by the hostess to M. Amédée Silvenoire, whose experiment in unromantic drama had not long ago gloriously failed at the Odéon ; and Madame Jacquelin, the violinist, was looked for.

Mrs. Lessingham had not passed a season in London for several years. When, at the end of April, she took this house, there came to live with her the widow and daughter of a man of letters who had died in poverty. She had known the Delphs in Paris, in the days when Cecily was with her, and in the winter just past she had come upon Irene Delph copying at the Louvre ; the girl showed a good deal of talent, but was hard beset by the difficulty of living whilst she worked. In the spirit of her generous brother, Mrs. Lessingham persuaded the two to come and live with her through the season ; a room in the house was a studio for Irene, who took to portraits. Mrs. Delph, a timid woman whose nerves had failed under her misfortunes, did not appear on formal occasions like the present, but Irene was becoming an ornament of the drawing-room. To be sure, but for her good looks and her artistic aptitude, she would not have been here—no reason, perhaps, for stinted praise of her friend's generosity.

An enjoyable thing to see Mrs. Lessingham in conversation with one of her French guests. She threw off full fifteen years, and looked thirty at most. Her handsome features had a vivid play of expression in harmony with the language she was speaking; her eyes were radiant as she phrased a thought which in English would have required many words for the—blunting of its point. M. Silvenoire, who—with the slight disadvantage of knowing no tongue but his own—was making a study of English social life, found himself at ease this evening for the first time since he had been in London. Encouraged to talk his best, he frankly and amusingly told Mrs. Lessingham of the ideas he had formed regarding conversation in the drawing-rooms of English ladies.

"Civilization is spreading among us," she replied, with a laugh. "Once or twice it has been my privilege to introduce young Frenchmen, who were studying our language, to English families abroad, and in those cases I privately recommended to them a careful study of Anthony Trollope's novels, that they might learn what is permissible in conversation and what is not. But here and there in London you will find it possible to discuss things that interest reasonable beings."

At the door sounded the name of "Mr. Bickerdike," and there advanced towards the hostess a tall, ugly young man, known by repute to all the English people present. He was the author of a novel called "A Crown of Lilies," which was much talked of just now, and excited no less ridicule than admiration, On the one hand, it was lauded for delicate purity and idealism; on the other, it was scoffed at for artificiality and affected refinement. Mrs. Lessingham had met him for the first time a week ago. Her invitation was not due to approval of his book, but to personal interest which the author moved in her; she was curious to discover how far the idealism of "A Crown of Lilies" was a genuine fruit of the man's nature. Mr. Bickerdike's countenance did not promise clarity of soul; his features were distinctly coarse, and the glance he threw round the room on entering made large demands.

Irene Delph was talking with a young married lady named Mrs. Travis; they both regarded Mr. Bickerdike with close scrutiny.

"Who could have imagined such an author for the book !" murmured the girl, in wonder.

"I could perfectly well," murmured back Mrs. Travis, with a smile which revealed knowledge of humanity.

"I pictured a very youthful man, with a face of effeminate beauty—probably a hectic colour in his cheeks."

"Such men don't write 'the novel of the season.' This gentleman is very shrewd; he gauges the public. Some day, if he sees fit, he will write a brutal book, and it will have merit."

Mr. Bickerdike unfortunately did not speak French, so M. Silvenoire was unable to exchange ideas with him. The Parisian, having learnt what this gentleman's claims were, regarded him through his *pince-nez* with a subtle smile. But in a few moments he had something more interesting to observe.

"Mrs. Elgar," cried the voice at the door.

Cecily was met half-way by her aunt.

"You are alone?"

"Reuben has a headache. Perhaps he will come to fetch me, but more likely not."

All the eyes in the room had one direction. Alike those who ingenuously admired and those who wished to seem indifferent paid the homage of observation to Mrs. Elgar, as she stood exchanging greetings with the friends who came forward. Yes, there was something more than attractive features and a pleasant facility of speech. In Cecily were blended a fresh loveliness and a grace as of maidenhood with the perfect charm of wedded youth. The air about her was charged with something finer than the delicate fragrance which caressed the senses. One had but to hear her speak, were it only the most ordinary phrase of courtesy, and that wonderful voice more than justified profound interest. Strangers took her for a few years older than she was, not judging so much by her face as the finished ease of her manners; when she conversed, it was hard to think of her as only one-and-twenty.

"She is a little pale this evening," said Irene to Mrs. Travis.

The other assented; then asked:

"Why don't you paint her portrait?"

"Heaven forbid! I have quite enough discouragement in my attempts at painting, as it is."

M. Silvenoire was bowing low, as Mrs. Lessingham presented him. To his delight, he heard his own language fluently, idiomatically spoken; he remarked, too, that Mrs. Elgar had a distinct pleasure in speaking it. She seated herself, and flattered him into ecstasies by the respect with which she received his every word. She had seen it mentioned in the *Figaro* that a new play of his was in preparation; when was it likely to be put on the stage? The theatre in London—of course, he understood that no one took it *au sérieux?*

The Parisian could do nothing but gaze about the room, following her movements, when their dialogue was at an end. Mon Dieu! And who, then, was Mr. Elgar? Might not one hope for an invitation to madame's assemblies? A wonderful people, these English, after all.

Mr. Bickerdike secured, after much impatience, the desired introduction. For reasons of his own, he made no mention of his earlier acquaintance with Elgar. Did she know of it? In any case she appeared not to, but spoke of things which did not interest Mr. Bickerdike in the least. At length he was driven to bring forward the one subject on which he desired her views.

"Have you, by chance, read my book, Mrs. Elgar?"

M. Silvenoire would have understood her smile; the Englishman thought it merely amiable, and prepared for the accustomed compliment.

"Yes, I have read it, Mr. Bickerdike. It seemed to me a charmingly written romance."

The novelist, seated upon too low a chair, leaning forward so that his knees and chin almost touched, was not in himself a very graceful object; the contrast with his neighbour made him worse than grotesque. His visage was disagreeably animal as it smiled with condescension.

"You mean something by that," he remarked, with awkward attempt at light fencing.

There was barely a perceptible movement of Cecily's brows.

"I try to mean something as often as I speak," she said, in an amused tone.

"In this case it is a censure. You take the side of those who find fault with my idealism."

"Not so; I simply form my own judgment."

Mr. Bickerdike was nervous at all times in the society of a refined woman; Mrs. Elgar's quiet rebuke brought the perspiration to his forehead, and made him rub his hands together. Like many a better man, he could not do justice to the parts he really possessed, save when sitting in solitude with a sheet of paper before him. Though he had a confused perception that Mrs. Elgar was punishing him for forcing her to speak of his book, he was unable to change the topic and so win her approval for his tact. In the endeavour to seem at ease, he became blunt.

"And what has your judgment to say on the subject?"

"I think I have already told you, Mr. Bickerdike."

"You mean by a romance a work that is not soiled with the common realism of to-day."

"I am willing to mean that."

"But you will admit, Mrs. Elgar, that my mode of fiction has as much to say for itself as that which you prefer?"

"In asking for one admission you take for granted another. That is a little confusing."

It was made sufficiently so to Mr. Bickerdike. He thrust out his long legs, and exclaimed:

"I should be grateful to you if you would tell me what your view of the question really is—I mean, of the question at issue between the two schools of fiction."

" But will you first make clear to me the characteristics of the school you represent ? "

"It would take a long time to do that satisfactorily. I proceed on the assumption that fiction is poetry, and that poetry deals only with the noble and the pure."

"Yes," said Cecily, as he paused for a moment, "I see that it would take too long. You must deal with so many prejudices—such, for example, as that which supposes 'King Lear' and 'Othello' to be poems."

Mr. Bickerdike began a reply, but it was too late ; Mrs. Lessingham had approached with some one else who wished to be presented to Mrs. Elgar, and the novelist could only bite his lips as he moved away to find a more reverent listener.

It was not often that Cecily trifled in this way. As a rule, her manner of speech was direct and earnest. She had a very uncommon habit of telling the truth whenever it was possible ; rather than utter smooth falsehoods, she would keep silence, and sometimes when to do so was to run much danger of giving offence. Beautiful women have very different ways of using the privilege their charm assures them ; Cecily chose to make it a protection of her integrity. She was much criticized by acquaintances of her own sex. Some held her presumptuous, conceited, spoilt by adulation ; some accused her of bad taste and blue-stockingism ; some declared that she had no object but to win men's admiration and outshine women. Without a thought of such comments, she behaved as was natural to her. Where she felt her superiority, she made no pretence of appearing femininely humble. Yet persons like Mrs. Delph, who kept themselves in shadow and spoke only with simple kindness, knew well how unassuming Cecily was, and with what deference she spoke when good feeling dictated it. Or again, there was her manner with the people who, by the very respect with which they inspired her, gave her encouragement to speak without false restraint; such as Mr. Bird, the art critic, a grizzle-headed man with whom she sat for a quarter of an hour this evening, looking her very brightest and talking in her happiest vein, yet showing all the time her gratitude for what she learnt from his conversation.

It was nearly twelve o'clock when Mrs. Travis, who had made one or two careless efforts to draw near to Cecily, succeeded in speaking a word aside with her.

" I hope you didn't go to see me yesterday ? I left home in the morning, and am staying with friends at Hampstead, not far from you."

" For long ? "

" I don't know. I should like to talk to you, if I could. Shall you be driving back alone ? "

" Yes. Will you come with me ? "

" Thank you. Please let me know when you are going."

And Mrs. Travis turned away. In a few minutes Cecily went to take leave of her aunt.

" How is Clarence ? " asked Mrs. Lessingham.

" Still better, I believe. I left him to-night without uneasiness."

" Oh, I had a letter this morning from Mrs. Spence. No talk of England yet. In the autumn they are going to Greece, then for the winter to Sicily."

" Miriam with them ? "

" As though it were a matter of course."

They both smiled. Then Cecily took leave of two or three other people, and quitted the room. Mrs. Travis followed her, and in a few minutes they were seated in the brougham.

Mrs. Travis had a face one could not regard without curiosity. It was not beautiful in any ordinary sense, but strange and striking and rich in suggestiveness. In the chance, flickering light that entered the carriage, she looked haggard, and at all times her thinness and pallor give her the appearance of suffering both in body and mind. Her complexion was dark, her hair of a rich brown; she had very large eyes, which generally wandered in an absent, restless, discontented way. If she smiled, it was with a touch of bitterness, and her talk was wont to be caustic. Cecily had only known her for a few weeks, and did not feel much drawn to her, but she compassionated her for sorrows known and suspected. Though only six and twenty, Mrs. Travis had been married seven years, and had had two children; the first died at birth, the second was carried off by diphtheria. Her husband Cecily had never seen, but she heard disagreeable things of him, and Mrs. Travis herself had dropped hints which signified domestic unhappiness.

After a minute or two of silence, Cecily was beginning to speak on some indifferent subject, when her companion interrupted her.

"Will you let me tell you something about myself?"

"Whatever you wish, Mrs. Travis," Cecily answered, with sympathy.

"I've left my husband. Perhaps you thought of that?"

"No."

The sudden disclosure gave her a shock. She had the sensation of standing for the first time face to face with one of the sterner miseries of life.

"I did it once before," pursued the other, "two years ago. Then I was foolish enough to be wheedled back again. That shan't happen this time."

"Have you really no choice but to do this?" Cecily asked, with much earnestness.

"Oh, I could have stayed if I had chosen. He doesn't beat me. I have as much of my own way as I could expect. Perhaps you'll think me unreasonable. A Turkish woman would."

Cecily sat mute. She could not but resent the harsh tone in which she was addressed, in spite of her pity.

"It's only that I suffer in my self-respect—a little," Mrs. Travis continued. "Of course, this is no reason for taking such a step, except to those who have suffered in the same way. Perhaps you would like to stop the carriage and let me leave you?"

"Your suffering makes you unjust to me," replied Cecily, much embarrassed by this strange impulsiveness. "Indeed I sympathize with you. I think it quite possible that you are behaving most rightly."

"You don't maintain, then, that it is a wife's duty to bear every indignity from her husband?"

"Surely not. On the contrary, I think there are some indignities which no wife *ought* to bear."

"I'm glad to hear that. I had a feeling that you would think in this way, and that's why I wanted to talk to you. Of course you have only the evidence of my word for believing me."

"I can see that you are very unhappy, and the cause you name is quite sufficient."

"In one respect, I am very lucky. I have a little money of my own, and that enables me to go and live by myself. Most women haven't this resource: many are compelled to live in degradation only for want of it. I should like to see how many homes would be broken up, if all women were suddenly made independent in the same way that I am. How I should enjoy that! I hate the very word 'marriage'!"

Cecily averted her face, and said nothing. After a pause, her companion continued in a calm voice:

"You can't sympathize with that, I know. And you are comparing my position with your own."

No answer was possible, for Mrs. Travis had spoken the truth.

"In the first year of my marriage, I used to do the same whenever I heard of any woman who was miserable with her husband."

"Is there no possibility of winning back your husband?" Cecily asked, in a veiled voice.

"Winning him back? Oh, he is affectionate enough. But you mean winning him back to faithfulness. My husband happens to be the average man, and the average man isn't a pleasant person to talk about, in this respect."

"Are you not too general in your condemnation, Mrs. Travis?"

"I am content you should think so. You are very young still, and there's no good in making the world ugly for you as long as it can seem rosy."

"Please don't use that word," said Cecily, with emphasis. It annoyed her to be treated as immature in mind. "I am the last person to take rosy views of life. But there is something between the distrust to which you are driven by misery and the optimism of foolish people."

"We won't argue about it. Every woman must take life as she finds it. To me it is a hateful weariness. I hope I mayn't have much of it still before me; what there is, I will live in independence. You know Mrs. Calder?"

"Yes."

"Her position is the same as mine has been, but she has more philosophy; she lets things take their course, just turning her eyes away."

"That is ignoble, hateful!" exclaimed Cecily.

"So I think, but women as a rule don't. At all events, they are content to whine a little, and do nothing. Poor wretches, what *can* they do, as I said?"

"They can go away, and, if need be, starve."

"They have children."

Cecily became mute.

"Will you let me come and see you now and then?" Mrs. Travis asked presently.

"Come whenever you feel you would like to," Cecily answered, rousing herself from reverie.

The house in which Mrs. Travis now lived was a quarter of an hour's drive beyond that of the Elgars; she would have alighted and walked, making nothing of it, but of course Cecily could not allow this. The coachman was directed to make the circuit. When Cecily reached home, it was after one o'clock.

CHAPTER II.

THE PROPRIETIES DEFENDED.

THE house was in Belsize Park. Light shone through the blind of one of the upper windows, but the rest of the front was lifeless. Cecily's ring at the bell sounded distinctly; it was answered at once by a maid-servant, who said that Mr. Elgar was still in the library. Having spoken a few words, ending with a kind good night, Cecily passed through the hall and opened the library door.

A reading-lamp made a bright sphere on the table, but no one sat within its rays. After a fruitless glance round the room, Cecily called her husband's name. There was a sound of moving, and she saw that Reuben was on a sofa which the shadow veiled.

"Have you been asleep?" she asked merrily, as she approached him.

He stood up and stretched himself, muttering.

"Why didn't you go to bed, poor boy? I'm dreadfully late; I went out of my way to take some one home."

"Who was that?" Elgar inquired, coming forward and seating himself on the corner of the writing-table.

"Mrs. Travis. She has come to stay with friends at Hampstead. But to bed, to bed! You look like Hamlet when he came and frightened Ophelia. Have you had an evil dream?"

" That's the truth ; I have."

" What about ? "

" Oh, a stupid jumble." He moved the lamp-shade, so that the light fell suddenly full upon her. " Why have you made such friends all at once with Mrs. Travis ? "

" How is your headache ? "

" I don't know—much the same. Did she ask you to take her home ? "

" Yes, she did—or suggested it, at all events."

" Why has she come to Hampstead ? "

" How can I tell, dear ? Put the lamp out, and let us go."

He sat swinging his leg. The snatch of uncomfortable sleep had left him pale and swollen-eyed, and his hair was tumbled.

" Who was there to-night ? "

" Several new people. Amédée Silvenoire—the dramatist, you know ; an interesting man. He paid me the compliment of refraining from compliments on my French. Madame Jacquelin, a stout and very plain woman, who told us anecdotes of George Sand ; remind me to repeat them to-morrow. And Mr. Bickerdike, the pillar of idealism."

" Bickerdike was there ? " Elgar exclaimed, with an air of displeasure.

" He didn't refer to his acquaintance with you. I wonder why not ? "

" Did you talk to the fellow ? "

" Rather pertly, I'm afraid. He was silly enough to ask me what I thought of his book, though I hadn't mentioned it. I put on my superior air and snubbed him ; it was like tapping a frog on the head each time it pokes up out of the water. He will go about and say what an insufferable person that Mrs. Elgar is."

Reuben was silent for a while.

" I don't like your associating with such people," he said suddenly. " I wish you didn't go there. It's all very well for a woman like your aunt to gather about her all the disreputable men and women who claim to be of some account; but they are not fit companions for you. I don't like it at all."

She looked at him in astonishment, with bewildered eyes, that were on the verge of laughter.

" What *are* you talking about, Reuben ? "

" I'm quite serious." He rose and began to walk about the room. " And it surprised me that you didn't think of staying at home this evening. I said nothing, because I wanted to see whether it would occur to you that you oughtn't to go alone."

" How should such a thing occur to me ? Surely I am as much at home in aunt's house as in my own ? I can hardly believe that you mean what you say."

" You will understand it if you think for a moment. A year ago you wouldn't have dreamt of going out at night when I stayed at home. But you find the temptation of society irresistible. People admire you and talk about you and crowd round you, and you enjoy it—never mind who the people are. Presently we shall be seeing your portrait in the shop-windows. I noticed what a satisfaction it was to you when your name was mentioned among the other people in that idiotic society journal."

Cecily laughed, but not quite so naturally as she wished it to sound.

" This is too absurd ! Your dream has unsettled your wits, Reuben. How could I imagine that you had begun to think of me in such a light ? You used to give me credit for at least average common sense. I can't talk about it; I am ashamed to defend myself."

He had not spoken angrily, but in a curiously dogged tone, with awkward emphasis, as if struggling to say what did not come naturally to his lips. Still walking about, and keeping his eyes on the floor, he continued in the same half-embarrassed way :

"There's no need for you to defend yourself. I don't exactly mean to blame you, but to point out a danger."

"Forgetting that you degrade my character in doing so."

"Nothing of the kind, Cecily. But remember how young you are. You know very little of the world, and often see things in an ideal light. It is your tendency to idealize. You haven't the, experience necessary to a woman who goes about in promiscuous society."

Cecily knitted her brows.

"Instead of using that vague, commonplace language— which I never thought to hear from *you*—I wish you would tell me exactly what you mean. What things do I see in an ideal light? That means, I suppose, that I am childishly ignorant of common evils in the world. You couldn't speak otherwise if I had just come out of a convent. And, indeed, you don't believe what you say. Speak more simply, Reuben. Say that you distrust my discretion."

"To a certain extent, I do."

"Then there is no more to be said, dear. Please to tell me in future exactly what you wish me to do, and what to avoid. I will go to school to your prudence."

The clock ticked very loudly, and, before the silence was again broken, chimed half-past one.

"Let me give you an instance of what I mean," said Elgar, again seating himself on the table and fingering his watch-chain nervously. "You have been making friends with Mrs. Travis. Now, you are certainly quite ignorant of her character. You don't know that she left home not long ago."

Cecily asked in a low voice:

"And why didn't you tell me this before?"

"Because I don't choose to talk with you about such disagreeable things."

"Then I begin to see what the difficulty is between us. It is not I who idealize things, but you. Unless I am much mistaken, this is the common error of husbands—of those who are at heart the best. They wish their wives to remain children, as far as possible. Everything 'disagreeable' must be shunned—and we know what the result often is. But I had supposed all this time that you and I were on other terms. I thought you regarded me as not quite the everyday woman. In some things it is certain you do; why not in the most important of all? Knowing that I was likely to see Mrs. Travis often, it was your duty to tell me what you knew of her."

Elgar kept silence.

"Now let me give you another version of that story," Cecily continued. "To-night she has been telling me about herself. She says that she left home because her husband was unfaithful to her. I think the reason quite sufficient, and I told her so. But there is something more. She has again been driven away. She has come to live at Hampstead because her home is intolerable, and she says that nothing will ever induce her to return."

"And this has been the subject of your conversation as you drove back? Then I think such an acquaintance is very unsatisfactory, and it must come to an end."

"Please to tell me why you spoke just now as if Mrs. Travis were to blame."

"I have heard that she was."

"Heard from whom?"

"That doesn't matter. There's a doubt about it, and she's no companion for you."

"As you think it necessary to lay commands on me, I shall of course obey you. But I believe Mrs. Travis is wronged by the rumours you have heard; I believe she acted then, and has done now, just as it behoved her to."

"And you have been encouraging her?"

"Yes, on the assumption that she told me the truth. She asked if she might come and see me, and I told her to do so whenever she wished. I needn't say that I shall write and withdraw this invitation."

Elgar hesitated before replying.

"I'm afraid you can't do that. You have tact enough to end the acquaintance gradually."

"Indeed I have not, Reuben. I either condemn her or pity her; I can't shuffle contemptibly between the two."

"Of course you prefer to pity her!" he exclaimed impatiently. "There comes in the idealism of which I was speaking. The vulgar woman's instinct would be to condemn her; naturally enough, you take the opposite course. You like to think nobly of people, with the result that more often than not you will be wrong. You don't know the world."

"And I am very young; pray finish the formula. But why do you prefer to take the side of 'the vulgar woman' of whom you speak? I see that you have no evidence against Mrs. Travis; why lean towards condemnation?"

"Well, I'll put it in another way. A woman who lives apart from her husband is always amid temptations, always in doubtful circumstances. Friends who put faith in her may, of course, keep up their intimacy; but a slight acquaintance, and particularly one in your position, will get harm by associating with her. This is simple and obvious enough."

"If you knew for certain that she was blameless, you would speak in the same way?"

"If it regarded you, I should. Not if Mrs. Lessingham were in question."

"That is a distinction which repeats your distrust. We won't say any more about it. I will bear in mind my want of experience, and in future never act without consulting you."

She moved towards the door.

"You are coming?"

"Look here, Ciss, you are not so foolish as to misunderstand me. When I said that I distrusted your discretion, I meant, of course, that you might innocently do things which

would make people talk about you. There is no harm in
reminding you of the danger."

"Perhaps not; though it would be more like yourself to
scorn people's talk."

"That is only possible if we chose to go back to our
life of solitude. I'm afraid it wouldn't suit you very well
now."

"No; I am far too eager to see my name in fashionable
lists. Has not all my life pointed to that noble ambition?"

She regarded him with a smile from her distance, a smile
that trembled a little about her lips, and in which her clear
eyes had small part. Elgar, without replying, began to turn
down the lamp.

"This is what has made you so absent and uneasy for the
last week or two?" Cecily added.

The lamp was extinguished

"Yes, it is," answered Elgar's voice in the darkness. "I
don't like the course things have been taking."

"Then you were quite right to speak plainly. Be at
rest; you shall have no more anxiety."

She opened the door, and they went upstairs together.
In the bedroom Cecily found her little boy sleeping quietly;
she bent above him for a few moments, and with soft
fingers smoothed the coverlet.

There was no further conversation between them—except
that Cecily just mentioned the news her aunt had received
from Mrs. Spence.

At breakfast they spoke of the usual subjects, in the
usual way. Elgar had his ride, amused himself in the
library till luncheon, lolled about the drawing-room whilst
Cecily played, went to his club, came back to dinner,—all in
customary order. Neither look nor word, from him or
Cecily, made allusion to last night's incident.

The next morning, when breakfast was over, he came
behind his wife's chair and pointed to an envelope she had
opened.

"What strange writing! Whose is it?"

"From Mrs. Travis."

He moved away, and Cecily rose. As she was passing him, he said:

"What has she to say to you?"

"She acknowledges the letter I sent her yesterday morning, that's all."

"You wrote—in the way you proposed?"

"Certainly."

He allowed her to pass without saying anything more.

CHAPTER III.

GRADATION.

During the first six months of her wedded life, Cecily wrote from time to time in a handsomely-bound book which had a little silver lock to it. She was then living at the seaside in Cornwall, and Reuben occasionally went out for some hours with the fishers, or took a long solitary ride inland, just to have the delight of returning to his home after a semblance of separation; in his absence, Cecily made a confidant of the clasped volume. On some of its fair pages were verses, written when verse came to her more easily than prose, but read not even to him who occasioned them. A passage or two of the unrhymed thoughts, with long periods of interval, will suggest the course of her mental history.

"I have no more doubts, and take shame to myself for those I ever entertained. Presently I will confess to him how my mind was tossed and troubled on that flight from Capri; I now feel able to do so, and to make of the confession one more delight. It was impossible for me not to be haunted by the fear that I had yielded to impulse, and acted unworthily of one who could reflect. I had not a doubt of my lover, but the foolish pride which is in a girl's heart whispered to me that I had been too eager—had allowed myself to be won too readily ; that I should have been more precious to him if more difficulty had been put in his way. Would it not have been good to give him proof of constancy through long months of waiting? But the secret was that I dreaded to lose him. I reproached him for want of faith in my steadfastness ; but just as well he might have reproached me. It was horrible to think of his going back into the world and living among people of whom I knew nothing. I knew in some degree what his life had been; by force of passionate love I understood, or thought I understood him ; and I feared most ignobly.

" And I was putting myself in opposition to all those older and more experienced people. How could I help distrusting myself at times ? I saw them all looking coldly and reproachfully at me. Here again my pride had something to say. They would smile among themselves, and tell each other that they had held a mistakenly high opinion of me. That was hard to bear. I like to be thought much of ; it is delicious to feel that people respect me, that they apply other judgments to me than to girls in general. Mr. Mallard hurt me more than he thought in pretending—I feel sure he only pretended —to regard my words as trivial. How it rejoices me that there are some things I know better than my husband does! I have read of women liking to humble themselves, and in a way I can understand it ; I do like to *say* that he is far above me—oh ! and I mean it, I believe it ; but the joy of joys is to see him look at me with admiration. I rejoice that I have beauty ; I rejoice that I have read much, and can think for myself now and then, and sometimes say a thing that every one would not think of. Suppose I were an uneducated girl, not particularly good-looking, and a man loved me ; well, in that case perhaps the one joy would be mere worship of him and intense gratitude—blind belief in his superiority to every other man that lived. But then Reuben would never have loved me; he must have something to admire, to stand a little in awe of. And for this very reason, perhaps I feel such constant—self-esteem, for that is the only word.". . .

"All the doubts and fears are over. I acted rightly, and because I obeyed my passion. The poets are right, and all the prudent people only grovel in their worldly wisdom. It may not be true for every one, but for me to love and be loved, infinitely, with the love that conquers everything, is the sole end of life. It is enough; come what will, if love remain nothing else is missed. In the direst poverty, we should be as much to each other as we are now. If he died, I would live only to remember the days I passed with him. What folly, what a crime, it would have been to waste two years, as though we were immortal!

"I never think of Capri but I see it in the light of a magnificent sunrise. Beloved, sacred island, where the morning of my life indeed began! No spot in all the earth has beauty like yours; no name of any place sounds to me as yours does!"

"I know that our life cannot always be what it is now. This is a long honeymoon; we do not walk on the paths that are trodden by ordinary mortals; the sky above us is not the same that others see as they go about their day's business or pleasure. By what process shall we fall to the common existence? We have all our wants provided for; there is no need for my husband to work that he may earn money, no need for me to take anxious thought about expenses; so that we are tempted to believe that life will always be the same. That cannot be; I am not so idle as to hope it.

"He certainly has powers which should be put to use. We have talked much of things that he might possibly do, and I am sure that before long his mind will hit the right path. I am so greedy of happiness that even what we enjoy does not suffice me ; I want my husband to distinguish himself among men, that I may glory in his honour. Yesterday he told me that my own abilities exceeded his, and that I was more likely to make use of them ; but in this case my ambition takes a humble form. Even if I were sure that I could, say, write a good book, I would infinitely prefer him to do it and receive the reward of it. I like him to *say* such things, but in fact he must be more than I. Do I need a justification of the love I bear him ? Surely not; that would be a con-tradiction of love. But it is true that I would gladly have him justify to others my belief in his superiority.

" And yet—why not be content with what is well ? If *he* could remain so ; but will he ? We have a long life before us, and I know that it cannot be all honeymoon."

" I have been reading a French novel that has made me angry—in spite of my better sense. Of course, it is not the first book of the kind that I have read, but it comes home to me now. What right has this author to say that no man was ever absolutely faithful ? It is a commonplace, but how can any one have evidence enough to justify such a state-ment? I shall not speak of it to Reuben, for I don't care to think long about it. Does that mean, I wonder, that I am afraid to think of it ?

" Well, I had rather have been taught to read and think about everything, than be foolishly ignorant as so many women are. This French author would laugh at my con-fidence, but I could laugh back at his narrow cynicism. He knows nothing of love in its highest sense. I am firm in my optimism, which has a very different base from that of ignor-ance.

" This does not concern me ; I won't occupy my mind with it ; I won't read any more of the cynics. My husband loves me, and I believe his love incapable of receiving a soil. If ever I cease to believe that, time enough then to be miserable and to fight out the problem."

The end of the six months found them still undecided as to where they should fix a permanent abode. In no part of England had either of them relatives or friends whose proximity would be of any value. Cecily inclined towards London, feeling that there only would her husband find incentives to exertion; but Reuben was more disposed to settle somewhere on the Continent. He talked of going back to Italy, living in Florence, and—writing something new about the Renaissance. Cecily shook her head; Italy she loved, and she had seen nothing of it north of Naples, but it was the land of lotus-eaters. They would go there again, but not until life had seriously shaped itself.

Whilst they talked and dreamed, decision came to them in the shape of Mrs. Lessingham. Without warning, she one day presented herself at their lodgings, having come direct from Paris. Her spirits were delightful; she could not have behaved more graciously had this marriage been the one desire of her life. The result of her private talk with Cecily was that within a week all three travelled down to London; there they remained for a fortnight, then went on to Paris. Mrs. Lessingham's quarters were in Rue de Belle Chasse, and the Elgars found a suitable dwelling in the same street.

Their child was born, and for a few months all questions were postponed to that of its health and Cecily's. The infant gave a good deal of trouble, was anything but robust; the mother did not regain her strength speedily. The first three months of the new year were spent at Bordighera; then came three months of Paris; then the family returned to England (without Mrs. Lessingham), and established themselves in the house in Belsize Park.

The immediate effect of paternity upon Elgar was amusing. His self-importance visibly increased. He spoke with more gravity; whatever step he took was seriously considered; if he read a newspaper, it was with an air of sober reflection.

" This is the turning-point in his life," Cecily said to her aunt. "He seems to me several years older; don't you notice it? I am quite sure that as soon as things are in order again he will begin to work."

And the prophecy seemed to find fulfilment. Not many days after their taking possession of the English home, Reuben declared a project that his mind had been forming. It was not, to be sure, thoroughly fashioned; its limits must necessarily be indeterminate until fixed by long and serious study; but what he had in view was to write a history of the English mind in its relation to Puritanism.

"I have a notion, Ciss, that this is the one thing into which I can throw all my energies. The one need of my intellectual life is to deal a savage blow at the influences which ruined all my early years. You can't look at the matter quite as I do; you don't know the fierce hatred with which I am moved when I look back. If I am to do literary work at all, it must be on some subject which deeply concerns me— me myself, as an individual. I feel sure that my bent isn't to fiction; I am not objective enough. But I enjoy the study of history, and I have a good deal of acuteness. If I'm not mistaken, I can make a brilliant book, a book that will excite hatred and make my name known."

They were sitting in the library, late at night. As usual when he was stirred, Reuben paced up and down the room and gesticulated.

"Do you mean it to be a big book?" Cecily asked, after reflection.

"Not very big. I should have French models before me, rather than English."

"It would take you a long time to prepare."

"Two or three years, perhaps. But what does that matter? I shall work a good deal at the British Museum. It will oblige me to be away from you a good deal, but——"

"You mustn't trouble about that. I have my own work. If your mornings are regularly occupied, I shall be able to make fixed plans of study ; there are so many things I want to work at."

"Capital! It's high time we came to that. And then, you know, you might be able to give me substantial help—reading, making notes, and so on—if you cared to."

Cecily smiled.

"Yes, if I care to.—But hasn't the subject been dealt with already?"

"Oh, of course, in all sorts of ways. But not in *my* way. No man ever wrote about it with such energy of hatred as I shall bring to the task."

Cecily was musing.

"It won't be a history in the ordinary sense," she said. "You will make no pretence of historic calm and impartiality."

"Not I, indeed! My book shall be cited as a splendid example of *odium antitheologicum.* There are passages of eloquence rolling in my mind! And this is just the time for such a work. Throughout intellectual England, Puritanism is dead ; but we know how vigorously it survives among the half-educated classes. My book shall declare the emancipation of all the better minds, and be a help to those who are struggling upwards. It will be a demand, also, for a new literature, free from the absurd restraints that Puritanism has put upon us. All the younger writers will rally about me. It shall be a 'movement.' The name of my book shall be a watchword."

They talked about it till one in the morning.

For several weeks Elgar was constantly at the Museum. He read prodigiously; he brought home a great quantity of notes; every night Cecily and he talked over his acquisitions, and excited themselves. But the weather grew oppressively hot, and it was plain that they could not carry out the project of remaining in town all through the autumn. Already Reuben was languishing in his zeal, when little Clarence had a sudden and alarming illness. As soon as possible, all went off to the seaside.

Since his work had begun, Reuben's interest in the child had fallen off. Its ailments were soon little more than an annoyance to him; Cecily perceived this, and seldom spoke on the subject. The fact of the sudden illness affording an opportunity for rest led him to express more solicitude than he really felt, but when the child got back into its normal state, Reuben was more plainly indifferent to it than ever. He spoke impatiently if the mother's cares occupied her when he wished for her society.

" A baby isn't a rational creature," he said once. " When he is old enough to begin to be educated, that will be a different thing. At present he is only a burden. Perhaps you think me an unfatherly brute ? "

" No ; I can understand you quite well. I should very often be impatient myself if I had no servants to help me."

" What a horrible thought ! Suppose, Ciss, we all of a sudden lost everything, and we had to go and live in a garret, and I had to get work as a clerk at five-and-twenty shillings a week. How soon should we hate the sight of each other, and the sound of each other's voices ? "

" It might come to that," replied Cecily, with half a smile. " Perhaps."

" There's no doubt about it."

Cecily remembered something she had written in the book with the silver lock—a book which had not been opened for a long time.

" I used to think nothing could bring that about. And I am not sure yet."

" I should behave like a ruffian. I know myself well enough."

" I think that would kill my love in time."

" Of course it would. How can any one love what is not lovable ? "

" Yet we hear," suggested Cecily, " of wretched women

remaining devoted to husbands who all but murder them now and then."

"You are not so foolish as to call *that* love ! That is mere unreasoning and degraded habit—the same kind of thing one may find in a dog."

"Has love anything to do with reason, Reuben ? "

"As I understand it, it has everything to do with reason. Animal passion has not, of course ; but love is made of that with something added. Can my reason discover any argument why I should not love you ? I won't say that it might not, some day, and then my love would by so much be diminished."

"You believe that reason is free to exercise itself, where love is in possession ? "

"I believe that love can only come when reason invites. Of course, we are talking of love between men and women ; the word has so many senses. In this highest sense, it is one of the rarest of things. How many wives and husbands love each other ? Not one pair in five thousand. In the average pair that have lived together as long as we have, there is not only mutual criticism, but something even of mutual dislike. That makes love impossible. Habit takes its place."

"Happily for the world."

"I don't know. Perhaps so. It is an ignoble necessity ; but then, the world largely consists of ignoble creatures."

Cecily reflected often on this conversation. Was there any significance in such reasonings ? It gave her keen pleasure to hear Reuben maintain such a view, but did it mean anything ? If, in meditating about him, she discovered characteristics of his which she could have wished to change, which in themselves were certainly not lovable, had she in that moment ceased to love him, in love's highest sense ?

But in that case love might be self-deception. In that case, perfect love was impossible save as a result of perfect knowledge.

What part had reason in the impulses which possessed her from her first meeting with Reuben in Italy, unless that name were given to the working of mysterious affinities, afterwards to be justified by experience?

Cecily had been long content to accept love as an ultimate fact of her being. But it was not Reuben's arguments only that led her to ponder its nature and find names for its qualities. By this time she had become conscious that her love as a wife was somehow altered, modified, since she had been a mother. The time of passionate reveries was gone by. She no longer wrote verses. The book was locked up and kept hidden; if ever she resumed her diary, it must be in a new volume, for that other was sacred to an undivided love. It would now have been mere idle phrasing, to say that Reuben was all in all to her. And she could not think of this without some sadness.

To the average woman maternity is absorbing. Naturally so, for the average woman is incapable of poetical passion, and only too glad to find something that occupies her thoughts from morning to night, a relief from the weariness of her unfruitful mind. It was not to be expected that Cecily, because she had given birth to a child, should of a sudden convert herself into a combination of wet and dry nurse, after the common model. The mother's love was strong in her, but it could not destroy, nor even keep in long abeyance, those intellectual energies which characterized her. Had she been constrained to occupy herself ceaselessly with the demands of babyhood, something more than impatience would shortly have been roused in her: she would have rebelled against the conditions of her sex; the gentle melancholy with which she now looked back upon the early days of marriage would have become a bitter protest against her slavery to nature. These possibilities in the modern woman correspond to that spirit in the modern man which is in revolt against the law of labour. Picture Reuben Elgar reduced to the necessity of toiling for daily bread—

that is to say, brought down from his pleasant heights of civilization to the dull plain where nature tells a man that if he would eat he must first sweat at the furrow; one hears his fierce objurgations, his haughty railing against the gods. Cecily did not represent that extreme type of woman to whom the bearing of children has become in itself repugnant; but she was very far removed from that other type which the world at large still makes its ideal of the feminine. With what temper would she have heard the lady in her aunt's drawing-room, who was of opinion that she should "stay at home and mind the baby"? Education had made her an individual; she was nurtured into the disease of thought. This child of hers showed in the frail tenure on which it held its breath how unfit the mother was for fulfilling her natural functions. Both parents seemed in admirable health, yet their offspring was a poor, delicate, nervous creature, formed for exquisite sensibility to every evil of life. Cecily saw this, and partly understood it; her heart was heavy through the long anxious nights passed in watching by the cradle.

When they returned to London, Reuben at first made a pretence of resuming his work. He went now and then to the reading-room, and at home shut himself up in the study; but he no longer voluntarily talked of his task. Cecily knew what had happened; the fatal lack of perseverance had once more declared itself. For some weeks she refrained from inviting his confidence, but of necessity they spoke together at last. Reuben could no longer disguise the ennui under which he was labouring. Instead of sitting in the library, he loitered about the drawing-room; he was often absent through the whole day, and Cecily knew that he had not been at the Museum.

"I'm at a stand-still," he admitted, when the opportunity came. "I don't see my way so clearly as at first. I must take up some other subject for a time, and rest my mind."

They had no society worth speaking of. Mrs. Lessingham

had supplied them with a few introductions, but these people were now out of town. Earlier in the year neither of them had cared to be assiduous in discharging social obligations, with the natural result that little notice was taken of them in turn. Reuben had resumed two or three of his old connections; a bachelor acquaintance now and then came to dine; but this was not the kind of society they needed. Impossible for them to utter the truth, and confess that each other's companionship was no longer all-sufficient. Had Reuben been veritably engaged in serious work, Cecily might have gone on for a long time with her own studies before she wearied for lack of variety and friendly voices; as it was, the situation became impossible.

"Wouldn't you like to belong to a club?" she one day asked.

And Reuben caught at the suggestion. Not long ago, it would have caused him to smile rather scornfully.

Cecily had lost her faith in the great militant book on Puritanism. Thinking about it, when it had been quite out of her mind for a few days, she saw the project in a light of such absurdity that, in spite of herself, she laughed. It was laughter that pained her, like a sob. No, that was not the kind of work for him. What was?

She would think rather of her child and its future. If Clarence lived—if he lived—she herself would take charge of his education for the first years. She must read the best books that had been written on the training of children's minds; everything should be smoothed for him by skilful methods. There could be little doubt that he would prove a quick child, and the delight of watching his progress! She imagined him a boy of ten, bright, trustful, happy; he would have no nearer friend than his mother; between him and her should exist limitless confidence. But a firm hand would be necessary; he would exhibit traits inherited from his father——

Cecily remembered the day when she first knew that she

did not wish him to be altogether like his father. Perhaps in no other way could she have come to so clear an understanding of Reuben's character—at all events, of those parts of it which had as yet revealed themselves in their wedded life. She thought of him with an impartiality which had till of late been impossible. And then it occurred to her: Had the same change come over his mind concerning her? Did he feel secret dissatisfactions? If he had a daughter, would he say to himself that in this and that he would wish her not to resemble her mother?

About once in three months they received a letter from Miriam, addressed always to Cecily. She was living still with the Spences, and still in Italy. Her letters offered no explanation of this singular fact; indeed, they threw as little light as was possible on the state of her mind, so brief were they, and so closely confined to statements of events. Still, it was clear that Miriam no longer shrank from the study of profane things. Of Bartles she never spoke.

Mrs. Spence also wrote to Cecily, the kind of letter to be expected from her, delightful in the reading and pleasant in the memory. But she said nothing significant concerning Miriam.

"Would they welcome us, if we went to see them?" Cecily asked, one cheerless day this winter—it was Clarence's birthday.

"You can't take the child," answered Reuben, with some discontent.

"No; I should not dare to. And it is just as impossible to leave him with any one. In another year, perhaps."

Mrs. Lessingham occasionally mentioned Miriam in her letters, and always with a jest. "I strongly suspect she is studying Greek. Is she, perchance, the author of that delightful paper on 'Modern Paganism,' in the current *Fortnightly?* Something strange awaits us, be sure of that."

T

The winter dragged to its end, and with the spring came Mrs. Lessingham herself. Instantly the life of the Elgars underwent a complete change. The vivacious lady from Paris saw in the twinkling of an eye how matters stood ; she considered the situation perilous, and set to work most efficaciously to alter it. With what result, you are aware. The first incident of any importance in the new life was that which has already been related, yet something happened one day at the Academy of which it is worth while speaking.

Cecily had looked in her catalogue for the name of a certain artist, and had found it ; he exhibited one picture only. Walking on through the rooms with her husband, she came at length to the number she had in mind, and paused before it.

" Whose is that? " Reuben inquired, looking at the same picture.

" Mr. Mallard's," she answered, with a smile, meeting his eyes.

" Old Mallard's? Really? I was wondering whether he had anything this year."

He seemed to receive the information with genuine pleasure. A little to Cecily's surprise, for the name was never mentioned between them, and she had felt uneasy in uttering it. The picture was a piece of coast-scenery in Norway, very grand, cold, desolate ; not at all likely to hold the gaze of Academy visitors, but significant enough for the few who see with the imagination.

"Nobody looks at it, you notice," said Elgar, when they had stood on the spot for five minutes.

" Nobody."

Yet as soon as they had spoken, an old and a young lady came in front of them, and they heard the young lady say, as she pointed to Mallard's canvas :

" Where is that, mamma ? "

" Oh, Land's End, or some such place," was the careless

reply. "*Do* just look at that *sweet* little creature playing with the dog! Look at its collar! And that ribbon!"

Reuben turned away and muttered contemptuous epithets; Cecily cast a haughty and angry glance at the speaker. They passed on, and for the present spoke no more of Mall..rd; but Cecily thought of him, and would have liked to return to the picture before leaving. There was a man who *did* something, and something worth the doing. Reuben must have had a thought not unlike this, for he said, later in the same day:

"I am sorry I never took up painting. I believe I could have made something of it. To a certain extent, you see, it is a handicraft that any man may learn; if one can handle the tools, there's always the incentive to work and produce. By-the-bye, why do you never draw nowadays?"

"I hold the opinion of Miss Denyer—I wonder what's become of her, poor girl?—that it's no use 'pottering.' Strange how a casual word can affect one. I've never cared to draw since she spoke of my 'pottering.'"

This day was the last on which Reuben was quite his wonted self. Cecily, who was not studying him closely just now, did not for a while observe any change, but in the end it forced itself upon her attention. She said nothing, thinking it not impossible that he was again dissatisfied with the fruitlessness of his life, and had been made to feel it more strongly by associating with so many new people. Any sign of that kind was still grateful to her.

She knew now how amiss was her interpretation. The truth she could not accept as she would have done a year ago; it would then have seemed more than pardonable, as proving that Reuben's love of her could drive him into grotesque inconsistencies. But now she only felt it an injury, and in sitting down to write her painful letter to Mrs. Travis, she acted for the first time in deliberate resentment of her husband's conduct.

When the reply from Mrs. Travis instructed him in what

had been done, Reuben left the house, and did not return till late at night. Cecily stayed at home, idle. Visitors called in the afternoon, but she received no one. After her solitary dinner, she spent weary hours, now in one room, now in another, unable to occupy herself in any way. At eleven o'clock she went down to the library, resolving to wait there for Reuben's return.

She heard him enter, and heard the servant speaking with him. He came into the room, closed the door, and sauntered forwards, his hands in his pockets.

"Why didn't you tell me you would be away all day?" Cecily asked, without stress of remonstrance.

"I didn't know that I should be."

He took his favourite position on the corner of the table. Examining him, Cecily saw that his face expressed ennui rather than active displeasure; there was a little sullenness about his lips, but the knitting of his brows was not of the kind that threatens tempest.

"Where have you been, dear?"

"At the Museum, the club, and a music-hall."

"A music-hall?" she repeated, in surprise.

"Why not? I had to get through the time somehow. I was in a surly temper; if I'd come home sooner, I should have raged at you. Don't say anything to irritate me, Ciss; I'm not quite sure of myself yet."

"But I think the raging would have been preferable; I've had the dreariest day I ever spent."

"I suppose some one or other called?"

"Yes, but I didn't see them. You have made me very uncertain of how I ought to behave. I thought it better to keep to myself till we had come to a clearer understanding."

"That is perversity, you know. And it was perversity that led you to write in such a way to Mrs. Travis."

"You are quite right. But the provocation was great. And after all I don't see that there is much difference between writing to her that she mustn't come, and giving directions to a servant that she isn't to be admitted."

"You said in the letter that *I* had forbidden it?"

"Yes, I did."

"And so made me ridiculous!" he exclaimed petulantly.

"My dear, you *were* ridiculous. It's better that you should see it plainly."

"The letter will be shown to all sorts of people. Your aunt will see it, of course. You are ingenious in revenging yourself."

Cecily bent her head, and could not trust herself to speak. All day she had been thinking of this, and had repented of her foolish haste. Yet confession of error was impossible in her present mood.

"As you make such a parade of obedience," he continued, with increasing anger, " I should think it would be better to obey honestly. I never said that I wished you to break with her in this fashion."

"Anything else would be contemptible. I can't subdue myself to that."

"Very well; then to be logical you must give up society altogether. It demands no end of contemptible things."

"Will you explain to me why you think that letter will make you ridiculous?"

Reuben hesitated.

"Is it ridiculous," she added, "for a man to forbid his wife to associate with a woman of doubtful character?"

"I told you distinctly that I had no definite charge to bring against her. Caution would have been reasonable enough, but to act as you have represented me is sheer Philistinism."

"Precisely. And it *was* Philistinism in you to take the matter as you did. Be frank with me. Why should you wish to have a name for liberal thinking among your

acquaintances, and yet behave in private like the most
narrow of men?"

"That is your misrepresentation. Of course, if you
refuse to understand me——"

He broke off, and went to another part of the room.

"Shall I tell you what all this means, Reuben?" said
Cecily, turning towards him. "We have lived so long in
solitude, that the common circumstances of society are
strange and disturbing to us. Solitary people are theoretical people. You would never have thought of forbidding
me to read such and such a book, on the ground that it took
me into doubtful company; the suggestion of such
intolerance would have made you laugh scornfully.
You have become an idealist of a curious kind; you
like to think of me as an emancipated woman, and yet,
when I have the opportunity of making my independence
practical, you show yourself alarmed. I am not sure that I
understand you entirely; I should be very sorry to explain
your words of the other night in the sense they would bear
on the lips of an ordinary man. Can't you help me out of
this difficulty?"

Reuben was reflecting, and had no reply ready.

"If there is to be all this difference between theory and
practice," Cecily continued, "it must either mean that you
think otherwise than you speak, or else that I have shown
myself in some way very untrustworthy. You say you
have been angry with me; I have felt both angry and
deeply hurt. Suppose you had known certainly that Mrs.
Travis was not an honourable woman, even then it was
wrong to speak to me as you did. Even then it would have
been inconsistent to forbid me to see her. You put yourself
and me on different levels. You make me your inferior—
morally your inferior. What should you say if I began to
warn you against one or other of the men you know—if I put
on a stern face, and told you that your morals were in
danger?"

" Pooh ! what harm can a man take ? "

" And pray what harm can a woman take, if her name happens to be Cecily Elgar ? "

She drew herself up, and stood regarding him with superb self-confidence.

" Without meaning it, you insult me, Reuben. You treat me as a vulgar husband treats a vulgar wife. What harm to me do you imagine ? Don't let us deal in silly evasions and roundabout phrases. Do you distrust my honour ? Do you think I can be degraded by association ? What woman living has power to make me untrue to myself ? "

" You are getting rhetorical, Cecily. Then at this rate I should *never* be justified in interfering ? "

" In interfering with mere command, never."

" Not if I saw you going to destruction ? "

She smiled haughtily.

" When it comes to that, we'll discuss the question anew. But I see that you think it possible. Evidently I have given proof of some dangerous weakness. Tell me what it is, and I shall understand you better."

" I'm afraid all this talk leads to nothing. You claim an independence which will make it very difficult for us to live on the old terms."

" I claim nothing more than your own theories have always granted."

" Then practice shows that the theories are untenable, as in many another case."

" You refuse me the right to think for myself."

" In some things, yes. Because, as I said before, you haven't experience enough to go upon."

Cecily cast down her eyes. She forced herself to keep silence until that rush of indignant rebellion had gone by. Reuben looked at her askance.

" If you still loved me as you once did," he said, in a lower voice, " this would be no hardship. Indeed, I should never have had to utter such words."

"I still do love you," she answered, very quietly. "If I did not, I should revolt against your claim. But it is too certain that we no longer live on the old terms."

They avoided each other's eyes, and after a long silence left the room without again speaking.

CHAPTER IV.

THE DENYERS IN ENGLAND.

"There!" said Mrs. Denyer, laying money on the table. "There are your wages, up to the end of April—notwithstanding your impertinence to me this morning, you see. Once more I forgive you. And now get on with your work, and let us have no more unpleasantness."

It was in the back parlour of a small house at Hampstead, a room scantily furnished and not remarkably clean. Mrs. Denyer sat at the table, some loose papers before her. She was in mourning, but still fresh of complexion, and a trifle stouter than when she lived at Naples, two years and a half ago. Her words were addressed to a domestic (most plainly, of all work), who without ceremony gathered the coins up in both her hands, counted them, and then said with decision:

"Now I'm goin', mum."

"Going? Indeed you are not, my girl! You don't leave this house without the due notice."

"Notice or no notice, I'm a-goin'," said the other, firmly. "I never thought to a' got even this much, an' now I've got it, I'm a-goin'. It's wore me out, has this 'ouse; what with——"

The conflict lasted for a good quarter of an hour, but the

domestic was to be shaken neither with threats nor prayers. Resolutely did she ascend to her bedroom, promptly did she pack her box. Almost before Mrs. Denyer could realize the disaster that had befallen, her house was servantless.

She again sat in the back parlour, gazing blankly at the table, when there came the sound of the house-door opening, followed by a light tread in the passage.

"Barbara!" called Mrs. Denyer.

Barbara presented herself. She also wore mourning, genteel but inexpensive. Her prettiness endured, but she was pale, and had a chronic look of discontent.

"Well, now, what do you think has happened? Shut the door. I paid Charlotte the wages, and the very first thing she did was to pack and go!"

"And you mean to say you let her? Why, you must be crazy!"

"Don't speak to me in that way!" cried her mother, hotly. "How could I prevent her, when she was determined? I did my utmost, but nothing could induce her to stay. Was ever anything so distracting? The very day after letting our rooms! How are we to manage?"

"I shall have nothing to do with it. The girl wouldn't have gone if I'd been here. You must manage how you can."

"It's no use talking like that, Barbara. You're bound to wait upon Mrs. Travis until we get another girl."

"I?" exclaimed her daughter. "Wait on her yourself! I certainly shall do nothing of the kind."

"You're a bad, cruel, undutiful girl!" cried Mrs. Denyer, her face on fire. "Neither of your sisters ever treated me as you do. You're the only one of the family that has never given the least help, and you're the only one that day by day insults me and behaves with heartless selfishness! I'm to wait on the lodger myself, am I? Very well! I will do so, and see if anything in the world will shame you. She shall know *why* I wait on her, be sure of that!"

Barbara swept out of the room, and ascended the stairs to the second floor. Here again she heard her name called, in a soft voice and interrogatively ; in reply, she entered a small bedroom, saying impatiently :

" What is it, Mad ? "

It was seen at the first glance that this had long been a sick-chamber. The arrangement of the furniture, the medicine-bottles, the appliances for the use of one who cannot rise from bed, all told their story. The air had a peculiar scent ; an unnatural stillness seemed to pervade it. Against the raised white pillow showed a face hardly less white.

" Isn't it provoking, Barbara ? " said the invalid, without moving in the least. " Whatever shall you do ? "

" As best we can, I suppose. I've to turn cook and house-maid and parlour-maid, now. Scullery-maid too. I suppose I shall clean the steps to-morrow morning."

" Oh, but you must go to the registry-office the very first thing. Don't upset yourself about it. If you can just manage to get that lady's dinner."

" It's all very well for you to talk ! How would *you* like to *wait* on people, like a girl in a restaurant ? "

" Ah, if only I could ! " replied Madeline, with a little laugh that was heart-breaking. " If only I could ! "

In a month it would be two years since Madeline stood and walked like other people ; live as long as she might, she would never rise from her bed. It came about in this way. Whilst the Denyers were living in the second-class hotel at Southampton, and when Mr. Denyer had been gone to Vera Cruz some five months, a little ramble was taken one day in a part of the New Forest. Madeline was in particularly good spirits ; she had succeeded in getting an engagement to teach some children, and her work was to begin the next day. In a frolic she set herself to jump over a fallen tree ; her feet slipped on the dry grass beyond, and she fell with her back upon the trunk.

This was pleasant news to send to her father! With him things were going as well as he had anticipated, and before long he was able to make substantial remittances, but his letters were profoundly sad. In a year's time, the family quitted Southampton and took the house at Hampstead; with much expense and difficulty Madeline was removed. Mrs. Denyer and Barbara were weary of provincial life, and considered nothing in their resolve to be within reach of London amusements. Zillah was living as governess with a family in Yorkshire.

They had been settled at Hampstead three weeks, when information reached them that Mr. Denyer was dead of yellow fever.

On the day when this news came, the house received no less important a visitor than Mr. Musselwhite. Long ago, Mrs. Denyer had written to him from Southampton, addressing her letter to the club in London of which he had spoken; she had received a prompt reply, dated from rooms in London, and thenceforth the correspondence was established. But Mr. Musselwhite never spoke of coming to Southampton; his letters ended with " Sincere regards to Miss Denyer and the other young ladies," but they contained nothing that was more to the point. He wrote about the weather chiefly. Arrived in London, Mrs. Denyer at once sent an invitation, and to her annoyance this remained unanswered. To-day the explanation was forthcoming; Mr. Musselwhite had been on a journey, and by some mistake the letter had only come into his hands when he returned. He was most gentlemanly in his expressions of condolement with the family in their distress; he sat with them, moreover, much longer than was permissible under the circumstances by the code of society. And on going, he begged to be allowed to see them frequently—that was all.

Barbara could not control herself for irritation; Mrs. Denyer was indignant. Yet, after all, was it to be expected that the visitor should say or do more on such an occasion as this ? In any case, he knew what their position was ; all had been put before him, as though he were a member of the family. If they succeeded in obtaining whatever Mr. Denyer had died possessed of, it would certainly be nothing more than a provision for the present. When they spoke of taking a lodger for their first floor, Mr. Musselwhite agreed that this was a good thought, whilst shaking his gentlemanly head over the necessity.

He came again and again, always sadly sympathetic. He would sit in the drawing-room for an hour, pulling his whiskers and moustaches nervously, often glancing at Barbara, making the kindest inquiries concerning Madeline, for whom he actually brought flowers. On one of these occasions, he told them that his brother the baronet was very ill, down at the "place in Lincolnshire." And after mentioning this, he fell into abstraction.

As for Madeline, she still received letters from Clifford Marsh. On first hearing of the accident, Clifford at once came to Southampton ; his distress was extreme. But it was useless for him to remain, and business demanded his return to Leeds. Neither he nor Madeline was yet aware of the gravity of what had happened ; they talked of recovery. Before long Madeline knew how her situation was generally regarded, but she could not abandon hope ; she was able to write, and not a word in her letters betrayed a doubt of the possibility that she might yet be well again. Clifford wrote very frequently for the first year, with a great deal of genuine tenderness, with compassion and encouragement. Never mind how long her illness lasted, let her be assured of his fidelity ; no one but Madeline should ever be his wife. A considerable part of his letters was always occupied with lamentation over the cursed fate that bound him to the Philistines, though he took care to repeat that this was the result of his own choice, and that he blamed no one—unless it were his gross-minded step-father, who had driven him to such an alternative. These bewailings grew less vehement as his letters became shorter and arrived at longer intervals ; there began to be a sameness in the tone, even in the words. When his yearly holiday came round, he promised to visit Southampton, but after all never did so. What was the use ? he wrote. It only meant keener misery to both. Instead of coming south, he had gone into Scotland.

And Madeline no longer expressed a wish to see him. Her own letters grew shorter and calmer, containing at length very little about herself, but for the most part news of family affairs. Every now and then Clifford seemed to rouse himself to the effort of repeating his protestations, of affirming his deathless faith ; but as a rule he wrote about trifles, sometimes even of newspaper matters. So did the second year of Madeline's martyrdom come to its close.

Quarrelling incessantly, Mrs. Denyer and Barbara prepared the lodger's dinner between them. This Mrs. Travis was not exacting ; she had stipulated only for a cutlet, or something of the kind, with two vegetables, and a milk pudding. Whatever was proposed seemed to suit her. The Denyers knew nothing about her, except that she was able to refer them to a lady who had a house in Mayfair ; her husband, she said, was abroad. She had brought a great deal of luggage, including books to the number of fifty or so.

When the moment for decision came, Barbara snatched up the folded white table-cloth, threw it with knives, forks, and plates upon a tray, and ascended to the lodger's sitting-room. Her cheeks were hot ; her eyes flashed. She had donned the most elegant attire in her possession, had made her hair magnificent. Her knock at the door was meant to be a declaration of independence ; it sounded peremptory.

Mrs. Travis was in an easy-chair, reading. She looked up absently ; then smiled.

"Good evening, Miss Denyer. How close it has been again ! "

"Very. I must ask you to excuse me, Mrs. Travis, if I do these things rather awkwardly. At a moment's notice, we have lost the servant whose duty it was."

"Oh, I am only sorry that you should have the trouble. Let us lay the table together. I've done it often enough for myself. No, that's the wrong side of the cloth. I'll put these things in order, whilst you go for the rest."

Barbara looked at Mrs. Travis with secret disdain. The girl's nature was plebeian; a little arrogance would have constrained her to respect, however she might have seemed to resent it. This good-natured indifference made her feel that her preparations were thrown away. She would have preferred to see herself as a martyr.

When dinner was over and the table being cleared, Mrs. Travis spoke of Madeline.

"Does she sleep well at night?"

"Never till very late," replied Barbara.

"Does she like to be read to?"

"Oh yes—reading of certain kinds. I often read Italian poetry to her."

Mrs. Travis had not now to learn for the first time of the family's superior attainments; it had been Mrs. Denyer's care to impress upon her that they were no ordinary letters of lodgings. Indeed, said Mrs. Denyer, they were rather *dépaysées* here in England; they had so long been accustomed to the larger intellectual atmosphere of Continental centres. "The poor girls pine for Italy; they have always adored Italy. My eldest daughter is far more Italian than English."

"Well, I don't read Italian," said Mrs. Travis to Barbara, "but if English would do, I should really like to sit with her for an hour sometimes. I never sleep myself if I go to bed before midnight. Do you think she would care for my company?"

"I am sure she would be grateful to you," answered Barbara, who felt that she might now exhibit a little politeness.

"Then please ask her if I may come to-night."

This request was readily granted, and at about half-past nine Mrs. Travis went into the sick-chamber, taking in her hand a volume of Browning. Madeline had not yet seen the lodger; she returned her greeting in a murmur, and examined her with the steady eyes of one whom great suffering has delivered from all petty embarrassments. Her face was not so calm as when Barbara came to speak to her in the afternoon; lines of pain showed themselves on her forehead, and her thin lips were compressed.

"It's very good of you to come," she said, when Mrs. Travis had taken a seat by the bed. "But please don't read anything to-night. I don't feel that I could take any interest. It is so sometimes."

"Naturally enough. But do you feel able to talk?"

"Yes; I had rather talk. Can you tell me something quite new and different from what I'm accustomed to hear? Do you know any country where I haven't been?"

"I haven't travelled much. Last autumn I was in Iceland for a few weeks; would you care to hear of that?"

"Very much. Just talk as if you were going over it in your memory. Don't mind if I close my eyes; I shan't be asleep; it helps me to imagine, that's all."

Mrs. Travis did as she was asked. Now and then Madeline put a question. When at length there came a pause, she said abruptly:

"I suppose it seems dreadful to you, to see me lying here like this?"

"It makes me wish I had it in my power to relieve you."

"But does it seem dreadful? Could you bear to imagine yourself in the same case? I want you to tell me truthfully. I'm not an uneducated girl, you know; I can think about life and death as people do nowadays."

Mrs. Travis looked at her curiously.

"I can imagine positions far worse," she answered.

"That means, of course, that you could not bear to picture

yourself in this. But it's strange how one can get used to it. The first year I suffered horribly—in mind, I mean. But then I still had hope. I have none now, and that keeps my mind calmer. A paradox, isn't it? It's always possible, you know, that I may feel such a life unendurable at last, and then I should hope to find a means of bringing it to an end. For instance, if we become so poor that I am too great a burden. Of course I wouldn't live in a hospital. I don't mean I should be too proud, but the atmosphere would be intolerable. And one really needn't live, after one has decided that it's no use."

"I don't know what to say about that," murmured Mrs. Travis.

"No; you haven't had the opportunity of thinking it over, as I have. I can imagine myself reaching the point when I should not care to have health again, even if it were offered me. I haven't come to that yet; oh no! To-night I am feeling dreadfully what I have lost—not like I used to, but still dreadfully. Will you tell me something about yourself? What kind of books do you like?"

"Pretty much the same as you do, I should fancy. I like to know what new things people are discovering, and how the world looks to clever men. But I can't study; I have no perseverance. I read the reviews a good deal."

"You'd never guess the last book I have read. It lies on the chest of drawers there—a treatise on all the various kinds of paralysis. The word 'paralysis' used to have the most awful sound to me; now I'm so familiar with it that it has ceased to be shocking and become interesting. What I am suffering from is called *paraplegia;* that's when the lower half of the body is affected; it comes from injury or disease of the spinal cord. The paralysis begins at the point in the vertebral column where the injury was received. But it tends to spread upward. If it gets as far as certain nerves upon which the movements of the diaphragm depend, then you die. I wonder whether that will be my case?"

Mrs. Travis kept her eyes on the girl during this singular little lecture; she felt the fascination which is exercised by strange mental phenomena.

"Do you know Italy?" Madeline asked, with sudden transition.

"I have travelled through it, like other tourists."

"You went to Naples?"

"Yes."

"If I close my eyes, how well I can see Naples! Now I am walking through the Villa Nazionale. I come out into the Largo Vittoria, where the palm-trees are—do you remember? Now I might go into the Chiatamone, between the high houses; but instead of that I'll turn down into Via Caracciolo and go along by the sea, till I'm opposite the Castel dell' Ovo. Now I'm turning the corner and coming on to Santa Lucia, where there are stalls with shells and ices and fish. I can smell the Santa Lucia. And to think that I shall never see it again, never again.—Don't stay any longer now, Mrs. Travis. I can't talk any more. Thank you for being so kind."

In a week's time it had become a regular thing for Mrs. Travis to spend an hour or two daily with Madeline. Their conversation was suitable enough to a sick-chamber, yet strangely unlike what is wont to pass in such places. On Madeline's side it was thoroughly morbid; on that of her visitor, a curious mixture of unhealthy speculation and pure feeling. Mrs. Travis was at first surprised that the suffering girl never seemed to think of ordinary religion as a solace. She herself had no fixity of faith; her mind played constantly with creeds of negation; but she felt it as an unnatural thing for one of Madeline's age to profess herself wholly without guidance on so dark a journey. And presently she began to doubt whether the profession were genuine. The characteristic of the family was pretence and posing; Mrs. Denyer and Barbara illustrated that every time they spoke. Not impossibly Madeline did but declare the

U

same tendency in her rambling and quasi-philosophic talk. She was fond of warning Mrs. Travis against attributing to her the common prejudices of women. And yet, were it affectation, then the habit must be so inextricably blended with her nature as to have become in practice a genuine motive in the mind's working. Madeline would speculate on the difference between one of her "culture" in the circumstances and the woman who is a slave of tradition; and a moment after she would say something so profoundly pathetic that it brought tears to her companion's eyes.

Mrs. Travis never spoke of her personal affairs; Madeline could supply no food for the curiosity of her mother and sister when they questioned her about the long private conversations. The lodger received no visitors, and seldom a letter. In the morning she went out for an hour, generally towards the heath; occasionally she was from home until late at night. About the quality of the attendance given her she was wholly indifferent; in spite of frequent inconveniences, she made her weekly payments without a word of dissatisfaction. She had a few eccentricities of behaviour which the Denyers found it difficult to reconcile with the refinement of her ordinary conduct. Once or twice, when the servant went into her sitting-room the first thing in the morning, she was surprised to find Mrs. Travis lying asleep on the couch, evidently just as she had come home the previous night, except that her bonnet was removed. It had happened, too, that when some one came and knocked at her door during the day, she vouchsafed no answer, and yet made the sound of moving about, as if to show that she did not choose to be disturbed, for whatever reason.

The household went its regular way. Mrs. Denyer sat in her wonted idle dignity, or scolded the hard-driven maid-of-all-work, or quarrelled fiercely with Barbara. Barbara was sullen, insolent, rebellious against fate, by turns. Up in the still room lay poor Madeline, seldom visited by either of the two save when it was necessary. All knew that the position of things had no security; before long there must come a crisis worse than any the family had yet experienced. Unless, indeed, that one hope which remained to them could be realized.

One afternoon at the end of July, mother and daughter were sitting over their tea, lamenting the necessity which kept them in London when the eternal fitness of things demanded that they should be preparing for travel. They heard a vehicle draw up before the house, and Barbara, making cautious espial from the windows, exclaimed that it was Mr. Musselwhite.

"He has a lot of flowers, as usual," she added, scornfully, watching him as he paid the cabman. "Go into the back room, mamma. Let's say you're not at home to-day. Send for the teapot, and get some more tea made."

There came a high-bred knock at the front door, and Mrs. Denyer disappeared.

Mr. Musselwhite entered with a look and bearing much graver than usual. He made the proper remarks, and gave Barbara the flowers for her sister; then seated himself, and stroked his moustache.

"Miss Denyer," he began, when Barbara waited wearily for the familiar topic, "my brother, Sir Grant, died a week ago."

"I am very grieved to hear it," she replied, mechanically, at once absorbed in speculation as to whether this would make any change that concerned her.

"It was a long and painful illness, and recovery was known to be impossible. Yet I too cannot help grieving. As you know, we had not seen much of each other for some years, but I had the very highest opinion of Sir Grant, and it always gave me pleasure to think of him as the head of our family. He was a man of great abilities, and a kind man."

"I am sure he was—from what you have told me of him."

"My nephew succeeds to the title and the estate; he is now Sir Roland Musselwhite. I have mentioned him in our conversations. He is about thirty-four, a very able man, and very kind, very generous."

There was a distinct tremor in his voice; he pulled his moustache vigorously. Barbara listened with painful eagerness.

"If you will forgive me for speaking of my private circumstances, Miss Denyer, I should like to tell you that for some years I have enjoyed only a very restricted income; a bachelor's allowance—really it amounted to nothing more than that. In consequence of that, my life has been rather unsettled; I scarcely knew what to do with myself, in fact; now and then time has been rather heavy on my hands. You may have noticed that, for I know you are observant."

He waited for her to say whether she had or had not observed this peculiarity in him.

"I have sometimes been afraid that was the case," said Barbara.

"I quite thought so." He smiled with gratification. "But now—if I may speak a little longer of these personal matters—all that is altered, and by the very great kindness, the generosity, of my nephew Sir Roland. Sir Roland has seen fit to put me in possession of an income just three times what I have hitherto commanded. This does not, Miss Denyer, make me a wealthy man; far from it. But it puts certain things within my reach that I could not think of formerly. For instance, I shall be able to take a modest house, either in the country, or here in one of the suburbs. It's my wish to do so. My one great wish is to settle down and have something to—to occupy my time."

Barbara breathed a faint approval.

"You may wonder, Miss Denyer, why I trouble you with these details. Perhaps I might be pardoned for doing so, if I spoke with— with a desire for your friendly sympathy.

But there is more than that in my mind. The day is come, Miss Denyer, when I am able to say what I would gladly have said before our parting at Naples, if it had been justifiable in me. That is rather a long time ago, but the feeling I then had has only increased in the meanwhile. Miss Denyer, I desire humbly to ask if you will share with me my new prosperity, such as it is ? "

The interview lasted an hour and a quarter. Mrs. Denyer panted with impatience in the back parlour. Such an extended visit could not but have unusual significance. On hearing the door of the other room open, she stood up and listened. But there was no word in the passage, no audible murmur.

The front door closed, and in two ticks of the clock Barbara came headlong into the parlour. With broken breath, with hysterical laughing and sobbing, she made known what had happened. It was too much for her; the relief of suspense, the absolute triumph, were more than she could support with decency. Mrs. Denyer shed tears, and embraced her daughter as if they had always been on the fondest terms.

"Go up and tell Maddy ! "

But, as not seldom befalls, happiness inspired Barbara with a delicacy of feeling to which as a rule she was a stranger.

"I don't like to, mamma. It seems cruel."

"But you can't help it, my dear ; and she must know to-morrow if not to-day."

So before long Barbara went upstairs. She entered the room softly. Madeline had her eyes fixed on the ceiling, and did not move them as her sister approached the bed.

"Maddy ! "

Then indeed she looked at the speaker, and with surprise, so unwonted was this tone on Barbara's lips. Surprise was quickly succeeded by a smile.

"I know, Barbara; I understand."

"What? How can you?"

"I heard a cab drive up, and I heard a knock at the door. 'That's Mr. Musselwhite,' I thought. He has been here a long time, and now I understand. You needn't tell me."

"But there's a good deal to tell that you can't have found out, quick as you are."

And she related the circumstances. Madeline listened with her eyes on the ceiling.

"We shall be married very soon," Barbara added; "as soon as a house can be chosen. Of course it must be in London, or very near. We shall go somewhere or other, and then, very likely, pay a formal visit to the 'place in Lincolnshire.' Think of that! Sir Roland seems a good sort of man; he will welcome us. Think of visiting at the 'place in Lincolnshire'! Isn't it all like a dream?"

"What will mamma do without you?"

"Oh, Zillah is to come home. We'll see about that."

"I suppose he forgot to bring me some flowers to-day?"

"No! But I declare I forgot to bring them up. I'll fetch them at once."

She did so, running downstairs and up again like a child, with a jump at the landings. The flowers were put in the usual place. Madeline looked at them, and listened to her sister's chatter for five minutes. Then she said absently:

"Go away now, please. I've heard enough for the present."

"You shall have all sorts of comforts, Maddy."

"Go away, Barbara."

The sister obeyed, looking back with compassion from the door. She closed it softly, and in the room there was the old perfect stillness. Madeline had let her eyelids fall, and the white face against the white pillows was like that of one dead. But upon the eyelashes there presently shone a tear; it swelled, broke away, and left a track of moisture. Poor white face, with the dark hair softly shadowing its temples! Poor troubled brain, wearying itself in idle questioning of powers that heeded not!

CHAPTER V.

MULTUM IN PARVO.

ELGAR's marriage had been a great success. For a year and a half, for even more than that, he had lived the fullest and most consistent life of which he was capable; what proportion of the sons of men can look back on an equal span of time in their own existence and say the same of it?

Life with Cecily gave predominance to all the noblest energies in his nature. He loved with absolute sincerity; his ideal of womanhood was for the time realized and possessed; the vagrant habit of his senses seemed permanently subdued; his mind was occupied with high admirations and creative fancies; in thought and speech he was ardent, generous, constant, hopeful. A happy marriage can do no more for man than make unshadowed revelation of such aspiring faculty as he is endowed withal. It cannot supply him with a force greater than he is born to; even as the happiest concurrence of healthful circumstances cannot give more strength to a physical constitution than its origin warrants. At this period of his life, Reuben Elgar could not have been more than, with Cecily's help, he showed himself. Be the future advance or retrogression, he had lived the possible life.

Whose the fault that it did not continue? Cecily's, if it

were blameworthy to demand too much; Elgar's, if it be wrong to learn one's own limitations.

His making definité choice of a subject whereon to employ his intellect was at one and the same time a proof of how far his development had progressed and a warning of what lay before him. However chaotic the material in which he proposed to work, however inadequate his powers, it was yet a truth that, could he execute anything at all, it would be something of the kind thus vaguely contemplated. His intellect was combative, and no subject excited it to such activity as this of Hebraic constraint in the modern world. Elgar's book, supposing him to have been capable of writing it, would have resembled no other; it would have been, as he justly said, unique in its anti-dogmatic passion. It was quite in the order of things that he should propose to write it; equally so, that the attempt should mark the end of his happiness.

For all that she seemed to welcome the proposal with enthusiasm, Cecily's mind secretly misgave her: She had begun to understand Reuben, and she foresaw, with a certainty which she in vain tried to combat, how soon his energy would fail upon so great a task. Impossible to admonish him; impossible to direct him on a humbler path, where he might attain some result. With Reuben's temperament to deal with, that would mean a fatal disturbance of their relations to each other. That the disturbance must come in any case, now that he was about to prove himself, she anticipated in many a troubled moment, but would not let the forecast discourage her.

Elgar knew how his failure in perseverance affected her; he looked for the signs of her disappointment, and was at no loss to find them. It was natural to him to exaggerate the diminution of her esteem; he attributed to her what, in her place, he would himself have felt; he soon imagined that she had as good as ceased to love him. He could not bear to be less in her eyes than formerly; a jealous shame stung him, and at length made him almost bitter against her.

In this way came about his extraordinary outbreak that night when Cecily had been alone to her aunt's. Pent-up irritation drove him into the extravagances which to Cecily were at first incredible. He could not utter what was really in his mind, and the charges he made against her were modes of relieving himself. Yet, as soon as they had once taken shape, these rebukes obtained a real significance of their own. Coincident with Cecily's disappointment in him had been the sudden exhibition of her pleasure in society. Under other circumstances, his wife's brilliancy among strangers might have been pleasurable to Elgar. His faith in her was perfect, and jealousy of the ignobler kind came not near him. But he felt that she was taking refuge from the dulness of her home; he imagined people speaking of him as "the husband of Mrs. Elgar;" it exasperated him to think of her talking with clever men who must necessarily suggest comparisons to her.

He himself was not the kind of man who shines in company. He had never been trained to social usages, and he could not feel at ease in any drawing-room but his own. The Bohemianism of his early life had even given him a positive distaste for social obligations and formalities. Among men of his own way of thinking, he could talk vigorously, and as a rule keep the lead in conversation; but where restraint in phrase was needful, he easily became flaccid, and the feeling that he did not show to advantage filled him with disgust. So there was little chance of his ever winning that sort of reputation which would have enabled him to accompany his wife into society without the galling sense of playing an inferior *rôle*.

In the matter of Mrs. Travis, he was conscious of his own arbitrariness, but, having once committed himself to a point of view, he could not withdraw from it. He had to find fault with his wife and her society, and here was an obvious resource. Its very obviousness should, of course, have warned him away, but his reason for attacking Mrs. Travis had an

intimate connection with the general causes of his discontent. Disguise it how he might, he was simply in the
position of a husband who fears that his authority over his
wife is weakening. Mrs. Travis, as he knew, was a rebel
against her own husband—no matter the cause. She would
fill Cecily's mind with sympathetic indignation; the effect
would be to make Cecily more resolute in independence.
Added to this, there was, in truth, something of that conflict
between theoretical and practical morality of which his wife
spoke. It developed in the course of argument; he recognized
that, whilst having all confidence in Cecily, he could not
reconcile himself to her associating with a woman whose
conduct was under discussion. The more he felt his inconsistency, the more arbitrary he was compelled to be. Motives
confused themselves and harassed him. In his present mood,
the danger of such a state of things was greater than he knew,
and of quite another kind than Cecily was prepared for.

"What is all this about Mrs. Travis?" inquired Mrs.
Lessingham, with a smile, when she came to visit Cecily.
Reuben was out, and the ladies sat alone in the drawing-
room.

Cecily explained what had happened, but in simple terms,
and without meaning to show that any difference of opinion
had arisen between her and Reuben.

"You have heard of it from Mrs. Travis herself?" she
asked, in conclusion.

"Yes. She expressed no resentment, however; spoke as
if she thought it a little odd, that was all. But what has
Reuben got into his head?"

"It seems he has heard unpleasant rumours about her."

"Then why didn't he come and speak to me? She is
absolutely blameless: I can answer for it. Her husband is the
kind of man——Did you ever read Fielding's 'Amelia'? To
be sure; well, you understand. I much doubt whether she
is wise in leaving him; ten to one, she'll go back again, and

that is more demoralizing than putting up with the other indignity. She has a very small income of her own, and what
is her life to be ? Surely you are the last people who should
abandon her. That is the kind of thing that makes such a
woman desperate. She seems to have made a sort of appeal
to you. I am but moderately in her confidence, and I believe
she hasn't one bosom friend. It's most fortunate that
Reuben took such a whim. Send him to me, will you ? "

Cecily made known this request to her husband, and there
followed another long dialogue between them, the only result of which was to increase their mutual coldness. Cecily
proposed that they should at once leave town, instead of
waiting for the end of the season ; in this way all their
difficulties would be obviated. Elgar declined the proposal ;
he had no desire to spoil her social pleasures.

"That is already done, past help," Cecily rejoined, with
the first note of bitterness. "I no longer care to visit, nor
to receive guests."

"I noticed the other day your ingenuity in revenging
yourself."

"I say nothing but the simple truth. Had you rather I
went out and enjoyed myself without any reference to your
wishes ? "

"From the first you made up your mind to misunderstand
me," said Reuben, with the common evasion of one who cannot defend his course.

Cecily brought the dispute to an end by her silence. The
next morning Reuben went to see Mrs. Lessingham, and
heard what she had to say about Mrs. Travis.

"What is your evidence against her ? " she inquired, after
a little banter.

"Some one who knows Travis very well assured me that
the fault was not all on his side."

"Of course. It is more to the point to hear what those
have to say who know his wife. Surely you acted with extraordinary haste."

With characteristic weakness, Elgar defended himself by detailing the course of events. It was not he who had been precipitate, but Cecily; he was never more annoyed than when he heard of that foolish letter.

"Go home and persuade her to write another," said Mrs. Lessingham. "Let her confess that there was a misunderstanding. I am sure Mrs. Travis will accept it. She has a curious character; very sensitive, and very impulsive, but essentially trustful and warm-hearted. You should have heard the pathetic surprise with which she told me of Cecily's letter."

"I should rather have imagined her speaking contemptuously."

"It would have been excusable," replied the other, with a laugh. "And very likely that would have been her tone had it concerned any one else. But she has a liking for Cecily. Go home, and get this foolish mistake remedied, there's a good boy."

Elgar left the house and walked eastward, into Praed Street. As he walked, he grew less and less inclined to go home at once. He could not resolve how to act. It would be a satisfaction to have done with discord, but he had no mind to submit to Cecily and entreat her to a peace.

He walked on, across Edgware Road, into Marylebone Road, absorbed in his thoughts. Their complexion became darker. He found a perverse satisfaction in picturing Cecily's unhappiness. Let her suffer a little; she was causing *him* uneasiness enough. The probability was that she derided his recent behaviour; it had doubtless sunk him still more in her estimation. The only way to recover his lost ground was to be as open with her as formerly, to confess all his weaknesses and foolish motives; but his will resisted. He felt coldly towards her; she was no longer the woman he loved and worshipped, but one who had asserted a superiority of mind and character, and belittled him to himself. He was tired of her society—the simple formula which sufficiently explains so many domestic troubles.

He would have lunch somewhere in town; then see whether he felt disposed to go home or not.

In the afternoon he loitered about the Strand, looking at portraits in shop-windows and at the theatre-doors. Home was more, instead of less, repugnant to him. He wanted to postpone decision; but if he returned to Cecily, it would be necessary to say something, and in his present mood he would be sure to make matters worse, for he felt quarrelsome. How absurd it was for two people, just because they were married, to live perpetually within sight of each other! Wasn't it Godwin who, on marrying, made an arrangement that he and his wife should inhabit separate abodes, and be together only when they wished? The only rational plan, that. Should he take train and go out of town for a few days? If only he had some one for company; but it was wearisome to spend the time in solitude.

To aggravate his dulness, the sky had clouded over, and presently it began to rain. He had no umbrella. Quite unable to determine whither he should go if he took a cab, he turned aside to the shelter of an archway. Some one was already standing there, but in his abstraction he did not know whether it was man or woman, until a little cough, twice or thrice repeated, made him turn his eyes. Then he saw that his companion was a girl of about five-and-twenty, with a pretty, good-natured face, which wore an embarrassed smile. He gazed at her with a look of surprised recognition.

"Well, it really *is* you!" she exclaimed, laughing and looking down.

"And it is really *you!*"

They shook hands, again examining each other.

"I thought you didn't mean to know me."

"I hadn't once looked at you. But you have changed a good deal."

"Not more than you have, I'm sure."

"And what are you doing? You look much more cheerful than you used to."

"I can't say the same of you."

"Have you been in London all the time?"

"Oh no. Two years ago I went back to Liverpool, and had a place there for nearly six months. But I got tired of it. In a few days I'm going to Brighton; I've got a place in a restaurant. Quite time, too; I've had nothing for seven weeks."

"I've often thought about you," said Elgar, after a pause.

"But you never came to see how I was getting on."

"Oh, I supposed you were married long since."

She laughed, and shook her head.

"You are, though, I suppose?" she asked.

"Not I!"

They talked with increasing friendliness until the rain stopped, then walked away together in the direction of the City.

About dinner-time, Cecily received a telegram. It was from her husband, and informed her that he had left town with a friend for a day or two.

This was the first instance of such a proceeding on Reuben's part. For a moment, it astonished her. Which of his friends could it be? But when the surprise had passed, she reflected more on his reasons for absenting himself, and believed that she understood them. He wished to punish her; he thought she would be anxious about him, and so come to adopt a different demeanour when he returned. Ever so slight a suspicion of another kind occurred to her once or twice, but she had no difficulty in dismissing it. No; this was merely one of his tactics in the conflict that had begun between them.

And his absence was a relief. She too wanted to think for a while, undisturbed. When she had seen the child in bed and asleep, she moved about the house with a strange sense of freedom, seeming to breathe more naturally than for several days. She went to the piano, and played some favourite pieces, among them one which she had learnt long ago in Paris. It gave her a curiously keen pleasure, like a revival of her girlhood; she lingered over it, and nursed the impression. Then she read a little—not continuously, but dipping into familiar books. It was holiday with her. And when she lay down to rest, the sense of being alone was still grateful. Sleep came very soon, and she did not stir till morning.

On the third day Elgar returned, at noon. She heard the cab that brought him. He lingered in the hall, opened the library door; then came to the drawing-room, humming an air. His look was as different as could be from that she had last seen on his face; he came towards her with his pleasantest smile, and first kissed her hand, then embraced her in the old way.

" You haven't been anxious about me, Ciss ? "

"Not at all," she replied quietly, rather permitting his caresses than encouraging them.

" Some one I hadn't met for several years. He was going down to Brighton, and persuaded me to accompany him. I didn't write because—well, I thought it would be better if we kept quite apart for a day or two. Things were getting wrong, weren't they ? "

" I'm afraid so. But how are they improved ? "

" Why, I had a talk with your aunt about Mrs. Travis. I quite believe I was misled by that fellow that talked scandal. She seems very much to be pitied, and I'm really sorry that I caused you to break with her."

Cecily watched him as he spoke, and he avoided her eyes. He was holding her hands and fondling them; now he bent and put them to his lips. She said nothing.

" Suppose you write to her, Ciss, and say that I made a fool of myself. You're quite at liberty to do so. Tell her exactly how it was, and ask her to forgive us."

She did not answer immediately.

" Will you do that ? "

"I feel ashamed to. I know very well how *I* should receive such a letter."

"Oh, you! But every one hasn't your superb arrogance!" He laughed. "And it's hard to imagine you in such a situation."

"I hope so."

"Aunt tells me that the poor woman has very few friends."

"It's very unlikely that she will ever make one of me. I don't see how it is possible, after this."

"But write the letter, just to make things simpler if you meet anywhere. As a piece of justice, too."

Not that day, but the following, Cecily decided herself to write. She could only frame her excuse in the way Reuben had suggested; necessarily the blame lay on him. The composition cost her a long time, though it was only two pages of note-paper; and when it was despatched, she could not think without hot cheeks of its recipient reading it. She did not greatly care for Mrs. Travis's intimacy, but she did desire to remove from herself the imputation of censoriousness.

There came an answer in a day or two.

"I was surprised that you (or Mr. Elgar) should so readily believe ill of me, but I am accustomed to such judgments, and no longer resent them. A wife is always in the wrong; when a woman marries, she should prepare herself for this. Or rather, her friends should prepare her, as she has always been kept in celestial ignorance by their care. Pray let us forget what has happened. I won't renew my request to be allowed to visit you; if that is to be, it will somehow come to pass naturally, in the course of time. If we meet at Mrs. Lessingham's, please let us speak not a word of this affair. I hate scenes."

In a week's time, the Elgars' life had resumed the course it held before that interruption—with the exception that

Reuben, as often as it was possible, avoided accompanying his wife when she went from home. His own engagements multiplied, and twice before the end of July he spent Saturday and Sunday out of town. Cecily made no close inquiries concerning his employment of his time; on their meeting again, he always gave her an account of what he had been doing, and she readily accepted it. For she had now abandoned all hope of his doing serious work; she never spoke a word which hinted regret at his mode of life. They were on placid terms, and she had no such faith in anything better as would justify her in endangering the recovered calm.

It became necessary at length to discuss what they should do with themselves during the autumn. Mrs. Lessingham was going with friends to the Pyrenees. The Delphs would take a short holiday in Sussex; Irene could not spare much time from her work.

"I don't care to be away long myself," Reuben said, when Cecily mentioned this. "I feel as if I should be able to get on with my Puritanic pursuits again when we return."

Cecily looked at him, to see if he spoke in earnest. In spite of his jesting tone, he seemed to be serious, for he was pacing the floor, his head bent as if in meditation.

"Make your own plans," was her reply. "But we won't go into Cornwall, I think."

"No, not this year."

They spent a month at Eastbourne. Some agreeable people whom they were accustomed to meet at Mrs. Lessingham's had a house there, and supplied them with society. Towards the end of the month, Reuben grew restless and uncertain of temper; he wandered on the downs by himself, and when at home kept silence. The child, too, was constantly ailing, and its cry irritated him.

"The fact of the matter is," he exclaimed one evening, "I don't feel altogether well! I ought to have had more change than this. If I go back and settle to work, I shall break down."

"What kind of change do you wish for?" Cecily asked.

"I should have liked to take a ramble in Germany, or Norway—some new part. But nothing of that is possible. Clarence makes slaves of us."

Cecily reflected.

"There's no reason why he should hinder you from going."

"Oh, I can't leave you alone," he returned impatiently.

"I think you might, for a few weeks—if you feel it necessary. I don't think Clarence ought to leave the seaside till the middle of September. The Robinsons will be here still, you know."

He muttered and grumbled, but in the end proposed that he should go over by one of the Harwich boats, and take what course happened to attract him. Cecily assented, and in a few hours he was ready to bid her good-bye. She had said that it wasn't worth while going with him to the station, and when he gave her the kiss at starting she kept perfectly tranquil.

"You're not sorry to get rid of me," he said, with a forced laugh.

"I don't wish you to stay at the expense of your health."

"I hope Clarence mayn't damage yours. These sleepless nights are telling on you."

"Go. You'll miss the train."

He looked back from the door, but Cecily had turned away.

He was absent for more than six weeks, during which he wrote frequently from various out-of-the-way places on the Rhine. On returning, he found Cecily in London, very anxious about the child, and herself looking very ill. He, on the other hand, was robust and in excellent spirits; in a day or two he began to go regularly to the British Museum —to say, at all events, that he went there. And so time passed to the year's end.

One night in January Reuben went to the theatre. He left Cecily sitting in the bedroom, by the fireside, with Clarence on her lap. For several weeks the child had been so ill that Cecily seldom quitted it.

Three hours later she was sitting in the same position, still bent forward, the child still on her lap. But no movement, no cry ever claimed her attention. Tears had stained her face, but they no longer fell. Holding a waxen little hand that would never again caress her, she gazed at the dying fire as though striving to read her destiny.

CHAPTER VI.

AT PÆSTUM.

The English artist had finished his work, and the dirty little inn at Pæstum would to-day lose its solitary guest.

This morning he rose much later than usual, and strolled out idly into the spring sunshine, a rug thrown over his shoulder. Often plucking a flower or a leaf, and seeming to examine it with close thoughtfulness, he made a long circuit by the old walls ; now and then he paused to take a view of the temples, always with eye of grave meditation. At one elevated point, he stood for several minutes looking along the road to Salerno.

March rains had brought the vegetation into luxurious life ; fern, acanthus, brambles, and all the densely intermingled growths that cover the ground about the ruins, spread forth their innumerable tints of green. Between shore and mountains, the wide plain smiled in its desolation.

At length he went up into the Temple of Neptune, spread the rug on a spot where he had been accustomed, each day at noon, to eat his salame and drink his Calabrian wine, and seated himself against a column. Here he could enjoy a view from both ends of the ruin. In the one direction it was only a narrow strip of sea, with the barren coast below, and the cloudless sky above it; in the other, a purple valley, rising far away on the flank of the Apennines; both pictures set between Doric pillars. He lit a cigar, and with a smile of contented thought abandoned himself to the delicious warmth, the restful silence. Within reach of his hand was a fern that had shot up between the massive stones; he gently caressed its fronds, as though it were a sentient creature. Or his eyes dwelt upon the huge column just in front of him—now scanning its superb proportions, now enjoying the hue of the sunny-golden travertine, now observing the myriad crevices of its time-eaten surface, the petrified forms of vegetable growth, the little pink snails that housed within its chinks.

It was not an artistic impulse only that had brought Mallard to Italy, after three years of work under northern skies. He wished to convince himself that his freedom was proof against memories revived on the very ground where he had suffered so intensely. He had put aside repeated invitations from the Spences, because of the doubt whether he could trust himself within sight of the Mediterranean. Liberty from oppressive thought he had long recovered; the old zeal for labour was so strong in him that he found it difficult to imagine the mood in which he had bidden good-bye to his life's purposes. But there was always the danger lest that witch of the south should again overcome his will and lull him into impotence of vain regret. For such a long time he had believed that Italy was for ever closed against him, that the old delights were henceforth converted into a pain which memory must avoid. At length he resolved to answer his friends' summons, and meet them on their return from Sicily. They had wished to have him with them in Greece, but always his departure was postponed; habits of solitude and characteristic diffidence kept him aloof as long as possible.

Evidently, his health was sound enough. He had loitered about the familiar places in Naples; he took the road by Pompeii to Sorrento, and over the hills to Amalfi; and at each step he could smile with contemptuous pity for the self which he had outlived. More than that. When he came hither three years ago, it was with the intention of doing certain definite work; this purpose he now at last fulfilled, thus completing his revenge upon the by-gone obstacles, and reinstating himself in his own good opinion, as a man who did that which he set himself to do. At Amalfi he had made a number of studies which would be useful; at Pæstum he had worked towards a picture, such a one as had from the first been in his mind. Yes, he was a sound man once more.

Tempestuous love is for boys, who have still to know themselves, and for poets, who can turn their suffering into song. But to him it meant only hindrance. Because he had been a prey to frantic desires, did he look upon earth's beauty with a clearer eye, or was his hand endowed with subtler craft? He saw no reason to suppose it. The misery of those first months of northern exile—his battling with fierce winds on sea and moorland and mountain, his grim vigils under stormy stars—had it given him new strength? Of body, perhaps; otherwise, he might have spent the time with decidedly more of satisfaction and profit.

Let it be accepted as one of the unavoidable ills of humanity —something that has to be gone through, like measles. But it had come disagreeably late. No doubt he had to thank the monastic habits of his life that it assailed him with such violence. That he had endured it, therein lay the happy assurance that it would not again trouble him.

If it be true that love ever has it in its power to make or mar a man, this love that he had experienced was assuredly not of such quality. From the first his reason had opposed it, and now that it was all over he tried to rejoice at the circumstances which had made his desire vain. Herein he went a little beyond sincerity; yet there were arguments which, at all events, fortified his wish to see that everything was well. It was not mere perversity that in the beginning had warned him against thinking of Cecily as a possible wife for him. Had she betrayed the least inclination to love him, such considerations would have gone to the winds; he would have called the gods to witness that the one perfect woman on the earth was his. But the fact of her passionate self-surrender to Reuben Elgar, did it not prove that the possibilities of her nature were quite other than those which could have assured *his* happiness? To be sure, so young a girl is liable to wretched errors—but of that he would take no account; against that he resolutely closed his mind. From Edward Spence he heard that she was delighting herself and others in a London season. Precisely; this justified his forethought; for this she was adapted. But as his wife nothing of the kind would have been within her scope. He knew himself too well. His notion of married life was inconsistent with that kind of pleasure. As his wife, perhaps she would have had no desire save to fit herself to him. Possibly; but that again was a reflection not to be admitted. He had only to deal with facts. Sufficient that he could think of her without a pang, that he could even hope to meet her again before long. And, best of Ila, no ungenerous feeling ever tempted him to wish her anything but wholly happy.

Stretched lazily in the Temple of Neptune, he once or twice looked at his watch, as though the hour in some way concerned him. How it did was at length shown. He heard voices approaching, and had just time to rise to his feet before there appeared figures, rising between the columns of the entrance against the background of hills. He moved forward, a bright smile on his face. The arrivals were Edward Spence, with his wife and Mrs. Baske.

All undemonstrative people, they shook hands much as if they had parted only a week ago.

"Done your work?" asked Spence, laying his palm on one of the pillars, with affectionate greeting.

"All I can do here."

"Can we see it?" Eleanor inquired.

"I've packed it for travelling."

Mallard took the first opportunity of looking with scrutiny at Mrs. Baske. Alone of the three, she was changed noticeably. Her health had so much improved that, if anything, she looked younger; certainly her face had more distinct beauty. Reserve and conscious dignity were still its characteristics—these were inseparable from the mould of feature; but her eyes no longer had the somewhat sullen gleam which had been wont to harm her aspect, and when she smiled it was without the hint of disdainful reticence. Yet the smile was not frequent; her lips had an habitual melancholy, and very often she knitted her brows in an expression of troubled thought. Whilst the others were talking with Mallard, she kept slightly in the rear, and seemed to be occupied in examining the different parts of the temple.

In attire she was transformed. No suggestion now of the lady from provincial England. She was very well, because most fittingly, dressed; neither too youthfully, nor with undue disregard of the fact that she was still young; a travelling-costume apt to the season and the country.

"They speak much of Signor Mal-lard at the osteria," said Spence. "Your departure afflicts them, naturally, no doubt. Do you know whether any other Englishman ever braved that accommodation?"

A country lad appeared, carrying a small hamper, wherein the party had brought their midday meal from Salerno.

"Why did you trouble?" said Mallard. "We have cheese and salame in abundance."

"So I supposed," Spence replied, drily. "I recall the quality of both. Also the *vino di Calabria*, which is villanously sweet. Show us what point of view you chose."

For an hour they walked and talked. Miriam alone was almost silent, but she paid constant attention to the ruins. Mallard heard her say something to Eleanor about the difference between the columns of the middle temple and those of the so-called Basilica; three years ago, such a remark would have been impossible on her lips, and when he glanced at her with curiosity, she seemed conscious of his look.

They at length opened the hamper, and seated themselves near the spot where Mallard had been reclining.

"There's a smack of profanity in this," said Spence. "The least we can do is to pour a libation to Poseidon, before we begin the meal."

And he did so, filling a tumbler with wine and solemnly emptying half of it on to the floor of the *cella*. Mallard watched the effect on Mrs. Baske; she met his look for an instant and smiled, then relapsed into thoughtfulness.

The only other visitors to-day were a couple of Germans, who looked like artists and went about in enthusiastic talk; one kept dealing the other severe blows on the chest, which occasionally made the recipient stagger—all in pure joy and friendship. They measured some of the columns, and in one place, for a special piece of observation, the smaller man mounted on his companion's shoulders. Miriam happened to see them whilst they were thus posed, and the spectacle struck her with such ludicrous effect that she turned away to disguise sudden laughter. In doing so, she by chance faced Mallard, and he too began to laugh. For the first time since they had been acquainted, they looked into each other's eyes with frank, hearty merriment. Miriam speedily controlled herself, and there came a flush to her cheeks.

"You may laugh," said Spence, observing them, "but when did you see two Englishmen abroad who did themselves so much honour?"

"True enough," replied Mallard. "One supposes that Englishmen with brains are occasionally to be found in Italy, but I don't know where they hide themselves."

" You will meet one in Rome in a few days," remarked
Eleanor, " if you go on with us—as I hope you intend
to ? "

" Yes, I shall go with you to Rome. Who is the man ? "

" Mr. Seaborne—your most reverent admirer."

" Ah, I should like to know the fellow."

Miriam looked at him and smiled.

" You know Mr. Seaborne ? " he inquired of her, abruptly.

" He was with us a fortnight in Athens."

As they were idling about, after their lunch, Mallard kept
near to Miriam, but without speaking. He saw her stoop to
pick up a piece of stone ; presently another. She glanced at
him.

" Bits of Pæstum," he said, smiling ; " perhaps of Posei-
donia. Look at the field over there, where the oxen are ;
they have walled it in with fragments dug up out of the
earth,—the remnants of a city."

She just bent her head, in sign of sympathy. A minute
or two after, she held out to him the two stones she had
taken up.

" How cold one is, and how warm the other ! "

One was marble, one travertine. Mallard held them for a
moment, and smiled assent ; then gave them back to her.
She threw them away.

When it was time to think of departure, they went to the
inn ; Mallard's baggage was brought out and put into the
carriage. They drove across the silent plain towards
Salerno. In a pause of his conversation with Spence,
Mallard drew Miriam's attention to the unfamiliar shape of
Capri, as seen from this side of the Sorrento promontory.
She looked, and murmured an affirmative.

" You have been to Amalfi ? " he asked.

" Yes ; we went last year."

" I hope you hadn't such a day as your brother and I
spent there—incessant pouring rain."

" No ; we had perfect weather."

At Salerno they caught a train which enabled them to reach Naples late in the evening. Mallard accompanied his friends to their hotel, and dined with them. As he and Spence were smoking together afterwards, the latter communicated some news which he had reserved for privacy.

" By-the-bye, we hear that Cecily and her aunt are at Florence, and are coming to Rome next week."

" Elgar with them ? " Mallard asked, with nothing more than friendly interest.

" No. They say he is so hard at work that he couldn't leave London."

" What work ? "

" The same I told you of last year."

Mallard regarded him with curious inquiry.

" His wife travels for her health ? "

" She seems to be all right again, but Mrs. Lessingham judged that a change was necessary. Won't you use the opportunity of meeting her ? "

" As it comes naturally, there's no reason why I shouldn't. In fact, I shall be glad to see her. But I should have preferred to meet them both together. What faith do you put in this same work of Elgar's ? "

" That he *is* working, I take it there can be no doubt, and I await the results with no little curiosity. Mrs. Lessingham writes vaguely, which, by-the-bye, is not her habit. Whether she is a believer or not, we can't determine."

" Did the child's death affect him much ? "

" I know nothing about it."

They smoked in silence for a few minutes. Then Mallard observed, without taking the cigar from his lips :

" How much better Mrs. Baske looks ! "

" Naturally the change is more noticeable to you than to us. It has come very slowly. I dare say you see other changes as well ? "

Spence's eye twinkled as he spoke.

" I was prepared for them. That she should stay abroad

with you all this time is in itself significant. Where does she propose to live when you are back in England?"

"Why, there hasn't been a word said on the subject. Eleanor is waiting; doesn't like to ask questions. We shall have our house in Chelsea again, and she is very welcome to share it with us if she likes. I think it is certain she won't go back to Lancashire; and the notion of her living with the Elgars is improbable."

"How far does the change go?" inquired Mallard, with hesitancy.

"I can't tell you, for we are neither of us in her confidence. But she is no longer a precisian. She has read a great deal; most of it reading of a very substantial kind. Not at all connected with religion; it would be a mistake to suppose that she has been going in for a course of modern criticism, and that kind of thing. The Greek and Latin authors she knows very fairly, in English or French translations. What would our friend Bradshaw say? She has grappled with whole libraries of solid historians. She knows the Italian poets. Really, no common case of a woman educating herself at that age."

"Would you mind telling me what her age is?"

"Twenty-seven, last February. To-day she has been mute; generally, when we are in interesting places, she rather likes to show her knowledge—of course we encourage her to do so. A blessed form of vanity, compared with certain things one remembers!"

"She looks as if she had by no means conquered peace of mind," observed Mallard, after another silence.

"I don't suppose she has. I don't even know whether she's on the way to it."

"How about the chapel at Bartles?"

Spence shook his head and laughed, and the dialogue came to an end.

The next morning all started for Rome.

CHAPTER VII.

LEARNING AND TEACHING.

EASTER was just gone by. The Spences had timed their arrival in Rome so as to be able to spend a few days with certain friends, undisturbed by bell-clanging and the rush of trippers, before at length returning to England. Their hotel was in the Babuino. Mallard, who was uncertain about his movements during the next month or two, went to quarters with which he was familiar in the Via Bocca di Leone. He brought his Pæstum picture to the hotel, but declined to leave it there. Mallard was deficient in those properties of the showman which are so necessary to an artist if he would make his work widely known and sell it for substantial sums; he hated anything like private exhibition, and dreaded an offer to purchase from any one who had come in contact with him by way of friendly introduction.

"I'm not satisfied with it, now I come to look at it again. It's nothing but a rough sketch."

"But Seaborne will be here this afternoon," urged Spence. "He will be grateful if you let him see it."

"If he cares to come to my room, he shall."

Miriam made no remark on the picture, but kept looking at it as long as it was uncovered. The temples stood in the light of early morning, a wonderful, indescribable light, perfectly true and rendered with great skill.

"Is it likely to be soon sold?" she asked, when the artist had gone off with his canvas.

"As likely as not, he'll keep it by him for a year or two, till he hates it for a few faults that no one else can perceive or be taught to understand," was Mr. Spence's reply. " I wish I could somehow become possessed of it. But if I hinted such a wish, he would insist on my taking it as a present. An impracticable fellow, Mallard. He suspects I want to sell it for him ; that's why he won't leave it. And if Seaborne goes to his room, ten to one he'll be received with growls of surly independence."

This Mr. Seaborne was a man of letters. Spence had made his acquaintance in Rome a year ago ; they conversed casually in Piale's reading-room, and Seaborne happened to say that the one English landscape-painter who strongly interested him was a little-known man, Ross Mallard. His own work was mostly anonymous ; he wrote for one of the quarterlies and one of the weekly reviews. He was a little younger than Mallard, whom in certain respects he resembled ; he had much the same way of speaking, the same reticence with regard to his own doings, even a slight similarity of feature, and his life seemed to be rather a lonely one.

When the two met, they behaved precisely as Spence predicted they would—with reserve, almost with coldness. For all that, Seaborne paid a visit to the artist's room, and in a couple of hours' talk they arrived at a fair degree of mutual understanding. The next day they smoked together in an odd abode occupied by the literary man near Porto di Ripetta, and thenceforth were good friends.

The morning after that, Mallard went early to the Vatican. He ascended the Scala Regia, and knocked at the little red door over which is written, " Cappella Sistina." On entering, he observed only a gentleman and a young girl, who stood in the middle of the floor, consulting their guide-book ; but when he had taken a few steps forward, he saw a lady come from the far end and seat herself to look at the ceiling through an opera-glass. It was Mrs. Baske, and he approached whilst she was still intent on the frescoes. The pausing of his footstep close to her caused her to put down the glass and regard him. Mallard noticed the sudden change from cold remoteness of countenance to pleased recognition. The brightening in her eyes was only for a moment; then she smiled in her usual half-absent way, and received him formally.

"You are not alone?" he said, taking a place by her as she resumed her seat.

"Yes, I have come alone." And, after a pause, she added, "We don't think it necessary always to keep together. That would become burdensome. I often leave them, and go to places by myself."

Her look was still turned upwards. Mallard followed its direction.

"Which of the Sibyls is your favourite?" he asked.

At once she indicated the Delphic, but without speaking.

"Mine too."

Both fixed their eyes upon the figure, and were silent.

"You have been here very often?" were Mallard's next words.

"Last year very often."

"From genuine love of it, or a sense of duty?" he asked, examining her face.

She considered before replying.

"Not only from a sense of duty, though of course I have felt that. I don't *love* anything of Michael Angelo's, but I am compelled to look and study. I came here this morning only to refresh my memory of one of those faces"—she pointed to the lower part of the Last Judgment—"and yet the face is dreadful to me."

She found that he was smiling, and abruptly she added the question:

"Do you love that picture?"

"Why, no; but I often delight in it. I wouldn't have it always before me (for that matter, no more would I have the things that I love). A great work of art may be painful at all times, and sometimes unendurable."

"I have learnt to understand that," she said, with something of humility, which came upon Mallard as new and agreeable. "But—it is not long since that scene represented a reality to me. I think I shall never see it as you do."

Mallard wished to look at her, but did not.

"I have sometimes been repelled by a feeling of the same kind," he answered. "Not that I myself ever thought of it as a reality, but I have felt angry and miserable in remembering that a great part of the world does. You see the pretty girl there, with her father. I noticed her awed face as I passed, and heard a word or two of the man's, which told me that from them there was no question of *art*. Poor child! I should have liked to pat her hand, and tell her to be good and have no fear."

"Did Michael Angelo believe it?" Miriam asked diffidently, when she had glanced with anxious eyes at the pair of whom he spoke.

"I suppose so. And yet I am far from sure. What about Dante? Haven't you sometimes stumbled over his grave assurances that this and that did really befall him? Putting aside the feeble notion that he was a deluded visionary, how does one reconcile the artist's management of his poem with the Christian's stern faith? In any case, he was more poet than Christian when he wrote. Milton makes no such claims; he merely prays for the enlightenment of his imagination."

Miriam turned from the great fresco, and again gazed at the Sibyls and Prophets.

"Do the Stanze interest you?" was Mallard's next question.

"Very little, I am sorry to say. They soon weary me."

"And the Loggia?"

"I never paid much attention to it."

"That surprises me. Those little pictures are my favourites of all Raphael's work. For those and the Psyche, I would give everything else."

Miriam looked at him inquiringly.

" Are you again thinking of the subjects ? " he asked.

" Yes. I can't help it. I have avoided them, because I knew how impossible it was for me to judge them only as art."

" Then you have the same difficulty with nearly all Italian pictures ? "

She hesitated ; but, without turning her eyes to him, said at length :

" I can't easily explain to you the distinction there is for me between the Old Testament and the New. I was taught almost exclusively out of the Old—at least, it seems so to me. I have had to study the New for myself, and it helps rather than hinders my enjoyment of pictures taken from it. The religion of my childhood was one of bitterness and violence and arbitrary judgment and hatred."

"Ah, but there is quite another side to the Old Testament —those parts of it, at all events, that are illustrated up in the Loggia. Will you come up there with me ? "

She rose without speaking. They left the chapel, and ascended the stairs.

" You are not under the impression," he said, with a smile, as they walked side by side, " that the Old Testament is responsible for those horrors we have just been speaking of ? "

"They are in *that* spirit. My reading of the New omits everything of the kind."

" So does mine. But we have no justification."

" We can select what is useful to us, and reject what does harm."

" Yes ; but then——"

He did not finish the sentence, and they went into the pictured Loggia. Here, choosing out his favourites, Mallard endeavoured to explain all his joy in them. He showed her how it was Hebrew history made into a series of exquisite and touching legends; he dwelt on the sweet, idyllic treatment, the lovely landscape, the tender idealism throughout, the perfect adaptedness of gem-like colouring.

Miriam endeavoured to see with his eyes, but did not pretend to be wholly successful. The very names were discordant to her ear.

"I will buy some photographs of them to take away," she said.

"Don't do that; they are useless. Colour and design are here inseparable."

They stayed not more than half an hour; then left the Vatican together, and walked to the front of St. Peter's in silence. Mallard looked at his watch.

"You are going back to the hotel?"

"I suppose so."

"Shall I call one of those carriages?—I am going to have a walk on to the Janiculum."

She glanced at the sky.

"There will be a fine view to-day."

"You wouldn't care to come so far?"

"Yes, I should enjoy the walk."

"To walk? It would tire you too much."

"Oh no!" replied Miriam, looking away and smiling. "You mustn't think I am what I was that winter at Naples. I can walk a good many miles, and only feel better for it."

Her tone amused him, for it became something like that of a child in self-defence when accused of some childlike incapacity.

"Then let us go, by all means."

They turned into the Borgo San Spirito, and then went by the quiet Longara. Mallard soon found that it was necessary to moderate his swinging stride. He was not in the habit of walking with ladies, and he felt ashamed of himself when a glance told him that his companion was put to overmuch exertion. The glance led him to observe Miriam's gait; its grace and refinement gave him a sudden sensation of keen pleasure. He thought, without wishing to do so, of

Cecily; her matchless, maidenly charm in movement was something of quite another kind. Mrs. Baske trod the common earth, yet with, it seemed to him, a dignity that distinguished her from ordinary women.

There had been silence for a long time. They were alike in the custom of forgetting what had last been said, or how long since.

" Do you care for sculpture ? " Mallard asked, led to the inquiry by his thoughts of form and motion.

" Yes ; but not so much as for painting."

He noticed a reluctance in her voice, and for a moment was quite unconscious of the reason for it. But reflection quickly explained her slight embarrassment.

" Edward makes it one of his chief studies," she added at once, looking straight before her. " He has told me what to read about it."

Mallard let the subject fall. But presently they passed a yoke of oxen drawing a cart, and, as he paused to look at them, he said :

" Don't you like to watch those animals ? I can never be near them without stopping. Look at their grand heads, their horns, their majestic movement ! They always remind me of the antique—of splendid power fixed in marble. These are the kind of oxen that Homer saw, and Virgil."

Miriam gazed, but said nothing.

" Does your silence mean that you can't sympathize with me ? "

" No. It means that you have given me a new way of looking at a thing ; and I have to think."

She paused ; then, with a curious inflection of her voice, as though she were not quite certain of the tone she wished to strike, whether playful or sarcastic :

" You wouldn't prefer me to make an exclamation ? "

He laughed.

" Decidedly not. If you were accustomed to do so, I should not be expressing my serious thoughts."

The pleasant mood continued with him, and, a smile still on his face, he asked presently :

"Do you remember telling me that you thought I was wasting my life on futilities ? "

Miriam flushed, and for an instant he thought he had offended her. But her reply corrected this impression.

" You admitted, I think, that there was much to be said for my view."

" Did I ? Well, so there is. But the same conviction may be reached by very different paths. If we agreed in that one result, I fancy it was the sole and singular point of concord."

Miriam inquired diffidently :

"Do you still think of most things just as you did then ? "

" Of most things, yes."

" You have found no firmer hope in which to work ? "

" Hope ? I am not sure that I understand you."

He looked her in the face, and she said hurriedly :

"Are you still as far as ever from satisfying yourself ? Does your work bring you nothing but a comparative satisfaction ? "

"I am conscious of having progressed an inch or two on the way of infinity," Mallard replied. "That brings me no nearer to an end."

"But you *have* a purpose ; you follow it steadily. It i much to be able to say that."

"Do you mean it for consolation ? "

"Not in any sense that you need resent," Miriam gave answer, a little coldly.

"I felt no resentment. But I should like to know what sanction of a life's effort you look for, now ? We talked once, perhaps you remember, of one kind of work being 'higher' than another. How do you think now on that subject ? "

She made delay before saying :

"It is long since I thought of it at all. I have been too

busy learning the simplest things to trouble about the most difficult."

"To learn, then, has been *your* object all this time. Let me question you in turn. Do you find it all-sufficient?"

"No; because I have begun too late. I am doing now what I ought to have done when I was a girl, and I have always the feeling of being behindhand."

"But the object, in itself, quite apart from your progress? Is it enough to study a variety of things, and feel that you make some progress towards a possible ideal of education? Does this suffice to your life?"

She answered confusedly:

"I can't know yet; I can't see before me clearly enough."

Mallard was on the point of pressing the question, but he refrained, and shaped his thought in a different way.

"Do you think of remaining in England?"

"Probably I shall."

"You will return to your home in Lancashire?"

"I haven't yet determined," she replied formally.

The dialogue seemed to be at an end. Unobservant of each other, they reached the Via Crucis, which leads up to S. Pietro in Montorio. Arrived at the terrace, they stood to look down on Rome.

"After all, you are tired," said Mallard, when he had glanced at her.

"Indeed I am not."

"But you are hungry. We have been forgetting that it is luncheon-time."

"I pay little attention to such hours. One can always get something to eat."

"It's all very well for people like myself to talk in that way," said Mallard, with a smile, "but women have orderly habits of life."

"For which you a little despise them?" she returned, with grave face fixed on the landscape.

"Certainly not. It's only that I regard their life as wholly different from my own. Since I was a boy, I have known nothing of domestic regularity."

"You sometimes visit your relatives?"

"Yes. But their life cannot be mine. It is domestic in such a degree that it only serves to remind me how far apart I am."

"Do you hold that an artist cannot live like other people, in the habits of home?"

"I think such habits are a danger to him. He *may* find a home, if fate is exceptionally kind."

Pointing northwards to a ridged hill on the horizon, he asked in another voice if she knew its name.

"You mean Mount Soracte?"

"Yes. You don't know Latin, or it would make you quote Horace."

She shook her head, looked down, and spoke more humbly than he had ever yet heard her.

"But I know it in an English translation."

"Well, that's more than most women do."

He said it in a grudging way. The remark itself was scarcely civil, but he seemed all at once to have a pleasure in speaking roughly, in reminding her of her shortcomings. Miriam turned her eyes in another quarter, and presently pointed to the far blue hills just seen between the Alban and the Sabine ranges.

"Through there is the country of the Volsci," she said, in a subdued voice. "Some Roman must have stood here and looked towards it, in days when Rome was struggling for supremacy with them. Think of all that happened between that day and the time when Horace saw the snow on Soracte; and then, of all that has happened since."

He watched her face, and nodded several times. They pursued the subject, and reminded each other of what the scene suggested, point by point. Mallard felt surprise, though he showed none. Cecily, standing here, would have spoken with more enthusiasm, but it was doubtful whether she would have displayed Miriam's accuracy of knowledge.

"Well, let us go," he said at length. "You don't insist on walking home?"

"There is no need to, I think. I could quite well, if I wished."

"I am going to run through a few of the galleries for a morning or two. I wonder whether you would care to come with me to-morrow?"

"I will come with pleasure."

"That is how people speak when they don't like to refuse a troublesome invitation."

"Then what am I to say? I spoke the truth, in quite simple words."

"I suppose it was your tone; you seemed too polite."

"But what is your objection to politeness?" Miriam asked naïvely.

"Oh, I have none, when it is sincere. But as soon as I had asked you, I felt afraid that I was troublesome."

"If I had felt that, I should have expressed it unmistakably," she replied, in a voice which reminded him of the road from Baiæ to Naples.

"Thank you; that is what I should wish."

Having found a carriage for her, and made an appointment for the morning, he watched her drive away.

A few hours later, he encountered Spence in the Piazza Colonna, and they went together into a *caffè*. Spence had the news that Mrs. Lessingham and her niece would arrive on the third day from now. Their stay would be of a fortnight at longest.

"I met Mrs. Baske at the Vatican this morning," said Mallard presently, as he knocked the ash off his cigar. "We had some talk."

"On Vatican subjects?"

"Yes. I find her views of art somewhat changed. But sculpture still alarms her."

"Still? Do you suppose she will ever overcome that feeling? Are you wholly free from it yourself? Imagine yourself invited to conduct a party of ladies through the marbles, and to direct their attention to the merits that strike you."

"No doubt I should invent an excuse. But it would be weakness."

"A weakness inseparable from our civilization. The nude in art is an anachronism."

"Pooh! That is encouraging the vulgar prejudice."

"No; it is merely stating a vulgar fact. These collections of nude figures in marble have only an historical interest. They are kept out of the way, in places which no one is obliged to visit. Modern work of that kind is tolerated, nothing more. What on earth is the good of an artistic production of which people in general are afraid to speak freely? You take your stand before the Venus of the Capitol; you bid the attendant make it revolve slowly, and you begin a lecture to your wife, your sister, or your young cousin, on the glories of the masterpiece. You point out in detail how admirably Praxiteles has exhibited every beauty of the female frame. Other ladies are standing by; you smile blandly, and include them in your audience."

Mallard interrupted with a laugh.

"Well, why not?" continued the other. "This isn't the *gabinetto* at Naples, surely?"

"But you are well aware that, practically, it comes to the same thing. How often is one half pained, half amused, at the behaviour of women in the Tribune at Florence! They are in a false position; it is absurd to ridicule them for what your own sensations justify. For my own part, I always leave my wife and Mrs. Baske to go about these galleries without my company. If I can't be honestly at my ease, I won't make pretence of being so."

"All this is true enough, but the prejudice is absurd. We ought to despise it and struggle against it."

"Despise it, many of us do, theoretically. But to make

practical demonstrations against it, is to oppose, as I said, all the civilization of our world. Perhaps there will come a time once more when sculpture will be justified; at present the art doesn't and can't exist. Its relics belong to museums —in the English sense of the word."

"You only mean by this," said Mallard, "that art isn't for the multitude. We know that well enough."

"But there's a special difficulty about this point. We come across it in literature as well. How is it that certain pages in literature, which all intellectual people agree in pronouncing just as pure as they are great, could never be read aloud, say, in a family circle, without occasioning pain and dismay? No need to give illustrations; they occur to you in abundance. We skip them, or we read mutteringly, or we say frankly that this is not adapted for reading aloud. Yet no man would frown if he found his daughter bent over the book. There's something radically wrong here."

"This is the old question of our English Puritanism. In France, here in Italy, there is far less of such feeling."

"Far less; but why must there be any at all? And Puritanism isn't a sufficient explanation. The English Puritans of the really Puritan time had freedom of conversation which would horrify us of to-day. We become more and more prudish as what we call civilization advances. It is a hateful fact that, from the domestic point of view, there exists no difference between some of the noblest things in art and poetry, and the obscenities which are prosecuted; the one is as impossible of frank discussion as the other."

"The domestic point of view is contemptible. It means the bourgeois point of view, the Philistine point of view."

"Then I myself, if I had children, should be both bourgeois and Philistine. And so, I have a strong suspicion, would you too."

"Very well," replied Mallard, with some annoyance, "then it is one more reason why an artist should have nothing to do with domesticities. But look here, you are wrong as regards me. If ever I marry, *amico mio*, my wife shall learn to make more than a theoretical distinction between what is art and what is grossness. If ever I have children, they shall from the first be taught a natural morality, and not the conventional. If I can afford good casts of noble statues, they shall stand freely about my house. When I read aloud, by the fire side, there shall be no skipping or muttering or frank omissions ; no, by Apollo ! If a daughter of mine cannot describe to me the points of difference between the Venus of the Capitol and that of the Medici, she shall be bidden to use her eyes and her brains better. I'll have no contemptible prudery in *my* house!"

"Bravissimo !" cried Spence, laughing. "I see that my cousin Miriam is not the only person who has progressed during these years. Do you remember a certain conversation of ours at Posillipo about the education of a certain young lady ? "

"Yes, I do. But that was a different matter. The question was not of Greek statues and classical books, but of modern pruriencies and shallowness and irresponsibility."

"You exaggerated then, and you do so now," said Spence ; "at present with less excuse."

Mallard kept silence for a space ; then said:

"Let us speak of what we have been avoiding. How has that marriage turned out ? "

"I have told you all I know. There's no reason to suppose that things are anything but well."

"I don't like her coming abroad alone; I have no faith in that plea of work. I suspect things are *not* well."

"A cynic—which I am not—would suggest that a wish had something to do with the thought."

"He would be cynically wrong," replied Mallard, with calmness.

"Why shouldn't she come abroad alone ? There's nothing alarming in the fact that they no longer need to see each other every hour. And one takes for granted that *they*, at all events, are not bourgeois; their life won't be arranged exactly like that of Mr. and Mrs. Jones the greengrocers."

"No," said the other, musingly.

"In what direction do you imagine that Cecily will progress? Possibly she has become acquainted with disillusion."

"Possibly?"

"Well, take it for certain. Isn't that an inevitable step in her education? Things may still be well enough, philosophically speaking. She has her life to live—we know it will be to the end a modern life. *Servetur ad imum*—and so on; that's what one would wish, I suppose? We have no longer to take thought for her."

"But we are allowed to wish the best."

"What *is* the best?" said Spence, sustaining his tone of impartial speculation. "Are you quite sure that Mr. and Mrs. Jones are not too much in your mind?"

"Whatever modern happiness may mean, I am inclined to think that modern unhappiness is not unlike that of old-fashioned people."

"My dear fellow, you are a halter between two opinions. You can't make up your mind in which direction to look. You are a sort of Janus, with anxiety on both faces."

"There's a good deal of truth in that," admitted the artist, with a growl.

"Get on with your painting, and whatever else of practical you have in mind. Leave philosophy to men of large leisure and placid pulses, like myself. Accept the inevitable.

"I do so."

"But not with modern detachment," said Spence, smiling.

"Be hanged with your modernity! I believe myself distinctly the more modern of the two."

"Not with regard to women. When you marry, you will be a rigid autocrat, and make no pretence about it. You don't think of women as independent beings, who must save or lose themselves on their own responsibility. You are not willing to trust them alone."

"Well, perhaps you are right."

"Of course I am. Come and dine at the hotel. I think Seaborne will be there."

"No, thank you."

Mallard had waited but a few minutes in the court of the Palazzo Borghese next morning, when Miriam joined him. There was some constraint on both sides. Miriam looked as if she did not wish yesterday's conversation to be revived in their manner of meeting. Her "Good-morning, Mr. Mallard," had as little reference as possible to the fact of this being an appointment. The artist was in quite another mood than that of yesterday; his smile was formal, and he seemed indisposed for conversation.

"I have the *permesso*," he said, leading at once to the door of the gallery.

They sauntered about the first room, exchanging a few idle remarks. In the second, a woman past the prime of life was copying a large picture. They looked at her work from a distance, and Miriam asked if it was well done.

"What do you think yourself?" asked Mallard.

"It seems to me skilful and accurate, but I know that perhaps it is neither one nor the other."

He pointed out several faults, which she at once recognized.

"I wonder I could not see them at first. That confirms me in distrust of myself. I am as likely as not to admire a thing that is utterly worthless."

"As likely as not—no; at least, I think not. But of course your eye is untrained, and you have no real knowledge to go upon. You can judge an original picture sentimentally, and your sentiment will not be wholly misleading. You can't judge a copy technically, but I think you have more than average observation. How would you like to spend your life like this copyist?"

"I would give my left hand to have her skill in my right."

"You would?"

"I should be able to *do* something—something definite and tolerably good."

"Why, so you can already; one thing in particular."

"What is that?"

"Learn your own deficiencies; a thing that most people neither will nor can. Look at this Francia, and tell me your thoughts about it."

She examined the picture for a minute or two. Then, without moving her eyes, she murmured:

"I can say nothing that is worth saying."

"Never mind. Say what you think, or what you feel."

"Why should you wish me to talk commonplace?"

"That is precisely what I don't wish you to talk. You know what is commonplace, and therefore you can avoid it. Never mind his school or his date. What did the man want to express here, and how far do you think he has succeeded? That's the main thing; I wish a few critics would understand it."

Miriam obeyed him, and said what she had to say diffidently, but in clear terms. Mallard was silent when she ceased, and she looked up at him. He rewarded her with a smile, and one or two nods—as his manner was.

"I have not made myself ridiculous?"

"I think not."

They had walked on a little, when Mallard said to her unexpectedly:

"Please to bear in mind that I make no claim to infallibility. I am a painter of landscape; out of my own sphere, I become an amateur. You are not bound to accept my judgment."

"Of course not," she replied simply.

"It occurred to me that I had been rather dictatorial."

"So you have, Mr. Mallard," she returned, looking at a picture.

"I am sorry. It's the failing of men who have often to be combative, and who live much in solitude. I will try to use a less offensive tone."

"I didn't mean that your tone was in the least offensive."

" A more polite tone, then—as you taught me yesterday."

" I had rather you spoke just as is natural to you."

Mallard laughed.

" Politeness is not natural to me, I admit. I am horribly uncomfortable whenever I have to pick my words out of regard to polite people. That is why I shun what is called society. What little I have seen of it has been more than enough for me."

" I have seen still less of it ; but I understand your dislike."

" Before you left home, didn't you associate a great deal with people ? "

" People of a certain kind," she replied coldly. " It was not society as you mean it."

" You will be glad to mix more freely with the world, when you are back in England ? "

" I can't tell. By whom is that Madonna ? "

Thus they went slowly on, until they came to the little hall where the fountain plays, and whence is the outlook over the Tiber. It was delightful to sit here in the shadows, made cooler and fresher by that plashing water, and to see the glorious sunlight gleam upon the river's tawny flow.

" Each time that I have been in Rome," said Mallard, " I have felt, after the first few days, a peculiar mental calm. The other cities of Italy haven't the same effect on me. Perhaps every one experiences it, more or less. There comes back to me at moments the kind of happiness which I knew as a boy—a freedom from the sense of duties and responsibilities, of work to be done, and of disagreeable things to be faced ; the kind of contentment I used to have when I was reading lives of artists, or looking at prints of famous pictures, or myself trying to draw. It is possible that this mood is not such a strange one with many people as with me ; when it comes, I feel grateful to the powers that rule life. Since boyhood, I have never known it in the north. Out of Rome, perhaps only in fine weather on the Mediterranean. But in Rome is its perfection."

"I thought you preferred the north," said Miriam.

"Because I so often choose to work there? I can do better work when I take subjects in wild scenery and stern climates, but when my thoughts go out for pleasure, they choose Italy. I don't enjoy myself in the Hebrides or in Norway, but what powers I have are all brought out there. Here I am not disposed to work. I want to live, and I feel that life can be a satisfaction in itself without labour. I am naturally the idlest of men. Work is always pain to me. I like to dream pictures; but it's terrible to drag myself before the blank canvas."

Miriam gazed at the Tiber.

"Do these palaces," he asked, "ever make you wish you owned them? Did you ever imagine yourself walking among the marbles and the pictures with the sense of this being your home?"

"I have wondered what that must be. But I never wished it had fallen to my lot."

"No? You are not ambitious?"

"Not in that way. To own a palace such as this would make one insignificant."

"That is admirably true! I should give it away, to recover self-respect. Shakespeare or Michael Angelo might live here and make it subordinate to him; I should be nothing but the owner of the palace. You like to feel your individuality?"

"Who does not?"

"In you, I think, it is strong."

Miriam smiled a little, as if she liked the compliment. Before either spoke again, other visitors came to look at the view, and disturbed them.

"I shan't ask you to come anywhere to-morrow," said Mallard, when they had again talked for awhile of pictures. "And the next day Mrs. Elgar will be here."

She looked at him.

"That wouldn't prevent me from going to a gallery—if you thought of it."

"You will have much to talk of. And your stay in Rome won't be long after that."

Miriam made no reply.

"I wish your brother had been coming," he went on. "I should have liked to hear from him about the book he is writing."

"Shall you not be in London before long?" she asked, without show of much interest.

"I think so, but I have absolutely no plans. Probably it is raining hard in England, or even snowing. I must enjoy the sunshine a little longer. I hope your health won't suffer from the change of climate."

"I hope not," she answered mechanically.

"Perhaps you will find you can't live there?"

"What does it matter? I have no ties."

"No, you are independent; that is a great blessing."

Chatting as if of indifferent things, they left the gallery.

CHAPTER VIII.

STUMBLINGS.

ROLLED tightly together, and tied up with string, at the bottom of one of Miriam's trunks lay the plans of that new chapel for which Bartles still waited. Miriam did not like to come upon them, in packing or unpacking; she had covered them with things which probably would not be moved until she was again in England.

But the thought of them could not be so satisfactorily hidden. It lay in a corner of her mind, and many were the new acquisitions heaped upon it; but in spite of herself she frequently burrowed through all those accumulations of travel, and sought the thing beneath. Sometimes the impulse was so harassing, the process so distressful, that she might have been compared to a murderer who haunts the burial-place of his victim, and cannot restrain himself from disturbing the earth.

It was by no methodic inquiry, no deliberate reasoning, that Miriam had set aside her old convictions and ordered her intellectual life on the new scheme. Of those who are destined to pass beyond the bounds of dogma, very few indeed do so by the way of studious investigation. How many of those who abide by inherited faith owe their steadfastness to a convinced understanding? Convictions, in the proper sense of the word, Miriam had never possessed; she accepted what she was taught, without reflecting upon it, and pride subsequently made her stubborn in consistency. The same pride, aided by the ennui of mental faculties just becoming self-conscious, and the desires of a heart for the first time humanly touched, constrained her to turn abruptly from the ideal she had pursued, and with unforeseen energy begin to qualify herself for the assertion of new claims. No barriers of logic stood in her way; it was a simple matter of facing round about. True, she still had to endure the sense of having chosen the wide way instead of that strait one which is authoritatively prescribed. It was a long time before she made any endeavour to justify herself; but the wide way ran through a country that delighted her, and her progress was so notable that self-commendation and the respect of others made her careless of the occasional stings of conscience.

She was able now to review the process of change, and to compare the two ideals. Without the support of a single argument of logical value, she stamped all the beliefs of her childhood as superstition, and marvelled that they had so long held their power over her. Her childhood, indeed, seemed to her to have lasted until she came to Naples; with hot shame she reflected on her speech and behaviour at that time. What did the Spences think of her? How did they speak of her to their friends? What impression did she make upon Mallard? These memories were torture; they explained the mixture of humility and assumption which on certain days made her company disagreeable to Eleanor, and the dark moods which now and then held her in sullen solitude.

But the word "superstition" was no guarantee against the haunting of superstition itself. Miriam was far from being one of the emancipated, however arrogantly she would have met a doubt of her freedom. Just as little as ever had she genuine convictions, capable of supporting her in hours of weakness and unsatisfied longing. Several times of late she had all but brought herself to speak plainly with Eleanor, and ask on what foundation was built that calm life which seemed independent of supernatural belief; but shame always restrained her. It would be the same as confessing that she had not really the liberty to which she pretended. There was, however, an indirect way of approaching the subject, by which her dignity would possibly be rather enhanced than suffer; and this she at length took. After her return from the Palazzo Borghese, she was beset with a confusion of anxious thoughts. The need of confidential or semi-confidential speech with one of her own sex became irresistible. In the evening she found an opportunity of speaking privately with Eleanor.

"I want to ask your opinion about something. It's a question I am obliged to decide now I am going back to England."

Eleanor smiled inquiringly. She was not a little curious to have a glimpse into her cousin's mind just now.

"You remember," pursued Miriam, leaning forward on a table by which she sat, and playing with a twisted piece of paper, "that I once had the silly desire to build a chapel at Bartles."

She reddened in hearing the words upon her own lips—so strange a sound they had after all this time.

"I remember you talked of doing so," replied Eleanor, with her usual quiet good-nature.

"Unfortunately, I did more than talk about it. I made a distinct promise to certain people gravely interested. The promise was registered in a Bartles newspaper. And you know that I went so far as to have my plans made."

"Do you feel bound by this promise, my dear?"

Miriam propped her cheek on one hand, and with the other kept rolling the piece of paper on the table.

"Yes," she answered, "I can't help thinking that I ought to keep my word. How does it strike you, Eleanor?"

"I am not quite clear how you regard the matter. Are you speaking of the promise only as a promise?"

It was no use. Miriam could not tell the truth; she could not confess her position. At once a smile trembled scornfully upon her lips.

"What else could I mean?"

"Then it seems to me that the obligation has passed away with the circumstances that occasioned it."

Miriam kept her eyes on the table, and for a few moments seemed to reflect.

"A promise is a promise, Eleanor."

"So it is. And a fact is a fact. I take it for granted that you are no longer the person who made the promise. I have a faint recollection that when I was about eight years old, I pledged myself, on reaching maturity, to give my nurse the exact half of my worldly possessions. I don't feel the least ashamed of having made such a promise, and just as little of not having kept it."

Miriam smiled, but still had an unconvinced face.

"I was not eight years old," she said, "but about four-and-twenty."

"Then let us put it in this way. Do you still feel a desire to benefit that religious community in Bartles? Would it distress you to think that they shook their heads in mentioning your name?"

"I do feel rather in that way," Miriam admitted slowly.

"But is this enough to justify you in giving them half or more of all you possess? You spoke of pulling down Redbeck House, and building on the site, didn't you?"

"Yes."

"In any case, should you ever live there again?"

"Never."

"You prefer to be with us in London?"

"I think you have been troubled with me quite long enough. Perhaps I might take rooms."

"If you are as willing to share our house as we are to have you with us, there can be no need for you to live alone."

"I can't make up my mind about that, Eleanor. Let us talk only about the chapel just now. Are you sure that other people would see it as you do?"

"Other people of my way of thinking would no doubt think the same—which is a pretty piece of tautology. Edward would be amazed to hear that you have such scruples. It isn't as if you had promised to support a family in dire need, or anything of that kind. The chapel is a superfluity."

"Not to them."

"They have one already."

"But very small and inconvenient."

"Suppose you ask Mr. Mallard for his thoughts on the subject?" said Eleanor, as if at the bidding of a caprice.

"Does Mr. Mallard know that I once had this purpose?"

"I think so," replied the other, with a little hesitation. "You know that there was no kind of reserve about it when you first came to Naples."

"No, of course not. Do you feel as sure of his opinion as of Edward's?"

"I can't say that I do. There's no foreseeing his judgment about anything. As you are such good friends, why not consult him?"

" Our friendship doesn't go so far as that."

" And after all, I don't see what use other people's opinions can be to you," said Eleanor, waiving the point. " It's a matter of sentiment. Strict obligation you see, of course, that there is none whatever. If it would please you to use a large sum of money in this way, you have a perfect right to do so. But, by-the-bye, oughtn't you to make the Bartles people clearly understand who it is that builds their chapel ? "

" Surely there is no need of that ? "

" I think so. The scruple, in my case, would be far more on this side than on the other."

Miriam did not care to pursue the conversation. The one result of it was that she had an added uncertainty. She had thought that her proposal to fulfil the promise would at least earn the respect which is due to stern conscientiousness ; but Eleanor clearly regarded it as matter for the smile one bestows on good-natured folly. Her questions even showed that she was at first in doubt as to the motives which had revived this project—a doubt galling to Miriam, because of its justification. She said, in going away :

" Please to consider that this was in confidence, Eleanor."

Confidence of a barren kind. It was the same now as it had ever been ; she had no one with whom she could communicate her secrets, no friend in the nearer sense. On this loneliness she threw the blame of those faults which she painfully recognized in herself—her frequent insincerity, her speeches and silences calculated for effect, her pride based on disingenuousness. If she could but have disclosed her heart in the humility of love and trust, how would its aching have been eased !

For a long time she had been absorbed, or nearly so, in studying and observing ; but Mallard's inquiry whether she found this sufficient touched the source whence trouble was again arising for her. Three years ago it did not cost her much to subdue a desire which had hopelessness for its birthright; the revival of this desire now united itself with disquietudes of the maturing intellect, and she looked forward in dread to a continuation of her loneliness. Some change in her life there must be. Sudden hope had in a day or two brought to full growth the causes of unrest which would otherwise have developed slowly.

It seemed to be her fate to live in pretences. As the mistress of Redbeck House, and the light of dissenting piety in Bartles, she knew herself for less than she wished to appear to others; not a hypocrite, indeed, but a pretender to extraordinary zeal, and at the same time a flagrant instance of spiritual pride. Now she was guilty of like simulation directed to a contrary end. In truth neither bond nor free, she could not suffer herself to seem less liberal-minded than those with whom she associated. And yet her soul was weary of untruth. The one need of her life was to taste the happiness of submission to a stronger than herself. Religious devotion is the resource of women in general who suffer thus and are denied the natural solace; but for Miriam it was impossible. Her temperament was not devout, and, however persistent the visitings of uneasy conscience, she had no longer the power of making her old beliefs a reality. The abstract would not avail her; philosophic comforts had as little to say to her as the Churches' creeds. Only by a strong human hand could she be raised from her unworthy position and led into the way of sincerity.

She had counted on having another morning with Mallard before Cecily's arrival. Disappointed in this hope, she invented a variety of tormenting reasons for Mallard's behaviour. As there was a chance of his calling at the hotel, she stayed in all day. But he did not come. The next afternoon Mrs. Lessingham and her companion reached Rome.

It was known that Cecily's health had suffered from her

watchings by the sick child, and from her grief at its death; so no one was surprised at finding her rather thin-faced. She had a warm greeting for her friends, and seemed happy to be with them again; but the brightness of the first hour was not sustained. Conversation cost her a perceptible effort; she seldom talked freely of anything, and generally with an unnatural weighing of her words, an artificiality of thought and phrase, which was a great contrast to the spontaneousness of former times. When Eleanor wanted her to speak about herself, she preferred to tell of what she had lately read or heard or seen. That the simple grace of the girl should be modified in the wife and mother was of course to be expected, but Cecily looked older than she ought to have done, and occasionally bore herself with a little too much consciousness, as if she felt the observation even of intimate friends something of a restraint.

Miriam, when she had made inquiries about her brother's health, took little part in the general conversation, and it was not till late in the evening that she spoke with Cecily in private.

"May I come and sit with you for a few minutes?" Cecily asked, when Miriam was going to her bedroom.

They were far less at ease with each other than when their differences of opinion were a recognized obstacle to intimacy. Cecily was uncertain how far her sister-in-law had progressed from the old standpoint, and she saw in her even an increase of the wonted reticence. On her own side there was no longer a warm impulse of sisterly affection. But her first words, when they were alone together, sounded like an appeal for tender confidence.

"I do so wish you had seen my poor little boy!"

"I wish I had been nearer," Miriam answered kindly. "It is very sad that you have suffered such a loss."

Cecily spoke of the child, and with simple feeling, which made her more like herself than hitherto.

" When a little thing dies at that age," she said presently, " it is only the mother's grief. The father cannot have much interest in so young a child."

" But Reuben wrote very affectionately of Clarence in one letter I had from him."

"Yes, but it is natural that he shouldn't feel the loss as I do. A man has his business in life; a woman, if she needn't work for bread, has nothing to do but be glad or sorry for what happens in her home."

"I shouldn't have thought you took that view of a woman's life," said Miriam, after a silence, regarding the other with uncertain eyes.

"'Views' have become rather a weariness to me," answered Cecily, smiling sadly. " Sorrow is sorrow to me as much as to the woman who never questioned one of society's beliefs; it makes me despondent. No doubt I ought to find all sorts of superior consolations. But I don't and can't. A woman's natural lot is to care for her husband and bring up children. Do you believe, Miriam, that anything will ever take the place of these occupations ? "

"I suppose not. But time will help you, and your interests will come back again."

"True. On the other hand, it is equally true that I am now seeing how little those interests really amount to. They are pastime, if you like, but nothing more. Some women do serious work, however; I wish I could be one of them. To them, perhaps, ' views ' are something real and helpful. But never mind myself; you were glad to hear that Reuben is working on ? "

" Very glad."

Cecily waited a little; then, watching the other's face, asked :

" You know what he is writing ? "

" In a general way," Miriam answered, averting her eyes. " Do you think he has made a wise choice ? "

"I dare say it is the subject on which he will write best," Cecily answered, smiling.

"I doubt whether he understands it sufficiently," said Miriam, with balanced tone. "He has really nothing but prejudice to go upon. There will be a great deal of mis-representation in his book—if he ever finishes it."

"Yes, I am afraid that is true. But it may be useful, after all. Here and there he will hit the mark."

Cecily was tentative. She saw Miriam's brows work uneasily.

"Perhaps so," was the reply. "But I know quite well that such a book would have been no use to me when I stood in need of the kind of help you mean."

"To be sure; it is for people who have already helped themselves," said Cecily, in a jesting tone.

Miriam turned to another subject, and very soon said good night. Reflecting on the conversation, she was annoyed with herself for having been led by her familiar weakness to admit that she had changed her way of thinking. Certainly she had no intention of disguising the fact, but this explicit confession had seemed to make her Cecily's inferior; she was like a school-girl claiming recognition of progress.

The next morning Mallard called. He came into a room where Mrs. Lessingham, Eleanor, and Miriam were waiting for Cecily to join them, that all might go out together. Miriam had never seen him behave with such ease of manner. He was in good spirits, and talked with a facility most unusual in him. Mrs. Lessingham said she would go and see why Cecily delayed; Eleanor also made an excuse for leaving the room. But Miriam remained, standing by the window and looking into the street; Mallard stood near her, but did not speak. The silence lasted for a minute or two; then Cecily entered, and at once the artist greeted her with warm friendliness. Miriam had turned, but did not regard the pair directly; her eye caught their reflection in a mirror, and she watched them closely without seeming to do so. Cecily had made her appearance with a face of pleased anticipation; she looked for the first moment with much earnestness at her old friend, and when she spoke to him it was with the unmistakable accent of emotion. Mallard was gentle, reverent; he held her hand a little longer than was necessary, but his eyes quickly fell from her countenance.

"Your husband is well?" he asked in a full, steady voice.

They seated themselves, and Miriam again turned to the window. Cecily's voice made a jarring upon her ear; it was so much sweeter and more youthful, so much more like the voice of Cecily Doran, than when it addressed other people. Mallard, too, continued in a soft, pleasant tone, quite different from his usual speech; Miriam thrilled with irritation as she heard him.

"They have told me of the picture you painted at Pæstum. When may Mrs. Lessingham and I come and see it?"

"I haven't a place in which I could receive you. I'll bring the thing here, whenever you like."

Miriam moved. She wished to leave the room, but could not decide herself to do so. In the same moment Mallard glanced round at her. She interpreted his look as one of impatience, and at once said to Cecily:

"I think I'll change my mind, and write some letters this morning. Perhaps you could persuade Mr. Mallard to take my place for the drive."

"Oh!" exclaimed Cecily, with a laugh, "I'm quite sure Mr. Mallard has no desire to go to the English cemetery." She added in explanation, to Mallard himself, "My aunt has promised to visit a certain grave, and copy the inscription for a friend at Florence."

Whilst she was speaking, Mrs. Lessingham and Eleanor returned. Mallard, rising, looked at Miriam with a singular smile; then talked a little longer, and, with a promise to come again, soon took his leave.

"Don't disappoint us," said Cecily to Miriam, in the most natural tone.

"It was only that I felt we were making Mr. Mallard's visit very short," answered Miriam, constrained by shame.

"He detests ceremony. You couldn't please him better than by saying, ' Please don't hinder me now, but come when I'm at leisure.' "

It was peculiarly distasteful to Miriam to have information concerning the artist's character offered her by Cecily, in spite of the playful tone. During the drive, she persuaded herself that Cecily's improved spirits were entirely due to the conversation with Mallard, and this stirred fresh resentment in her. She had foreseen the effect upon her own feelings of the meeting which had just come about; it was extreme folly, but she could not control it.

The next day Mallard brought his picture again to the hotel, and spent nearly an hour with Mrs. Lessingham and Cecily in their sitting-room. Miriam heard of this on her return from a solitary walk, and heard, moreover, that Mallard had been showing his friends a number of little drawings which he had never offered to let her or the Spences see. In the afternoon she again went out by herself, and, whilst looking into a shop-window in the Piazza di Spagna, became aware of Mallard's face reflected in the glass. She drew aside before looking round at him.

"That is a clever piece of work," he said, indicating a water-colour in the window, and speaking as if they had already been in conversation. He had not even made the hat-salute.

"I thought so," Miriam replied, very coldly, looking at something else.

"Are you going home, Mrs. Baske ? "

"Yes. I only came out to buy something."

"I am just going to see the studio of an Italian to whom Mr. Seaborne introduced me yesterday. It's in the Quattro-Fontane. Would it interest you ? "

" Thank you, Mr. Mallard; I had rather not go this afternoon."

He accepted the refusal with a courteous smile, raised his hat in approved manner, and turned to cross the Piazza as she went her way.

This evening they had a visit from Seaborne, who met Mrs. Lessingham and Cecily for the first time. These ladies were predisposed to like him, and before he left they did so genuinely. In his pleasantly quiet way, he showed much respectful admiration of Mrs. Elgar.

" Now, isn't there a resemblance to Mr. Mallard ? " asked Eleanor, when the visitor was gone.

" Just—just a little," admitted Cecily, with fastidiousness and an amused smile. " But Mr. Seaborne doesn't impress me as so original, so strong."

" Oh, that he certainly isn't," said Spence. " But acuter, and perhaps a finer feeling in several directions."

Miriam listened, and was tortured.

She had suffered all the evening from observing Cecily, whose powers of conversation and charms of manner made her bitterly envious. How far she herself was from this ideal of the instructed and socially trained woman ! The presence of a stranger had banished Cecily's despondent mood, and put all her capacities in display. With a miserable sense of humiliation, Miriam compared her own insignificant utterances and that bright, often brilliant, talk which held the attention of every one. Beside Cecily, she was still indeed nothing but a school-girl, who with much labour was getting a smattering of common knowledge; for, though Cecily had no profound acquirements, the use she made of what she did know was always suggestive, intellectual, individual.

What wonder that Mallard brought out his drawings to show them to Cecily ? There would be nothing commonplace in *her* remarks and admiration.

She felt herself a paltry pretender to those possibilities of modern womanhood which were open to Cecily from her birth. In the course of natural development, Cecily, whilst still a girl, threw for ever behind her all superstitions and harassing doubts; she was in the true sense "emancipated"—a word Edward Spence was accustomed to use jestingly. And this was Mallard's conception of the admirable in woman.

CHAPTER IX.

SILENCES.

CECILY was seeing Rome for the first time, but she could not enjoy it in the way natural to her. It was only at rare moments that she *felt* Rome. One of the most precious of her life's anticipations was fading into memory, displaced by a dull experience, numbered among disillusionings. Not that what she beheld disappointed her, but that she was not herself in beholding. Had she stayed here on her first visit to Italy, on what a strong current of enthusiasm would the hours and the days have borne her! What a light would have glowed upon the Seven Hills, and how would every vulgarity of the modern streets have been transformed by her imagination! But now she was in no haste to visit the most sacred spots; she was content to take each in its turn, and her powers of attention soon flagged. It had been the same in Florence. She felt herself reduced to a lower level of existence than was native to her. Had she lived her life—all that was worth calling life?

Her chief solace was in the society of Mrs. Spence. Formerly she had not been prepared for appreciating Eleanor, but now she felt the beauties of that calm, self-reliant character, rich in a mode of happiness which it seemed impossible for herself ever to attain. Fortune had been Eleanor's friend. Disillusion had come to her only in the form of beneficent wisdom; no dolorous dead leaves rustled about her feet and clogged her walk. Happy even in the fact that she had never been a mother. She was a free woman; free in the love of her husband, free in the pursuit of knowledge and the cultivation of all her tastes. She had outlived passion without mourning it; what greater happiness than that can a woman expect? Cecily had once believed that life was to be all passion, or a failure. She understood now that there was a middle path. But against her it was closed.

In a few days she could talk with Eleanor even of bygone things in a perfectly simple tone, without danger of betraying the thoughts she must keep secret. One such conversation reminded her of something she had learnt shortly before she left London.

"Do you remember," she asked, "a family named Denyer, who were at Mrs. Gluck's?"

Eleanor recollected the name, and the characteristics attached to it.

"An acquaintance of mine who has rooms at Hampstead happened to speak of the people she is with, and it surprised me to discover that they were those very Denyers. One of the daughters is paralyzed, poor girl; I was shocked to remember her, and think of her visited by such a fate. I believe she was to have married that artist, Mr. Marsh, who gave Mr. Bradshaw so much amusement. And the eldest——"

She broke off to inquire why Eleanor had looked at her so expressively.

"I'll tell you when you have finished your story. What of the eldest?"

"She has recently married Mr. Musselwhite, who was also one of our old acquaintances. Mrs. Travis—the lady who tells me all this—says that Mrs. Denyer is overjoyed at this marriage, for Mr. Musselwhite is the brother of a baronet!"

"Very satisfactory indeed. Well, now for Mr. Marsh. Edward heard from Mr. Bradshaw when we were in Sicily, and this young gentleman had a great part in the letter. It seems he has long abandoned his artistic career, and gone into commerce."

"That most superior young man? But I remember something about that."

"His business takes him often to Manchester, and he has been cultivating the acquaintance of the Bradshaws. And now there is an engagement between him and their eldest daughter."

"Charlotte? What a queer thing to happen! Isn't she about my age?"

"Yes; and, if she fulfils her promise, one of the plainest girls in existence. Her father jokes about the affair, but evidently doesn't disapprove."

It was Thursday, and the Spences had decided to start for London on Friday night. Miriam had been keeping much alone these last few days, and this morning was out by herself in the usual way. Spence was engaged with Seaborne. Mrs. Lessingham, Eleanor, and Cecily went to the Vatican.

Where also was Mallard. He had visited the chapel, and the Stanze, and the Loggia, and the picture-gallery, not looking at things, but seeming to look for some one; then he came out, and walked round St. Peter's to the Museum. In the Sala Rotonda he encountered his friends.

They talked about the busts. Cecily was studying them with the catalogue, and wished Mallard to share her pleasure.

"The empresses interest me most," she said. "Come and do homage to them."

They look with immortal eyes, those three women who

once saw the world at their feet: Plotina, the wife of
Trajan; Faustina, the wife of Antoninus Pius; Julia, the
wife of Septimius Severus. Noble heads, each so unlike
the other. Plotina, with her strong, not beautiful, features,
the high cheek-bones, the male chin; on her forehead a
subdued anxiety. Faustina, the type of aristocratic self-
consciousness, gloriously arrogant, splendidly beautiful,
with her superb coronet of woven hair. Julia Domna, a
fine, patrician face, with a touch of idleness and good-
natured scorn about her lips, taking her dignity as a matter
of course.

"These women awe me," Cecily murmured, as Mallard
stood beside her. "They are not of our world. They make
me feel as if I belonged to an inferior race."

"Glorious barbarians," returned Mallard.

"We of to-day have no right to say so."

Then the Antinous, the finest of all his heads. It must
be caught in profile, and one stands marvelling at the
perfection of soulless beauty. And the Jupiter of Otricoli,
most majestic of marble faces; in that one deep line across
the brow lies not only profound thought, but something of
the care of rule, or something of pity for mankind; as
though he had just uttered his words in Homer: "For
verily there is no creature more afflicted than man, of all
that breathe and move upon the earth." But that other,
the Serapis, is above care of every kind; on his countenance
is a divine placidity, a supernal blandness; he gazes for
ever in sublime and passionless reverie.

Thence they passed to the Hall of the Muses, and spoke
of Thalia, whose sweet and noble face, with its deep, far-
looking eyes, bears such a weary sadness. Comedy? Yes;
comedy itself, when comedy is rightly understood.

And whilst they stood here, there came by a young
priest, holding open a missal or breviary or some such book,
and muttering from it, as if learning by heart. Cecily
followed him with her gaze.

"What a place for study of that kind!" she exclaimed, looking at Mallard.

He also had felt the incongruity, and laughed.

Two or three chambers of the Vatican sufficed for one day. Cecily would not trust herself to remain after her interest had begun to weary; it was much that she had won two hours of intellectual calm. Her companions had no wish to stay longer. Just as they came again into the Sala Rotonda, they found themselves face to face with Miriam.

"Did you know we were coming here?" asked Eleanor.

"I thought it likely."

She shook hands with Mallard, but did not speak to him. Eleanor offered to stay with her, as this would be their last visit, but Miriam said in a friendly manner that she preferred to be alone. So they left her.

At the exit, Mallard saw his companions into a carriage, and himself walked on; but as soon as the carriage was out of sight, he turned back. He had taken care to recover his *permesso* from the attendant, in the common way, when he came out, so that he could enter again immediately. He walked rapidly to the place where they had left Miriam, but she was gone. He went forward, and discovered her sitting before the Belvedere Apollo. As his entrance drew her attention, he saw that she had an impulse to rise; but she overcame it, and again turned her eyes upon him, with a look in which self-control was unconsciously like defiance.

He sat down by her, and said:

'I came to the Vatican this morning for the chance of meeting you."

"I hope that was not your only reason for coming," she returned, in a voice of ordinary civility.

"It was, in fact. I should have asked you to let me have your company for an hour to-day, as it is practically your last in Rome; but I was not sure that you would grant it, so I took my chance instead."

She waited a moment before replying.

"I am afraid you refer to your invitation of a few days ago. I didn't feel in the mood for going to a studio, Mr. Mallard."

"Yes, I was thinking of that. You refused in a way not quite like yourself. I began to be afraid that you thought me too regardless of forms."

His return had gratified her; it was unexpected, and she set her face in a hard expression that it might not betray her sudden gladness. But the look of thinly-masked resentment which succeeded told of what had been in her mind since she encountered him in the company of Cecily. That jealous pain was uncontrollable; the most trivial occasions had kept exciting it, and now it made her sick at heart. The effort to speak conventionally was all but beyond her strength.

They had in common that personal diffidence which is one of the phases of pride, and which proves so fruitful a source of misunderstandings. For all her self-esteem, Miriam could not obtain the conviction that, as a woman, she strongly interested Mallard; and the artist found it very hard to persuade himself that Miriam thought of him as anything but a man of some talent, whose attention was agreeable, and perhaps a little flattering. Still, he could not but notice that her changed behaviour connected itself with Cecily's arrival. It seemed to him extraordinary, almost incredible, that she should be jealous of his relations with her sister-in-law. Had she divined his passion for Cecily at Naples? (He cherished a delusion that the secret had never escaped him.) But to attribute jealousy to her was to assume that she set a high value on his friendship.

Miriam had glanced at the Apollo as he spoke. Conscious of his eyes upon her, she looked away, saying in a forced tone:

"I had no such thought. You misunderstood me."

"It was all my fault, then, and I am sorry for it. You said just now that you preferred to be alone. I shall come to the hotel to-morrow, just to say good-bye."

A A

He rose ; and Miriam, as she did the same, asked formally :

" You are still uncertain how long you remain here ? "

" Quite," was his answer, cheerfully given.

" You are not going to work ? "

" No ; it is holiday with me for a while. I wish you were staying a little longer."

" You will still have friends here."

Mallard disliked the tone of this.

" Oh yes," he replied. " I hope to see Mrs. Lessingham and Mrs. Elgar sometimes."

He paused ; then added :

" I dare say I shall return to England about the same time that they do. May I hope to see you in London ? "

" I am quite uncertain where I shall be."

" Then perhaps we shall not meet for a long time.—Will you let me give you one or two little drawings that may help to remind you of Italy ? "

Miriam's cheeks grew warm, and she cast down her eyes.

" Your drawings are far too valuable to be given as one gives trifles, Mr. Mallard."

" I don't wish you to receive them as trifles. One of their values to me is that I can now and then please a friend with them. If you had rather I did not think of you as a friend, then you would be right to refuse them."

" I will receive them gladly."

" Thank you. They shall be sent to the hotel."

They shook hands, and he left her.

On the morrow they met again for a few minutes, when he came to say good-bye. Miriam made no mention of the packet that had reached her. She was distant, and her smile at leave-taking very cold.

So the three travelled northwards.

Their departure brought back Cecily's despondent mood. With difficulty she restrained her tears in parting from

Eleanor; when she was alone, they had their way. She felt vaguely miserable—was troubled with shapeless apprehensions, with a sense of desolateness.

The next day brought a letter from her husband, "Dear Ciss," he wrote, "I am sorry its so long since I sent you a line, but really there's no news. I foresee that I shall not have much manuscript to show you; I am reading hugely, but I don't feel ready to write. Hope you are much better; give me notice of your return. My regards to Mallard; I expect you will see very little of him." And so, with a "yours ever," the epistle ended.

This was all Reuben had to say to her, when she had been absent nearly a month. With a dull disappointment, she put the arid thing out of her sight. It had been her intention to write to-day, but now she could not. She had even less to say than he.

He expressed no wish for her return, and felt none. Perhaps, it was merely indifferent to him how long she stayed away; but she had no assurance that he did not prefer to be without her. And, for her own part, had she any desire to be back again? Here she was not contented, but at home she would be even less so.

The line in his letter which had reference to the much-talked-of book only confirmed her distrust. She had no faith in his work. The revival of his energy from time to time was no doubt genuine enough, but she knew that its subsequent decline was marked with all manner of pretences. Possibly he was still " reading hugely," but the greater likelihood was that he had fallen into mere idleness. It was significant of her feeling towards him that she never made surmises as to how he spent his leisure; her thoughts, consciously and unconsciously, avoided such reflections; it was a matter that did not concern her. He had now a number of companions, men of whom her own knowledge was very vague; that they were not considered suitable acquaintances for her, of course meant that Reuben could have no profit from them, and would probably suffer from their contact. But in these things she had long been passive, careless. Experience had taught her how easy it was for husband and wife to live parted lives, even whilst their domestic habits seemed the same as ever; in books, that situation had formerly struck her as inconceivable, but now she suspected that it was the commonest of the results of marriage. Habit, habit; how strong it is!

And how degrading! To it she attributed this bluntness in her faculties of perception and enjoyment, this barrenness of the world about her. It was dreadful to look forward upon a tract of existence thus vulgarized. Already she recognized in herself the warnings of a possible future in which she would have lost her intellectual ambitions. There is a creeping paralysis of the soul, and did she not experience its symptoms? Already it was hard to apply herself to any study that demanded real effort; she was failing to pursue her Latin; she avoided German books, because they were more exacting than French; her memory had lost something of its grasp. Was she to become a woman of society, a refined gossip, a pretentious echo of the reviews and of clever people's talk? If not, assuredly she must exert a force of character which she had begun to suspect was not in her.

Strange that the one person to whom she had disclosed something of her real mind was also the one who seemed at the greatest distance from her in this circle of friends. Involuntarily, she had spoken to Miriam as to no one else. This might be a result of old associations. But had it a connection with that curious surmise she had formed during the first hour of her conversation with the Spences, and with Miriam herself—that an unexpected intimacy was coming about between Miriam and Mallard? For, in her frequent thoughts of Mallard, she had necessarily wondered whether he would ever perceive the true issue of her self-will; and, so far from desiring to blind him, she had almost a hope that one day he might know how her life had shaped itself. Mallard's position in her mind was a singular one; in some such way she might have regarded a brother who had always lived remote from her, but whom she had every reason to love and reverence. Her esteem for him was boundless; he was the ideal of the artist, and at the same time of the nobly strong man. Had such a thing been possible, she would have sought to make *him* her confidant. However it was to be explained, she felt no wound to her self-respect in supposing him cognizant of all her sufferings; rather, a solace, a source of strength.

Was it, in a measure, woman's gratitude for love? In the course of three years she had seen many reasons for believing that Reuben was right; that the artist had loved her, and gone through dark struggles when her fate was being decided. That must have added tenderness to her former regard and admiration. But she was glad that he had now recovered his liberty; the first meeting, his look and the grasp of his hand, told her at once that the trouble was long gone by. She was glad of this, and the proof of her sincerity came when she watched the relations between him and Miriam.

On the last evening, Miriam came to her room, carrying a small portfolio, which she opened before her, disclosing three water-colours.

"You have bought them?" Cecily asked, as the other said nothing.

"No. Mr. Mallard has given me them," was the answer, in a voice which affected a careless pleasure.

"They are admirable. I am delighted that you take such a present away with you."

Cecily expected no confidences, and received none; she could only puzzle over the problem. Why did Miriam behave with so strange a coldness? Her new way of regarding life ought to have resulted in her laying aside that austerity. Mrs. Lessingham hinted an opinion that the change did not go very deep; Puritanism, the result of birth and breeding, was not so easily eradicated.

Mallard stayed on in Rome, but during this next week Cecily only saw him twice—the first time, for a quarter of an hour on the Pincio; then in the Forum. On that second occasion he was invited to dine with them at the hotel the next day, Mr. Seaborne's company having also been requested. The result was a delightful evening. Seaborne was just now busy with a certain period of Papal history; he talked of some old books he had been reading in the Vatican library, and revealed a world utterly strange to all his hearers.

Here were men who used their lives to some purpose; who not only planned, but executed. When the excitement of the evening had subsided, Cecily thought with more bitterness than ever yet of the contrast between such workers and her husband. The feeling which had first come upon her intensely when she stood before Mallard's picture at the Academy was now growing her habitual mood. She had shut herself out for ever from close communion with this world of genuine activity; she could only regard it from behind a barrier, instead of warming her heart and brain in free enjoyment of its emotions. And the worst of it was that these glimpses harmed her, injured her morally. One cannot dwell with discontent and keep a healthy imagination. She knew her danger, and it increased the misery with which she looked forward.

Another week, and again there was a chance meeting with Mallard, this time on the Via Appia, where Cecily and her aunt were driving. They spent a couple of hours together. At the parting, Mallard announced that the next day would see him on his journey to London

CHAPTER X.

ELGAR AT WORK.

At Dover it was cold and foggy; the shore looked mildewed, the town rain-soaked and mud-stained. In London, a solid leaden sky lowered above the streets, neither threatening rain nor allowing a hope of sunlight. What a labour breathing had become!

"My heart warms to my native land," said Spence. "This is a spring day that recalls one's youth."

Eleanor tried to smile, but the railway journey had depressed her beneath the possibility of joking. Miriam was pallid and miserable; she had scarcely spoken since she set foot on the steamboat. Cab-borne through the clangorous streets, they seemed a party of exiles.

The house in Chelsea, which the Spences held on a long lease, had been occupied during their absence by Edward's brother-in-law and his family. Vacated, swept, and garnished, the old furniture from the Pantechnicon re-established somewhat at haphazard, it was not a home that welcomed warmly; but one could heap coals on all the fires, and draw down the blinds as soon as possible, and make a sort of Christmas evening. If only one's lungs could have free play! But in a week or so such little incommodities would become natural again.

Miriam had decided that in a day or two she would go down to Bartles; not to stay there, but merely to see her relative, Mrs. Fletcher, and Redbeck House. Before leaving London, she must visit Reuben; she had promised Cecily to do so without delay. This same evening she posted a card to her brother, asking him to be at home to see her early the next morning.

She reached Belsize Park at ten o'clock, and dismissed the cab as soon as she had alighted from it. Her ring at the door was long in being answered, and the maid-servant who at last appeared did small credit to the domestic arrangements of the house—she was slatternly, and seemed to resent having her morning occupations, whatever they were, thus disturbed. Miriam learnt with surprise that Mr. Elgar was not at home.

"He is out of town?"

The servant thought so; he had not been at the house for two days.

"You are unable to tell me when he will return?"

Mr. Elgar was often away for a day or two, but not for longer than that. The probability was that he would, at all events, look in before evening, though he might go away again.

Miriam left a card—which the servant inspected with curiosity before the door was closed—and turned to depart. It was raining, and very windy. She had to walk some distance before she could find a conveyance, and all the way she suffered from a painful fluttering of the heart, an agitation like that of fear. All night she had wished she had never returned to England, and now the wish became a dread of remaining.

By the last post that evening came a note from Reuben. He wrote in manifest hurry, requesting her to come again next morning; he would have visited her himself, but perhaps she had not a separate sitting-room, and he preferred to talk with her in privacy.

So in the morning she again went to Belsize Park. This time the servant was a little tidier, and behaved more conventionally. Miriam was conducted to the library, where Reuben awaited her.

They examined each other attentively. Miriam was astonished to find her brother looking at least ten years older than when she last saw him; he was much sparer in body, had duller eyes and, it seemed to her, thinner hair.

"But why didn't you write sooner to let me know you were coming?" was his first exclamation.

"I supposed you knew from Cecily."

"I haven't heard from her since the letter in which she told me she had got to Rome. She said you would be coming soon, but that was all. I don't understand this economy of postage!"

He grew more annoyed as he spoke. Meeting Miriam's eye, he added, in the tone of explanation:

"It's abominable that you should come here all the way from Chelsea, and be turned away at the door! What did the servant tell you?"

"Only that your comings and goings were very uncertain," she replied, looking about the room.

"Yes, so they are. I go now and then to a friend's in Surrey and stop overnight. One can't live alone for an indefinite time. But sit down. Unless you'd like to have a look at the house, first of all?"

"I'll sit a little first."

"This is my study, when I'm working at home," Reuben continued, walking about and handling objects, a book, or a pen, or a paper-knife. "Comfortable, don't you think? I want to have another bookcase over there. I haven't worked here much since Cecily has been away; I have a great deal of reading to do at the Museum, you know.—You look a vast deal better, Miriam. What are you going to do?"

"I don't know. Most likely I shall continue to live with the Spences."

"You wouldn't care to come here?"

"Thank you; I think the other arrangement will be better."

"Perhaps so. For one thing, it's quite uncertain whether we shall keep this house. It's really a good deal too large for us; an unnecessary expense. If Cecily is often to be away like this, there's no possibility of keeping the place in order. How the servants live, or what they do, I have no idea. How can I be expected to look after such things?"

"But surely it is not expected of you? I understood that Cecily had left a housekeeper."

"Oh yes; but I have a suspicion that she does little but eat and drink. I know the house is upside down. It's long enough since I had a decent meal here. Practically I have taken to eating at restaurants. Of course I say nothing about it to Cecily; what's the use of bothering her? By-the-bye, how is she? How did you leave her?"

"Not very well, I'm afraid."

"She never says a word about her health. But then, practically, she never writes. I doubt whether London suits her. We shall have to make our head-quarters in Paris, I fancy; she was always well enough there. Of course I can't abandon London entirely; at all events, not till I've—till my materials for the book are all ready; but it's simple enough for me to come and take lodgings for a month now and then."

Miriam gave an absent "Yes."

"You don't seem to have altered much, after all," he resumed, looking at her with a smile. "You talk to me just like you used to. I expected to find you more cheerful."

Miriam showed a forced smile, but answered nothing.

"Well, did you see much of Mallard?" he asked, throwing himself into a seat impatiently, and beginning to rap his knee with the paper-knife.

"Not very much."

"Has he come back with you?"

"Oh no; he is still in Rome. He said that he would most likely return when the others did."

"How do he and Cecily get on together?"

"They seemed to be quite friendly."

"Indeed? Does he go about with them?"

"I don't know."

" But did he when you were there ? "

" I think he was with them at the Vatican once."

Elgar heard it with indifference. He was silent for a minute or two ; then, quitting his chair, asked :

" Had you much talk with her ? "

" With Cecily ?   We were living together, you know."

" Yes, but had she much to tell you ?   Did she talk about how things were going with us—what I was doing, and so on ? "

He was never still.   Now he threw himself into another chair, and strummed with his fingers on the arm of it.

" She told me about your work."

" And showed that she took very little interest in it, no doubt ? "

Miriam gazed at him.

" Why do you think that ? "

" Oh, that's tolerably well understood between us." Again he rose, and paced with his hands in his pockets.   " It was a misfortune that Clarence died.   Now she has nothing to occupy herself with.   She doesn't seem to have any idea of employing her time.   It was bad enough when the child was living, but since then——"

He spoke as though the hints fell from him involuntarily ; he wished to be understood as implying no censure, but merely showing an unfortunate state of things.   When he broke off, it was with a shrug and a shake of the head.

" But I suppose she reads a good deal ? " said Miriam ; " and has friends to visit ? "

" She seems to care very little about reading nowadays. And as for the friends—yes, she is always going to some house or other.   Perhaps it would have been better if she had had no friends at all."

" You mean that they are objectionable people ? "

" Oh no ; I don't mean to say anything of that kind. But—well, never mind, we won't talk about it."

He threw up an arm, and began to pace the floor again.

His nervousness was increasing. In a few moments he broke out in the same curious tone, which was half complaining, half resigned.

"You know Cecily, I dare say. She has a good deal of—well, I won't call it vanity, because that has a vulgar sound, and she is never vulgar. But she likes to be admired by clever people. One must remember how young she still is. And that's the very thing of which she can't endure to be reminded. If I hint a piece of counsel, she feels it an insult. I suppose I am to blame myself, in some things. When I was working here of an evening, now and then I felt it a bore to have to dress and go out. I don't care much for society, that's the fact of the matter. But I couldn't bid her stay at home. You see how things get into a wrong course. A girl of her age oughtn't to be going about alone among all sorts of people. Of course something had to precede that. The first year or two, she didn't want any society. I suppose a man who studies much always runs the danger of neglecting his home affairs. But it was her own wish that I should begin to work. She was incessantly urging me to it. One of the inconsistencies of women, you see."

He laughed unmelodiously, and then there was a long silence. Miriam, who watched him mechanically, though her eyes were not turned directly upon him, saw that he seated himself on the writing-table, and began to make idle marks with a pencil on the back of an envelope.

"Why didn't you go abroad with her?" she asked in a low voice.

"I would have gone, if it hadn't been quite clear that she preferred not to have my company."

"Are you speaking the truth?"

"What do you mean, Miriam? She preferred to go alone; I know she did."

"But didn't you make the excuse to her that you couldn't leave your work?"

"That's true also. Could I say plainly that I saw what she wished?"

"I think it very unlikely that you were right," Miriam rejoined in a tone of indecision.

"What reason have you for saying that?"

"You ought to have a very good reason before you believe the contrary."

She waited for him to reply, but he had taken another piece of paper, and seemed absorbed in covering it with a sort of pattern of his own design.

"Right or wrong, what does it matter?" he exclaimed at length, flinging the pencil away. "The event is the same, in any case. Does it depend on myself how I act, or what I think? Do you believe still that we are free agents, and responsible for our acts and thoughts?"

Miriam avoided his look, and said carelessly:

"I know nothing about it."

He gave a short laugh.

"Well, that's better and more honest than saying you believe what is contrary to all human experience. Look back on your life. Has its course been of your own shaping? Compare yourself of to-day with yourself of four years ago; has the change come about by your own agency? If you are *wrong*, are you to blame? Imagine some fanatic seizing you by the arm, and shouting to you to beware of the precipice to which you are advancing——"

He suited the action to the word, and grasped her wrist. Miriam shook him off angrily.

"What do you know of *me*?" she exclaimed, with suppressed scorn.

"True. Just as little as you know of me, or any one person of any other. However, I was speaking of what you know of yourself. I suppose you can look back on one or two things in your life of which your judgment doesn't approve? Do you imagine they could have happened otherwise than they did? Do you think it lay in your own power to take the course you now think the better?"

Miriam stood up impatiently, and showed no intention of replying. Again Elgar laughed, and waved his arm as if dismissing a subject of thought.

"Come up and look at the drawing-room," he said, walking to the door.

"Some other time. I'll come again in a few days."

"As you please. But you must take your chance of finding me at home, unless you give me a couple of days' notice."

"Thank you," she answered coldly. "I will take my chance."

He went with her to the front door. With his hand on the latch, he said in an undertone:

"Shall you be writing to Cecily?"

"I think not; no."

"All right. I'll let her know you called."

For Miriam, this interview was confirmative of much that she had suspected. She believed now that Reuben and his wife, if they had not actually agreed to live apart, were practically in the position of people who have. The casual reference to a possible abandonment of their house meant more than Reuben admitted. She did not interpret the situation as any less interested person, with her knowledge of antecedents, certainly would have done; that is to say, conclude that Reuben was expressing his own desires independently of those which Cecily might have formed. Her probing questions, in which she had seemed to take Cecily's side, were in reality put with a perverse hope of finding that such a view was untenable, and she came away convinced that this was the case. The state of things at home considered, Cecily would not have left for so long an absence but on her own wish.

And, this determined, she thought with increased bitterness of Mallard's remaining in Rome. He too could not but suspect the course that Cecily's married life was taking; by this time he might even know with certainty. How would that affect him? In her doubt as to how far the exchange of confidences between Cecily and Mallard was a possible thing, she tortured herself with picturing the progress of their intercourse at Rome, inventing chance encounters, imagining conversations. Mrs. Lessingham was as good as no obstacle to their intimacy; her, Miriam distrusted profoundly. Judging by her own impulses, she attributed to Cecily a strong desire for Mallard's sustaining companionship; and on the artist's side, she judged all but inevitable, under such circumstances, a revival of that passion she had read in his face long ago. Her ingenuity of self-torment went so far as to interpret Mallard's behaviour to herself in a dishonourable sense. It is doubtful whether any one who loves passionately fulfils the ideal of being unable to see the object of love in any but a noble light; this is one of the many conventions, chiefly of literary origin, which to the eyes of the general make cynicism of wholesome truth. Miriam deemed it not impossible that Mallard had made her his present of pictures simply to mislead her thought when she was gone. Jealousy can sink to baser imaginings than this. It is only calm affection that judges always in the spirit of pure sympathy.

On the following day, the Spences dined from home, and Miriam, who had excused herself from accompanying them, sat through the evening in their drawing-room. The weather was wretched; a large fire made the comfort within contrast pleasantly enough with sounds of wind and rain against the house. Miriam's mind was far away from Chelsea; it haunted the Via del Babuino, and the familiar rooms of the hotel where Cecily was living. Just after the clock had struck ten, a servant entered and said that Mr. Elgar wished to see her.

Reuben was in evening dress.

"What! you are alone?" he said on entering. "I'm glad

of that. I supposed I should have to meet the people. I want to kill half an hour, that's all."

He drew a small low chair near to hers, and, when he had seated himself, took one of her hands. Miriam glanced at him with surprise, but did not resist him. His cheeks were flushed, perhaps from the cold wind, and there was much more life in his eyes than the other morning.

"You're a lonely girl, Miriam," he let fall idly, after musing. "I'm glad I happened to come in, to keep you company. What have you been thinking about ?"

"Italy," she answered, with careless truth.

"Italy, Italy! Who doesn't think of Italy ? I wish I knew Italy as well as you do. Isn't it odd that I should be saying that to you ? I believe you are now far my superior in all knowledge that is worth having. Did I mention that Ciss wrote an account of you in the letter just after she had reached Rome ?"

Miriam made an involuntary movement as if to withdraw her hand, but overcame herself before she had succeeded.

"How did she come to know me so quickly ?" was her question, murmured absently.

"From Mrs. Spence, it seemed. Come, tell me what you have been doing this long time. You have seen Greece too. I must go to Greece—perhaps before the end of this year. I'll make a knapsack ramble: Greece, Egypt, Asia Minor, Constantinople."

Miriam kept silence, and her brother appeared to forget that he had said anything that required an answer. Presently he released her hand, after patting it, and moved restlessly in his chair; then he looked at his watch, and compared it curiously with the clock on the mantelpiece.

"Ciss," he began suddenly, and at once with a laugh corrected himself—"Miriam, I mean."

"What ?"

"I forget what I was going to say," he muttered, after delaying. "But that reminds me; I've been anxious lest you should misunderstand what I said yesterday. You didn't think I wished to make charges against Cecily ? "

" It's difficult to understand you," was all she replied.

" But you mustn't think that I misjudge her. Cecily has more than realized all I imagined her to be. There are few women living who could be called her equals. I say this in the gravest conviction ; this is the simple result of my knowledge of her. She has an exquisite nature, an admirable mind. I have never heard her speak a sentence that was unworthy of her, not one ! "

His voice trembled with earnestness. Miriam looked at him from under her eyebrows.

" If any one," he pursued, " ever threw doubt on the perfect uprightness of Cecily's conduct, her absolute honour, I would gage my life upon the issue."

And in this moment he spoke with sincerity, whatever the mental process which had brought him to such an utterance· Even Miriam could not doubt him. His clenched fist quivered as it lay on his knee, and the gleam of firelight showed that his eyes were moist.

" Why do you say this ? " his sister asked, still scrutinizing him.

" To satisfy myself ; to make you understand once for all what I *do* believe. Have you any other opinion of her, Miriam ? "

She gave a simple negative.

" I am not saying this," he pursued, " in the thought that you will perhaps repeat it to her some day. It is for my own satisfaction. If I could put it more strongly, I would ; but I will have nothing to do with exaggerations. The truth is best expressed in the simplest words."

" What do you mean by honour ? " Miriam inquired, when there had been a short silence.

" Honour ? "

" Your definitions are not generally those accepted by most people."

"I hope not." He smiled. "But you know sufficiently what I mean. Deception, for instance, is incompatible with what I understand as honour."

He spoke it slowly and clearly, his eyes fixed on the fire.

"You seem to me to be attributing moral responsibility to her."

"What I say is this: that I believe her nature incapable of admitting the vulgar influences to which people in general are subject. I attach no merit to her high qualities—no more than I attach merit to the sea for being a nobler thing than a muddy puddle. Of course I know that she cannot help being what she is, and cannot say to herself that in future she will become this or that. How am I inconsistent? Suppose me wrong in my estimate of her. I might then lament that she fell below what I had imagined, but of course I should have no right to blame her."

Miriam reflected; then put the question:

"And does she hold the same opinion—with reference to you, for instance?"

"Theoretically she does."

"Theoretically? If she made her opinions practical, I suppose there would be no reason why you shouldn't live together in contentment?"

Reuben glanced at her.

"I can't say," he replied gloomily. "That is quite another matter."

"Speaking of honour," said Miriam, "you would attach no blame to yourself if you fell below it."

He replied with deliberation:

"One often blames one's self emotionally, but the understanding is not affected by that. Unless your mind is unsteadied by excess of feeling."

"I believe you are a victim of sophistry—sophistry of the most dangerous kind. I can't argue with you, but I pity you, and fear for you."

The words were uttered so solemnly that Reuben for a

moment was shaken; his features moved in a way which indicates a sudden failure of self-possession. But he recovered himself immediately, and smiled his least amiable smile.

"I see you are not yet past the half-way house on the way of emancipation, Miriam. These things sound disagreeable, and prompt such deliverances as this of yours. But can I help it if a truth is unpalatable? What better should I be if I shut my eyes against it? You will say that this conviction makes me incapable of struggle for the good. Nothing of the kind. Where I am destined to struggle, I do so, without any reference to my scientific views. Of course, one is unhappier with science than without it. Who ever urged the contrary, that was worth listening to? I believe the human race will be more and more unhappy as science grows. But am I on that account likely to preach a crusade against it? Sister mine, we are what we are; we think and speak and do what causation determines. If you can still hold another belief, do so, and be thrice blessed. I would so gladly see you happy, dear Miriam."

Again he took her hand, and pressed it against his cheek Miriam looked straight before her with wide, almost despairing eyes.

"I must go, this moment," Elgar said, happening to notice the time. "Say I have been here, and couldn't wait for their return; indeed, they wouldn't expect it."

"Wait a few minutes, Reuben."

She retained his hand.

"I can't dear; I can't." His cheeks were hot. "I have an appointment."

"What appointment? With whom?"

"A friend. It is something important. I'll tell you another time."

"Tell me now. Your sister is more to you than a friend. I ask you to stay with me, Reuben."

In his haste, he did not understand how great an effort

over herself such words as these implied. The egoist rarely is moved to wonder at unusual demonstrations made on his own behalf. Miriam was holding his hand firmly, but he broke away. Then he turned back, took her in his arms, and kissed her more tenderly than he ever had done since he was a child. Miriam had a smile of hope, but only for a moment. After all, he was gone.

CHAPTER XI.

IN DUE COURSE.

A CHANGE of trains, and half an hour's delay, at Manchester, then on through Lancashire civilization, through fumes and evil smells and expanses of grey-built hideousness, as far as the station called Bartles.

Miriam remarked novelties as she alighted. The long wooden platform, which used to be almost bare, was now in part sheltered by a structure of iron and glass. There was a bookstall. Porters were more numerous. The old stationmaster still bustled about; he recognized her with a stare of curiosity, but did not approach to speak, as formerly he would have done. Miriam affected not to observe him; he had been wont to sit in the same chapel with her.

The wooden stairs down into the road were supplanted by steps of stone, and below waited several cabs, instead of the two she remembered. "To Redbeck House." The local odours were, at all events, the same as ever; with what intensity they revived the past! Every well-known object, every familiar face, heightened the intolerable throbbing of her heart; so that at length she drew herself into a corner of the cab and looked at nothing.

In the house itself nothing was new; even the servants

were the same Miriam had left there. Mrs. Fletcher lived
precisely the life of three and a half years ago, down to the
most trivial habit; used the same phrases, wore the same
kind of dress. To Miriam everything seemed unreal,
visionary; her own voice sounded strange, for it was out of
harmony with this resuscitated world. She went up to the
room prepared for her, and tried to shake off the nightmare
oppression. The difficulty was to keep a natural consciousness of her own identity. Above all, the scents in the air
disturbed her, confused her mind, forced her to think in
forgotten ways about the things on which her eyes fell.

The impressions of every moment were disagreeable, now
and then acutely painful. To what purpose had she faced
this experience? She might have foreseen what the result
would be, and her presence here was unnecessary.

But in an hour, when her pulse again beat temperately,
she began to adjust the relations between herself and these
surroundings. They no longer oppressed her; the sense of
superiority which had been pleasant at a distance re-
established itself, and gave her a defiant strength such as
she had hoped for. So far from the anxieties of her conscience being aggravated by return to Bartles, she could not
recover that mode of feeling which had harassed her for the
last few months. Like so many other things, it had become
insubstantial. It might revive, but for the present she was
safe against it.

And this self-possession was greatly aided by Mrs.
Fletcher's talk. From her sister-in-law's letters, though for
the last two years they had been few, Miriam had formed
some conception of the progress of Bartles opinion concerning
herself. Now she led Mrs. Fletcher to converse with native
candour on this subject, and in the course of the evening,
which they spent alone, all the town's gossip since Miriam's
going abroad was gradually reported. Mrs. Fletcher was
careful to prevent the inference (which would have been
substantially correct) that she herself had been the source

of such rumours as had set wagging the tongues of dissident Bartles; she spoke with much show of reluctance, and many protestations of the wrath that had been excited in her by those who were credulous of ill. Miriam confined herself to questioning; she made no verbal comments. But occa sionally she averted her face with a haughty smile.

Mrs. Welland, the once-dreaded rival, had established an unassailable supremacy. From her, according to Mrs. Fletcher, proceeded most of the scandalous suggestions which had attached themselves to Mrs. Baske's name. This lady had not scrupled to state it as a fact in her certain knowledge that Mrs. Baske was become a Papist. To this end, it seemed, was the suspicion of Bartles mainly directed —the Scarlet Woman throned by the Mediterranean had made a victim of her who was once a light in the re-reformed faith. That was the reason, said Mrs. Welland, why the owner of Redbeck House continued to dwell in foreign parts. If ever she came back at all, it would be as an insidious enemy; but more likely she would never return; possibly her life would close in a convent, like that of other hapless Englishwomen whose personal property excited the covetous-ness of the Pope. In the Bartles newspaper there had appeared, from time to time, enigmatic paragraphs, which Mrs. Welland and her intimates made the subject of much gossip; these passages alluded either to a certain new chapel which seemed very long in getting its foundations laid, or to a certain former inhabitant of Bartles, who found it neces-sary, owing to the sad state of her health, to make long residence in Roman Catholic countries. Mrs. Fletcher had preserved these newspapers, and now produced them. Miriam read and smiled.

"Why didn't it occur to them to suggest that I had become an atheist?"

Mrs. Fletcher screamed with horror. No, no; Bartles did not contain any one so malicious as that. After all, what-ever had been said was merely the outcome of a natural disappointment. All would be put right again. To-morrow was Sunday, and when Miriam appeared in the chapel——

" I have no intention of going to chapel."

On Monday morning she returned to London. Excepting Mrs. Fletcher and her daughters, she had spoken with no one in Bartles. She came away with a contemptuous hatred of the place—a resolve never to see it again.

This had been the one thing needed to make Miriam as intolerant in agnosticism as she formerly was in dogma. Henceforth she felt the animosity of a renegade. In the course of a few hours her soul had completed its transformation, and at the incitement of that pride which had always been the strongest motive within her. Her old faith was now identified with the cackle of Bartles, and she flung it behind her with disdain.

Not that she felt insulted by the supposition that she had turned Romanist. No single reason would account for her revolt, which, coming thus late, was all but as violent as that which had animated her brother from his boyhood. Intellectual progress had something to do with it, for on approaching with new eyes that narrow provincial life, she could scarcely believe it had once been her own, and resented the memory of such a past. But less worthy promptings were more strongly operative. The Bartles folk had a certain measure of right against her ; she had ostentatiously promised them a chapel, and how was her failure in keeping the promise to be accounted for ? This justification of theirs chafed her ; she felt the ire of one who has no right to be angry. It shamed her, moreover, to be reminded of the pretentious spirit which was the origin of this trouble ; and to be shamed by her inferiors was to Miriam a venomed stab. Then, again, she saw no way of revenging herself. Had she this morning possessed the power of calling down fire from heaven, Lancashire would shortly have missed one of its ugliest little towns ; small doubt of that.

No wonder a grave old gentleman who sat opposite on the journey to London was constrained frequently to look at her. As often as she forgot herself, the wrathful arrogance which boiled in her heart was revealed on her features; the strained brow, the flashing eyes, the stern-set lips, made a countenance not often to be studied in the railway-carriage.

It was with distinct pleasure that she found herself again in London. Contrasted with her homes in the south, London had depressed and discouraged her; but in this also did the visit to Bartles change her feeling. She understood now what had determined the Spences to make their abode once more in London. She too was in need of tonics for the mind. The roar of the streets was grateful to her; it seemed to lull the painful excitement in which she had travelled, and at the same time to stimulate her courage. Yes, she could face miseries better in London, after all. She could begin to work again, and make lofty that edifice of anti-dogmatic scorn which had now such solid foundations.

She allowed nearly a week to pass before writing to Reuben. When at length she sent a note, asking him either to come and see her or to make an appointment, it remained unanswered for three days; then arrived a few hurried lines, in which he said that he had been out of town, and was again on the point of leaving home, but he hoped to see her before long. She waited, always apprehensive of ill. What she divined of her brother's life was inextricably mingled with the other causes of her suffering.

One afternoon she returned from walking on the Chelsea Embankment, and, on reaching the drawing-room door, which was ajar, heard a voice that made her stand still. She delayed an instant; then entered, and found Eleanor in conversation with Mallard.

He had been in London, he said, only a day or two. Miriam inquired whether Mrs. Lessingham and Cecily had also left Rome. Not yet, he thought, but certainly they would be starting in a few days. The conversation then went on between Mallard and Eleanor; Miriam, holding a cup of tea, only gave a brief reply when it was necessary.

"And now," said Eleanor, "appoint a day for us to come and see your studio."

"You shall appoint it yourself."

"Then let us say to-morrow."

In speaking, Eleanor turned interrogatively to Miriam, who, however, said nothing. Mallard addressed her.

"May I hope that you will come, Mrs. Baske?"

His tone was, to her ear, as unsatisfying as could be; he seemed to put the question under constraint of civility. But, of course, only one answer was possible.

So next day this visit was paid; Spence also came. Mallard had made preparations. A tea-service which would not have misbecome Eleanor's own drawing-room stood in readiness. Pictures were examined, tea was taken, artistic matters were discussed.

And Miriam went away in uttermost discontent. She felt that henceforth her relations with Mallard were established on a perfectly conventional basis. Her dreams were left behind in Rome. Here was no Vatican in which to idle and hope for possible meetings. The holiday was over. Everything seemed of a sudden so flat and commonplace, that even her jealousy of Cecily faded for lack of sustenance.

Then she received a letter from Cecily herself, announcing return within a week. From Reuben she had even yet heard nothing.

A few days later, as she was reading in her room between tea and dinner-time, Eleanor came in; she held an evening newspaper, and looked very grave—more than grave. Miriam, as soon as their eyes met, went pale with misgiving.

"There's something here," Eleanor began, "that I must show you. If I said nothing about it, you would see it all the same. Sooner or later, we should speak of it."

" What is it? About whom? " Miriam asked, with fearful impatience, half rising.

" Your brother."

Miriam took the paper, and read what was indicated. It was the report of a discreditable affair—in journalistic language, a *fracas*—that had happened the previous night at Notting Hill. A certain music-hall singer, a lady who had of late achieved popularity, drove home about midnight, accompanied by a gentleman whose name was also familiar to the public—at all events, to that portion of it which reads society journals and has an interest in race-horses. The pair had just alighted at the house-door, when they were hurriedly approached by another gentleman, who made some remark to the songstress; whereupon the individual known to fame struck him smartly with his walking-stick. The result was a personal conflict, a rolling upon the pavement, a tearing of shirt-collars, and the opportune arrival of police. The gentleman whose interference had led to the *rencontre*—again to borrow the reporter's phrase—and who was charged with assault by the other, at first gave a false name; it had since transpired that he was a Mr. R. Elgar, of Belsize Park.

Miriam laid down the paper. She had overcome her extreme agitation, but there was hot shame on her cheeks. She tried to smile.

" One would think he had contrived it for his wife's greeting on her return."

Eleanor was silent.

" I am not much surprised," Miriam added. "Nor you either, I dare say? "

" I have felt uneasy; but I never pictured anything like this. Can we do anything? Shall you go and see him? "

" No."

They sat for some minutes without speaking; then Miriam exclaimed angrily:

" What right had she to go abroad alone? "

"For anything we know, Miriam, she may have had only too good a reason."

"Then I don't see that it matters."

Eleanor sighed, and, after a little lingering, but without further speech, went from the room.

In the meantime, Spence had entered the house. Eleanor met him in the drawing-room, and held the paper to him, with a silent indication of the paragraph. He read, and with an exclamation of violent disgust threw the thing aside. His philosophy failed him for once.

"What a blackguardly affair! Does Miriam know?"

"I have just shown it her. Evidently she had a suspicion of what was going on."

Spence muttered a little; then regained something of his usual equanimity.

"Our conjectures may be right," he said. "Perhaps no revelation awaits her."

"I begin to think it very likely. Oh, it is hateful, vile! She oughtn't to return to him."

"Pray, what is she to do?"

"I had rather she died than begin such a life!"

"I see no help for her. Her lot is that of many a woman no worse than herself. We both foresaw it; Mallard foresaw it."

"I am afraid to look forward. I don't think she is the kind of woman to forgive again and again. This will revolt her, and there is no telling what she may do."

"It is the old difficulty. Short of killing herself, whatever she does will be the beginning of worse things. In this respect, there's no distinction between Cecily and the wife of the costermonger. Civilization is indifferent. Her life is marred, and there's an end on't."

Eleanor turned away. Her eyes were wet with tears of indignant sympathy.

CHAPTER XII.

CECILY'S RETURN.

On alighting at Charing Cross, Cecily searched the platform for Reuben. There could be no doubt of his coming to meet her, for she had written to tell him that Mrs. Lessingham would at once go into the country from another station, and she would thus be alone. But she looked about and waited in vain. In the end she took a cab, parted with her companion, and drove homewards.

It was more than a trivial disappointment. On the journey, she had felt a longing for home, a revival of affection; she had tried to persuade herself that this long separation would have made a happy change, and that their life might take a new colour. Had Reuben appeared at the station, she would have pressed his hand warmly. Her health had improved; hope was again welcome. It came not like the hope of years ago, radiant, with eyes of ecstasy; but sober, homely, a gentle smile on its compassionate lips.

His failure would easily be explained; either he had mistaken the train, or something inevitable had hindered him; possibly she had made a slip of the pen in writing. Nearing home, she grew tremulous, nervously impatient. Before the cab had stopped, she threw the door open.

The servant who admitted her wore an unusual expression, but Cecily did not observe this.

"Mr. Elgar is at home?"

"No, ma'am."

"When did he go out?"

"He has not been at home for three days, ma'am."

Cecily controlled herself.

"There are some parcels in the cab. Take them up-stairs."

She went into the study, and stood looking about her. On the writing-table lay some unopened letters, all addressed to her husband; also two or three that had been read and thrown aside. Whilst she was still at the mercy of her confused thoughts, the servant came and asked if she would pay the cabman.

Then she ascended to the drawing-room and sat down. Had her letter gone astray? But if he had not been home for three days, and, as appeared, his letters were not forwarded to him, did not this prove (supposing a miscarriage of what she had written) that he was not troubling himself about news from her? If he had received her letter—and it ought to have arrived at least four days ago—what was the meaning of his absence?

She shrank from questioning the servants further. Presently, without having changed her dress, she went down again to the library, and re-examined the letters waiting to be read; and the handwriting was in each case unknown to her. Then she took up the letters that were open. One was an invitation to dine, one the appeal of some charitable institution; last, a few lines from Mallard. He wrote asking Elgar to come and see him—seemingly with no purpose beyond a wish to re-establish friendly relations. Cecily read the note again and again, wondering whether it had led to a meeting.

Why had not the housekeeper made her appearance? She rang the bell, and the woman came. With as much composure as she could command, Cecily inquired whether Mr. Elgar had spoken of her expected arrival. Yes, he had done so; everything had been made ready. And had he left word when he himself should be back? No; he had said nothing.

Naturally, she thought of going to the Spences'; but her dignity resisted. How could she seek information about her husband from friends? It was difficult to believe that he kept away voluntarily. Would he not in any case have sent word, even though the excuse were untruthful? What motive could he have for treating her thus? His last letter was longer and kinder than usual.

She was troubling herself needlessly. The simple explanation was of course the true one. He had been away in the country, and had arranged to be back in time to meet her at the station; then some chance had intervened. Doubtless he would very soon present himself. Her impatience and anxiety would never occur to him; what difference could a few hours make? They were not on such lover-like terms nowadays.

Compelling herself to rest in this view, she made a change of clothing, and again summoned the housekeeper, this time for discussion of domestic details. Cecily had no feminine delight in such matters for their own sake; the butcher, the baker, and the candlestick-maker were necessary evils, to be put out of mind as soon as possible. She learned incidentally that Reuben had been a great deal from home; but this did not surprise her. She had never imagined him leading a methodical life, between Belsize Park and the British Museum. That was not in his nature.

At the usual hour she had luncheon. Shortly after, when her patience was yielding to fears—fears which, in truth, she had only masked with the show of explanation—a letter was brought in. But nothing to the purpose. It came from Zillah Denyer, who began with apologies for writing, and expressed uncertainty whether Mrs. Elgar had yet returned from abroad; then went on to say that her sister Madeline had been suffering dreadfully of late. " Perhaps you know that Mrs. Travis has left us. Madeline has missed her company very much, and often longs to see the face of some visitor. She speaks of the one visit you paid her, and would so like to see you again. Forgive me for asking if you could spare half an hour. The evening is best; I venture to say this, as you came in the evening before,"

Cecily forgot herself for a few minutes in sorrows graver than her own. Her impression after the one visit had been that Madeline would not greatly care for her to repeat it; this, it seemed, was a mistake. So Mrs. Travis had left her lodgings? She heard of it for the first time.

About half-past three there sounded the knock of a visitor at the house door. Expecting no one, Cecily had given no directions; the parlour-maid hurried upstairs to ask if she was "at home." She replied that the name must first be announced to her.

It was Mrs. Travis. Cecily hesitated, but decided to receive her.

Though the intercourse between them had been resumed, it was with a restraint on both sides that seemed to forbid the prospect of friendship. They had met two or three times only; once it was in the Denyers' house, and on that occasion Cecily had renewed her acquaintance with the family and sat a little with Madeline. Interest in each other they certainly felt, but not in like degrees; Mrs. Travis showed herself more strongly attracted to Cecily than Cecily was to her, as it had been from the first. That this was the attraction of simple liking and goodwill, Cecily could never quite convince herself. Mrs. Travis always seemed to be studying her, and sometimes in a spirit of curiosity that was disagreeable. But at the same time she was so manifestly in need of sympathetic companionship, and allowed such sad glimpses into her own wrecked life, that Cecily could not reject her, nor even feel with actual coldness.

"Have you been home long?" the visitor asked, as they shook hands.

"A few hours only."

"Indeed? You have arrived to-day?"

They sat down. Mrs. Travis fixed her eyes on Cecily.

"I hardly hoped to find you."

"I should have let you know that I was back."

Their conversations were accustomed to begin awkwardly,

constrainedly. They never spoke of ordinary topics, and each seemed to wait for a suggestion of the other's mood. At present Cecily was uneasy under her visitor's gaze, which was stranger and more inquisitive than usual.

"So you have left the Denyers'?" she said.

"From whom did you hear?"

"I have just had a note from Zillah Denyer, about Madeline. She merely mentions that you are no longer there."

"I ought to go and see them; but I can't to-day."

"Have you been in London all the time?"

"Yes.—I have gone back to my husband."

It was spoken in a matter-of-fact tone (obviously assumed) which was very incongruous with the feeling it excited in Cecily. She could not hear the announcement without an astonished look.

"Of your own free will?" she asked, in a diffident voice.

"Oh yes. That is to say, he persuaded me."

Their eyes met, and Cecily had an impulse of distrust, more decided than she had ever felt. She could not find anything to say, and by keeping silence she hoped the interview might be shortened.

"You are disposed to feel contempt for me," Mrs. Travis added, after a few moments.

"No one can judge another in such things. It is your own affair, Mrs. Travis."

"Yes, but you despise me for my weakness, naturally you do. Had you no suspicion that it would end again in this way?"

"I simply believed what you told me."

"That nothing would induce me to return to him. That is how women talk, you know. We are all very much the same."

Again Cecily kept silence. Mrs. Travis, observing her, saw an offended look rise to her face.

"I mean, we are few of us, us women, strong enough to hold out against natural and social laws. We feel indignant, we suffer more than men can imagine, but we have to yield. But it is true that most women are wise enough not to act in my way. You are quite right to despise me."

"Why do you repeat that? It is possible you are acting quite rightly. How should I be able to judge?"

"I am not acting rightly," said the other, with bitterness. "Two courses are open to a woman in my position. Either she must suffer in silence, care nothing for the world's talk, take it for granted that, at any cost, she remains under her husband's roof; or she must leave him once and for ever, and regard herself as a free woman. The first is the ordinary choice; most women are forced into it by circumstances; very few have courage and strength for the second. But to do first one thing, then the other, to be now weak and now strong, to yield to the world one day and defy it the next, and then to yield again,—that is base. Such a woman is a traitor to her sex."

Cecily did not lift her eyes. She heard the speaker's voice tremble, and could not bear to look at her face. Her heart was sinking, though she knew not exactly what oppressed her. There was a long silence; then Cecily spoke.

"If your husband persuaded you to return, it must have been that you still have affection for him."

"The feeling is not worthy of that name."

"That is for yourself to determine. Why should we talk of it?"

Looking up, Cecily found the other's eyes again fixed on her. It was as though this strange gaze were meant to be a reply.

"Would it not be better," she continued, "if we didn't speak of these things? If it could do any good—— But surely it cannot."

"Sympathy is good—offered or received."

"I do sympathize with you in your difficulties."

"But you do not care to receive mine," replied Mrs. Travis, in an undertone.

C C

Cecily gazed at her with changed eyes, inquiring, offended, fearful.

"What need have I of your sympathy, Mrs. Travis?" she asked distantly.

"None, I see," answered the other, with a scarcely perceptible smile.

"I don't understand you. Please let us never talk in this way again."

"Never, if you will first let me say one thing. You remember that Mr. Elgar once had doubts about my character. He was anxious on your account, lest you should be friendly with a person who was not all he could desire from the moral point of view. He did me justice at last, but it was very painful, as you will understand, to be suspected by one who embodies such high morality."

There was no virulence in her tone; she spoke as though quietly defending herself against some unkindness. But Cecily could not escape her eyes, which searched and stabbed.

"Why do you say this?"

"Because I am weak, and therefore envious. Why should you reject my sympathy? I could be a better friend to you than any you have. I myself have no friend; I can't make myself liked. I feel dreadfully alone, without a soul who cares for me. I am my husband's plaything, and of course he scorns me. I am sure he laughs at me with his friends and mistresses. And you too scorn me, though I have tried to make you my friend. Of course it is all at an end between us now. I understand your nature; it isn't quite what I thought."

Cecily heard, but scarcely with understanding. The word for which she was waiting did not come.

"Why," she asked, "do you speak of offering me sympathy? What do you hint at?"

"Seriously, you don't know?"

"I don't," was the cold answer.

" Why did you go abroad without your husband ? "

It came upon Cecily with a shock. Were people discussing her, and thus interpreting her actions ?

"Surely that is my own business, Mrs. Travis. I was in poor health, and my husband was too busy to accompany me."

" That is the simple truth, from *your* point of view ? "

" How have you done me the honour to understand me ? "

Mrs. Travis examined her; then put another question.

" Have you seen your husband since you arrived ? "

" No, I have not."

" And you don't know that he is being talked about every-where—not exactly for his moral qualities ? "

Cecily was mute. Thereupon Mrs. Travis opened the little sealskin-bag that lay on her lap, and took out a newspaper. She held it to Cecily, pointing to a certain report. It was a long account of lively proceedings at a police-court. Cecily read. When she had come to the end, her eyes remained on the paper. She did not move until Mrs. Travis put out a hand and touched hers; then she drew back, as in repugnance.

" You had heard nothing of this ? "

Cecily did not reply. Thereupon Mrs. Travis again opened her little bag, and took out a cabinet photograph. It represented a young woman in tights, her arms folded, one foot across the other; the face was vulgarly piquant, and wore a smile which made eloquent declaration of its price.

" That is the 'lady,'" said Mrs. Travis, with a slight emphasis on the last word.

Cecily looked for an instant only. There was perfect silence for a minute or two after that; then Cecily rose. She did not speak; but the other, also rising, said :

" I shouldn't have come if I had known you were still ignorant. But now you can, and will, think the worst of me ; from this day you will hate me."

" I am not sure," replied Cecily, " that you haven't some

strange pleasure in what you have been telling me; but I know you are very unhappy, and that alone would prevent me from hating you. I can't be your friend, it is true; we are too unlike in our tempers and habits of thought. Let us shake hands and say good-bye."

But Mrs. Travis refused her hand, and with a look of bitter suffering, which tried to appear resignation, went from the room.

Cecily felt a cold burden upon her heart. She sat in a posture of listlessness, corresponding to the weary misery, numbing instead of torturing, which possessed her now that the shock was over. Perhaps the strange manner of the re-velation tended to produce this result; the strong self-con-trol which she had exercised, the mingling of incongruous emotions, the sudden end of her expectation, brought about a mood resembling apathy.

She began presently to reflect, to readjust her view of the life she had been living. It seemed to her now unaccountable that she had been so little troubled with fears. Ignorance of the world had not blinded her, nor was she unaware of her husband's history. But the truth was that she had not cared to entertain suspicion. For a long time she had not seriously occupied her mind with Reuben. Self-absorbed, she was practically content to let happen what would, pro-vided it called for no interference of hers. Her indifference had reached the point of idly accepting the present, and taking for granted that things would always be much the same.

Yet she knew the kind of danger to which Reuben was exposed from the hour when her indifference declared itself; it was present to her imagination when he chose to remain alone in London. But such thoughts were vague, impalpa-ble. She had never realized a picture of such degradation as this which had just stamped itself upon her brain. In her surmises jealousy had no part, and therefore nothing was conceived in detail. In the certainty that he no longer loved her with love of the nobler kind, did it matter much what he concealed ? But this flagrant shame had never threatened her. This was indeed the " experience " in which, as Reuben had insisted, she was lacking.

No difficulty in understanding now why he kept away. Would he ever come ? Or had he determined that their life in common was no longer possible, and resolved to spare her the necessity of saying that they were no longer husband and wife ? Doubtless that was what he expected to hear from her ; his view of her character, which she understood sufficiently well, would lead him to think that.

But she had no impulse to leave his house. The example of Mrs. Travis was too near. Escape, with or without melo-dramatic notes of farewell, never suggested itself. She knew that it was a practical impossibility to make that absolute severance of their lives without which they were still man and wife, though at a distance from each other ; they must still be linked by material interests, by common acquaint-ances. The end of sham heroics would come, sooner or later, in the same way as to Mrs. Travis. How was her life different from what it had been yesterday ? By an addition of shame and scorn, that was all ; actually, nothing was altered. When Reuben heard that she was remaining at home, he would come to her. Perhaps they might go to live in some other place ; that was all.

Tea was brought in, but she paid no heed to it. Sunset and twilight came ; the room grew dusk ; then the servants appeared with lamps. She dined, returned to the drawing-room, and took up a book she had been reading on her jour-ney. It was a volume of Quinet, and insensibly its interest concentrated her attention. She read for nearly two hours.

Then she was tired of it, and began to move restlessly about. Again she grew impatient of the uncertainty whether Reuben would return to-night. She lay upon a couch and tried to forget herself in recollection of far-off places and people. But instead of the pictures she wished to form, there kept coming before her mind the repulsive photograph which Mrs. Travis had produced. Though she had barely glanced at it, she saw it distinctly—the tawdry costume, the ignoble attitude, the shameless and sordid face. It polluted her imagination.

Jealousy, of a woman such as that? Had she still loved him, she must have broken her heart to think that he could fall so low. If it had been told her that he was overcome by passion for a woman of some nobleness, she could have heard it with resignation; in that there would have been nothing base. But the choice he had made would not allow her even the consolation of reflecting that she felt no jealousy; it compelled her to involve him in the scorn, if not in the loathing, with which that portrait inspired her.

That he merely had ceased to love her, what right had she to blame him? The very word of "blame" was unmeaning in such reference. In this, at all events, his fatalism had become her own way of thinking. To talk of controlling love is nonsensical; dead love is dead beyond hope. But need one sink into a slough of vileness?

At midnight she went to her bedroom. He would not come now.

Sleep seemed far from her, and yet before the clock struck one she had fallen into a painful slumber. When she awoke, it was to toss and writhe for hours in uttermost misery. She could neither sleep nor command a train of thoughts. At times she sobbed and wailed in her suffering.

No letter arrived in the morning. She could no longer read, and knew not how to pass the hours. In some way she must put an end to her intolerable loneliness, but she could not decide how to act. Reuben might come to-day; she wished it, that the meeting might be over and done with.

But the long torment of her nerves had caused a change of mood. She was feverish now, and impatience grew to resentment. The emotions which were yesterday so dulled began to stir in her heart and brain. Walking about the room, unable to occupy herself for a moment, she felt as though fetters were upon her; this house had become a prison; her life was that of a captive without hope of release.

There came in her a sudden outbreak of passionate indignation at the unequal hardships of a woman's lot. Often as she had read and heard and talked of this, she seemed to understand it for the first time; now first was it real to her, in the sense of an ill that goads and tortures. Not society alone was chargeable with the injustice; nature herself had dealt cruelly with woman. Constituted as she is, limited as she is by inexorable laws, by what refinement of malice is she endowed with energies and desires like to those of men? She should have been made a creature of sluggish brain, of torpid pulse; then she might have discharged her natural duties without exposure to fever and pain and remorse such as man never knows.

She asked no liberty to be vile, as her husband made himself; but that she was denied an equal freedom to exercise all her powers, to enrich her life with experiences of joy, this fired her to revolt. A woman who belongs to the old education readily believes that it is not to experiences of joy, but of sorrow, that she must look for her true blessedness; her ideal is one of renunciation; religious motive is in her enforced by what she deems the obligation of her sex. But Cecily was of the new world, the emancipated order. For a time she might accept misery as her inalienable lot, but her youthful years, fed with the new philosophy, must in the end rebel.

Could she live with such a man without sooner or later taking a taint of his ignobleness? His path was downwards, and how could she hope to keep her own course in independence of him? It shamed her that she had ever loved him. But indeed she had not loved the Reuben that now was; the better part of him was then predominant. No matter that he was changed; no matter how low he descended; she must still be bound to him. Whereas he acknowledged no mutual bond; he was a man, and therefore in practice free.

Yet she was as far as ever from projecting escape. The unjust law was still a law, and irresistible. Had it been her case that she loved some other man, and his return of love claimed her, then indeed she might dare anything and break her chains. But the power of love seemed as dead in her as the passion she had once, and only once, conceived. She was utterly alone.

Morning and noon went by. She had exhausted herself with ceaseless movement, and now for two or three hours lay on a couch as if asleep. The fever burned upon her forhead and in her breath.

But at length endurance reached its limits. As she lay still, a thought had taken possession of her—at first rejected again and again, but always returning, and with more tempting persistency. She could not begin another night without having spoken to some one. She seemed to have been forsaken for days; there was no knowing how long she might live here in solitude. When it was nearly five o'clock, she went to her bedroom and prepared for going out.

When ready, she met the servant who was bringing up tea.

"I shall not want it," she said. "And probably I shall not dine at home. Nothing need be prepared."

She entered the library, and took up from the writing-table Mallard's note; she looked at the address that was on it.

Then she left the house, and summoned the first vacant cab.

CHAPTER XIII.

ONWARD TO THE VAGUE.

THE cab drew up in a quiet road in Chelsea, by a gateway opening into a yard. Cecily alighted and paid the driver.

"Be good enough to wait a minute or two," she said. "I may need you again at once. But if I am longer, I shall not be coming."

Entering the yard, she came in front of a row of studios ; on the door of each was the tenant's name, and she easily discovered that of Ross Mallard. This door was half open ; she looked in and saw a flight of stairs. Having ascended these, she came to another door, which was closed. Here her purpose seemed to falter ; she looked back, and held her hand for a moment against her cheek. But at length she knocked. There was no answer. She knocked again, more loudly, leaning forward to listen ; and this time there came a distant shout for reply. Interpreting it as summons to enter, she turned the handle ; the door opened, and she stepped into a little ante-chamber. From a room within came another shout, now intelligible.

"Who's there ?"

She advanced, raised a curtain, and found herself in the studio, but hidden behind some large canvases. There was a sound of some one moving, and when she had taken another step, Mallard himself, pipe in mouth, came face to face with her. With a startled look, he took the pipe from his lips, and stood regarding her ; she met his gaze with the same involuntary steadiness.

"Are you alone, Mr. Mallard ? " fell at length from her.

"Yes. Come and sit down."

There was a gruffness in the invitation which under ordinary circumstances would have repelled a visitor. But Cecily was so glad to hear the familiar voice that its tone mattered nothing; she followed him, and seated herself where he bade her. There was much tobacco-smoke in the air; Mallard opened a window. She watched him with timid, anxious eyes. Then, without looking at her, he sat down near an easel on which was his painting of the temples of Pæstum. This canvas held Cecily's gaze for a moment.

"When did you get home?" Mallard asked abruptly.

"Yesterday morning."

"Mrs. Lessingham went on, I suppose?"

"Yes. I have been alone ever since, except that a visitor called."

"Alone?"

She met his eyes, and asked falteringly:

"You know why? You have heard about it?"

"Do you mean what happened the other day?" he returned, in a voice that sounded careless, unsympathetic.

"Yes."

"I know that, of course. Where is your husband?"

"I have neither seen him nor heard from him. I shouldn't have understood why he kept away but for the visitor that came—a lady; she showed me a newspaper."

Mallard knit his brows, and now scowled at her askance, now looked away. His visage was profoundly troubled. There was silence for some moments. Cecily's eyes wandered unconsciously over the paintings and other objects about her.

"You have come to ask me if I know where he is?"

She failed in her attempt to reply.

"I am sorry that I can't tell you. I know nothing of him. But perhaps Mrs. Baske does. You know their address?"

"I didn't come for that," she answered, with decision, her features working painfully. "It is not my part to seek for him."

"Then how can I help you?" Mallard asked, still gruffly, but with more evidence of the feeling that his tone disguised.

"You can't help me, Mr. Mallard. How could any one help me? I was utterly alone, and I wanted to hear a friend's voice."

"That is only natural. It is impossible for you to remain alone. You don't feel able to go to Mrs. Baske?"

She shook her head.

"But your aunt will come? You have written to her?"

"No. I had rather she didn't come. It seems strange to you that I should bring my troubles here, when it can only pain you to see me, and to have to speak. But I am not seeking comfort or support—not of the kind you naturally think I need."

As he watched the workings of her lips, the helpless misery in her young eyes, the endeavour for self-command and the struggles of womanly pride, Mallard remembered how distinctly he had foreseen this in his past hours of anguish. It was hard to grasp the present as a reality; at moments he seemed only to be witnessing the phantoms of his imagination. The years that had vanished were so insubstantial in memory; *now* and *then*, what was it that divided the two? This that was to-day a fact, was it not equally so when Cecily walked by his side at Baiæ? That which is to come, already is. In the stress of a deep emotion we sometimes are made conscious of this unity of things, and the effect of such spiritual vision is a nobler calm than comes of mere acquiescence in human blindness.

"I came here," Cecily was continuing, "because I had something to say to you—something I shall never say to any one else. You were my guardian when I was a child, and I have always thought of you as more than a simple friend. I want to fulfil a duty to you. I owe you gratitude, and I shall have no rest till I have spoken it—told you how deeply I feel it."

Mallard interrupted her, for every word seemed to be wrung from her by pain, and he felt like one who listens to a forced confession.

"Don't give way to this prompting," he said, with kind firmness. "I understand, and it is enough. You are not yourself; don't speak whilst you are suffering so."

"My worst suffering would be *not* to speak," she replied, with increased agitation. "I must say what I came to say; then I can go and face whatever is before me. I want to tell you how right you were. You told me through Mrs. Lessingham how strongly you disapproved of my marrying at once; you wished me to take no irrevocable step till I knew myself and him better. You did everything in your power to prevent me from committing a childish folly. But I paid no regard to you. I ought to have held your wish sacred; I owed you respect and obedience. But I chose my own foolish way, and now that I know how right you were, I feel the need of thanking you. You would have saved me if you could. It is a simple duty in me to acknowledge this, now I know it."

Mallard rose and stood for a minute looking absently at the temples. Then he turned gravely towards her.

"If it has really lightened your mind to say this, I am content to have heard it. But let it end there; there is no good in such thoughts and speeches. They are hysterical, and you don't like to be thought that. Such a service as you believe I might have rendered you is so very doubtful, so entirely a matter of suppositions and probabilities and possibilities, that we can't talk of it seriously. I acted as any guardian was bound to act, under the circumstances. You, on the other hand, took the course that young people have taken from time immemorial. The past is past; it is worse than vain to revive it. Come, now, let us talk for a few minutes quietly."

Cécily's head was bent. He saw that her bosom heaved, but on her face there was no foreboding of tears. The strong impulse having had its way, she seemed to be recovering self command.

"By the bye," he asked, "how did you know where to find me?"

"I found a letter of yours lying open. Did he answer your invitation?"

"Yes; he wrote a few lines saying he would come before long. But I haven't seen him. What do you intend to do when you leave me?"

"Go home again and wait," she answered, with quiet sadness.

"In solitude? And what assurance have you that he means to come?"

"None whatever. But where else should I go, but home? My place is there, until I have heard his pleasure."

It was mournfully unlike her, this bitter tone. Her eyes were fixed upon the picture again. Looking at her, Mallard was moved by something of the same indignant spirit that was still strong in her heart. Her pure and fine-wrought beauty, so subtle in expression of the soul's life, touched him with a sense of deepest pathos. It revolted him to think of her in connection with those brutalities of the newspaper; he had a movement of rebellion against the undiscerning rigour of social rule. Disinterested absolutely, but he averted his face lest she should have a suspicion of what he thought.

In spite of that, he was greatly relieved to hear her purpose. He had feared other things. It was hateful that she should remain the wife of such a man as Elgar, but what refuge was open to her? The law that demands sacrifice of the noble few on behalf of the ignoble many is too swift and sure in avenging itself when defied. It was well that she had constrained herself to accept the inevitable.

"You will write this evening to Mrs. Lessingham?" he said, in a tone of assuredness.

"Why do you wish me to do that?" she asked, looking at him.

"Because of the possibility of your still being left alone. You are not able to bear that."

"Yes, I can bear anything that is necessary now," she answered firmly. "If it was weakness to come here and say what I have said, then my weakness is over. Mrs. Lessingham is enjoying herself with friends; why should I disturb her? What have I to say to her, or to any one?"

"Suppose an indefinite time goes by, and you are still alone?"

"In that case, I shall be able to arrange my life as other such women do. I shall find occupation, the one thing I greatly need. My gravest misfortune is, that I feel the ability to do something, but do not know what. Since the death of my child, that is what has weighed upon me most."

Mallard reflected upon this. He could easily understand its truth. He felt assured that Miriam suffered in much the same way, having reached the same result by so very different a process of development. But it was equally clear to him that neither of these women really could *do* anything; it was not their function to do, but to *be*. Eleanor Spence would in all likelihood have illustrated the same unhappy problem had it been her lot to struggle against adverse conditions; she lived the natural life of an educated woman, and therefore was beset by no questionings as to her capacities and duties. So long, however, as the educated woman is the exceptional woman, of course it will likewise be exceptional for her life to direct itself in a calm course.

To discuss such questions with Cecily was impossible. How should he say to her, "You have missed your chance of natural happiness, and it will only be by the strangest good fortune if you ever again find yourself in harmony with fate"? Mallard had far too much discretion to assume the part of lay preacher, and involve himself in the dangers of suggesting comfort. The situation was delicate enough, and all his efforts were directed to subduing its tone. After a pause, he said to her:

" Have you taken your meals to-day ? "

She smiled a little.

"Yes. But I am thirsty. Can you give me a glass of water ? "

" Are you *very* thirsty ? Can you wait a quarter of an hour ? "

With a look of inquiry as to his meaning, she answered that she could. Mallard nodded, and began to busy himself in a corner of the studio. She saw that he was lighting a spirit-lamp, and putting a kettle over it. She made no remark; it was soothing to sit here in this companionship, and feel the feverish heat in her veins gradually assuaged. Mallard kept silence, and when he saw her beginning to look around at the pictures, he threw out a word or two concerning them. She rose, to see better, and moved about, now and then putting a question. In little more than the stipulated time, tea was prepared. After a short withdrawal to the ante-room, Mallard produced some delicate slices of bread and butter. Cecily ate and drank. As it was growing dusk, the artist lit a lamp.

" You know," she said, again turning her eyes to the pictures, " that I used to pretend to draw, to make poor little sketches. Would there be any hope of my doing anything, not good, but almost good, if I began again and worked seriously ? "

He would rather have avoided answering such a question ; but perhaps the least dangerous way of replying was to give moderate approval.

" At all events, you would soon find whether it was worth while going on or not. You might take some lessons ; it would be easy to find some lady quite competent to help you in the beginning."

She kept silence for a little ; then said that she would think about it.

Mallard had left his seat, and remained standing. When

both had been busy with their thoughts for several minutes, Cecily also rose.

"I must ask a promise from you before you go," Mallard said, as soon as she had moved. "If you are still alone to-morrow, you promise me to communicate with Mrs. Lessingham. Whether you wish to do so or not is nothing to the point."

She hesitated, but gave her promise.

"That is enough; your word gives me assurance. You are going straight home? Then I will send for a cab."

In a few minutes the cab was ready at the gate. Mallard, resolved to behave as though this were the most ordinary of visits, put on his hat and led the way downstairs. They went out into the road, and then Cecily turned to give him her hand. He looked at her, and for the first time spoke on an impulse.

"It's a long drive. Will you let me come a part of the way with you?"

"I shall be very glad."

They entered the hansom, and drove off.

The few words that passed between them were with reference to Mrs. Lessingham. Mallard inquired about her plans for the summer, and Cecily answered as far as she was able. When they had reached the neighbourhood of Regent's Park, he asked permission to stop the cab and take his leave; Cecily acquiesced. From the pavement he shook hands with her, seeing her face but dimly by the lamplight; she said only "Thank you," and the cab bore her away.

Carried onward, with closed eyes as if in self-abandonment to her fate, Cecily thought with more repugnance of home the nearer she drew to it. It was not likely that Reuben had returned; there would be again an endless evening of misery in solitude. When the cab was at the end of Belsize Park, she called the driver's attention, and bade him drive on to a certain other address, that of the Denyers. Zillah's letter of appeal, all but forgotten, had suddenly come to

mind and revived her sympathies. Was there not some resemblance between her affliction and that of poor Madeline ?
Her own life had suffered a paralysis ; helpless amid the
ruin of her hopes, she could look forward to nothing but
long endurance.

On arriving, she asked for Mrs. Denyer, but that lady was
from home. Miss Zillah, then. She was led into the front
room on the ground floor, and waited there for several
minutes.

At length Zillah came in hurriedly, excusing herself for
being so long. This youngest of the Denyers was now a
tall, awkward, plain girl, with a fixed expression of trouble ;
in talking, she writhed her fingers together and gave other
signs of nervousness ; she spoke in quick, short sentences,
often breaking off in embarrassment. During the years of
her absence from home as a teacher, Zillah had undergone a
spiritual change ; relieved from the necessity of sustaining
the Denyer tone, she had by degrees ceased to practise
affectation with herself, and one by one the characteristics
of an " emancipated " person had fallen from her. Living
with a perfectly conventional family, she adopted not only
the forms of their faith—in which she had, of course, no
choice—but at length the habit of their minds ; with a profound sense of solace, she avowed her self-deceptions, and
became what nature willed her to be—a daughter of the
Church. The calamities that had befallen her family had
all worked in this direction with her, and now that her daily
life was in a sick-chamber, she put forth all her best qualities, finding in accepted creeds that kind of support which
only the very few among women can sincerely dispense
with.

" She has been very, very ill the last few days," was her
reply to Cecily's inquiry. " I don't venture to leave her for
more than a few minutes."

" Mrs. Denyer is away ? "

" Yes ; she is staying at Sir Roland's, in Lincolnshire.

D D

Barbara and her husband are there, and they sent her an invitation."

"But haven't you a nurse?"

"I'm afraid I shall be obliged to find one."

"Can I help you to-night? Do let me. I have only been home two days, and came in reply to your letter as soon as I could."

They went up to Zillah's room, and Cecily threw aside her out-of-door clothing. Then they silently entered the sick-chamber.

Madeline was greatly changed in the short time since Cecily had seen her. Ceaseless pain had worn away the last traces of her girlish beauty; the drawn features, the deadened eyes, offered hope that an end must come before long. She gave a look of recognition as the visitor approached her, but did not attempt to speak.

"Are you easier again, dear?" Zillah asked, bending over her.

"Yes."

"Mrs. Elgar would like to stay with you a little. She won't ask you to talk."

"Very well. Go and rest while she stays."

"Yes, go and lie down," urged Cecily. "Please do! I will call you at once if it is necessary."

Zillah was persuaded, and Cecily took her seat alone by the bedside. She had lost all thought of herself. The tremor which possessed her when she entered was subsiding; the unutterable mournfulness of this little room made everything external to it seem of small account. She knew not whether it was better to speak or remain mute, and when silence had lasted for a few minutes, she could not trust her voice to break it. But at length the motionless girl addressed her.

"Have you enjoyed yourself in Italy?"

"Not much. I have not been very well," Cecily answered, leaning forward.

" Did you go to Naples ? "

" Only as far as Rome."

" How can any one be in Italy, and not go to Naples ? " said Madeline, in a low tone of wonder.

Silence came again. Cecily listened to the sound of breathing. Madeline coughed, and seemed to make a fruitless effort to speak; then she commanded her voice.

" I took a dislike to you at Naples," she said, with the simple directness of one who no longer understands why every thought should not be expressed. " It began when you showed that you didn't care for Mr. Marsh's drawings. It is strange to think of that now. You know I was engaged to Mr. Marsh ? "

" Yes."

" He used to write me letters; I mean, since *this*. But it is a long time since the last came. No doubt he is married now. It would have been better if he had told me, and not just ceased to write. I want Zillah to write to him for me; but she doesn't like to."

" Why do you think he is married ? " Cecily asked.

" Isn't it natural ? I'm not so foolish as to wish to prevent him. It's nothing to me now. I should even be glad to hear of it. He ought to marry some good-natured, ordinary kind of girl, who has money. Of course you were right about his drawings; he was no artist, really. But I had a liking for him."

Cecily wondered whether it would be wise or unwise to tell what she knew. The balance seemed in favour of holding her peace. In a few minutes, Madeline moaned a little.

" You are in pain ? "

" That's nothing; pain, pain—I find it hard to understand that life is anything but pain. I can't live much longer, that's the one comfort. Death doesn't mean pain, but the end of it. Yesterday I felt myself sinking, sinking, and I said, ' Now this is the end,' and I could have cried with joy. But

Zillah gave me something, and I came back. That's cruelty, you know. They ought to help us to die instead of keeping us alive in pain. If doctors had any sense they would help us to die; there are so many simple ways. You see the little bottle with the blue label; look round; the little bottle with the measure near it. If only it had been left within my reach! They call it poison when you take too much of it; but poison means sleep and rest and the end of pain."

Cecily listened as though some one spoke from beyond the grave; that strange voice made all the world unreal.

"Do you believe in a life after this?" asked Madeline, with earnestness.

"I know nothing," was the answer.

"Neither do I. It matters nothing to me. All I have to do is to die, and then whatever comes will come. Poor Zillah does her best to persuade me that she *does* know. I shall try to seem as if I believed her. Why should I give her pain? What does it matter if she is wrong? She is a kind sister to me, and I shall pretend that I believe her. Perhaps she is right? She may be, mayn't she?"

"She may be."

"It's good of you to come and sit here while she rests. She hasn't gone to bed for two nights. She's the only one of us that cares for me. Barbara has got her husband; well, I'm glad of that. And there's no knowing; she might live to be Lady Musselwhite. Sir Roland hasn't any children. Doesn't it make you laugh?"

She herself tried to laugh—a ghostly sound. It seemed to exhaust her. For half an hour no word was spoken. Then Cecily, who had fallen into brooding, heard herself called by a strange name.

"Miss Doran!"

She rose and bent over the bed, startled by this summons from the dead past.

"Can I do anything for you, Madeline?"

The heavy eyes looked at her in a perplexed way. They seemed to be just awaking, and Madeline smiled faintly.

"Didn't I call you, Miss Doran? I was thinking about you, and got confused. But you are married, of course. What is your name now? I can't remember."

"Mrs. Elgar."

"How silly of me! Mrs. Elgar, of course. Are you happily married?"

"Why do you ask?"

For the first time, she remembered the possibility that the Denyers knew of her disgrace. But Madeline's reply seemed to prove that she, at all events, had no such thing in mind.

"I was only trying to remember whom you married. Yes, yes; you told us about it before. Or else Mrs. Travis told me."

"What did she say?"

"Only that you had married for love, as every woman ought to. But *she* is very unhappy. Perhaps that would have been my own lot if I had lived. I dare say I should have been married long ago. What does it matter? But as long as one is born at all, one might as well live life through, see the best as well as the worst of it. It's been all worst with me.—Oh, that's coming again! That wishing and rebelling and despairing! I thought it was all over. You stand there and look at me; that is you and this is I, this, this! I am lying here waiting for death and burial. You have the husband you love, and long years of happy life before you.—Do you feel sorry for me? Suppose it was you who lay here?"

The same question she had put to Mrs. Travis, but now spoken in a more anguished voice. The tears streamed from Cecily's eyes.

"You cry, like Zillah does when she tries to persuade me. I don't know whether I had rather be pitied, or lie quite alone. But don't cry. You shan't go away and be made miserable by thinking of me. I can bear it all well enough; there can't be much more of it, you know. Sit down again, if you have time. Perhaps you want to go somewhere to-night—to see friends?"

"No. I will stay with you as long as ever you wish."

Presently the conversation ceased, and then for nearly three hours Cecily listened to the sound of breathing. At length the door softly opened, and Zillah came in. She was distressed; it had struck twelve long since, and only now had she awoke from sleep. Cecily entreated her to go and sleep again; she herself had no desire to close her eyes.

"But what will Mr. Elgar think has become of you?"

"He is not at home to-night. Let me have my way, there's a good girl."

Zillah, whose eyelids could scarcely be supported, at length went back to her room. Madeline still slept, with unusual calmness. The vigil was resumed, and nothing again disturbed it until white dawn began to glimmer at the windows.

Then Madeline awoke with a sudden loud cry of anguish. Cecily, aroused from slumber which was just beginning, sprang up and spoke to her. But the cry seemed to have been the end of her power of utterance; she moved her lips and looked up fearfully. Cecily hastened to summon Zillah.

CHAPTER XIV.

SUGGESTION AND ASSURANCE.

When Miriam went out by herself to walk, either going or returning she took the road in which was Mallard's studio. She kept on the side opposite the gateway, and, in passing, seemed to have no particular interest in anything at hand.

A model who one day came out of the gate, and made inspection of the handsomely attired lady just going by, little suspected for what purpose she walked in this locality.

And so it befell that Miriam was drawing near to the studios at the moment when a cab stopped there, at the moment when Cecily alighted from it. Instantly recognizing her sister-in-law, Miriam thought it inevitable that she herself must be observed; for an instant her foot was checked. But Cecily paid the driver without looking this way or that, and entered the gateway. Miriam walked on for a few paces; then glanced back and saw the cab waiting. She reached the turning of the road, and still the cab waited. Another moment, and it drove away empty.

She stood and watched it, until it disappeared in the opposite direction. Heedless of one or two people who came by, she remained on the spot for several minutes, gazing towards the studios. Presently she moved that way again. She passed the gate, and walked on to the farther end of the road, always with glances at the gate. Then she waited again, and then began to retrace her steps.

How many times backwards and forwards? She neither knew nor cared; it was indifferent to her whether or not she was observed from the windows of certain houses. She felt no weariness of body, but time seemed endless. The longer she stood or walked, the longer was Cecily there within. For what purpose? Yesterday she was to arrive in London; to-day she doubtless knew all that had been going on in her absence. And dusk fell, and twilight thickened. The street-lamps were lit. But Cecily still remained within.

Twice or thrice some one entered or left the studio-yard, strangers to Miriam. At length there came forth a man who, after looking about, hurried away, and in a few minutes returned with a hansom following him. Seeing that it stopped at the gateway, she approached as close as she durst, keeping in shadow. There issued two persons, whom at once she knew—Cecily with Mallard. They spoke together a moment; then both got into the vehicle and drove away.

That evening Miriam had an engagement to dine out, together with the Spences. When she reached home, Eleanor, dressed ready for departure and not a little impatient, met her in the entrance-hall.

"Have you forgotten?"

"No. I am very sorry that I couldn't get back sooner. What is the time?"

It was too late for Miriam to dress and reach her destination at the appointed hour.

"You must go without me. I hope it doesn't matter. They are not the kind of people who plan for their guests to go like the animals of Noah's ark."

This was a sally of unwonted liveliness from Miriam, and it did not suit very well with her jaded face.

"Will you come after dinner?" Eleanor asked.

"Yes, I will. Make some excuse for me."

So Miriam dined alone, or made a pretence of doing so, and at nine o'clock joined her friends. Through the evening she talked far more freely than usual, and with a frequency of caustic remark which made one or two mild ladies rather afraid of her.

At half-past nine next morning, when she and Eleanor were talking over a letter Mrs. Spence had just received from Greece, a servant came into the drawing-room to say that Mr. Elgar wished to speak with Mrs. Baske. The ladies looked at each other; then Miriam directed that the visitor should go up to her own sitting-room.

"This has something to do with Cecily," said Eleanor in a low voice.

"Probably."

And Miriam turned away.

As she entered her room, Reuben faced her, standing close by. He looked miserably ill, the wreck of a man compared with what he had been at his last visit. When the door was shut, he asked without preface, and in an anxious tone:

"Can you tell me where Cecily is?"

Miriam laid her hand on a chair, and met his gaze.

"Where she is?"

"She isn't at home. Haven't you heard of her?"

"Since when has she been away?"

Her manner of questioning seemed to Elgar to prove that her own surprise was as great as his.

"I only went there last night," he said, "about eleven o'clock. She had been in the house since her arrival the day before yesterday; but in the afternoon she went out and didn't return. She left no word, and there's nothing from her this morning. I thought it likely you had heard something."

"I have heard many things, but not about *her*."

"Of course, I know that!" he exclaimed impatiently, averting his eyes for a moment. "I haven't come to talk, but to ask you a simple question. You have no idea where she is?"

Miriam moved a few steps away and seated herself. But almost at once she arose again.

"Why didn't you go home before last night?" she asked harshly.

"I tell you, I am not going to talk of my affairs," he answered, with a burst of passion. "If you want to drive me mad——! Can't you answer me? Do you know anything, or guess anything, about her?"

"Yes," said Miriam, after some delay, speaking deliberately, "I can give you some information."

"Then do so, and don't keep me in torment."

"Yesterday afternoon I happened to be passing Mr. Mallard's studio, and I saw her enter it; she came in a cab. She stayed there an hour or two; it grew dark whilst she was there. Then I saw them both go away together."

Elgar stared, half incredulously.

"You saw this? Do you mean that you waited about and watched?"

"Yes."

"You had suspicions?"

"I knew what a happy home she had returned to."

Again she seated herself.

"She went there to ask about me," said Elgar, in a forced voice.

"You think so? Why to him? Wouldn't she rather have come to me? Why did she stay so long? Why did he go away with her? And why hasn't she returned home?"

Question followed question with cold deliberateness, as if the matter barely concerned her.

"But Mallard? What is Mallard to her?"

"How can I tell?"

"Were they together much in Rome?"

"I think very likely they were."

"Miriam, I can't believe this. How could it happen that you were near Mallard's studio just then? How could you stand about for hours, spying?"

"Perhaps I dreamt it."

"Where is this studio?" he asked. "I knew the other day, but I have forgotten."

She told him the address.

"Very well, then I must go there. You still adhere to your story?"

"Why should I invent it?" she exclaimed bitterly. "And what is there astonishing in it? What right have *you* to be astonished?"

"Every right!" he answered, with violence. "What warning have I had of such a thing?"

She rose and moved away with a scornful laugh. For a minute he looked at her as she stood apart, her face turned from him.

"If I find Mallard," he said, "of course I shall tell him who my authority is."

She turned.

"No; that you will not do!"

"And why not?"

"Because I forbid you. You will not dare to mention my name in any such conversation! Besides"—her voice fell to a tone of indifference—"if you meet him, there will be no need. You will ask your question, and that will be enough. There is very little chance of his being at the studio."

"I see that your Puritan spirit is gratified," he said, looking at her with fierce eyes.

"Naturally."

He went towards the door. Miriam, raising her eyes and following him a step or two, said sternly:

"In any case, you understand that my name is not to be spoken. Show at least some remnant of honour. Remember who I am, and don't involve me in your degradation."

"Have no fear. Your garment of righteousness shall not be soiled."

When he was gone, Miriam sat for a short time alone. She had not foreseen this sequel of yesterday's event. In spite of all the promptings of her jealous fear, she had striven to explain Cecily's visit in some harmless way. Mean what it might, it tortured her; but, in her ignorance of what was happening between Cecily and her husband, she tried to believe that Mallard was perhaps acting the part of reconciler—not an unlikely thing, as her better judgment told her. Now she could no longer listen to such calm suggestions. Cecily had abandoned her home, and with Mallard's knowledge, if not at his persuasion.

She thought of Reuben with all but hatred. He was the cause of the despair which had come upon her. The abhorrence with which she regarded his vices—no whit less strong for all her changed habits of thought—blended now with the sense of personal injury; this only had been lacking to destroy what natural tenderness remained in her feeling towards him. Cecily she hated, without the power of condemning her as she formerly would have done. The old voice of conscience was not mute, but Miriam turned from it with sullen scorn. If Cecily declared her marriage at an end, what fault could reason find with her? If she acted undisguisedly as a free womam, how was she to blame? Reuben's praise of her might still keep its truth. And the unwilling conviction of this was one of Miriam's sharpest torments. She would have liked to regard her with disdainful condemnation, or a fugitive wife, a dishonoured woman. But the power of sincerely judging thus was gone. Reuben had taunted her amiss.

Presently she left her room and went to seek Eleanor. Mrs. Spence was writing; she laid down her pen, and glanced at Miriam, but did not speak.

"Cecily has left her home," Miriam said, with matter-of-fact brevity.

Eleanor stood up.

"Parted from him?"

"It seems he didn't go to the house till late last night. She had left in the afternoon, and did not come back."

"Then they have not met?"

"No."

"And had Cecily heard?"

"There's no knowing."

"Of course, she has gone to Mrs. Lessingham."

"I think not," replied Miriam, turning away.

"Why?"

But Miriam would give no definite answer. Neither did she hint at the special grounds of her suspicion. Presently she left the room as she had entered, dispirited and indisposed for talk.

Elgar walked on to the studios. He found Mallard's door, and was beginning to ascend the stairs, when the artist himself appeared at the top of them, on the point of going out. He recognized his visitor with a grim movement of brows and lips, and without speaking turned back. Reuben reached the door, which remained open, and entered. Mallard, who stood there in the ante-room, looked at him inquiringly.

"I want a few minutes' talk with you, if you please," said Elgar.

"Come in."

They passed into the studio. The last time they had seen each other was more than three years ago, at Naples ; both showed something of curiosity, over and above the feelings of graver moment. Mallard, observing the signs of mental stress on Elgar's features, wondered to what they were attributable. Was the fellow capable of suffering remorse or shame to this degree ? Or was it the outcome of that other affair, sheer ignoble passion ? Reuben, on his part, could not face the artist's somewhat rigid self-possession without feeling rebuked and abashed. The fact of Mallard's being here at this hour seemed all but a disproval of what Miriam had hinted, and when he looked up again at the rugged, saturnine, energetic countenance, and met the calmly austere eyes, he felt how improbable it was that this man should be anything to Cecily save a conscientious friend.

"I haven't come in answer to your invitation," Reuben began, glancing uneasily at the pictures, and endeavouring to support an air of self-respect. "Something less agreeable has brought me."

They had not shaken hands, nor did Mallard offer a seat.

"What may that be ? " he asked.

"I believe you have seen my wife lately ? "

"What of that ? "

Mallard began to knit his brows anxiously. He put up one foot on a chair, and rested his arm on his knee.

"Will you tell me when it was that you saw her ? "

"If you will first explain why you come with such questions," returned the other, quietly.

"She has not been home since yesterday; I think that is reason enough."

Mallard maintained his attitude for a few moments, but at length put his foot to the ground again, and repeated the keen look he had cast at the speaker as soon as that news was delivered.

"When did you yourself go home?" he asked gravely.

"Late last night."

Mallard pondered anxiously.

"Then," said he, "what leads you to believe that I have seen Mrs. Elgar?"

"I don't merely believe; I know that you have."

Elgar felt himself oppressed by the artist's stern and authoritative manner. He could not support his dignity; his limbs embarrassed him, and he was conscious of looking like a man on his trial for ignoble offences.

"How do you know?" came from Mallard, sharply.

"I have been told by some one who saw her come here yesterday, in the late afternoon."

"I see. No doubt, Mrs. Baske?"

The certainty of this flashed upon Mallard. He had never seen Miriam walk by, but on the instant he comprehended her doing so. It was even possible, he thought, that, if she had not herself seen Cecily, some one in her employment had made the espial for her. The whole train of divination was perfect in his mind before Elgar spoke.

"It is nothing to the purpose who told me. My wife was here for a long time, and when she went away, you accompanied her."

"I understand."

"That is more than I do. Will you please to explain it?"

"You are accurately informed. Mrs. Elgar came here, naturally enough, to ask if I knew what had become of you."

"And why should she come to you?"

"Because my letter to you lay open somewhere in your house, and she thought it possible we had been together."

Elgar reflected. Yes, he remembered that the letter was left on his table.

"And where did she go afterwards? Where did you conduct her?"

"I went rather more than half-way home with her, in the cab," replied Mallard, somewhat doggedly. "I supposed she was going on to Belsize Park."

"Then you know nothing of her reason for not doing so?"

"Nothing whatever."

Elgar became silent. The artist, after moving about quietly, turned to question him with black brows.

"Hasn't it occurred to you that she may have joined Mrs. Lessingham in the country?"

"She has taken nothing—not even a travelling-bag."

"You come, of course, from the Spences' house?"

Elgar replied with an affirmative. As soon as he had done so, he remembered that this was as much as corroborating Mallard's conjecture with regard to Miriam; but for that he cared little. He had begun to discern something odd in the relations between Miriam and Mallard, and suspected that Cecily might in some way be the cause of it.

"Did they not at once suggest that she was with Mrs. Lessingham?"

Elgar muttered a "No," averting his face.

"What *did* they suggest, then?"

"I saw only my sister," said Reuben, irritably.

"And your sister thought I was the most likely person to know of Mrs. Elgar's whereabouts?"

"Yes, she did."

"I am sorry to disappoint you," said Mallard, coldly. "I have given you all the information I can."

"All you *will*," replied Elgar, whose temper was exasperated by the firmness with which he was held at a scornful distance. He began now to imagine that Mallard, from reasons of disinterested friendship, had advised Cecily to seek some retreat, and would not disclose the secret. More than that, he still found incredible.

Mallard eyed him scornfully.

"I said 'all I *can*,' and I don't deal in double meanings. I know nothing more than I have told you. You are probably unaccustomed, of late, to receive simple and straightforward answers to your questions; but you'll oblige me by remembering where you are."

Elgar might rage inwardly, but he had no power of doubting what he heard. He understood that Mallard would not even permit an allusion to anything save the plain circumstances which had come to light. Moreover, the artist had found a galling way of referring to the events that had brought about this juncture. Reuben was profoundly humiliated; he had never seen himself in so paltry a light. He could have shed tears of angry shame.

"I dare say the tone of your conversation," he said acridly, "was not such as would reconcile her to remaining at home. No doubt you gave her abundant causes for self-pity."

"I did not congratulate her on her return home; but, on the other hand, I said nothing that could interfere with her expressed intention to remain there."

"She told you that she had this intention?" asked Reuben, with some eagerness.

"She did."

As in the dialogue of last evening, so now, Mallard kept the sternest control upon himself. Had he obeyed his desire, he would have scarified Elgar with savage words; but of that nothing save harm could come. His duty was to smooth, and not to aggravate, the situation. It was a blow to him to learn that Cecily had passed the night away from home, but he felt sure that this would be explained in some way that did no injury to her previous resolve. He would not admit the thought that she had misled him. What had happened, he could not with any satisfaction conjecture, but he was convinced that a few hours would solve the mystery. Had she really failed in her determination, then assuredly she would write to him, even though it were without saying where she had taken refuge. But he persisted in hoping that it was not so.

"Go back to your house, and wait there," he added gravely, but without harshness. "For some reason best known to yourself, you kept your wife waiting for nearly two days, in expectation of your coming. I hope it was reluctance to face her. You can only go and wait. If I hear any news of her, you shall at once receive it. And if she comes, I desire to know of it as soon as possible."

Elgar could say nothing more. He would have liked to ask several questions, but pride forbade him. Turning in silence, he went from the studio, and slowly descended the stairs. Mallard heard him pause near the foot, then go forth.

Reuben had no choice but to obey the artist's directions. He walked a long way, the exercise helping him to combat his complicated wretchedness, but at length he felt weary and threw himself into a cab.

The servant who opened the door to him said that Mrs. Elgar had been in for a few minutes, about an hour ago; she would be back again by lunch-time.

CHAPTER XV.

PEACE IN SHOW AND PEACE IN TRUTH.

At first so much relieved that he was able to sit down and quietly review his thoughts, Elgar could not long preserve this frame of mind; in half an hour he began to suffer from impatience, and when the time of Cecily's return approached, he was in a state of intolerable agitation. Mallard's severity lost its force now that it was only remembered. He accused himself of having been, as always, weakly sensitive to the moment's impression. The fact remained that Cecily had spent a long time alone with Mallard, had made him the confidant of her troubles; was it credible in human nature—the past borne in mind—that Mallard had never exceeded a passionless sympathy? Did not Miriam say distinctly that suspicion had been excited in her by the behaviour of the two when they were in Rome? Why had he not stayed to question his sister on that point? As always, he had lost his head, missed the essential, obeyed impulses instead of proceeding on a rational plan.

He worked himself into a sense of being grossly injured. The shame he had suffered in this morning's interviews was now a mortification. What had *he* to do with vulgar rules and vulgar judgments? By what right did these people pose as his superiors and look contemptuous rebuke? His anger concentrated itself on Cecily; the violence of jealousy and the brute instinct of male prerogative plied his brain to frenzy as the minutes dragged on. Where had she passed the night? How durst she absent herself from home, and keep him in these tortures of expectation?

At a few minutes past one she came. The library door was ajar, and he heard her admit herself with a latch-key; she would see his hat and gloves in the hall. But instead of coming to the library she went straight upstairs; it was Cecily, for he knew her step. Almost immediately he followed. She did not stop at the drawing-room; he followed, and came up with her at the bedroom door. Still she paid no attention, but went in and took off her hat.

"Where have you been since yesterday afternoon?" he asked, when he had slammed the door.

Cecily looked at him with offended surprise—almost as she might have regarded an insolent servant.

"What right have you to question me in such a tone?"

"Never mind my tone, but answer me."

"What right have you to question me at all?"

"Every right, so long as you choose to remain in my house."

"You oblige me to remind you that the house is at least as much mine as yours. For what am I beholden to you? If it comes to the bare question of rights between us, I must meet you with arguments as coarse as your own. Do you suppose I can pretend, now, to acknowledge any authority in you? I am just as free as you are, and I owe you no account of myself."

Physical exhaustion had made her incapable of self-control. She had anticipated anything but such an address as this with which Elgar presented himself. The insult was too shameless; it rendered impossible the cold dignity she had purposed.

"What do you mean by 'free'?" he asked, less violently.

"Everything that you yourself understand by it. I am accountable to no one but myself. If I have allowed you to think that I held the old belief of a woman's subjection to her husband, you must learn that that is at an end. I owe no more obedience to you than you do to me."

"I ask no obedience. All I want to know is, whether it is possible for us to live under the same roof or not."

Cecily made no reply. Her anger had involved her in an inconsistency, yet she was not so far at the mercy of blind impulses as to right herself by taking the very course she had recognized as impossible.

"That entirely depends," added Elgar, "on whether you choose to explain your absence last night."

"In other words," said Cecily, "it can be of no significance to me where you go or what you do, but if you have a doubt about any of my movements, it at once raises the question whether you can continue to live with me or not. I refuse to admit anything of the kind. I have chosen, as you put it, to remain in your house, and in doing so I know what I accept. By what right do you demand more of me than I of you?"

"You know that you are talking absurdly. You know as well as I do the difference."

"Whatever laws I recognize, they are in myself only. As regards your claims upon me, what I have said is the simple truth. I owe you no account. If you are not content with this, you must form whatever suppositions you will, and act as you think fit."

"That is as much as telling me that our married life is at an end. I suppose you meant that when you kindly reminded me that it was your money I have been living on. Very well. Let it be as you wish."

Cecily regarded him with resentful wonder.

"Do you dare to speak as if it were I who had brought this about?"

Reuben was not the man to act emotion and contrive scenes. Whenever it might have seemed that he did so, he was, in truth, yielding to the sudden revulsions which were characteristic of his passionate nature. In him, harshness and unreason inevitably led to a reaction in which all the softer of his qualities rose predominant. So it was now. Those last words of his were not consciously meant to give him an opportunity of changing his standpoint. Inconstant, incapable of self-direction, at the mercy of the moment's will, he could foresee himself just as little as another could foresee him. His impetuous being prompted him to utter sincerely what a man of adroit insincerity would have spoken with calculation.

"Yes," he exclaimed. "it *is* you who have done most towards it!"

"By what act? what word?" she asked, in astonishment.

"By all your acts and words for the year past, and longer. You had practically abandoned me long before you went abroad. When you discovered that I was not everything you imagined, when you found faults and weaknesses in

me, you began to draw away, to be cold and indifferent,
to lose all interest in whatever I did or wished to do.
When I was working, you showed plainly that you had no
faith in my powers ; it soon cost you an effort even to listen
to me when I talked on the subject. I looked to you for
help, and I found none. Could I say anything ? The help
had to come spontaneously, or it was no use. Then you
gave yourself up entirely to the child ; you were glad of that
excuse for keeping out of my way. If I was away from
home for a day or two, you didn't even care to ask what I
had been doing; that was what proved to me how completely indifferent you had become. And when you went
abroad, what a pretence it was to ask me to come with you !
I knew quite well that you had much rather be without me.
And how did you suppose I should live during your absence ?
You never thought about it, never cared to think. Don't
imagine I am blaming you. Everything was at an end
between us, and which of us could help it? But it is as
well to show you that I am not the cause of all that has
happened. You have no justification whatever for this tone
of offence. It is foolish, childish, unworthy of a woman
who claims to think for herself."

Cecily listened with strange sensations. She knew that
all this had nothing to do with the immediate point at issue,
and that it only emphasized the want of nobility in
Reuben's character, but, as he proceeded, there was so much
truth in what he attributed to her that, in spite of everything, she could not resist a feeling of culpability. However
little it really signified to her husband, it was undoubtedly true
that she had made no effort with herself when she became
conscious of indifference towards him. To preserve love
was not in her power, but was he not right in saying that
she might have done more, as a wife, to supply his defects ?
Knowing him weak, should she not have made it a duty
to help him against himself? Had she not, as he said,
virtually " abandoned " him ?

Elgar observed her, and recognized the effect of his words.

"Of course," he pursued, "if you have made up your mind to be released, I have neither the power nor the will to keep you. But you must deal plainly with me. You can't both live here and have ties elsewhere. I should have thought you would have been the first to recognize that."

"Of what ties do you speak?"

"I don't know that you have any; but you say you hold yourself free to form them."

"If I had done so, I should not be here."

"Then what objection can you have to telling me where you have been?"

How idle it was, to posture and use grandiose words! Why did she shrink from the complete submission that her presence here implied? No amount of self-assertion would do away with the natural law of which he had contemptuously reminded her, the law which distinguishes man and woman, and denies to one what is permitted to the other.

"I passed the night by a sick-bed," she replied, letting her voice drop into weariness—"Madeline Denyer's."

"Did you go there directly on leaving home?"

"No."

"Will you tell me where else you went?"

"I went first of all to see Mr. Mallard. I talked with him for a long time, and he gave me some tea. Then he came part of the way back with me. Shall I try and remember the exact spot where he got out of the cab?"

"What had you to do with Mallard, Cecily?"

"I had to tell him that my life was a failure, and to thank him for having wished to save me from this fate."

Her answers were given in a dull monotone; she seemed to be heedless of the impression they made.

"You said that to Mallard?"

"Yes. It can be nothing to me what you think of it. I

had waited here till I could bear loneliness no longer; I knew I had one true friend, and I went to him."

"You behaved as no self-respecting woman could!" Elgar exclaimed passionately.

"If so," she answered, meeting his look, "the shame falls only on myself."

"That is not true! You yourself seem to be unconscious of the shame; to me it is horrible suffering. I thought you incapable of anything of the kind. I looked up to you as a high-minded woman, and I loved you for your superiority to myself."

"You loved me?" she asked, with a bitter smile.

"Yes; believe it or not, as you like. Because I was maddened by sensual passion for a creature whom I never one moment respected, how did that lessen my love for you? You complain that I kept away from you; I did so because I was still racked by that vile torment, and shrank in reverence from approaching you. You might have known me well enough to understand this. Have I not told you a thousand times that in me soul and body have lived separate lives? Even when I seemed sunk in the lowest depths, I still loved you purely and truly; I loved you all the more because I was conscious of my brutal faults. Now you have destroyed my ideal; you have degraded yourself in my esteem. It is nothing to me now, do what you may! I can never forgive you. By doing yourself wrong, you have wronged me beyond all words!"

Cecily could not take her eyes from him. She marvelled at such emotion in him. But the only way in which it affected her own feeling was to make her question herself anxiously as to whether she had really fallen below her self-respect. Had she led Mallard to think of her with like disapproval?

Life is so simple to people of the old civilization. The rules are laid down so broadly and plainly, and the conscience they have created answers so readily when appealed to. But for these poor instructed persons, what a complex affair has morality become! Hard enough for men, but for women desperate indeed. Each must be her own casuist, and without any criterion save what she can establish by her own experience. The growth of Cecily's mind had removed her further and further from simplicity of thought; this was in part the cause of that perpetual sense of weariness to which she awoke day after day. Communion with such a man as Elgar strengthened the natural tendency, until there was scarcely a motive left to which she could yield without discussing it in herself, consciously or unconsciously. Her safeguard was an innate nobleness of spirit. But it is not to every woman of brains that this is granted.

"What I did," she said at length slowly, "was done, no doubt, in a moment of weakness; I gave way to the need of sympathy. Had my friend been a man of less worth, he might have misunderstood me, and then I might indeed have been shamed. But I knew him and trusted him."

"Which means, that you were false to me in a way I never was to you. It is you who have broken the vow we made to be faithful to each other."

"I cannot read in your heart. If you still love me, it is a pity; I can give you no love in return."

He drew nearer, and looked at her despairingly.

"Cecily! when I came last night, I had a longing to throw myself at your feet, and tell you all my misery—everything, and find strength again with your help. I never feared *this*. You, who are all love and womanliness, you cannot have put me utterly from your heart!"

"I am your wife still; but I ask nothing of you, and you must not seek for more than I can give."

"Well, I too ask for nothing. But I will prove——"

She checked him.

"Don't forget your philosophy. We both of us know that it is idle to make promises of that kind."

" You will leave London with me ? "

" I shall go wherever you wish."

" Then we will make our home again in Paris. The sooner the better. A few days, and we will get rid of everything except what we wish to take with us. I don't care if I never see London again."

In the evening, Cecily was again at the Denyers' house. Madeline lay without power of speech, and seemed gradually sinking into unconsciousness. Mrs. Denyer had been telegraphed for; a reply had come, saying that she would be home very soon, but already a much longer time than was necessary had passed, and she did not arrive. Zillah sat by the bed weeping, or knelt in prayer.

" If your mother does not come," Cecily said to her, " I will stay all night. It's impossible for you to be left alone."

" She must surely come; and Barbara too. How can they delay so long ? "

Madeline's eyes were open, but she gave no sign of recognition. The look upon her face was one of suffering, there was no telling whether of body or mind. Hitherto it had changed a little when Zillah spoke to her, but at length not even this sign was to be elicited. Cecily could not take her gaze from the blank visage; she thought unceasingly of the bright, confident girl she had known years ago, and the sunny shore of Naples.

The doctor looked in at nine o'clock. He stayed only a few minutes.

At half-past ten there came a loud knocking at the house-door, and the servant admitted Mrs. Denyer, who was alone. In the little room above, the two watchers were weeping over the dead girl.

CHAPTER XVI.

THE TWO FACES.

MALLARD, when he had taken leave of Cecily by Regent's Park, set out to walk homewards. He was heavy-hearted, and occasionally a fit of savage feeling against Elgar took hold of him, but his mood remained that of one who watches life's drama from a point of vantage. Sitting close by Cecily's side, he had been made only more conscious of their real remoteness from each other—of his inability to give her any kind of help. He wished she had not come to him, for he saw she had hoped to meet with warmer sympathy, and perhaps she was now more than ever oppressed with the sense of abandonment. And yet such a result might have its good; it might teach her that she must look for support to no one but herself. Useless to lament the necessity; fate had brought her to the hardest pass that woman can suffer, and she must make of her life what she could. It was not the kind of distress that a friend can remedy; though she perished, he could do nothing but stand by and sorrow.

Coming to his own neighbourhood, he did not go straight to the studio, but turned aside to the Spences' house. He had no intention of letting his friends know of Cecily's visit, but he wished to ask whether they had any news of Elgar. No one was at home, however.

The next morning, when surprised by the appearance of Elgar himself, he was on the point of again going to the Spences'. The interview over, he set forth, and found Eleanor alone. She had just learnt from Miriam what news Reuben had brought, and on Mallard's entrance she at once repeated this to him.

"I knew it," replied the artist. "The fellow has been with me."

"He ventured to come? Before or after his coming here?"

"After. I think," he added carelessly, "that Mrs. Baske suggested it to him."

"Possibly. I know nothing of what passed between them."

"Do you think Mrs. Baske has any idea on the subject?" Mallard inquired, again without special insistence.

"She spoke rather mysteriously," Eleanor replied. "When I said that Mrs. Lessingham probably could explain it, she said she thought not, but gave no reasons."

"Why should she be mysterious?"

"That is more than I can tell you. Mystery rather lies in her character, I fancy."

"Would you mind telling me whether she is in the habit of going out alone?"

Eleanor hesitated a little, surprised by the question.

"Yes, she is. She often takes a walk alone in the afternoon."

"Thank you. Never mind why I wished to know. It throws no light on Cecily's disappearance."

They talked of it for some time, and were still so engaged when Spence came in. In him the intelligence excited no particular anxiety; Cecily had gone to her aunt, that was all. What else was to be expected when she found an empty house?

"But," remarked Eleanor, "the question remains whether or not she has heard of this scandal."

Mallard could have solved their doubts on this point, but to do so involved an explanation of how he came possessed of the knowledge; he held his peace.

It was doubtful whether Elgar would keep his promise

and communicate any news he might have. Mallard worked through the day, as usual, but with an uneasy mind. In the morning he walked over once more to the Spences', and learnt that anxieties were at an end; Mrs. Baske had received a letter from her brother, in which Cecily's absence was explained. Elgar wrote that he was making preparations for departure; in a few days they hoped to be in Paris, where henceforth they purposed living.

He went away without seeing Miriam, and there passed more than a fortnight before he again paid her a visit. In the meantime he had seen Spence, who reported an interview between Eleanor and Mrs. Lessingham; nothing of moment, but illustrating the idiosyncrasies of Cecily's relative. When at length, one sunny afternoon, Mallard turned his steps towards the familiar house, it was his chance to encounter Eleanor and her husband just hastening to catch a train; they told him hurriedly that Miriam had heard from Paris.

"Go and ask her to tell you about it," said Eleanor. "She is not going out."

Mallard asked nothing better. He walked on with a curious smile, was admitted, and waited a minute or two in the drawing-room. Miriam entered, and shook hands with him, coldly courteous, distantly dignified.

"I am sorry Mrs. Spence is not at home."

"I came to see you, Mrs. Baske. I have just met them, and heard that you have news from Paris."

"Only a note, sending a temporary address."

He observed her as she spoke, and let silence follow.

"You would like to know it—the address?" she added, meeting his look with a rather defiant steadiness.

"No, thank you. It will be enough if I know where they finally settle. You saw Mrs. Elgar before she left?"

"No."

"I'm sorry to hear that."

Miriam's face was clouded. She sat very stiffly, and

averted her eyes as if to ignore his remark. Mallard, who had been holding his hat and stick in conventional manner, threw them both aside, and leaned his elbow on the back of the settee.

"I should like," he said deliberately, "to ask you a question which sounds impertinent, but which I think you will understand is not really so. Will you tell me how you regard Mrs. Elgar? I mean, is it your wish to be still as friendly with her as you once were? Or do you, for whatever reason, hold aloof from her?"

"Will you explain to me, Mr. Mallard, why you think yourself justified in asking such a question?"

In both of them there were signs of nervous discomposure. Miriam flushed a little; the artist moved from one attitude to another, and began to play destructively with a tassel.

"Yes," he answered. "I have a deep interest in Mrs. Elgar's welfare—*that* needs no explaining—and I have reason to fear that something in which I was recently concerned may have made you less disposed to think of her as I wish you to. Is it so or not?"

Her answer was uttered with difficulty.

"What can it matter how I think of her?"

"That is the point. To my mind it matters a great deal. For instance, it seems to me a deplorable thing that you, her sister in more senses than one, should have kept apart from her when she so much needed a woman's sympathy. Of course, if you had no true sympathy to give her, there's an end of it. But it seems to me strange that it should be so. Will you put aside conventionality, and tell me if you have any definite reason for acting as if you and she were strangers?"

Miriam was mute. Her questioner waited, observing her. At length she spoke with painful impulsiveness.

"I can't talk with you on this subject."

"I am very sorry to distress you," Mallard continued, his voice growing almost harsh in its determination, "but talk of it we must, once for all. Your brother came to my studio one morning, and demanded an explanation of something about his wife which he had heard from you. He didn't *say* that it came from you, but I have the conviction that it did. Please to tell me if I am wrong."

She kept an obstinate silence, sitting motionless, her hands tightly clasped together on her lap.

"If you don't contradict me, I must conclude that I am right. To speak plainly, it had come to his knowledge that Mrs. Elgar—no; I will call her Cecily, as I used to do when she was a child—that Cecily had visited my studio the evening before. You told him of that. How did you know of it, Mrs. Baske?"

Miriam answered in a hard, forced voice.

"I happened to be passing when she drove up in a cab."

"I understand. But you also told him how long she remained, and that when she left I accompanied her. How could you be aware of those things?"

She seemed about to answer, but her voice failed. She stood up, and began to move away. Instantly Mallard was at her side.

"You must answer me," he said, his voice shaking. "If I detain you by force, you must answer me."

Miriam turned to face him. She stood splendidly at bay, her eyes gleaming, her cheeks bloodless, her lithe body in an attitude finer than she knew. They looked into each other's pupils, long, intensely, as if reading the heart there. Miriam's eyes were the first to fall.

"I waited till she came out again."

"You waited all that time? In the road?"

"Yes."

"And when you heard that Cecily had not returned home that night, you believed that she had left her husband for ever?"

"Yes."

Mallard drew back a little, and his voice softened.

"Forgive me for losing sight of civility. Knowing this, it was perhaps natural that you should inform your brother of it. You took it for granted that Cecily—however unwise it was of her—had come to tell me of her resolve to leave home, and that I, as her old friend, had seen her safely to the place where she had taken refuge?"

He uttered this with a peculiar emphasis, gazing steadily into her face. Miriam dropped her eyes, and made no reply.

"You represented it to your brother in this light?" he continued, in the same tone.

She forced herself to look at him; there was awed wonder on her face.

"There is no need to answer in words. I see that I have understood you. But of course you soon learnt that you had been in part mistaken. Cecily had no intention of leaving her husband, from the first."

Miriam breathed with difficulty. He motioned to her to sit down, but she gave no heed.

"Then why did she come to you?" fell from her lips.

"Please to take your seat again, Mrs. Baske."

She obeyed him. He took a chair at a little distance, and answered her question.

"She came because she was in great distress, and had no friend in whom she could confide so naturally. This was a misfortune; it should not have been so. It was to *you* that she should have gone, and I am afraid it was your fault that she could not."

"My fault?"

"Yes. You had not behaved to her with sisterly kindness. You had held apart from her; you had been cold and unsympathetic. Am I unjust?"

"Can one command feelings?"

"That is to say, you *felt* coldly to her. Are you conscious of any reason? I believe religious prejudice no longer influences you?"

"No."

"Then I am obliged to recall something to your mind. Do you remember that you were practically an agent in bringing about Cecily's marriage? No doubt things would have taken much the same course, however you had acted. But is it not true that you gave what help was in your power? You acted as though your brother's suit had your approval. And I think you alone did so."

"You exaggerate. I know what you refer to. Reuben betrayed my lack of firmness, as he betrays every one who trusts in him."

"Let us call it lack of firmness. The fact is the same, and I feel very strongly that it laid an obligation on you. From that day you should have been truly a sister to Cecily. You should have given her every encouragement to confide in you. She loved you in those days, in spite of all differences. You should never have allowed this love to fail."

Miriam kept her eyes on the floor.

"I am afraid," he added, after a pause, "that you won't tell me why you cannot think kindly of her?"

She hesitated, her lips moving uncertainly.

"There *is* a reason?"

"I can't tell you."

"I have no right to press you to do so. I will rather ask this—I asked it once before, and had no satisfactory answer —why did you allow me to think for a few days, in Italy, that you accepted my friendship and gave me yours in return, and then became so constrained in your manner to me that I necessarily thought I had given you offence?"

She was silent.

"That also you can't tell me?"

She glanced at him—or rather, let her eyes pass over his face—with the old suggestion of defiance. Her firm-set lips gave no promise of answer.

Mallard rose.

"Then I must still wait. Some day you will tell me, I think."

He held his hand to her, then turned away; but in a moment faced her again.

"One word—a yes or no. Do you believe what I have told you? Do you believe it absolutely? Look at me, and answer."

She flushed, and met his gaze almost as intensely as when he compelled her confession.

"Do you put absolute faith in what I have said?"

"I do."

"That is something."

He smiled very kindly, and so this dialogue of theirs ended.

A few days later, the Spences gathered friends about their dinner-table. Mallard was of the invited. The necessity of donning society's uniform always drew many growls from him; he never felt at his ease in it, and had a suspicion that he looked ridiculous. Indeed it suited him but ill; it disguised the true man as he appeared in his rough travelling apparel, and in the soiled and venerable attire of the studio.

As he entered the drawing-room, his first glance fell on Seaborne, who sat in conversation with Mrs. Baske. The man of letters was just returned from Italy. Going to shake hands with Miriam, Mallard exchanged a few words with him; then he drew aside into a convenient corner. He noticed that Miriam's eyes turned once or twice in his direction. Informed that she was to be his partner in the solemn procession, he approached her when the moment arrived. They had nothing to say to each other, until they had been seated some time; then they patched together a semblance of talk, a few formalities, commonplaces, all but imbecilities. Finding this at length intolerable, each turned to the person on the other side. In Mallard's case this was a young lady whom he had once before met, a pretty, bright, charming girl; without hesitation, she abandoned her companion proper, and drew the artist into lively dialogue. It was

F F

continued afterwards in the drawing-room, until Mallard, observing that Miriam sat alone, went over to her.

"What's the matter?" he asked, as he seated himself.

"The matter? Nothing."

"I thought you looked unusually well and cheerful early in the evening. Now you are the opposite."

"Society soon tires me."

"So it does me."

"You seem anything but tired."

"I have been listening to clever and amusing talk. Do you like Miss Harper?"

"I don't know her well enough to like or dislike her."

Mallard was looking at her hands, as they lay folded together; he noticed a distinct tension of the muscles, a whitening of the knuckles.

"She has just the qualities to put me in good humour. Often when I have got stupid and bearish from loneliness, I wish I could talk to some one so happily constituted."

Miriam had become mute, and in a minute or two she rose to speak to a lady who was passing. As she stood there, Mallard regarded her at his ease. She was admirably dressed to-night, and looked younger than of wont. Losing sight of her, owing to people who came between, Mallard fell into a brown study, an anxious smile on his lips.

On the second morning after that, he interrupted his work to sit down and pen a short letter. "Dear Mrs. Baske," he began; then pondered, and rose to give a touch to the picture on which his eyes were fixed. But he seated himself again, and wrote on rapidly. "Would you do me the kindness to come here to-morrow early in the afternoon? If you have an engagement, the day after would do. But please to come, if you can; I wish to see you."

There was no reply to this. At the time he had mentioned, Mallard walked about his room in impatience. Just before three o'clock, his ear caught a footstep outside, and a knock at the door followed.

"Come in!" he shouted.

From behind the canvases appeared Miriam.

"Ah! How do you do? This is kind of you. Are you alone?"

The question was so indifferently asked, that Miriam stood in embarrassment.

"Yes. I have come because you asked me."

"To be sure.—Can you sew, Mrs. Baske?"

She looked at him in confusion, half indignant.

"Yes, I can sew."

"I hardly like to ask you, but—would you mend this for me? It's the case in which I keep a large volume of engravings; the seams are coming undone, you see."

He took up the article in question, which was of glazed cloth, and held it to her.

"Have you a needle and thread?" she asked.

"Oh yes; here's a complete work-basket."

He watched her as she drew off her gloves.

"Will you sit here?" He pointed to a chair and a little table. "I shall go on with my work, if you will let me. You don't mind doing this for me?"

"Not at all."

"Is that chair comfortable?"

"Quite."

He moved away and seemed to be busy with a picture; it was on an easel so placed that, as he stood before it, he also overlooked Miriam at her needlework. For a time there was perfect quietness. Mallard kept glancing at his companion, but she did not once raise her eyes. At length he spoke.

"I have never had an opportunity of asking you what your new impressions were of Bartles."

"The place was much the same as I left it," she answered naturally.

"And the people? Did you see all your old friends?"

"I saw no one except my sister-in-law and her family."

"You felt no inclination?"

"None whatever."

"By-the-bye"—he seemed to speak half absently, looking closely at his work—"hadn't you once some thought of building a large new chapel there?"

"I once had."

She drew her stitches nervously.

"That has utterly passed out of your mind?"

"Must it not necessarily have done so?"

He stepped back, held his head aside, and examined her thoughtfully.

"H'm. I have an impression that you went beyond thinking of it as a possibility. Did you not make a distinct promise to some one or another—perhaps to the congregation?"

"Yes, a distinct promise."

He became silent; and Miriam, looking up for the first time, asked:

"Is it your opinion that the promise is still binding on me?"

"Why, I am inclined to think so. Your difficulty is, of course, that you don't see your way to spending a large sum of money to advance something with which you have no sympathy."

"It isn't only that I have no sympathy with it," broke from Miriam. "The thought of those people and their creeds is hateful to me. Their so-called religion is a vice. They are as far from being Christians as I am from being a Mahometan. To call them Puritans is the exaggeration of compliment."

Mallard watched and listened to her with a smile.

"Well," he said, soberly, "I suppose this only applies to the most foolish among them. However, I see that you can hardly be expected to build them a chapel. Let us think a moment.—Are there any public baths in Bartles?"

"There were none when I lived there."

" The proverb says that after godliness comes cleanliness. Why should you not devote to the establishing of decent baths what you meant to set apart for the chapel ? How does it strike you ? "

She delayed a moment ; then——

" I like the suggestion."

" Do you know any impartial man there with whom you could communicate on such a subject ? "

" I think so."

" Then suppose you do it as soon as possible ? "

" I will."

She plied her needle for a few minutes longer ; then looked up and said that the work was done.

" I am greatly obliged to you. Now will you come here and look at something ? "

She rose and came to his side. Then she saw that there stood on the easel a drawing-board ; on that was a sheet of paper, which showed drawings of two heads in crayon.

" Do you recognize these persons ? " he asked, moving a little away.

Yes, she recognized them. They were both portraits of herself, but subtly distinguished from each other. The one represented a face fixed in excessive austerity, with a touch of pride that was by no means amiable, with resentful eyes, and lips on the point of becoming cruel. In the other, though undeniably the features were the same, all these harsh characteristics had yielded to a change of spirit ; austerity had given place to grave thoughtfulness, the eyes had a noble light, on the lips was sweet womanly strength.

Miriam bent her head, and was silent.

" Now, both these faces are interesting," said Mallard. " Both are uncommon, and full of force. But the first I can't say that I like. It is that of an utterly undisciplined woman, with a possibility of great things in her, but likely to be dangerous for lack of self-knowledge and humility ; an ignorant woman, moreover ; one subjected to superstitions, and aiming at unworthy predominance. The second is obviously her sister, but how different! An educated woman, this; one who has learnt a good deal about herself and the world. She is 'emancipated,' in the true sense of the hackneyed word; that is to say, she is not only freed from those bonds that numb the faculties of mind and heart, but is able to control the native passions that would make a slave of her. Now, this face I love."

Miriam did not stir, but a thrill went through her.

"One of the passions that she has subdued," Mallard went on, "is, you can see, particularly strong in this sister of hers. I mean jealousy. This first face is that of a woman so prone to jealousy of all kinds that there would be no wonder if it drove her to commit a crime. The woman whom I love is superior to idle suspicions; she thinks nobly of her friends; she respects herself too much to be at the mercy of chance and change of circumstance."

He paused, and Miriam spoke humbly.

"Do you think it impossible for the first to become like her sister?"

"Certainly not impossible. The fact is that she has already made great progress in that direction. The first face is not that of an actually existing person. She has changed much since she looked altogether like this, so much, indeed, that occasionally I see the sister in her, and then I love her for the sister's sake. But naturally she has relapses, and they cannot but affect my love. That word, you know, has such very different meanings. When I say that I love her, I don't mean that I am ready to lose my wits when she is good enough to smile on me. I shouldn't dream of allowing her to come in the way of my life's work; if she cannot be my helper in it, then she shall be nothing to me at all. I shall never think or call her a goddess, not even if she develop all the best qualities she has. Still, I think the love is true love; I think so for several reasons, of which I needn't speak."

Miriam again spoke, all but raising her face.

"You once loved in another way."

"I was once out of my mind, which is not at all the same as loving."

He moved to a distance; then turned, and asked:

"Will you tell me now why you became so cold to Cecily?"

"I was jealous of her."

"And still remain so?"

"No."

"I am glad to hear that. Now I think I'll get on with my work. Thank you very much for the sewing.—By-the-bye, I often feel the want of some one at hand to do a little thing of that kind."

"If you will send for me, I shall always be glad to come."

"Thank you. Now don't hinder me any longer. Good-bye for to-day."

Miriam moved towards the door.

"You are forgetting your gloves, Mrs. Baske," he called after her.

She turned back and took them up.

"By-the-bye," he said, looking at his watch, "it is the hour at which ladies are accustomed to drink tea. Will you let me make you a cup before you go?"

"Thank you. Perhaps I could save your time by making it myself."

"A capital idea. Look, there is all the apparatus. Please to tell me when it is ready, and I'll have a cup with you."

He painted on, and neither spoke until the beverage was actually prepared. Then Miriam said:

"Will you come now, Mr. Mallard?"

He laid down his implements, and approached the table by which she stood.

"Do you understand," he asked, "what is meant when one says of a man that he is a Bohemian?"

" I think so."

" You know pretty well what may be fairly expected of him, and what must *not* be expected ? "

" I believe so."

" Do you think you could possibly share the home of such a man ? "

" I think I could."

" Then suppose you take off your hat and your mantle, or whatever it's called, and make an experiment—see if you can feel at home here."

She did so. Whilst laying the things aside, she heard him step up to her, till he was very close. Then she turned, and his arms were about her, and his heart beating against hers.

CHAPTER XVII.

END AND BEGINNING.

IN the autumn of this year, Mrs. Lessingham died. Owing to slight ailments, she had been advised to order her life more restfully, and with a view to this she took a house at Richmond, where Mrs. Delph and Irene again came to live with her. Scarcely was the settlement effected, when grave illness fell upon her, the first she had suffered since girlhood. She resented it; her energies put themselves forth defiantly; two days before her death she had no suspicion of what was coming. Warned at length, she made her will, angrily declined spiritual comfort, and with indignation fought her fate to the verge of darkness.

Cecily and her husband arrived a few hours too late; when the telegram of summons reached them, they were in Denmark. The Spences attended the funeral. Mallard and Miriam, who were in the north of Scotland—they had been married some two months—did not come. By Mrs. Lessingham's will, the greater part of her possessions fell to Cecily; there was a legacy of money to Irene Delph, and a London hospital for women received a bequest.

Eleanor wrote to Miriam:

"They went back to Paris yesterday. I had Cecily with me for one whole day, but of herself she evidently did not wish to speak, and of course I asked no questions. Both she and her husband looked well, however. It pleased me very much to hear her talk of you; all her natural tenderness and gladness came out; impossible to imagine a more exquisite sincerity of joy. She is a noble and beautiful creature; I do hope that the shadow on her life is passing away, and that we shall see her become as strong as she is lovable. She said she had written to you. Your letter at the time of your marriage was a delight to her.

"It happened that on the day when she was here we had a visit from—whom think you? Mr. Bradshaw, accompanied by his daughter Charlotte and her husband. The old gentleman was in London on business, and had met the young people, who were just returning from their honeymoon. He is still the picture of health, and his robust, practical talk seemed to do us good. How he laughed and shouted over his reminiscences of Italy! Your marriage had amazed him; when he began to speak of it, it was in a grave, puzzled way, as if there must be something in the matter which required its being touched upon with delicacy. The substitution of baths for a chapel at Bartles obviously gave him more amusement than he liked to show; he chuckled inwardly, with a sober face. 'What has Mallard got to say to that?' he asked me aside. I answered that it met with your husband's entire approval. 'Well,' he said, 'I feel that I can't keep up with the world; in my day, you didn't begin married life by giving away half your income. It caps me, but no doubt it's all right.' Mrs. Bradshaw by-the-bye, shakes her head whenever you are mentioned.

"You will like to hear of Mr. and Mrs. Marsh. Charlotte is excessively plain, and I am afraid excessively dull, but it is satisfactory to see that she regards her husband as a superior being, not to be spoken of save with bated breath. Mr. Marsh is rather too stout for his years, and I should think very self-indulgent; whenever his wife looks at him, he unconsciously falls into the attitude of one who is accustomed to snuff incense. He speaks of 'my Bohemian years' with a certain pride, wishing one to understand that he was a wild, reckless youth, and that his present profound knowledge of the world is the result of experiences which do not fall to the lot of common men. With Cecily he was superbly gracious—talked to her of art in a large, fluent way, the memory of which will supply Edward with mirth for some few weeks. The odd thing is that his father-in-law seems more than half to believe in him."

Time went on. Cecily's letters to her friends in England grew rare. Writing to Eleanor early in the spring, she mentioned that Irene Delph, who had been in Paris since Mrs. Lessingham's death, was giving her lessons in painting, but said she doubted whether this was anything better than a way of killing time. "You know Mr. Seaborne is here?" she added. "I have met him two or three times at Madame Courbet's, whom I was surprised to find he has known for several years. She translated his book on the revolutions of '48 into French."

Never a word now of Elgar. The Spences noted this cheerlessly, and could not but remark a bitterness that here and there revealed itself in her short, dry letters. To Miriam she wrote only in the form of replies, rarely even alluding to her own affairs, but always with affectionate interest in those of her correspondent.

Another autumn came, and Cecily at length was mute; the most pressing letters obtained no response. Miriam wrote to Reuben, but with the same result. This silence was unbroken till winter; then, one morning in November,

Eleanor received a note from Cecily, asking her to call as soon as she was able at an address in the far west of London —nothing more than that.

In the afternoon, Eleanor set out to discover this address. It proved to be a house in a decent suburban road. On asking for Mrs. Elgar, she was led up to the second floor, and into a rather bare little sitting-room. Here was Cecily, alone.

"I knew you would come soon," she said, looking with an earnest, but not wholly sad, smile at her visitor. "I had very nearly gone to you, but this was better. You understand why I am here?"

"I am afraid so, after your long silence."

"Don't let us get into low spirits about it," said Cecily, smiling again. "All that is over; I can't make myself miserable any more, and certainly don't wish any one to be so on my account. Come and sit nearer the fire. What a black, crushing day!"

She looked out at the hopeless sky, and shook her head.

"You have lodgings here?" asked Eleanor, watching the girl with concern.

"Irene and her mother live here; they were able to take me in for the present. He left me a month ago. This time he wrote and told me plainly—said it was no use, that he wouldn't try to deceive me any longer. He couldn't live as I wish him to, so he would have done with pretences and leave me free. I waited there in my 'freedom' till the other day; he might have come back, in spite of everything, you know. But at last I wrote to an address he had given me, and told him I was going to London—that I accepted his release, and that henceforth all his claims upon me must be at end."

"Is he in Paris?"

"In the south of France, I believe. But that is nothing to me. What I inherited from my aunt makes me independent; there is no need of any arrangements about money, fortunately. I dare say he foresaw this when he expressed a wish that I should keep this quite apart from our other sources of income, and manage it myself."

Eleanor felt that the last word was said. There was no distress in Cecily's voice or manner, nothing but the simplicity of a clear decision, which seemed to carry with it hardly a regret.

"A tragedy can go no further than its fifth act," Cecily pursued. "I have shed all my tears long since, exhausted all my indignation. You can't think what an everyday affair it has become with me. I am afraid that means that I am in a great measure demoralized by these experiences. I can only hope that some day I shall recover my finer feeling."

"You haven't seen Miriam?"

"No, and I don't know whether I can. There is no need for you to keep silence about me when you see her; what has happened can't be hidden. I thought it possible that Reuben might have written and told her. If she comes here, I shall welcome her, but it is better for me not to seek her first."

"If he writes to her," asked Eleanor, with a grave look, "is it likely that he will try to defend himself?"

"I understand you. You mean, defend himself by throwing blame of one kind or another on me. No, that is impossible. He has no desire to do that. What makes our relations to each other so hopeless, is that we can be so coldly just. In me there is no resentment left, and in him no wish to disguise his own conduct. We are simply nothing to each other. I appreciate all the good in him and all the evil; and to him my own qualities are equally well known. We have reached the point of studying each other in a mood of scientific impartiality—surely the most horrible thing in man and wife."

Eleanor had a sense of relief in hearing that last comment. For the tone of the speech put her painfully in mind of that which characterizes certain French novelists — all very well in its place, but on Cecily's lips an intolerable discord. It was as though the girl's spirit had been materialized by Parisian influences; yet the look and words with which she ended did away with, or at least mitigated, that fear.

"He is pursued by a fate," murmured the listener.

"Listen to my defence," said Cecily, after a pause, with more earnestness. "For I have not been blameless throughout. Before we left London, he charged me with contributing to what had befallen us, and in a measure he was right. He said that I had made no effort to keep him faithful to me; that I had watched the gulf growing between us with indifference, and allowed him to take his own course. A jealous and complaining wife, he said, would have behaved more for his good. Hearing this, I recognized its truth. I had held myself too little responsible. When our life in Paris began, I resolved that I would accept my duties in another spirit. I did all that a wife can do to strengthen the purer part in him. I interested myself in whatever he undertook ; I suggested subjects of study which I thought congenial to him, and studied them together with him, putting aside everything of my own for which he did not care. And for a time I was encouraged by seeming success. He was grateful to me, and I found my one pleasure in this absolute devotion of myself. I choose my words carefully ; you must not imagine that there was more in either his feeling or mine than what I express. But it did not last more than six months. Then he grew tired of it. I still did my utmost ; believe that I did, Mrs. Spence, for it is indeed true. I made every effort in my power to prevent what I knew was threatening. Until he began to practise deceit, trickery of every kind. What more could I do ? If he was determined to deceive me, he would do so ; what was gained by my obliging him to exert more cunning ? Then I turned sick at heart, and the end came."

"But, Cecily," said Eleanor, "how can the end be yet?"

"You mean that he will once more wish to return."

"Once more, or twenty times more."

"I know; but——"

She broke off, and Eleanor did not press her to continue.

It was not long before the news reached Miriam. In a few days Eleanor paid one of her accustomed visits to a little house out at Roehampton, externally cold and bare enough in these days of November, but inwardly rich with whatsoever the heart or brain can desire. Hither came no payers of formal calls, no leavers of cards, no pests from the humdrum world to open their mouths and utter foolishness. It was a dwelling sacred to love and art, and none were welcome across its threshold save those to whom the consecration was of vital significance. To Eleanor the air seemed purer than that of any other house she entered; to breathe it made her heart beat more hopefully, gave her a keener relish of life.

Mallard was absent to-day, held by business in London. The visitor had, for once, no wish to await his return. She sat for an hour by the fireside, and told what she had to tell; then took her leave.

When the artist entered, Miriam was waiting for him by the light of the fire; blinds shut out the miserable gloaming, but no lamp had yet been brought into the room. Mallard came in blowing the fog and rain off his moustache; he kicked off his boots, kicked on his slippers, and then bent down over the chair to the face raised in expectancy.

"A damnable day, Miriam, in the strict and sober sense of the word."

"Far too sober," she replied. "Eleanor came through it, however."

"Wonderful woman! Did she come to see if you bore it with the philosophy she approves?"

"She had a more serious purpose, I'm sorry to say.

Cecily is in London. He has left her—written her a good-bye."

Mallard leaned upon the mantelpiece, and watched his wife's face, illumined by the firelight. A healthier and more beautiful face than it had ever been; not quite the second of those two faces that Mallard drew, but with scarcely a record of the other. They talked in subdued voices. Miriam repeated all that Eleanor had been able to tell.

"You must go and see her, of course," Mallard said.

"Yes; I will go to-morrow."

"Shall you ask her to come here?"

"I don't think she will wish to," answered Miriam.

"That brother of yours!" he growled.

"Isn't it too late even to feel angry with him, dear? We know what all this means. It is absolutely impossible for them to live together, and Reuben's behaviour is nothing but an assertion of that. Sooner or later, it would be just as impossible, even if he preserved the decencies."

"Perhaps true; perhaps not. Would it be possible for him to live for long with *any* woman?"

Miriam sighed.

"Well, well; go and talk to the poor girl, and see if you can do anything. I wish she were an artist, of whatever kind; then it wouldn't matter much. A woman who sings, or plays, or writes, or paints, can live a free life. But a woman who is nothing but a woman, what the deuce is to become of her in this position? What would become of *you*, if I found you in my way, and bade you go about your business?"

"We are not far from the Thames," she answered, looking at him with the fire-glow in her loving eyes.

"Oh, you!" he muttered, with show of contempt. "But other women have more spirit. They get over their foolish love, and then find that life in earnest is just beginning."

"I shall never get over it."

"Pooh!—How long to dinner, Miriam?"

Miriam went to see her sister-in-law, and repeated the visit at intervals during the next few months; but Cecily would not come to Roehampton. Neither would she accept the invitations of the Spences, though Eleanor was with her frequently, and became her nearest friend. She seemed quite content with the society of Irene and Mrs. Delph; her health visibly improved, and as spring drew near there was a brightening in her face that told of thoughts in sympathy with the new-born hope of earth.

The Mallards were seldom in town. Excepting the house at Chelsea, their visits were only to two or three painters, who lived much as Mallard had done before his marriage. In these studios Miriam at first inspired a little awe; but as her understanding of the art-world increased, she adapted herself to its habits in so far as she could respect them, and where she could not, the restraint of her presence was recognized as an influence towards better things.

At the Spences', one day in April, they met Seaborne. They had heard of his being in London again (after a year mostly spent in Paris), but had not as yet seen him. He was invited to visit them, and promised to do so before long. A month or more passed, however, and the promise remained unfulfilled. At Chelsea the same report was made of him; he seemed to be living in seclusion.

In mid-May, as Miriam was walking by herself at a little distance from home, she was overtaken by a man who had followed her over the heath. When the step paused at her side, she turned and saw Reuben.

"Will you speak to me?" he said.

"Why not, Reuben?"

She gave him her hand.

"That is kinder than I hoped to find you. But I see how changed you are. You are so happy that you can afford to be indulgent to a poor devil."

"Why have you made yourself a poor devil?"

"Why, why, why! Pooh! Why is anything as it is?

Why are you what you are, after being what you were?"

It pained her to look at him. At length she discerned unmistakably the fatal stamp of degradation. When he came to her two years ago, his face was yet unbranded; now the darkening spirit declared itself. Even his clothing told the same tale, in spite of its being such as he had always worn.

"Where are you living?" she asked.

"Anywhere; nowhere. I have no home."

"Why don't you make one for yourself?"

"It's all very well for you to talk like that. Every one doesn't get a home so easily.—Does old Mallard make you a good husband?"

"Need you ask that?" Miriam returned, averting her eyes, and walking slowly on.

"You have to thank me for it, Miriam, in part."

She looked at him in surprise.

"It's true. It was I who first led him to think about you, and interested him in you. We were going from Pompeii to Sorrento—how many years ago? thirty, forty?—and I talked about you a great deal. I told him that I felt convinced you could be saved, if only some strong man would take you by the hand. It led him to think about you; I am sure of it."

Miriam had no reply to make. They walked on.

"I didn't come to the house,' he resumed presently, "because I thought it possible that the door might be shut in my face. Mallard would have wished to do so."

"He wouldn't have welcomed you; but you were free to come in if you wished."

"Have you thought it likely I might come some day?"

"I expected, sooner or later, to hear from you."

He had a cane, and kept slashing with it at the green growths by his feet. When he missed his aim at any particular object, he stopped and struck again, more fiercely.

" Does Cecily come to see you ? " was his next question, uttered as if unconcernedly.

" No."

" But you know about her ? You know where she is ? "

" Yes."

" Tell me what you know, Miriam. How is she living ? "

" I had much rather not speak of her. I don't feel that I have any right to."

" Why not ? " he asked quickly, standing still. " What is there to hide ? Why had you rather not speak ? "

" For reasons that you understand well enough. What is it to you how she lives ? "

He searched her face, like one suspecting a studied ambiguity. His eyes, which were a little bloodshot, grew larger and more turbid ; a repulsive animalism came out in ll his features.

" Do tell me what you know, Miriam," he pleaded. " Of course it's nothing to me ; I know that. I have no wish to interfere with her ; I promise you to do nothing of the kind ; I promise solemnly ! "

" You promise ? " she exclaimed, not harshly, but with stern significance. " How can you use such words ? Under what circumstances could I put faith in a promise of yours, Reuben ? "

He struck violently at the trunk of a tree, and his cane broke ; then he flung it away, still more passionately.

" You're right enough. What do I care ? I lie more often than I tell the truth. I have a sort of pride in it. If a man is to be a liar, let him be a thorough one.—Do you know why I smashed the stick ? I had a devilish tempta- tion to strike you across the face with it. That would have been nice, wouldn't it ? "

" You had better go your own way, Reuben, and let me go mine."

She drew apart, and not without actual fear of him, so

brutal he looked, and so strangely coarse had his utterance become.

"You needn't be afraid. If I *had* hit you, I'd have gone away and killed myself; so perhaps it's a pity I didn't. I felt a savage hatred of you, and just because I wanted you to take my hand and be gentle with me. I suppose you can't understand that? You haven't gone deep enough into life."

His voice choked, and Miriam saw tears start from his eyes.

"I hope I never may," she answered gently. "Have done with all that, and talk to me like yourself, Reuben."

"Talk! I've had enough of talking. I want to rest somewhere, and be quiet."

"Then come home with me."

"Dare you take me?"

"There's no question of daring. Come with me, if you wish to."

They walked to the house almost in silence. It was noon; Mallard was busy in his studio. Having spoken a word with him, Miriam rejoined her brother in the sitting-room. He had thrown himself on a couch, and there he lay without speaking until luncheon-time, when Mallard's entrance aroused him. The artist could not be cordial, but he exercised a decent hospitality.

In the afternoon, brother and sister again sat for a long time without conversing. When Reuben began to speak, it was in a voice softened by the influences of the last few hours.

"Miriam, there's one thing you will tell me; you won't refuse to. Is she still living alone?"

"Yes."

"Then there is still hope for me. I must go back to her, Miriam. No—listen to me! That is my one and only hope. If I lose that, I lose everything. Down and down, lower and lower into bestial life—that's my fate, unless she saves

me from it. Won't you help me? Go and speak to her for
me, dear sister, you can't refuse me that. Tell her how
helpless I am, and implore her to save me, only out of pity.
I don't care how mean it makes me in your eyes or hers; I
have no self-respect left, nor courage—nothing but a desire
to go back to her and ask her to forgive me."

Miriam could scarcely speak for shame and distress.

"It is impossible, Reuben. Be man enough to face what
you have brought on yourself. Have you no understanding
left? With her, there is no hope for you. She and you
are no mates; you can only wreck each other's lives. Surely,
surely you know this by now! She could only confirm your
ruin, strive with you as she might; you would fall again
into hateful falsity. Forget her, begin a life without
thought of her, and you may still save yourself—yourself;
no one else can save you. Begin the struggle alone, man-
like. You have no choice but to do so."

"I tell you I can't live without her. Where is she? I
will go myself——"

"You will never know from me. What right have you to
ask her to sink with you? That's what it means. There
are people who think that a wife's obligation has no bounds,
that she *must* sink, if her husband choose to demand it.
Let those believe it who will. What motive should render
such a sacrifice possible to her? You know she cannot love
you. Pity? How can she pity you in such a sense as to
degrade herself for your sake? Neither you nor she nor I
hold the creed that justifies such martyrdom. Am *I* to
teach you such things? Shame! Have the courage of your
convictions. You have released her, and you must be
content to leave her free. The desire to fetter her again is
ignoble, dastardly!"

He would neither be shamed nor convinced. With
desperate beseechings, with every argument of passion, no
matter how it debased him, he strove frantically to subdue
her to his purpose. But Miriam was immovable. At length

she could not even urge him with reasonings; his prostrate frenzy revolted her, and she drew away in repugnance. Reuben's supplication turned on the instant into brutal rage.

"Curse your obstinacy!" he shouted, in a voice that had strained itself to hoarseness.

The door opened, and Mallard, who had come to see whether Elgar was still here, heard his exclamation.

"Out of the house!" he commanded sternly. "March! And never let me see you here again."

Reuben rushed past him, and the house-door closed violently.

Then Miriam's overstrung nerves gave way, and for the first time Mallard saw her shed tears. She described to him the scene that had passed.

"What ought I to do? She must be warned. It is horrible to think that he may find her, and persuade her."

They agreed that she should go to Cecily early next morning. In the meantime she wrote to Eleanor.

But the morning brought a letter from Reuben, of a tenor which seemed to make it needless to mention this incident to Cecily.

"I had not long left you," he wrote, "when I recovered my reason, and recognized your wisdom in opposing me. For a week I have been drinking myself into a brutal oblivion—or trying to do so; I came to you in a nerveless and half imbecile state. You were hard with me, but it was just what I needed. You have made me understand—for to-day, at all events—the completeness of my damnation. Thank you for discharging that sisterly office. I observe, by-the-bye, that Mallard's influence is strengthening your character. Formerly you were often rigorous, but it was spasmodic. You can now persevere in pitilessness, an essential in one who would support what we call justice. Don't think I am writing ironically. Whenever I am free from passion, as now—and that is seldom enough—I can see myself precisely as you and all those on your side of the gulf see me. The finer qualities I once had survive in my memory, but I know it is hopeless to try and recover them. I find it interesting to study the processes of my degradation. I should like to write a book about it, but it would be of the kind that no one would publish.

"I hope I may never by chance see Cecily; I have a horrible conviction that I should kill her. Why shouldn't I tell you all the truth? My feeling towards her is a strange and vile compound of passions, but I believe that hatred predominates. If she were so unfortunate as to come again into my power, I should make it my one object to crush her to my own level; and in the end I should kill her. Perhaps that is the destined close of our drama. Even to you, as I confessed, I felt murderous impulses. I haven't yet been quite successful in analyzing this state of mind. The vulgar would say that, having chosen the devil's part, I am receiving a share of the devil's spirit. But to give a thing a bad name doesn't help one to understand it.

"Don't let this terrify you. I am going away again, to be out of reach of temptation. I know, I know with certainty, that the end in some form or other draws near. I have thought so much of Fate, that I seem to have got an unusual perception of its course, as it affects me. Keep this letter as a piece of curious human experience. It may be the last you receive from me."

Something less than a month after this, Edward Spence, examining his correspondence at the breakfast-table, found a French newspaper, addressed to him in a hand he recognized.

"This is from Seaborne," he said to Eleanor, as he stripped off the wrapper.

He discovered a marked paragraph. It reported a tragic occurrence in a street near the Luxembourg. The husband of an actress at one of the minor theatres in Paris had encountered his wife's lover, and shot him dead. The victim was "un jeune Anglais, nommé Elgare."

The sender of this newspaper had also written; his letter contained fuller details. He had seen the corpse, and identified it. Could he do anything? Or would some friend of Mrs. Elgar come over?

Eleanor carried the intelligence first of all to Roehampton. In her consultation with the Mallards, it was decided that she, rather than Miriam, should visit Cecily. She left them with this purpose.

It was possible that Cecily had already heard. On arriving at the house, Eleanor was at once admitted, and went up to the sitting-room on the second floor; she entered with a tremulous anxiety, and the first glance told her that her news had not been anticipated. Cecily was seated with several books open before her ; the smile of friendly welcome slowly lighting her grave countenance, showed that her mind detached itself with difficulty from an absorbing subject.

" Welcome always," she said, "and most so when least expected."

The room was less bare than when she first occupied it. Pictures and books were numerous; the sunlight fell upon an open piano ; an easel, on which was a charcoal drawing from a cast, stood in the middle of the floor. But the plain furniture remained, and no mere luxuries had been introduced. It was a work-room, not a boudoir.

" You are still content in your hermitage ? " said Eleanor, seating herself and controlling her voice to its wonted tone.

" More and more. I have been reading since six o'clock this morning, and never felt so quiet in mind."

Her utterance proved it; she spoke in a low, sweet voice, its music once more untroubled. But in looking at Eleanor, she became aware of veiled trouble on her countenance.

" Have you come only to see me ? Or is there something—— ? "

Eleanor broke the news to her. And as she spoke, the

beautiful face lost its calm of contemplation, grew pain-shadowed, stricken with pangs of sorrow. Cecily turned away and wept—wept for the past, which in these moments had lived again and again perished.

It seemed to Spence that his wife mourned unreasonably. A week or more had passed, and yet he chanced to find her with tears in her eyes.

"I have still so much of the old Eve in me," replied Eleanor. "I am heavy-hearted, not for him, but for Cecily's dead love. We all have a secret desire to believe love imperishable."

"An amiable sentiment; but it is better to accept the truth."

"True only in some cases."

"In many," said Spence, with a smile. "First love is fool's paradise. But console yourself out of Boccaccio. 'Bocca baciata non perde ventura; anzi rinnuova, come fa la luna.'"

THE END.

Notes to the Text

In compiling these notes, I was greatly helped by P. F. Krop-holler's preparatory work (*Gissing Newsletter*, April 1977, pp. 16-17).

Page 4, line 8:
Forestieri: foreigners.

Page 8, line 10:
'Revue des Deux Mondes': the leading French review at the time *The Emancipated* was published. It was founded in 1828 and is still published.

Page 14, line 17:
The Girton girl: Girton College, a college for women, was opened at Hitchin in 1869 and transferred to Cambridge in 1873. Girton girls had a reputation for being forward-thinking. Herminia Barton, the heroine of Grant Allen's *The Woman Who Did* (1895), was educated at Girton College.

Page 14, line 22:
Sarcey: Francisque Sarcey (1827-99), French dramatic critic and a regular contributor to *Le Temps*. Gissing attended lectures he gave in Paris in October 1888.

Page 14, line 24:
Sarah Bernhardt: the famous French actress (1844-1923) scored her earliest successes in plays by Hugo, Coppée and Racine. *La Dame aux Camélias*, by Alexandre Dumas the younger, was not drama-

tised in France until 1882. The action of *The Emancipated* beginning
in 1878, it appears that Gissing was guilty of an anachronism.
The Goncourt brothers, Edmond (1822-96) and Jules (1830-70),
pioneers of French naturalism, were disliked by Gissing. The
present reference to them is the only one in Gissing's fiction; so is
that to Charles Baudelaire (1821-67), the author of *Les Fleurs
du Mal* (1857).

Page 16, line 7:
Mrs. Grundy: this symbolic figure of conventional propriety is a
minor background character in *Speed the Plough*, a play by Thomas
Morton, produced in 1798.

Page 22, line 19:
Goethe's 'Italienische Reise': Gissing bought his copy of the book
in Paris on 9 October 1888. The allusion to Goethe's desire
to see Italy having become an illness with him refers to Goethe's
memoirs (12 October 1786). See also Gissing's *Commonplace Book*,
p. 40, in which *Italienische Reise* is listed among his favourite
books, *The Unclassed* (ch. VI) and *The Private Papers of Henry
Ryecroft* (Autumn XIX).

Page 27, line 15:
Pococurantism: the character, spirit, or style of a pococurante,
i.e. a careless or indifferent person (OED). Pococurante appears,
in French, in *Born in Exile*, Part V, ch. I.

Page 32, line 29:
John Murray's guide-books were nearly as famous as Baedeker's.
In 1820 he published Mrs. Mariana Starke's *Guide for Travellers
on the Continent*, which was the starting-point of the series.

Page 34, line 24:
John Lemprière (1765?-1824), the classical scholar, author of the
standard work of reference, *Bibliotheca Classica* (1788), or Classical
Dictionary.

Page 35, line 12:
Karl Baedeker (1801-59), German editor and publisher of the
guidebooks so popular in Victorian England.

Page 38, line 6:
Going up to the wall of Casa Guidi and kissing it: a reference to the Brownings' home in Florence opposite the Pitti Palace. They stayed there for thirteen years (1848-61).

Page 38, line 12:
Less given to the melting mood: 'albeit unused to the melting mood' (Shakespeare, *Othello*, V, ii, 348).

Page 42, line 28:
Gazing with lack-lustre eye: 'looking on it with lack-lustre eye' (Shakespeare, *As You Like It*, II, vii, 21).

Page 43, line 35:
In what region were the kine of Sir Grant Musselwhite unknown to fame? Perhaps an echo from Gray's *Elegy* (XXX): 'A youth to fortune and to fame unknown.'

Page 50, line 5:
She becomes the millstone about their neck: 'it were better for him that a millstone were hanged about his neck' (*St. Matthew*, XVIII. 6).

Page 52, line 30:
Daudet's 'Les Femmes d'Artistes': Alphonse Daudet (1840-97), one of Gissing's favourite authors, published these short sketches of character in 1874. The reference is most appropriate since the moral of the book is that finding a suitable mate for the artistic temperament is no easy matter. Gissing dealt with the subject in his next novel, *New Grub Street* (1891).

Page 55, line 10:
The conflict between the children of this world and the children of light: 'for the children of this world are in their generation wiser than the children of light' (*St. Luke*, XVI. 8).

Page 56, line 11:
'The Improvisatore': Hans Christian Andersen (1805-75) published *The Improvisatore; or, Life in Italy*, in 1834. The book expresses his delight in Italy which he had just visited. It is a vividly imaginative volume, full of poetic colour. Francis Turner Palgrave

(1824-97) is mainly remembered for his *Golden Treasury of Songs and Lyrics* (1861; second series, 1896).

Page 71, line 11:
He belonged to the unclassed and the unclassable: an ironical reference to a human category which Gissing had analysed in *The Unclassed* (1884) and defined in his preface to the second revised edition (1895; Harvester Press, 1976).

Page 72, line 32:
In forma pauperis: in pauper's garb.

Page 73, line 9:
The last refuge of a scoundrel: 'patriotism is the last refuge of a scoundrel' (Boswell's *Life of Johnson*, 7 April 1775). The same quotation occurs in ch. XXI of *The Crown of Life* (1899).

Page 73, line 13:
And is Miriam killing the fatted calf?: an echo from *St. Luke*, XV. 23: 'And bring hither the fatted calf, and kill it.'

Page 73, line 25:
I feel like a giant refreshed: 'so the Lord awaked as one out of sleep; and like a giant refreshed with wine' (*Book of Common Prayer*, Psalm LXXVIII, 66).

Page 74, *passim:*
Cocchieri: cabmen; *lo sventramento; il risanamento:* slum-clearance.

Page 76 and 77, *passim:*
Due soldi: twopence; *sorbe:* sorb-apples; *pomidori:* tomatoes; *bettola:* tavern, wineshop.

Page 77, line 9:
Carelessness of what might come hereafter: perhaps an echo from Swinburne's *The Garden of Proserpine:* 'Of what may come hereafter.'

Page 79, line 4:
Defoe's [*Political*] *History of the Devil:* published in 1726.

Page 90, line 20:
Mancia: tip.

Page 98, lines 4-5, 13 and 14:
Io ti voglio bene assaje/E tu non pienz'a me!: I am very fond of you/
And you don't care for me! – *Albergo del Sole, signore?:* The
Sun, sir? – *Prendi, bambino!:* Take this, child! – *Avanti:* Lead the
way!

Page 99, line 9:
All hail! From Shakespeare, *Macbeth,* I, iii, 48.

Page 100-101, *passim:*
Faktisch! Der Herr hat Recht!: Quite true! The gentleman is right!
– *Gewisz!:* Certainly! – *Nimmermehr!:* Never more! – *Vortrefflich!:*
Excellent! *Ach!:* Ah! Alas! – *Wie kann man so etwas sagen!:* How
can one speak like that! – *Hoch!:* Hear, hear! – *Verissime!:*
quite right! – *Doch!:* Indeed! – *Erlauben Sie!:* Allow me! –
Dummkopf: a fool, a blockhead.

Page 101, line 20:
In your hand a mantling goblet: Milton (*Paradise Lost,* IV, 258)
refers to 'mantling wine'.

Page 101, line 25:
Nunc est bibendum: Now we must drink (Horace, *Odes,* I, XXXVII,
1).

Page 105, line 6:
Kneipe: drinking bout.

Page 108, line 29:
Un sordo, signori!: a penny, gentlemen!

Page 109, lines 17-18:
Sordibus abstersis. . .: Cleaned and with its marble restored, the
old fountain shines again, and the water flows more pleasantly
for you.

Page 110, line 12:
That slough of despond: from Bunyan, *The Pilgrim's Progress.*

Page 111, line 12:
Marina: harbour.

Page 113, line 27:
'Company, villanous company', is the first thing to be avoided:'Company, villanous company, hath been the spoil of me' (Shakespeare, *Henry IV*, Part I, III, iii, 10).

Page 117, line 18:
Shall I the spigot wield?: 'Wilt thou the spigot wield?' (Shakespeare, *The Merry Wives of Windsor*, I, iii, 21).

Page 127, line 3:
He spoke not in anger, but in sorrow: 'a countenance more in sorrow than in anger' (Shakespeare, *Hamlet*, I, ii, 231).

Page 133, line 21:
Portone: Main entrance.

Page 144, line 11:
Amor ch'a null'amato amar perdona: 'Love, that absolves from love no one beloved' (transl. Henry Johnson). Dante, *Inferno*, Canto V, 103.

Page 145, line 1:
Oggi é festa: to-day is a holiday, a day of rejoicing.

Page 148, line 8:
Avanti, cocchiere!: Go on, driver!

Page 149, line 18:
Ore rotundo: fluently, with fluency (Horace, *Ars Poetica*, 323).

Page 152, line 22:
The Judgment of Paris: Paris, a son of Priam, King of Troy, and of Hecuba, was appointed by the gods to adjudge the prize of beauty among the three goddesses, Hera, Aphrodite and Athene. He awarded the prize to Aphrodite, who offered him Helen, the fairest woman in the world, for wife, and helped him to elope with her.

Page 169, line 12:
Hic intus. . .: Herein I lie, a truthful, reliable and virtuous man, Publius Octavius Rufus, decurion.

Page 169, line 18:
The faith that would have bidden him write himself a miserable sinner: an echo from the General Confession in *The Book of Common Prayer* ('But thou, o Lord, have mercy upon us, miserable offenders').

Page 186, line 25:
Silvio Pellico: Italian writer (1789-1854), playwright and poet, whose best known title is *My Prisons* (1832).

Page 198, line 8:
Satis superque: More than enough (Cicero, *Pro Q. Roscio Comoedo*, 11).

Page 211, chapter heading:
On the wings of the morning: 'If I take the wings of the morning' (*Book of Common Prayer*, Psalm CXXXIX. 8).

Page 230, line 5:
Of being able some day to find rest for the sole of his foot: 'But the dove found no rest for the sole of her foot' (*Genesis*, VIII. 9).

Page 234, line 17:
You remind me of the woman whose price is above rubies: 'Who can find a virtuous woman? for her price is far above rubies' (*Proverbs*, XXXI. 10).

Page 239, line 1:
You are of the salt of the earth: from *St. Matthew*, V. 13. Gissing used the phrase as a title for one of his short stories (*The House of Cobwebs*, 1906).

Page 243, line 19:
N'en sais rien: Don't know.

Page 245, line 11:
Anthony Trollope (1815-1882): Gissing had mixed feelings about

him. They are recorded in *Henry Ryecroft* (Autumn XXII), in his *Commonplace Book*, p. 29, and in a letter to Eduard Bertz of 17 April 1887: 'Trollope? Ah, I cannot read him, the man is such a terrible Philistine.'

Page 254, line 25:
You look like Hamlet . . . frightened Ophelia: an allusion to *Hamlet*, Act II, i, in which Ophelia tells her father Polonius how much 'affrighted' she has been by Lord Hamlet, 'with his doublet all unbrac'd; No hat upon his head; his stockings foul'd, ungarter'd, and down-gyved to his ancle. . .'

Page 263, line 10:
With the love that conquers everything: 'Omnia vincit amor' (Virgil, *Eclogue* X. 69).

Page 269:
Gissing expressed similar thoughts on love in other works, especially *The Odd Women:* 'Love – love – love; a sickening sameness of vulgarity. What is more vulgar than the ideal of novelists? They won't represent the actual world; it would be too dull for their readers. In real life, how many men and women *fall in love?* Not one in every ten thousand, I am convinced. . . There is the sexual instinct, of course, but that is quite a different thing.' Thus speaks Rhoda Nunn in ch. VI.

Page 286, line 25:
Dépaysées: out of their element.

Page 295, chapter heading:
Multum in parvo: much in a short time.

Page 298, line 33:
Fielding's Amelia: in this novel, published in 1751, Amelia's husband, Captain Booth, is a gambler.

Cella: sanctuary.

Page 322, line 24:
These are the kind of oxen that Homer saw, and Virgil: the same remark occurs in Gissing's diary (11 December 1888) and in his

correspondence (letter to Eduard Bertz of 3 January 1889 in particular).

Page 325, line 14:
'You mean Mount Soracte? . . . Horace.' A reference to 'Vides ut alta stet nive candidum/Soracte – ?' Horace, *Carmina*, I, VIII, 1-2. The same passage is quoted in a letter to Bertz of 7 December 1888 and referred to in the diary for 29 December 1888.

Page 327, line 25:
The gabinetto at Naples: an allusion to the small room containing a pornographic collection at the National Museum in Naples. In Gissing's time men only were admitted.

Page 329, line 1:
Amico mio: my friend.

Page 330, line 10:
Servetur ad imum [qualis ab incepto processerit, et sibi constet]: See that it [a character in a play] is kept to the end as it starts at the beginning and is self-consistent (Horace, *Ars Poetica*, 126).

Page 331, line 14:
Permesso: a pass.

Page 336, line 22:
The sense of having chosen . . . authoritatively described: 'Enter ye in at the strait gate: for wide is the gate, and broad is the way, that leadeth to destruction, and many there be which go in thereat' (*St. Matthew*, VII. 13).

Page 351, first paragraph:
The description of the three heads of empresses in the Sala Rotunda is based on a detailed description in Gissing's diary for 21 December 1888.

Page 351, line 23:
For verily . . . upon the earth: from Homer, *Odyssey*, Book XVIII. 130.

Page 374, line 14:
The Scarlet Woman throned by the Mediterranean: a reference to

Revelation XVII.

Page 389, line 30:
Edgar Quinet (1803-75): French philosopher, historian and poet. He wrote a number of volumes on Italy, in particular *Italy and its Revolutions* (1848-51).

Page 437, line 1:
The proverb says that after godliness comes cleanliness: from John Wesley's *Sermons* (no XCIII, 'On Dress': Cleanliness is, indeed, next to godliness).

Page 456, line 17:
Bocca . . . luna: lips that have been kissed do not lose their chances; they renew themselves like the moon (Boccacio, *Decamerone*, end of the seventh story of the second day).

Bibliography

I - Articles and reviews dealing with the first English edition (all published in 1890). *Indicates a reprint in *Gissing: The Critical Heritage.*

Athenaeum, 12 April, p. 466
Academy, 12 April, p. 263 (G. Barnett Smith)*
Illustrated London News, 19 April, p. 498*
Vanity Fair, 19 April, pp. 352-53
Graphic, 26 April, p. 488
Morning Post, 30 April, p. 2
Deutsche Presse, 4 May, p. 143 [Eduard Bertz]
St. James's Gazette, 8 May, p. 6
Guardian, 28 May, p. 882
Daily News, 30 May, p. 6
Saturday Review, 21 June, p. 772*
Spectator, 21 June, p. 875
Westminster Review, September, pp. 333-34*

II - Reviews of the second English edition

Star, 20 December 1893, p. 1
Manchester Guardian, 2 January 1894, p. 7
Saturday Review, 20 January 1894, p. 71
Spectator, 11 August 1894, pp. 183-84*

III - Reviews of the first American edition

Literary Era, October 1895, p. 272
Dial, 1 November 1895, p. 255 (William Morton Payne)

Book Buyer, December 1895, p. 697
Nation, 6 February 1896 (Annie R. M. Logan)
Critic, 22 February 1896, p. 123*

IV - Books containing material on The Emancipated

Coustillas, P. (ed.), *Collected Articles on George Gissing* (1968)

Coustillas, P. and Partridge, C. (eds.), *Gissing: The Critical Heritage* (1972). Contains reviews of *The Emancipated* and a number of articles in which the novel is discussed

Davis, Oswald H., *George Gissing. A Study in Literary Leanings* (1966, reprinted by Kohler & Coombes, Dorking, 1975, with an introduction by P. Coustillas)

Donnelly, Mabel Collins, *George Gissing, Grave Comedian* (1954)

Gissing, Algernon and Ellen (eds.), *Letters of George Gissing to Members of his Family* (1927)

Gordan, John D., *George Gissing 1857-1903. An Exhibition from the Berg Collection* (1954)

Hardy, Barbara, *The Appropriate Form: An Essay on the Novel* (1964)

Korg, Jacob, *George Gissing, a Critical Biography* (1963)

McKay, Ruth Capers, *George Gissing and his Critic Frank Swinnerton* (1933)

Milner, Earl (ed.), *English Criticism in Japan* (1972). Contains an essay, 'The Education of George Gissing', by Shigeru Koike

Murry, J. Middleton, *Katherine Mansfield and Other Literary Studies* (1959)

Poole, Adrian, *Gissing in Context* (1975)

Roberts, Morley, *The Private Life of Henry Maitland* (1912; new editions, 1923 and 1958)

Spiers, J. and Coustillas, P., *The Rediscovery of George Gissing* (1971)

Swinnerton, Frank, *George Gissing, a Critical Study* (1912; new editions, 1923 and 1966)

Tindall, Gillian, *The Born Exile: George Gissing* (1974)

Weber, Anton, *George Gissing und die soziale Frage* (1932; reprinted New York, 1967)

Wolff, Joseph J., *George Gissing: An Annotated Bibliography of Writings about Him* (1974)

Young, Arthur (ed.), *The Letters of George Gissing to Eduard Bertz* (1961)

V - Articles containing material on The Emancipated

Michaelis, Kate Woodbridge, 'Who is George Gissing?', *Boston Evening Transcript*, 21 February 1896, p. 11*

Wells, H. G., 'The Novels of Mr. George Gissing', *Contemporary Review*, August 1897, pp. 192-201*

Dolman, Frederick, 'George Gissing's Novels', *National Review*, October 1897, pp. 258-66*

More, Paul Elmer, 'George Gissing', *Shelburne Essays* (Fifth Series), 1908, pp. 45-65*

Francis, C. J., 'The Emancipated', *Gissing Newsletter*, January and April 1975, pp. 1-12 and 12-21

VI - Other related material

Allen, Walter, *The English Novel* (1954)

Baker, Ernest A., *The History of the English Novel*, vol. IX (1936)

Ford, Boris (ed.), *From Dickens to Hardy* (1958)

Korg, Jacob (ed.), *George Gissing's Commonplace Book* (1962)

Pollard, Arthur (ed.) , *The Victorians* (1970)

Williams, Raymond, *Culture and Society 1780-1950* (1958)

Young, W. T., *Cambridge History of English Literature*, vol. XIII, ch. XIV (1916)